# Tales
# of the
# Tea Shoppe

## Nik Kirimizi

*Everyone deserves to be loved as they are.*

*No exceptions.*

*Dedicated to those who love adventure, romance, and the thrill of the unexpected.*

I

Before the time of recorded history once stood a great empire, vast along both land and sea. Beyond a mere continent, took over a majority of land, all the way past the neighboring seas. Among this mass of land, all had been equal under the united name of Alqueris, a title that had its chokehold for lifetimes. Peace was not a priority within their reign. Instead, it was the need for a strong force that could lead without opposition, one that would leave the scattered people of the land alone.

It was once a singular monarchic family that the people of the ancient continent tolerated, so long as the humble people of the land were left alone. So long as those with heightened abilities and affinities were allowed to lead their lives.

Until the monarchy no longer reigned with its people in mind, abdicating responsibility for them entirely.

Affinities were once a gift in itself, a connection between humanity and magic. Elemental powers, though rare and many lost to time, sat as the most powerful of them all. Those that remained were of water, fire, earth, and wind. Various other affinic powers were so drastic from the last, there were no limits to what could be discovered. Some people could move faster than wind, strength to where some could lift boulders with no hesitation. Some affinities were advantageous, while other powers could be simply strange and unusable, even causing affliction to its user.

Out of a rising fear of discontent and rumors of overthrow, the royal family of Alqueris made a choice that would begin the end of their reign. They stole away those with known affinities, regardless of their power, and forced them into labor, prisons, and fates much worse than death itself.

The tradition of hiding one's affinity, or going as far as to remove them, had been born out of fear, to protect themselves and their families from these fates. All to evade capture from the empire.

Three hundred years ago, the monarchic chokehold of a reign came to a forceful end at the hands of the people, who no longer tolerated the violence that came from the sudden volatile reign. But what was supposed to bring freedom became a war zone. Out of the destruction of those who kept them captive and killed their own, more carnage and bloodshed than Alqueris empire had seen at the hands of the royal family. Where wars and battles for order and control took place in every corner of the continent, blood had eventually birthed borders and nations in its place.

Born from the times of bloodshed, rose the surviving clans we know today; The hillside Rooiboux to the south, the flatland, industrial Matxha to the west, the mountainous Oolonxg to the north, and the seaside Cxai to the east. Each of which have survived and maintained order in their respective nations since the great fall.

Life carries on, and in modern time, these nations continue to tolerate one another within their respective borders, as they once did the royal family of Alqueris.

As much as the stem of the flower tolerates the harsh wind as the storm approaches.

Beneath the modern scope, the Matxha territory thrived in both technology and industry alike, quickly finding itself to be the most populated section of the world, where people came to start their lives anew in its cities. In the Matxha capital of Densriel, many found opportunity in the heart of the territory. People from all over came to the western territory, in hopes for a better life and the privilege of freedom.

A local tea shoppe had popped up in the eastern section of the city, becoming a popular location among a particularly quiet neighborhood. Their popularity skyrocketed soon after opening one late spring, a combined effort of advertisement and hard work between the three workers who owned and ran the establishment amongst themselves.

Once a year, the grand capital went wild on the longest night of the year. The winter solstice had always been a popular holiday associated with magic that everyone in Densriel celebrated, especially those of affinic origin.

There was always something to do in the Matxha territory's capital city.

Osiris spotted the tea shoppe from across the busy street. The shoppe was so well tucked away in the dead shopping district to be so popular. He adjusted his circular rimless glasses, seeing the mob of people take over the inside from afar through the glass windows, being sure to be careful on the icy sidewalk beneath him. His chest length box braids swept to one side, fell over his forest colored hounds tooth scarf and part of his dark copper complexion. The feeling of the rough breeze burnt his brown cheeks and his warm breath left instant clouds whenever he moved.

The weather no longer took its toll on him after being outside for so long. Osiris watched the overflowing tea shoppe and the line beginning to form outside, threatening to spill over to the abandoned building to the left. He tried to make out the forms of those that rushed from both ends of the shop inside, their speed being an incredible attribute he could barely comprehend. With their constant movement, he watched the servers duck and sway around the shop, passing out multiple kettles, utensils, and plates of treats alike with the utmost grace. He felt his chest tighten from the cold, a part of him wanting to get closer to the warmth of the tea shoppe.

Osiris looked at the embellishments of the shop from the outside. The expanse of the hanging sign had a subtle glow of worn-out lights, but remained eye-catching to all who passed by, likely their goal as their name was enough to gain business. The windows were littered with dead ivy vines on the bottom brick lining, an orange door opening and closing continuously to accent the dark colors outside.

He wandered over towards the small line outside and found himself oddly patient, willing to wait to gain entry. The odd feeling inside him yearned for a warm tea on such a cold day.

A large party left their shop, allowing the line outside to enter the tea shoppe. As Osiris entered the doorway, he was met with a gentle wave of warmth, aromas of fresh tea leaves and floral perfumes lining the air. It was almost overwhelming.

A small group of women dressed in formal black attire, complete with matching wide-brim hats, left the shop giggling to themselves, ready to enjoy the remainder of their night elsewhere. Osiris heard a distant comment leave the group, something about the aloof owner of the shop.

Osiris hesitantly made it to the front of the line, as the tea shoppe was overflowing with people. He was immediately overwhelmed by the atmosphere, so full of magic and the beings who held them. He could barely distinguish who held what and where. He saw the tables cluttered with people and teacups in the middle of the shoppe, booths against the windows dedicated to privacy that did not exist that night, and a bar at the other end of the entrance that had run out of seats long ago. The back wall took his breath away. The whole section housed glass canisters on each illuminated black shelf, some full and others close to empty. Every glass was labeled with its own blend in calligraphic writing.

"Hey there, how are you tonight?" A bubbly middle-aged server rushed over to him and stood only briefly, her long dirty blonde hair pushed to the back in a loose ponytail. She wielded an empty black tray to her side. Though she was slowly losing her breath, she still managed a smile and walked him over to a booth by the windows.

The noise was nowhere near as bad after he settled into his seat. Once the first server left, another one with short black hair appeared to take her place, promptly handing Osiris a leather menu, face serious and full of thought before rushing away again.

"I'll be right with you." They quickly walked off to the next table behind him, taking their empty cups in both hands. He watched as they sped off with the empty ones towards the back of the bar, quickly unpacking and placing them into the dishwasher.

The bartender beside them was just as quick, making drinks and tallying up tabs almost simultaneously. Her pale blue oval glasses sat above her head before she flicked them down to read the receipts more clearly.

Osiris couldn't help but find his gaze returning to the second server throwing everything around with no hesitation in their movements. Their short, black, pin straight hair was kept to the back with thin symmetrical strands over each shoulder, a reddish apron sitting atop the black uniform the other two wore, and a silver necklace fixed together a far more formal outfit than he expected for a local tea shoppe. He watched the server run out from the back towards the middle tables, carrying a fresh kettle, six matching teacup sets, and a small black tray beside them. They smoothly caught a falling green teacup from a rowdy table, relieved it was empty, but shaking their head as they placed it back and hurried off towards their next goal. They dropped off the set of cups and made their way back over to his table, only meeting his eyes when they approached. Their hazel brown eyes fixed on his table, placing the delicate black porcelain tea set in front of him. Part of him wondered if a blush could be noticeable against his dark complexion like it would against their pale olive toned face.

"I apologize for the wait, my name is Ayale, what can I get you tonight?" Ayale asked with a rushed tone of voice. He froze up, trying to come up with an answer, even though his menu lay unopened in front of him.

"Hello! I..." Osiris trailed off, even more so unable to answer. "Have no idea what to order. What do you recommend?" He asked earnestly. Ayale's stoic face turned up with a half-smile, amused and maybe pleasantly surprised.

"Well," They looked around the busy shop, spotting the other server standing at the hostess desk, then looking at their bartender behind the black marble top. "I have a minute." Ayale grabbed the menu from him, opening it up and guiding him through it.

"Right here is our specialty blend section, can come as is or with alcohol. It will be good either way, Lau knows how to mix a drink like you wouldn't believe." They gestured with a nod to the bartender. "Over here is our seasonal selection, to the left is white tea, black tea, green tea, then regular blends."

Osiris nodded along, trying to keep his eyes on the menu and off the server, but was less than subtle about his glance.

"If you could drink anything right now, what would it be?" He looked up with a playful smile. Ayale raised a brow in confusion, but Osiris was unsure if he was being too forward. The seconds passed by and suddenly, he wondered if he was amusing or annoying to them. It certainly had to be one of the two for that expression to grace their face.

"I would want something simple, a jasmine tea. Could use the peace tonight as you can see." They huffed, clearly worn out from the busy night. "Look over the menu for a bit and I'll come back." Ayale rushed off to the next table and their brief time together had run out.

Osiris peeked down at the menu, feeling his heart beating a million miles a minute. The eclectic server left a strange feeling in his chest. He waited patiently for their return, rehearsing his order in his head. He hoped he could shed his nerves when they inevitably returned.

Until then, he watched for the graceful server as they extinguished issue after issue. A true powerhouse as they went around cleaning empty tables and replacing tea sets, all while the bartender took her own good look at Osiris. When he felt her eyes on him, Lau the bartender left a harsh stare that seemed to delve into his soul. His anxiety heightened, not knowing how long she had been staring at him for before he noticed. Life was already uncertain as it were, and he didn't want to make more enemies than he already had.

Lau held a cautious expression. A faded-out scar started from her forehead to the side of her face, the remainder of it stretching beneath her wispy brown hair. Clearly a person who had seen a thing or two in her lifetime.

Osiris gave a short wave to her before her attention had been taken by some patrons to her left. He sighed with relief and began to go through the menu, thinking to himself what he might want to order. There was no plan when he entered the tea shoppe.

His heart was suddenly set on jasmine tea, thinking of the night flower associated with the name. Would it be weird to order that after the server went through the menu with him? He felt strands of anxiety creeping up his back, beginning to overthink his choice.

Ayale finished clearing off a table and hurried back over as if they could hear his struggling thoughts. "Figure out what you wanted yet?"

"Jasmine will be just fine. Bring two cups though?" Osiris flashed a confident smile at them.

"Sounds good, expecting someone?"

"Maybe if they have time." He looked up expectedly, unable to stop his spontaneous flirting.

"Got it, I'll be back with your tea." Ayale nodded and wrote his order down before they walked off to the back to brew his tea.

Osiris' smile dropped, as did his face when he realized it went right over their head. He shifted in his seat, uncomfortable with what he had just done, having flirted with someone he just met who was working. His life was in shambles as it were, he didn't need to add onto his or their issues. Life was difficult but letting his playful persona out felt somehow worse.

In a quick instance, he took out his sketchbook and pulled off his glasses. The lenses were necessary for him, but he placed them onto the table, using the moment of partial blindness to reset himself. He rubbed his eyes, not realizing how exhausted he was from the events of the last few days.

Osiris took a few breaths in and out, centering himself amongst the commotion of the tea shop. He opened his sketchbook and pushed himself to make something, anything to keep himself distracted. His hands moved with small strokes, drawing whatever was on his mind. A flower stem came to mind, a trellis beneath it, and small, six petal flowers reached up and down the page.

He felt his quickened heart begin to slow down as he drew in his notebook. Plants always had a way to keep him in place.

Ayale sat in the back, impatiently waiting for multiple kettles of tea to finish brewing. While the night had begun to slow down, the need to rush around and make sure everything was okay remained as fervent as it did when they opened.

Rae was quick as lightning, but they didn't feel right leaving her out there by herself. Lau seemed to have a handle on everything at the bar, though they felt Lau would never speak up if she needed help to begin with.

Ayale wondered if they had ever seen the anxious man in their booth before. He seemed far more nervous than most, noting the odd twitch of his hand when he admitted he didn't know what to order. But he was in a tea shoppe, he would likely find something. Whatever his reason for his nerves, Ayale didn't care enough on such a busy night. They only hoped everyone coming in tonight would come back again, preferably not all at once like the winter solstice shift they were currently working.

The steamers finally stopped, signaling Ayale they were done. In no sooner than seconds, they had the kettles prepared and another black tea set to the side, walking out of the back room and back to Osiris' table. His focused expression broke, promptly closing his sketchbook up, and placing it to the side.

"Alright, here's that extra cup you ordered, did you want anything else or is the tea enough?" Ayale put the kettle up on the table as quickly as they brought it.

"Nope, that was it. Thank you." Osiris' shy voice said, already regretting the idea entirely. Ayale nodded, leaving the bill before going to walk away.

"Wait! Uh," He exclaimed. "My friend canceled on me if you want to take their place. I won't be able to drink all this myself."

"Oh! I'm sorry they canceled." Ayale apologized honestly. They looked over at the bar and the tables to the middle. It was certainly not as busy as before, but they definitely didn't have the time to sit down.

"I don't think I can join you either, it's a very busy night for us. Maybe another time." They nodded before rushing off to the next table, leaving Osiris with ideas for next time.

If he made it next time.

Osiris left his bill paid towards the edge of the table. Mortality was not a concept he wanted to consider tonight. So, he spent the remaining time on his sketchbook, drawing. He had a particular love for art, an outlet that grew with him throughout the good times and the bad. Even if the bad turned worse this week.

He practiced each stroke thousands of times. His sketchbook had nearly been filled primarily with drawings of plants and flowers. Nature had been his lifeblood, always involved in one way or another.

To have his affinity in nature was an added plus.

Osiris smiled as he thought of his half filled book. There was a sense of serenity in drawing where his power had come from. A full circle, just as nature intended.

He was unsure how much time had passed while he continued his drawing. He filled the page with jasmine flowers, stretched over a trellis in some imaginary garden.

"What are you making?" Ayale approached to grab the paid bill and quickly looked over at the sketchbook. Osiris almost jolted up at the sound of their voice, having to gently erase his last pencil mark.

"It's nothing. Just flowers." He responded with an anxious chuckle.

"Very talented." They commented. "I couldn't do that if I tried."

"I imagine you have your own talents elsewhere." He packed his unfinished art away into his faded green backpack.

"Maybe and maybe not." Ayale said back, refusing to elaborate.

"Perhaps a writer of some sort?"

"Pft! Me and words don't get along."

"Words and I, you mean."

"Look at you being funny." Ayale half smiled. "And also proving my point."

"Everyone has something they're good at." Osiris enjoyed seeing them smile, a sight he hoped was real and not just a customer service facade. "I don't believe I introduced myself, my name is Osiris."

"It was nice talking, Osiris. Stay hopeful and have a good night." They tapped the table and walked off with the bill. Lau and Rae slowly began to clean up tables and the bar counter, taking advantage of the crowds thinning out. As Ayale made their way into the backroom, they worried whether they were awkward during the busy shift.

The night wore on into the midnight hour before Osiris had finally left for the night. The tea shoppe remained open well past three am, keeping Ayale, Lau, and Rae later than they had ever stayed before.

It was unanimously decided that tomorrow would be a well-deserved day off for everyone.

# II

A full day of rest later, the three took their days off with no responsibilities to fill. All had agreed it was well-deserved time off.

Ayale found themself unable to get any decent sleep the night before opening the tea shoppe again. Between waking up multiple times through the night, they eventually settled in for a few hours of straight rest to grace the final half of their sleep.

Ayale eventually awoke at one in the afternoon.

So, there they laid, the noon light trickling through their loose blinds, staring up at the ceiling wondering what tonight would bring to the shop.

An hour before opening, both Ayale and Lau cleaned and prepared for the night shift ahead. Tea canisters were wiped down, cup and saucer sets were put in their rightful places, and the bar behind the marble countertops were to be fully stocked with whatever was necessary. There was a large customer base that enjoyed tea in other forms than by itself, an especially popular drink being their house blend of tea with sweet liquor. Ayale really didn't mind some of these drink combinations but found that their classic blends without alcohol was enough for them. They did not entirely favor the concept or taste of liquor, but certainly did not judge those who did. They asked Lau to create a new combination every week, making sure to find the best tea leaves Densriel had to offer in exchange for her effort.

Lau took charge in filling the glass case by the register with freshly baked pastries. From croissants to tea cakes, every space was filled to the brim with some variety of bakery items every night. Ayale had no talent when it came to baking, but Lau took no issue in filling the gaps of knowledge and taught them the skills they needed to learn along the way.

Lau had been nothing but kind since Ayale arrived in Densriel three years ago, with nowhere to go and no place to sleep. Only a few months after being taken in by her, Ayale offered a proposition to open this very shop they both stood within.

As the young tea shop owner reminisced, anxiety began to fill their chest. A sense of foreboding fluttered before being taken away by the sound of Lau crossing the room, mumbling a complaint about the warm weather leaving puddles all over the sidewalk.

The shop in the daytime was far less magical and required a lot of work to prepare for the night to come. Ayale put on a plain outfit in order to clean; a pair of black pants and an open collar black sweater, complete with a small, white jade amulet on their neck.

Ayale looked at the bar, listing off whether every task was complete before opening.

"Lau, what is going on back there?" Ayale asked. Lau popped up from behind the bar, dressed in plain black as well, the desolate look turning from a permanent fixture on her face into a partial smile.

"You're one to talk. Did you finish putting back the sets on the shelf?"

"Done." Ayale hopped up onto a bar stool at the black marble counter, yawning at the thought of opening tonight.

"All the tea sets are polished?"

"Yep."

"And the tables?"

"Set and ready, Lau."

Ayale held the side of the bar top and stretched their back out, then their legs. The day was already so very long, Lau already making her way to the backdoor. She fussed with her metal case, snatching and lighting up a cigarette in annoyance. One quick exhale and soon enough, Lau felt far more human again. Ayale followed behind her, looking up at their beloved bartender in hopes that she were in a sharing mood.

As the gentle drizzle began to come from the dreary sky, Lau and Ayale looked at one another, sharing an expressionless stare.

"One of these days, you should buy your own." Lau hesitantly rolled one over for the excited shop owner. Ayale happily accepted the item, lighting and smoking their own cigarette.

"Nah, that would start a bad habit." They shrugged, exhaling a thin layer of smoke from their mouth into the misty air. Lau frequently made it a point that Ayale should quit smoking, but if the day came that they would give back a cigarette, it would leave her more concerned for their wellbeing.

"Seriously?" Lau took another long drag in the process. "Be better, would you?" Her tone turned serious. The intense look in her eyes was overshadowed by the soft rumble coming from the sky.

As the two watched the sky begin to shift to make room for an incoming storm, the two of them quickly finished their cigarettes in silence before they both went back inside to continue to prepare for the night.

"Did Rae call out?" Lau asked, replacing one of the polished tea sets back to its rightful place in the display case above the shelf of alcohol behind the bar counter.

"Yup," Ayale muttered, picking up a few sets from the drying mat. They polished each cup and saucer, placing them nicely onto the shelves going horizontal. "Just us tonight. She's handling some issues at home."

"I heard she's planning to kick her husband out of the house."

"She's been done with his shit for a while." They dropped onto one of the bar stools. "He always sounded like a deadbeat to me."

Lau nodded slowly. She wanted to add to the conversation, but declined to comment. Instead, she checked the time, which prompted her to place her hair up.

"It's almost opening time." She mumbled with a hair tie in her mouth.

Ayale yawned, not entirely sure how they got out of bed that morning. To be met with news that they were alone on the floor was disgruntling, leaving them ready to melt out of the chair. They would rather be helping Rae and the liberation of her home from her ex-husband than serve customers all night alone. They knew better than to assume Rae needed help, being there would get in her way more than anything.

Lau knew this best, especially after their experience closing with Rae one cold night in February.

The two of them had only a handful of customers between them. It was one of Rae's usual tables that had become disorderly, three older men from the town south of Densriel. They had refused to pay, or leave for that matter. As Lau was readying to head over to the other end of the tea shop, Rae kicked off a chair leg from the unoccupied table nearest her and slammed each cup like a baseball. She finished off the last set, chair leg in hand, and stared at the table of frightened men, waiting with wild eyes to be paid. When no one in the whole bar made so much as a sound, she swung the wooden leg at the tabletop with all the power in her body, cracking it in half down the middle.

"Who's ready to pay?" Lau heard Rae ask the group. They fearfully emptied their wallets, paying their bill before scurrying out of the building.

As if nothing happened, Rae began to clean up the glass shards and wood pieces littering the floor. Before she could throw away the broken chair leg halves, Lau scooped them away, taping them back together with silver tape, and proudly displaying it behind the bar. No word of the incident came out of her mouth until well past closing time. But the smile across her face was one of utmost pride for her coworker and close friend.

It was not until the next day that Ayale came in and saw the broken table and the taped-up leg behind the bar. That was the last time they called out of work for a long time.

"Are you ready?" Lau interrupted their train of thought and motioned to the front door, keys in hand.

"Sure." Ayale mumbled. They put on their black apron, adorned with a few buttons gifted by customers over the years. They peered out the door from behind Lau, wondering if the impending storm from earlier would hit soon. The evening sky had its fill of clouds, streetlights beginning to turn on up and down the street. The tea shoppe wedged between far worse off buildings, but left its impact against the seemingly abandoned neighborhood.

The moon began to glow behind the clouds in the distance, trying to rise above them in their region. If luck would find them, Ayale considered expansion into the building next to them, hopefully in the next few years if they grew their customer base. They were unsure on how to get Lau to agree, attempting to come up with an angle as they watched her turn the lights on.

Tonight was going to be a long night.

The nighttime crowd seemed to come and go, similar to the last few weeks, and identical to this time last year. The only difference was their increased volume, thanks to Rae's bubbly personality drawing in a few extras from a recently closed bar down the street. At some point, every customer tonight became a blur to Ayale, every request the same. Nothing about the night shift stood out, leaving Ayale and Lau going through the motions.

An hour prior to closing, something interesting took everyone's attention.

Ayale was in the midst of cleaning off a table and noticed a friendly face. At the table nearest them, sat the young man from two nights ago. Odder than that, he already seemed to have ordered a setup, with a teapot and two cups across from one another, as though someone was to be seated across from him. They made brief eye contact as Ayale brought the dishes from the table they worked on to the area behind the bar.

Lau stared at the stranger's setup, taking Ayale's attention before they recognized where her eyes lingered. The look on her face was nothing they had ever seen on her before. They figured it would be best to ask later before cautiously heading over to his booth.

"Why are you buying from the bar and not me?" Ayale approached the tableside and leaned against the edge, part joking but also genuinely curious. The table had been set up for two indeed, to Ayale's surprise. Osiris smiled as he gestured to the seat across from him. They obliged and sat down, wondering if they were making a mistake doing so.

"I ordered your jasmine tea from Rae actually. I was hoping we could continue where we left off and talk some more tonight." Osiris first poured into the black ceramic teacup, decorated in shimmering mint-colored clovers, before sliding the cup across to them. He then poured for himself into a similar cup, though the clovers were replaced with forest colored flowering vines that wove around in an infinite circle around the cup.

Ayale darted their eyes to Lau, who dared to stare back with her dark eyes narrowed. There was a clear agitation in the way she watched them both.

"Thank you. I would love to." Ayale partly smiled, something Osiris smiled to himself over. He sipped his jasmine tea and did his best to begin where the two had left off. Osiris blushed, nervously adjusting his glasses. He did not expect his forward request to work out. Especially with the way the bartender behind the bar stared daggers at him. His luck this week had been anything but good to him.

Yet he wanted to try. It wasn't every day that he felt so enamored by someone in such dire circumstances.

"So, do you enjoy the arts? Painting or anything like that?" Osiris pulled a topic out of thin air, hoping for the best.

"I do not. I'm a bit plain, I'm sorry." Ayale apologized, not sure what else to say.

"That's okay, there is nothing wrong with that. Do you make the tea that you serve here?" He asked with a sense of excitement, genuinely wondering if any tea shops still observed growing their own leaves.

"Well, it depends on the plant. We try to stay local, that is if we can't grow it ourselves. I'm not personally great with plants, but our bartender happens to know a thing or two." Ayale fought against their awkward habits, trying their best to make genuine conversation and turning off their customer service voice. Something that wasn't their strongest suit.

"That sounds difficult," Osiris commented, looking at the tea canisters on display above the bar area. He wanted to ask something that popped up into his mind, yet he struggled to put it into words. In his time here, he had the sense of magic being around the tea shoppe. It would make perfect sense considering the amount of people that came to the area for the last major holiday.

"Ayale, are you..." Osiris trailed off. He thought it would come to him if he started, but now he sat there with empty words and a silent, staring server across from him. With nothing coming out, he froze in his seat, looking like a nervous wreck. His anxiety flooded him at that moment.

Ayale felt their own anxiety rise in their throat, feeling Lau's intense stare while waiting for Osiris to finish asking his question. They stood promptly from the booth, unable to take the pressure of waiting, taking Osiris aback.

"Is everything okay?" He asked, interrupting his question.

"I'll be right back." They hurried toward the bar area. To their surprise, Rae sat at the bar in front of Lau, drinking tea with a side eye following Ayale, before she followed them around to the back of the shoppe.

"Who is that lovely lad there? He requested a double tea set from me a bit ago." Rae wiggled her aged blonde brows, immediately making Ayale cringe.

"A spy for the Matxha clan family." Lau appeared from behind, roughly placing a pint glass on a nearby prep table. She couldn't quite prove her concerns, but her certainty was fierce, nonetheless.

"Well hold on, what makes you say that?" Rae put her cup down on the same table, trying to reason with her.

"Isn't it obvious to either of you?" Lau muttered, hoping no one could hear her. But Rae wasn't having it.

"Aya, go back and chat with him some more. What Matxha clan member would make a tea setup for two like that? Go be young and talk! I'll keep Lau at bay." Rae made her way back to the bar, taking Lau with her. Ayale looked horrified at the singular word talk. Were they supposed to be this terrified?

Although.

Maybe a part of them did want to go back. They couldn't recall the last time they had a friend, or even considered anyone as such outside of Lau and Rae.

They shuffled awkwardly from the backroom but stopped at the bar, their face turning back to their normal stoic expression.

All three took turns looking at Osiris, who was none the wiser and patiently pulled out his sketchbook from his bag to draw.

Rae stifled her giggle, coughing instead.

Lau refused to amuse either of them with anything but a scowl.

Ayale fiddled with their hands, holding their breath as they turned back to Rae with a worried look.

"Go back over, what's the worst that could happen?" Rae shooed them with a low voice.

"What if Lau is right?" Ayale frantically whispered back.

"I doubt it. No clan people have come here since we've opened, and they won't start now." Rae slapped Ayale's shoulder as the two of them looked back to Osiris' table.

"Talk to him. I can clean up." Rae winked at the stiff tea shoppe owner, but Lau shook her head in response.

Ayale took a deep breath and walked back over to Osiris, taking their apron off and folding it, leaving it on a nearby empty table.

"Sorry about that." They apologized as they sat back down. Osiris' face lit back up from his sketchbook when they sat back down, the excitement in his eyes was all the evidence they needed.

"Not a problem," He nodded, trying not to show his relief that they came back at all. "I kept your tea warm, I hope that's okay." Osiris drew a quick circle with his index finger on the table, which surged a small amount of heat into the cups and pot atop them. They rumbled softly in response.

Ayale's eyes widened, unaware that Osiris had an affinity or could do magic, let alone such a spell in public of all places. They stared at him with a mixture of fascination and terror.

"Osiris!" They quietly scolded, trying to stifle their surprise.

"Did you prefer your drink cold?" He asked, but Ayale held back their rising reaction.

"This is just fine, thank you." Ayale picked up their teacup, hesitantly sipping the warm tea. "Where did you learn that? You know that's dangerous right? You can't be doing that in public."

"Self-taught but it's a small trick, no affinity work. And I am very aware of the danger."

"Yet here you are. Using your talents for warming up tea." They commented, tired of social interaction already.

"Thank you." Osiris played with his braids before pushing them to one side, attempting to hide his flustered expression. "What about you?" He asked, intrigued by Ayale's reaction.

"I hold my expertise elsewhere. Like I said before." They replied, short and sweet, before taking another sip.

"I would love to see it someday, if you don't mind it."

"Only time will tell." They snickered, amused by his request. Ayale looked to the bar area, hoping to see Lau and Rae occupied. Instead, Rae was attempting to climb the side of the display case, before Lau took hold of Rae and placed her onto her shoulders. Rae stretched out to the top shelf to grab her legendary wooden stick. It wasn't soon after that the few patrons sitting bar-side were in a small uproar over the legendary chair leg.

Ayale and Osiris watched as Rae took the chair leg in hand and had the bar patrons chanting her name, holding it up with pride above her head like a gladiator holding their sword after a victory.

"They're very lively." Osiris laughed, unsure what the leg symbolized but enjoying the atmosphere all the same.

"Welcome to the tea shoppe, Osiris. Where the lively come to meet and tell their tales." Ayale peered over to the two workers, parading the leg around and showing it off to everyone left in the tea bar. Osiris glanced at Ayale, content with everything in the shoppe, pretending tomorrow would never come.

# III

The next morning came and went faster than Ayale had expected. They could not help but feel an unplaced excitement for the night to come. The rain began to pour down on the city of Densriel. That was until the evening sky washed over the rain and the tea shoppe opened for the night. Lau turned to the door but hesitated to unlock it. Ayale and Rae set up each table with candles, hoping for the Friday night rush to set them well off for the week.

Rae lit a candle with the wick of another lit one nearby. "Lau, have you opened yet?" But Lau didn't say a word, instead turning to look at Rae and Ayale, both visibly confused.

Lau shot a concerned glare at Ayale. "I don't think Osiris is safe to be around."

"This again?" Rae sighed heavily. Lau's pointed expression turned towards Rae.

"Our lives are not a joke. Do you think these clans play games?"

"No, I just think that he's some kid who's smitten by our dear Ayale. Harmless flirting is what young adults are supposed to do."

"He could have orders from the other clans too, Rae!"

Rae crossed her arms over her chest. "You need to stop assuming that any of the clans are after us."

"I'm just worried Rae. I want to be sure that we're left alone and keep it that way. We deserve peace after everything we have all been through." Lau defended herself, her voice growing quiet.

"I won't let anything happen to either of you. No clans will get in the way of our peace, with or without their magical tirades. I promise." Rae walked over to Lau's side, placing a comforting arm around her back. She placed her head on her shoulder, feeling Lau relax beneath her.

"I just want to protect you, too. Prison doesn't need you a second time." Lau sighed.

"If anyone from the clans tries to find me, I won't let them near either of you." Ayale chimed in with a low voice, fixing their dark messy hair in the front, their serious expression unchanged. Lau and Rae shared a look before concern crossed them.

Rae wandered over to Ayale, placing her arm around their shoulders and pulling them close. "We know. But we won't have you deal with it alone."

"If it comes down to it, I will make sure they can't do anything. Whatever it takes." Ayale vowed, grabbing one of Lau's stolen cigarettes out from their apron pocket before walking out the back door.

Osiris found himself wandering the humidity that made up the air around the lesser-known neighborhoods of Densriel. Some part of him knew to be careful, unsure who or what could be around the corner, but the other told him it was no use being frightened. Not after knowing the Matxha clan was coming after him.

He walked through one of the alleys, the solid brick walls on both sides stained with colors and designs he hadn't seen before. For a moment, Osiris stopped to admire the work. If things had been different, perhaps he could have followed a different path instead of the one that led him to where he was being hunted down by one of the most dangerous clans in the continent.

His eyes traced the line work, noting a few smaller details, ones he could easily fix if he had the materials on him. The only thing in his backpack had been whatever money he had left over from his savings, clothes, and whatever he could fit of his sketching supplies.

The incoming wind pulled him away from the mural on the wall. His mind wandered back to the tea shoppe, going back and forth between whether he should go again. There were quite a few reasons to go, after all. Not that he was willing to admit all of those reasons, but he did yearn for the jasmine tea from a few nights ago.

Walking by the alley at the same time was Ayale in their work uniform, the server he invited all too enthusiastically to sit with him, lying about how his friend didn't show up for tea. They turned almost instantly, meeting Osiris with a defensive glare before sighing in relief. "Ah, Osiris." A partial smile upturned on their lips.

Osiris' eyes lit up, relieved to see a somewhat friendly face. "Ayale, it's been so long." He joked, returning the smile as they came down the alley.

"Very funny." They scoffed, putting their lighter back into their pocket and turning to look at the mural on the wall. "Do you come down here often?"

"Not as often as I would like to," Osiris sighed, turning with them. "And you? I didn't think you were much into art."

"I can appreciate the talent and creativity behind it. Besides, the artist alley is too good not to come down occasionally. Seems someone updated the mural recently."

"That they did." Osiris looked over the newly added pieces to the art on the brick wall. New line-work had been added, extra shading and the like. His eyes peered over to Ayale, their neutral expression barely piqued with intrigue as it looked at every corner of the piece. Before they turned to Osiris, he shot his eyes back to the artwork in front of the two of them. "It takes a lot of effort to make things like this."

"That's the beauty of art. The hard work. The constant practice. I commend anyone who can create something so ephemeral." Ayale commented, nodding off at their watch. "Shit, I should get back." They met his uncertain expression with a barebones smile before hurrying out of the alley. "Nice to see you again, Osiris. Hopefully I'll see you at the tea shoppe soon?" They asked before making their way around the corner, running back to the tea shoppe for opening.

Osiris found himself wishing they stayed, even just a minute longer so he could say a proper goodbye.

*

The rain came back later in the nighttime, turning torrential so quickly that Osiris did not prepare for the shift in weather while he walked across the busy street. He sought out anything nearby to wait out the edges of the storm. With his hands above his eyes to shield his vision, he wandered toward one of many abandoned buildings in the district. He ducked beneath the overhang, sitting pretty on the dry concrete beneath.

Osiris put down his backpack to the space left of him, taking the hair tie from his wrist and holding it in his mouth while he put his braids up into a ponytail. Not long after he took out a small notebook from his bag and began to draw, making a small, intricate circle with symbols of flames in patterns around the page. As he completed the sketch, it was then a clap of thunder rumbled heavily above him, contrasting the previous nights' weather forecast.

He ripped the piece of paper out of his notebook, taking out another set of papers from his bag which he placed beneath his crude drawing. With a concentrative look on his face and a wave of his hand, the two papers burned up together, setting his fate aflame with them.

*

Ayale felt the clap of thunder shake the tea shoppe. With a tray in hand, they placed a new set of cloud themed white cups onto a table for two. Both people sitting down by the window stopped their conversation to greet Ayale.

"Hello!" The pale haired customer greeted them with enthusiasm before Ayale could say anything. The tall man sitting across from them stood out far less than his counterpart, putting his dark curls into a low bun while his eyes fixed on the menu. His hand reached over for the other person's, his darker skin tone contrasting with the intriguing person across from him, who practically paled against the candlelight in the middle of the table. The couple was a bit cute, Ayale thought.

"How are you two tonight?" Ayale asked, noting the loving gaze of the man sitting across. His serious expression melted away at the sight of his significant other, his poise and affection hand in hand.

"We are lovely, thank you," The person across from him responded, looking to their partner. "Amare, what did you have in mind?"

"Not sure yet, Taiya. But, if I had to pick... spiced chai perhaps?"

"Sounds like we'll take a pot of that then." Taiya looked up at Ayale a moment too long. Though it was only seconds between them, Ayale felt as though they could be seen from miles away.

Did the couple know Ayale from anywhere? Why did it feel as though Taiya knew something they shouldn't?

Ayale shook their thoughts away and cleared their throat.

30

"One pot of spiced chai, anything else?" They scribbled down their order and forced a smile to the surface.

"Nope! Thank you!" Taiya returned the smile with a tenfold grin. Ayale left the couple behind, making their way to the back of the bar to begin on their order. They weren't sure why, but a tinge of anxiety made its way into their head, almost certain that the cute couple were anything other than strange.

"What was that about?" The man sitting across asked, nervously shifting around the silver band on his ring finger. It took a minute for Taiya to respond, lost in their thoughts. The white strands laid about loose over their shoulders, still just as they sat. They pushed away a few of the strands that had fallen over their face, returning to his confused gaze.

"Just felt something, but nothing of concern. Stop worrying so much." They commented, playfully squeezing his hand.

As the rain began its descent into the city streets, the only evidence was visible by the fluorescent streetlights that lined up the road outside of the tea shoppe. The light drizzle turned back into a demanding downpour. Ayale watched the rain come down through the window nearest the couple, before noticing their cute exchanges with one another.

Ayale couldn't stop themself from staring. Their energy was something otherworldly. So soothing and sweet. Their clear trust for one another had them a touch envious. But to trust someone like that was not an option for Ayale, at least no one outside of Lau and Rae.

They noticed the front door open and close. At that moment, Ayale had hoped it was the friendly face who had been visiting them as of late. But instead, it was a mere breeze of wind that passed through the creaking door, to their disappointment.

Ayale picked up the finished brewing chai and picked up the pot, bringing it back over to the cute couple, feeling odd as they approached. They placed the pot down without a word, going on their way before Taiya's loud voice froze them in place.

"Wait!" Taiya accidentally yelled much louder than they intended. Amare would have been more embarrassed if he wasn't used to their behavior.

"Please, take this, too." Taiya handed them a raw purple stone from their pocket and pressed it into their hand, along with money for their bill. It was jagged across the top and smooth beneath. A geode of some sort. "Stay strong and keep resilient." Their empathetic golden eyes truly saw Ayale for what they were; a person just trying to rebuild their life.

"Thank you?" Ayale answered in a low, confused voice, a grateful look mixed with confusion on their expression. They made their way back to the bar, holding the aforementioned geode in one hand and an empty tray in the other.

"What the hell is that?" Lau asked, placing a drink in front of a distracted patron at the bar. Ayale leaned onto the bar beside a busy Lau, still straightening out what happened themself. They put the stone from their hand onto the display and simply shrugged.

"I have no idea, it's neat though." Ayale smiled and tilted their head to take a better look, wondering if what the couple had together was possible for anyone.

"Speaking of weird, have you seen Rae?" Lau asked, beginning to clean and polish a teacup set from the set drying in the shelves hidden below the bar side.

"Not for a bit, probably went out to smoke." Ayale said, craving a cigarette themself. The temptation grew when they looked over at the couple again. "Can I have one in the meantime?" They asked, hoping to make a run for it into the rainy night. They enjoyed the thunder accompanying the storm above them and wanted an excuse to watch it. Lau grumbled but did not refuse the request as she handed off her case to Ayale.

"Just be quick about it." Lau stated, signaling with a nod to the back door.

Ayale did not hesitate, making their way out the back, with a lighter stolen from the kitchen. They settled beneath the doorframe, setting off the lighter, and igniting a cigarette out of the case. The rain began to lessen, to Ayale's luck. They took the spare moments as something unhindered, unable to be interrupted by anything except the reflection of the city lights on the wet pavement behind the tea shoppe. The subtle sounds of the rain hitting roofs, concrete, and the awning above them was all the evidence that they existed in this world.

Above all, the only people who mattered to Ayale were Rae and Lau. No one else. It was their first meeting almost three full years ago, on a night so similar to this one, but far colder. Yet, it was the first time they felt warmth from another person. As the two of them risked everything for taking in Ayale, they wanted to thank the pair by creating something that pulled them up from only survival. The idea of opening the shop was thus born.

With all their money pooled together, hopes, and talents, L'Ayale's Tea Shoppe was born.

Ayale's distant frown turned back up. The fire glowing from the lighter radiated far more than the light of the streetlamps across. The smoke billowed from their lips and the gentle breeze took away their excessive thoughts.

"Honey, we should talk." Rae ran up in front Ayale with an umbrella overhead and a piece of paper in hand.

When Ayale looked down, they took a nervous inhale of their cigarette. Rae closed her umbrella and joined them beneath the protective awning. Rae fixed her blonde hair back behind her ears, her hesitant expression ripping the anxiety out of Ayale's chest before finally handing over the roughly folded up piece of paper.

Ayale unraveled the folded-up poster, revealing a 'wanted' sign in capital letters at the very bottom, with an official stamp from the desk of the Matxha clan themselves. Their heart sank into their throat as they unfolded part of it, going face to face with a photo of their local tea shoppe visitor, Osiris. Their stare was blank and unyielding to any emotion.

Rae braced herself, waiting for even a single word to leave Ayale's mouth. It was Rae who spoke instead.

"Aya, I don't know what to say. I'm so sorry." Rae put her arm across their shoulder to comfort them. But Ayale simply handed back the note and took another drag of their cigarette. They looked out beyond the cloudy sky and streetlights, wishing they could be a part of the calm rain rather than the incoming thunder.

Anything to ignore the poster in Rae's hands.

# IV

The next day came and went so quickly that the night seemed almost infinite. Ayale worked their shift alongside Lau and Rae in their typical black uniform. Their focus remained on the shoppe and for the weekend that was slowly creeping up on the trio. But the night was nowhere near as busy as their holiday last week. The oddly quiet night allowed everyone on shift to let loose for a bit, engaging more casually with the bar scene.

Lau offered the two of them alcohol, on or off the menu. The offer was politely declined from Ayale. It didn't stop them from thinking about the poster from the other night. That much was clear to Rae, who didn't dare bring it up in front of Lau.

As hour after hour passed by, the slow night progressed. Ayale was allowed time to decompress, the lack of customers bringing the two of them a quiet, ambient night. Rae and Ayale made themselves comfortable at the bar, sitting beside one another. Rae took her drink in hand, courtesy of Lau, bumping into Ayale's shoulder to catch their attention. "What are you thinking about?"

"Absolutely nothing." Ayale lied, sipping their plain ginger tea in a black teacup.

"Talk to me, would you?"

"If you must know," They started, but a frustrated sigh left their lips, struggling to put their thoughts into words. "I'm worried that Lau was right. Maybe I should have kept my head down." They sank onto the table.

"What do you mean?"

Ayale shot her a torn glance.

"I wish I didn't see that poster, Rae. I wish I had listened to Lau and walked away. I'm embarrassed more than anything."

"People your age, they do things like this. I don't ever want you to regret doing anything as mundane as trying to make friends. You deserve normalcy." Rae pulled them into a half embrace.

"You guys took a huge risk on me. I almost screwed it all up. How could you act like I did nothing wrong?"

"Easy. I think I speak for us both when I say we love you more than we fear the clans. More than the Matxha family, more than any of them. Especially me, what are they going to do? Take away my affinity? Like they left me any last time? Besides," Rae put her drink down on the black marble top and walked around to the other side of the bar. It took a few attempts, but she jumped up trying to reach the shelf display where the chair leg sat on.

"Who would try me if I wielded this thing?" Rae pretended to swing it around, using it as a fencing sword. But Lau quickly stepped in and confiscated the leg, placing it back on the high shelf.

"No one in their right mind would dare." Lau crossed her arms with a hint of a smile growing on her rough features.

Ayale watched as the bartender and waitress bicker, as if they were an old couple in public. They felt right at home, a smile returning on their face.

Whether they were ready to admit it or not, the tea shoppe itself truly felt like home. Ayale hoped to have many more years of peace, for the prosperity of the tea shoppe. They would happily work alongside the two that took them in for as long as Lau and Rae would have them.

The bell at the orange door jingled. Two well-dressed men in charcoal suits and green undershirts peeking from their necks entered the tea shoppe, carefully looking around the empty tables and even more discreetly at the handful of patrons that sat at the bar. Ayale stole a glance from the reflection of the glass bar display and looked at the deep green from the chest pockets. The stitched white flower buds were only a couple inches in diameter that decorated their collars. They were quickly identified as lower members of the Matxha clan.

Lau stood still behind the bar, narrowing her eyes as she carefully watched them make their way to the seats beside Ayale, who managed to maintain their stoic expression.

"Can I help you gentlemen?" Lau asked, walking further down the bar to draw attention towards her and no one else. Ayale sat still and silent, not wanting to stand out in any way possible.

The two men had matching tattoos peeking from their neck, lines stretching around each shoulder and likely down their back. Lau quietly sought out each exit and recalled the emergency plan the trio came up with in the tea shoppe's earlier days.

"Have any of you seen this man?" The first suited man with a dark, straight cut beard that ended halfway up his cheek stepped closest to the bar, handing Lau a photo of who was certainly Osiris.

"No." Without so much as a blink, she handed the photo back, patiently waiting for the two to leave her shop. Ayale and Rae both kept quiet, as did the other patrons.

"Mind if I ask around?" The same man began to circle around the bar, asking everyone regardless of Lau's response. She had no choice but to allow it with a quick nod.

Ayale only shook their head and shrugged, feigning his existence in the shoppe within the last few days.

The pair went around the scarcely taken tables and managed to avoid a few others sitting at the bar. It only took a few minutes before the two clan members left the tea shoppe. Ayale visibly decompressed, their shoulders sinking back down from their stiff position prior.

They could finally breathe easy. Rae exhaled, having held in her own breath unknowingly. She reached her hand into Lau's coat pocket and retrieved the cigarette case, taking out three sticks from the metal case.

"I think we deserve a breather after this, let's go out the back." Rae muttered, annoyed that she would have to face a Matxha member this late at night. She led the two out the back door, waiting for Lau to object, to no avail. Both followed her to the backdoor, standing beneath the awning. Lau would never endorse smoking, finding herself almost constantly scolding the others for doing so.

Instead, all she could think about was Osiris' face on the picture she was shown moments ago.

"Rae," Lau began, taking the cigarette from Rae's hand.

"Don't start." Rae retorted with, nowhere near in the mood to hear I told you so.

The three stood side by side, lighting one another's cigarettes, and letting the cool night air refresh them from the situation only moments ago. A more understood feeling had never come across the trio. The Matxha clan had never entered their beloved tea shoppe, let alone looking for someone wanted across the territory.

And of course, it had to be the man who showed interest in their Ayale. Someone who actively wanted to be their friend, for the first time since they moved to Densriel.

The three of them had adversely different thoughts on the situation.

Rae felt a sense of guilt for pushing the two to speak, yet felt equally bad for Ayale, who seemed to never get the chance to explore new things, nor interact with others their age, unless as a server.

Lau only felt a sense of protectiveness over the other two. Nothing and no one would ever be enough to justify putting either of them in danger.

Ayale was only numb. Being a fun-loving adult with a carefree attitude did not come easily and, after this, probably never would again.

"Do we know what they wanted with him?" Rae asked, basking in the misty air.

"No." Lau finished their cigarette off before heading back inside to tend to the tea shoppe. "Less is more. I don't want to know."

"Well shit. Makes you wonder what he did to piss off the Matxha family. Those goons were ready to shake him down." Rae hypothesized, a few theories coming to mind.

"Mhhm." Ayale grumbled, cigarette in mouth. It had been some time since any of them heard of the Matxha clan looking for someone. Regardless, Ayale wanted nothing to do with it, absolving themself from thinking about the clans for the rest of the night.

"Can I be honest with you, Rae?" Ayale asked. Rae peered over, seeing their vision stare into the distant alleyway.

"He seemed alright." Ayale said. They took a long drag of their cigarette and refused to make any eye contact with her. Not after admitting something like that. Rae nodded slowly, feeling the guilt well up far more than before. She just wanted Ayale to be happy. Instead, she managed to cause more harm than help.

The tired servers stood side by side, finishing off whatever was left of their cigarettes.

The trio closed up the shoppe for the night. Lau locked the door and placed the last of the teacups and plate sets from the dishwasher to the shelves behind her. Ayale grabbed chairs across the room and placed them upside down on each table, tending to the floor immediately after. Rae hung around in one of the remote booths, telling yet another rare tale to Ayale and Lau about a time in her life when she still held a fiery elemental affinity. She was one of the first in her hometown and held great pride for that matter.

Ayale would never admit it, but these riveting tales were easy to lose themself into. Rae being there made work some nights so much more bearable.

Lau seemed to wave off these unspoken adventures, but Ayale could tell she was just as interested in the tales of her youth. Those particular tales reminded them both of their pasts, long gone for many years. Any mention of affinities was a sensitive topic to each of the three, for vastly different reasons. Lau may have been the only one who looked upon the topic with silence. Her own past was a taboo subject, never to be asked or questioned about unless she brought it up herself.

Ayale and Rae knew very little of Lau's time prior to bartending, or if she held an affinity of her own. All anyone needed to know was that she had done her time, as Lau once said.

Rae had displayed her hardships with absolute honesty, hoping that those who listened would learn the lessons she wished she knew years ago. She was an open book, which made her the easiest to speak to, as both a friend and a colleague. Such was why both cared so greatly for Rae and her mischief. The only issue was her short-tempered behavior. Many of her stories wove tales of intrigue, but the one she did not dare to touch was the day her affinity had been forcefully taken away as sentencing for a crime. One that no one had been told how or what happened.

Both knew better than to ask questions upon the topic, and in response, Lau and Ayale seldom spoke of their own.

Affinities, in their day and age, was dangerous. Use of it came with consequences. Whether it was the past monarchical government or the clan families that rose up after it, no time had ever been safe to be a user of magic. There were two kinds of affinities; a common occurrence was a well of magic born inside of the person, giving them way to a plethora of possibilities and of curses, equally. The raw affinity magic that came from the land's most sacred forces itself, known as elementals, were far more uncommon though, and equally as dangerous.

Ayale knew better than to ask either of their affinities and in turn, would not be asked about their own.

The three of them understood this unspoken rule, to never force anyone to speak of their pasts, unless willing or, in one rare case, necessary.

The untimely rain quietly pattered against the glass windows. Every day so far had given way to rain, sort of bringing down the mood and leaving both staff and customers equally lethargic. Ayale continued cleaning the floors, thinking this week would finish off slowly in the tea shoppe, especially right after their solstice celebration. They could handle a few slow days, but secretly hoped the crowd would pick up again.

Ayale's life, at that very moment, stood to be completely average. Nothing could have told them they would be here at this shop. A newly twenty-five-year-old who strove to live underneath the radar.

The last big event brought in enough business to make any entrepreneur happy. They had the busiest holiday since opening the tea shoppe a few years ago, boding well for the days to come. When Ayale began to clean off the tables between each booth, they approached the distant corner and worked their way down the line. No thoughts crossed their mind, up until they reached the booth they had sat in with Osiris just two nights ago. They recalled the tea setup he made for them both, the way their conversation barely flowed, yet his attempt to speak in place of their silence.

The mere idea of enjoying someone left them frustrated and annoyed.

Someone on the loose from the Matxha clan and an affinity user of some sort.

What a combination.

They only wished they could have ignored him the first time and not have listened to Rae. The idea of crossing paths again made them even more annoyed, scrubbing the table a little harder against their own irritation.

Ayale solemnly wondered if hiding away was the right thing to do. But at the same time, they worked hard for the life they created in Densriel. For the first time in their life, they were safe, they had free will, and most importantly, people who cared about them. They could never see themself willing to throw it all away.

They never wished for the lifestyle of these clans, nor desired to take any part in them.

The humble tea shoppe owner continued to clean the remaining tables, letting go of the heavy thoughts, as the rain continued to drizzle down on the cloudy city of Densriel.

V

A few days had come and passed, each slowly bringing an increase in volume at the tea shoppe since the solstice event. While business was thriving, Ayale moved with the flow of things. They couldn't stop thinking if those men in suits would come back, whether they would find out about the young man who frequented their shop.

Whether they would find out Lau and Ayale lied right to their faces.

Every morning and every night, Ayale was defensive and ready for anything to happen. They found themself exhausted constantly, but unable to find a way to sleep through the night. That was a common occurrence, even with the varieties of tea at their disposal. They only hoped their fear would end at a certain point and allow them the rest they truly needed. Those particular nights bode to be some of the worst, because no matter how much they craved to sleep, it was only achieved for a few hours before abruptly waking up.

Ayale gave up altogether and left the small apartment building above the tea shoppe, an hour after midnight. They snatched Lau's cigarette case and lighter, placing it in their coat pocket. It was better than being in a stuffy room, alone with their thoughts.

As they walked down the back stairs, they crossed a short distance to the abandoned alleyway. The chilly night air left a tender red hue on both cheeks, already far better off than the other option of staying inside. Nothing but the noise of the city and the fine mist in the air, collecting into foggy patches, could ever bring this kind of peace. Alone and unbothered, Ayale took out a cigarette, shielding it from the breeze as they lit it away from the shifting wind. The tentative strand of smoke left their mouth, dissipating against the clouds in the night sky.

Moments where they could simply walk outside were freeing. Though they fought long and hard for their self-preserving peace, it did not take away any of their uncertainty. Ayale had been approaching three full years since their initial run towards freedom.

When they had the chance to be alone, they were instantly reminded what they fled home for.

Ayale remembered the feeling so clearly, recalling a night just like that one. The only difference being the sinking feeling in their chest when they arrived. Out of the hardship of their past, it made them all the more thankful for where they stood at that moment.

After spending a week on the road, taking trains and hitching rides from strangers, Ayale ended up in Densriel, an older mill city of the Matxha territory.

Lau, having been a bartender in a dying restaurant, watched as Ayale frequented their bar, night after night. A simple conversation had turned into many, and soon enough, they told Lau the fact that they were a runaway.

The same night Lau would take them in, Ayale had been served some of the best tea they ever had in the restaurant. An earthy jasmine tea. The waitress was just as warm and bubbly, checking in on Ayale throughout the night and sharing her own tales of triumph after running away herself. Something about her was an instant source of comfort, even if Ayale didn't know Rae at the time.

As the days went by, they refused to sit around Lau's tiny upstairs apartment and picked up a job in the same restaurant. When the time came for it to close its doors, Ayale convinced Lau to buy it out alongside them, renovate, and open the city's first tea shoppe. The place was falling apart when they arrived in Densriel, the floor ridden with loose planks, discoloration, and scuffs beneath each table. Blotches of paint were coming off the walls. It was an ordeal in and of itself. It took quite a bit of convincing, a day short of a month.

Ayale and Lau went to work, doing all the renovations themselves. There was no question to bring in Rae, and everything took off from there. While the decision to buy the shop was a huge choice, it was not one of regret for any of them.

A nearby tree out front of the alley crashed into the middle of the wet street, nearly taking the cigarette out of Ayale's mouth. The torn-up trunk was barely in their view before voices were heard in the distance.

They quietly stepped over to the edge of the alley, keeping wary of their surroundings, until they spotted the two Matxha men from the bar attempting to restrain someone. It had been a while since Ayale witnessed such a brawl between the clan and a citizen.

The fight escalated as they tried to pin the person against the building behind them. The solid metal door behind was left with indentations before the other person fell to the ground.

Ayale was too far to distinguish the other person involved, finishing their cigarette and beginning to walk back towards the apartment. It wasn't until they heard a far too familiar scream that they froze right then and there.

They looked back towards the scene ahead and crept closer, matching the voice to the face.

They watched as Osiris was pinned down onto a shoddily drawn magic circle, blood streaming down the side of his face and into the glowing symbols surrounding him, Ayale knew those signs well, as would anyone else, in or out of the Matxha territory.

A disintegration ritual, one meant to pull out a person's affinity.

In an instant, they turned from the scene, feeling around inside their pocket. No one deserved such a fate.

They didn't think twice before taking out the knife from their jacket pocket and barging into the altercation. Ayale rushed into the alley, tackling the first suited man, the glowing circle dissolving into mist when his concentration broke. No sooner did the man's head hit the concrete, rendering him unconscious on the ground.

Osiris watched Ayale struggle to take on the second Matxha member, blocking his flurry of aimless punching with their forearms and ducking back before swinging their knife forward, aiming for his shoulder. Before Ayale could pin him down, he threw them across the alley against a brick wall.

Ayale stood back up and charged at the last standing Matxha clan member again.

As soon as they saw him brandish a knife of his own, they knew there was no reason to hold back, that their last stand was life or death. Ayale swiftly grabbed the small blade and lodged it into his right side before he could even register where they stood. His dark eyes widened, a scream ripping from his throat as they took the blade out and kicked him into a nearby window, boarded up with mounted plywood.

Everything moved far too quickly for Osiris to register. He was beyond exhausted, dizzy, and unable to catch his breath from the initial struggle. Ayale spared no time grabbing his hand and pulling him up from the ground.

"We need to leave now, get up!" Ayale shouted, watching the suited man writhe in pain on the ground in a puddle of his own blood. Osiris nodded and let Ayale take him down the alleyway and down the street, trying desperately to get away from the crime scene they just created. They took to a side street and moved as fast as possible from the leer of streetlights. Even as they hurried down the street, Ayale maintained their composure until they turned into the alley. They were met with the second man they had stabbed, clutching his side, awaiting them at the other end.

Ayale came to an abrupt stop, swinging back out towards the dark street they came from. But the first Matxha member stood solemnly at the entryway.

With little choice left in the matter, Ayale froze up in fear. Osiris tried to pull them away, but they refused until both men started to descend from either end of the alley, though one slower than the other.

Ayale's wide hazel eyes fixated on the ground beneath them. The strange feeling that welled up within them overflowed, swinging their vision up at the first person across the alley. With no hesitation, they waved their hands upward before the tea shoppe owner slammed the heel of their right boot onto the concrete. The alleyway began to shake on command. Both men at each end struggled to stand before shards of concrete and rock came up from the ground, tossing shrapnel towards their individual directions.

Ayale grabbed Osiris once more and ran past one of the fallen men, into another nearby alleyway, crossing into different parts of the sleeping city. They started to slow down and hid away in one narrow alley, streets away from where the tea shoppe. Both Ayale and Osiris hid quietly, until they were no longer being tailed. Within their first breaths of relief, no words could be said. How could either of them come up with an explanation for what the other saw?

Osiris' hand remained tight around Ayale's, before they began their slow walk back to the tea shoppe. Ayale swore under their breath, wishing they didn't drop their cigarette earlier.

Lau was at a loss for words. Absolutely taken aback by Ayale's tale, she paced around the living room. It was far from organized, books and teacups strewn around from their hectic week.

Osiris sat ever so still in the couch beside Ayale as he felt the bandages on the side of his face, having been given first aid by the angry bartender from the tea shoppe. He tilted his head slightly to catch the titles of the books on the table. A few novels he had not heard of were up top of the pile. He wondered if these were Ayale's books and took it upon himself to guess the genres from the few titles. His attention was quickly stolen back when Lau spoke those fine words;

"Do you have any idea what you two have done?"

Ayale avoided her line of sight, leaning forward on their elbows, head in their hands, in disbelief for their own actions. They remained silent to the incoming scolding, knowing they deserved every last bit of it. Osiris felt his heart drop, no longer feeling the adrenaline from earlier in his veins.

"Are you both dense? Especially you," she looked directly at Ayale. "What about your new start? Everything you worked for? Everything we worked for! For a boy you don't even know!" Lau's voice began to rise, infuriated with every passing moment. "Did you at least kill them? That would buy us more time to figure something out." She reasoned. Osiris didn't know how to answer the question, looking to Ayale for a response.

"We didn't stay to find out. They almost completed their spell, and I would rather not experience that myself. I know Osiris would rather not lose his affinity either, I presume." Their exhausted expression didn't change as they looked at him, hoping to lighten up their situation.

"Are you out of it?" Lau asked, unable to meet their eyes.

"I didn't want him to end up like Rae."

Those words were enough to take Lau out of her anger. She sighed, a flurry of different emotions running through her face until she placed a hand on her forehead and through her disheveled brown hair.

"Alright," Lau snatched a cigarette and lit it up in seconds, breaking her rule of no smoking inside the house. "Stay the night, by dawn we'll have a plan." Lau said, straight faced but avoiding eye contact with either of them.

"I think I should take him home." Ayale said, face shifting with disgust at the words. "Maybe if I go back, they can get us the help we need."

Lau froze. Her sullen expression instantly changed to one of disbelief.

"You can't possibly be serious."

"If the Matxha are coming after him and I, we won't make it. You and Rae would be in danger because of me. The least I can do is leave."

"Please think this through. You worked hard these last three years, I don't want you to throw it all away. Not for him." Lau nodded sharply in his direction, and Osiris sheepishly fixed his braids to the side.

"I'm going home and asking the Cxai clan for help. They won't say no to me."

"If you're lucky," Lau finished off her cigarette. "Let's get some rest, please think about this...this plan of yours." Lau stormed out of the room, thinking to herself what other options could be available to them. Anything to avoid losing Ayale to either clan. The Matxha clan would never think to spare them or anyone they considered an enemy. She entered her bedroom and slammed the door shut behind her.

Ayale and Osiris were left on the living room couch amongst themselves. Both were horrified beyond belief for their situation.

Osiris' brow rose, curious as to what their plan was. He heard the keywords 'home' and 'Cxai family' in the same breath.

"What is it?" Ayale felt his stare, looking up with clear frustration written in their eyes.

"Do you work for the Cxai family?" He whispered as though the mere mention of the name would summon their wrath.

"I-I do." Ayale hesitated, not entirely lying but also not saying the full tale.

"But...?" Osiris urged, able to feel there was more.

"I'm more of a blood relative. Probably." Ayale said. "My mom hates my dad, so you never know." They shrugged.

Osiris would have found that humorous, but the dire situation beyond it held more weight than their dark humor.

"Not to sound ungrateful but," Osiris felt his heart in his throat before the next words left him. "Do we really have to leave Densriel? Is there no way to contact your family from here and have them do something from wherever they are?"

Ayale let out a long breath. "If only it were that easy. As far as I know, the Cxai clan has no contacts in the Matxha territory. And if they did, I wouldn't know where to begin to find them without raising suspicion with the Matxha clan."

"I just–this is a lot for me to take in."

Ayale nodded, wincing when they felt the ache in their back from the Matxha grunt who threw them against the brick walls of the alley.

"I was so sure I was going to die. And now, I have to flee the only place I've ever known. Everything I know is here." Osiris placed his hands on his face, pulling them over his eyes. "And yet, I am still, very much alive." He dropped his hands from his face, a serious face gracing his tired expression when he looked to Ayale beside him. "I didn't get a chance to say it but thank you. Thank you for saving my life. No one else would have done what you did."

Ayale would have spoken but the idea of saying anything after that was difficult. They had as much to lose, if not more than Osiris. But to comment on it would likely make the already anxious man beside them worse. Instead, they nodded to acknowledge his gratitude and promptly changed the subject.

"Want some wipes for the blood?" Ayale took out some makeup wipes from the side of the couch, taking a handful for themself then handing them off to Osiris. He simply nodded, silent in his seat as he wiped off the blood dried to the side of his face. He laid his back against the couch. The exhaustion caught up to him after the insane events of the night started to turn in his head. As he fell asleep, beside him sat the silent tea shoppe owner he no longer recognized.

## VI

At the first sign of daybreak, both Ayale and Osiris were given keys to a car, a stash of food, water, and a wad of cash that Ayale soon determined was every month of rent they had paid Lau since their initial stay.

Lau didn't dare acknowledge Osiris with anything besides a glare more threatening than the one she gave him on his first night in the tea shoppe. After Rae had come by to send off Ayale, her only words with Osiris had been in the living room while Ayale and Lau had gone on the balcony to smoke. She sat beside him on the couch, leaned in close, and whispered to him. "Please keep my Ayale safe. Make sure nothing happens to them. They've seen enough." Rae finished, getting up and heading out to the balcony.

A better part of an hour passed by, and before Lau and Rae could let them go, she couldn't help but stop Ayale from going down the back stairs.

"What's wrong?" Ayale asked, ready to get in the car and escape the city. Lau struggled to speak and simply sighed, letting her hand drop to her side.

"I'm sorry. This wasn't...this wasn't how I wanted things to go. This wasn't what I wanted for you. I failed to keep you safe." She said in front of Ayale, her tone oddly quiet. "You did the right thing, saving his life like that. Goes to show, right? No good deed going unpunished or whatever." Lau smiled, before noticing their eyes watering. They sniffled and before Ayale knew it, Lau's arms wrapped tightly around their back.

"Aya, you are your own person. I watched you grow the last few years, and I can't help myself from crying here." Lau squeezed her tighter. "You brought me happiness unlike any other. No matter what happens out there, don't forget your home is always here." As the words hit the air, so began the crying for them both.

Osiris had watched the tender moment from the car, sinking into his seat, and feeling far worse than last night. He felt Rae's eyes on him in the car, as if reminding him of her request with her somber stare.

"You will never be like your parents." Lau said to them with finality. Ayale was not one to cry but leaving behind everything they had built with Lau and Rae beside them, the truth couldn't be more obvious; they didn't want to do this.

"When you get back to Nalira, please call me when it's safe. Don't forget us, whatever you end up doing." Lau practically had Ayale in a hold, unable to let them go. "And if you come back, Rae will want to hear the stories."

Ayale pressed their forehead into her shoulder, tears melting into the soft cotton of her shirt. But soon it was replaced with their snickering, thinking of the stories Rae had told them both over the course of three years since their unexpected arrival in Densriel. The probability of being able to come back was slim, nothing Ayale would not figure out when the time came.

Lau felt Osiris' somber stare from the passenger side of her car, letting Ayale go once she realized how long she held onto them. In a quiet tone, she gave them one last piece of advice.

"If that kid starts causing you trouble, get rid of him. Do you understand?" Lau muttered in their ear quietly. Ayale hesitantly nodded, both looking at the running car sitting stagnant behind the tea shoppe. They felt something slide into their pocket from Lau before being sent off to the car.

Before they could make it there, Rae grabbed Ayale, tears streaming down her face, and seemingly unwilling to let go of their dear Aya until Lau pried them out of her embrace.

The moment Ayale drove off was the time they needed to remain strong.

The sun began to rise just slightly above the clouds that bore over the city.

Ayale silently drove. Osiris watched the buildings blur as they drove. A few cafes bustling with patrons, sidewalks full of pedestrians, and streets becoming infested with commuters. The local river weaved the plethora of bridges, almost following them out of the city they had just made their home. The view only lasted until they exited the city, watching as Densriel became further away.

The first day on the road was quiet and uneventful so far. Neither opted to speak to one another, letting the music on the radio play in the background. As Ayale drove, mourning the new life they had to leave behind, Osiris drowned in guilt. The quick flutter in his chest that accompanied every glance at them had left him feeling more anxious than ever.

There was no going back for either of them.

Their time on the road was just as quiet, with only the sounds of Lau's sedan and the bare minimum radio playing a ballad in the background. Unfortunately for both of them, it was the only station that played on the radio. As the hours went by, the only background on the highway was the seemingly infinite road in front of them. The closest looking mountain was at least a full day's drive before they were anywhere near it.

As Ayale looked to the dashboard, they noticed the gas gauge linger just over the quarter marker. Their first stop would be at whatever gas station came up next.

To their luck, a diner to their left came up, with a gas station across the way. Ayale pulled over to the side, parking next to the gas pump. They sank in their seat, placing their forehead on the steering wheel. When they peeked over to the clock on the dashboard, they sighed. They had been driving for almost ten hours non-stop.

"Are you alright?" Osiris asked in a soft voice.

"Mm. Just tired. Leg is a little numb, too." They groaned.

"Sounds like a good time to take a break. Need some help getting out?"

"No, I'll be fine. Let's just get gas and maybe some food. It's been hours since we ate anything besides snacks."

"That didn't even cross my mind." He yawned, reaching over to fix his side swept braids. A habit he picked up whenever his nerves got the best of him.

Ayale hopped out of the car with a pained groan followed by a yawn, holding their lower back as they started to put the gas nozzle into the car. They held it in place, waiting for the car to fill up.

Osiris watched from the inside, giving himself small mental cues to remember to breathe. This was only day one and he already struggled to keep it together, nervously smoothing out his braids while trying to breathe. It wasn't as if he lost much to begin with, but every time he looked over at the tea shoppe owner, the tired look in their eyes told him how badly he fucked up. He hoped to keep the jumble of uncertainty in his chest to himself and remain as strong and stoic as Ayale, until they made it to their end goal.

Maybe Ayale wouldn't understand the issue he dealt with. He didn't want to bother them over it, scared to hear what they would say after the fact.

The driver's side door opened and Ayale pointed their tired gaze at him.

"Do you want to get food at the place next door after this?"

"Oh! Sure, that's fine." He forced his hands away from his hair and a smile to his face. Ayale nodded, filling up the gas tank before getting back into the car. They drove a few seconds to the parking lot nearby, leaving the car to the furthest spot possible out of habit. Something Lau taught them when they first arrived in Densriel.

When the two of them entered the diner, they took a few steps through the run-down diner and sat themselves down in a distant booth by the window, with a perfect view of the barren highway and its scarce trees and shrubs. Not much was said, not even as much as a single glance passed between them. Ayale stared out the window, their hazel eyes reflecting part of the sunset across the horizon. In that short instance, Osiris was taken aback by the reflection of orange and red in their eyes. His heart fell into a small frenzy, but his brain quickly reminded him of the circumstances.

"Know what you want yet?" Ayale interrupted his thought before looking down at their own menu.

"Barely. Maybe fruit. I don't like eating too much if I'm going to be in a car."

"Honestly, me too. Never understood how people did that. Maybe a green tea, if this place has any." They muttered, looking up and down the menu in hopes of seeing tea at all. Their heavy eyes settled over the menu. After being spoiled by the quality of their tea shoppe for so long, they weren't sure how they would react to any tea from elsewhere anymore. Though it wasn't meant to be a jab, Osiris felt his heart sink a little.

The server walked over and took their order, and within ten minutes, both had something in their stomachs for the first time in hours. Ayale took the paper cup that housed their tea, hesitantly lifting the lid to see the damage. They cringed, noting the questionable beverage lacked any steam coming from the opening. To their chagrin, the tea was made with lukewarm water. If anything, the audacity of their shit luck was strong, and it was only day one.

"Damn it. This can't be real, this isn't even hot." They laughed weakly and placed the cover back on, irritation building on their face.

Osiris had never seen them so disappointed before. He reached over to their cup, taking it in hand when he tapped the bottom twice. He slid it back over and took the cover back off for them, revealing the gentle steam that rose over their drink, and soon, as did a short smile on their face.

"I forgot you could do that." They looked up at him.

"Good thing I remembered. That's no way to have tea." He adjusted his glasses.

Ayale brought the drink up to their lips, taking a quick sip. Not nearly as good as the quality they were used to, but it would have to do. They found their eyes wandering out at the sunset over the incoming plains once more, its sherbet colors drifting across the barely lit sky. They had to admit, the view was unlike anything they had seen in Densriel.

"Do you draw things like this?" Ayale asked, keeping their eyes on the sun setting in the horizon.

"It depends. Though I do draw quite a variety of scenes, if inspiration strikes." Osiris perked back up.

"Don't ever let me stop you if you decide to make anything. We can stay for a bit if you would like." Their voice softened, dreading the idea of driving again.

Osiris went to reach for one of his smaller sketchbooks from his inner coat pocket, but froze up when he saw two suited men enter the diner. In an instant, he recognized them as Matxha members, the distinctive green color popping from their collars and the pins over their heart that signaled their ranks based on leaves. One being the highest and three being the lower-level men that mostly handled dirty work.

And dirty work, they were here to handle.

Ayale noticed his terrified expression, taking a moment to look at the reflection on the glass windows adjacent from their seat. The emblem was all they needed to see before they realized who the two men were.

There was only one exit, being the one door they entered from. Though the timing was awful, there was no choice otherwise. Ayale inhaled a calm breath and took their tea in hand once more. They wouldn't do anything until the two of them were physically approached.

Osiris remained frozen for a moment before sinking into his seat. Ayale held his gaze with the stoic expression he began to grow used to. He wasn't sure how to keep it together the way they did, partly jealous they could hide their fear, if they had any to begin with.

That was the moment the two Matxha members approached their table. One was pale as could be with green eyes and bright red hair with a matching beard. The man next to him shared the same complexion with blond hair and similar green eyes with brown closest to the core. Ayale didn't so much as turn to acknowledge them.

"Evening to you both, might you be traveling from Densriel by chance?" The redhead asked, pointing the question to Ayale.

"Simply traveling through."

"Travelers? Come to stop at a Matxha meeting point?"

"Not sure about that. Like I said, we are just traveling through." They shrugged, watching through the same reflecting window of all the nervous servers suddenly making their way into the backroom area. A rough hand grabbed their shoulder, lingering close to their ear.

"Come with us quietly, we don't need to cause a scene." The blond muttered quietly.

"You don't want me to cause a scene?" They asked them, pointing their confused expression at Osiris.

The two men shared a look.

"A Matxha diner. Smart." Ayale looked up at them. The statement alone was enough to send adrenaline spiking in Osiris.

A second later, they shot a glance at Osiris before standing from the booth. Ayale swung their fist into the throat of the blond man, aiming for the jugular veins as best they could. Before anyone could react, they elbowed the redhead in the nose, watching him stumble backward into a nearby barstool.

Osiris' jaw dropped, feeling Ayale's hand pulling his own, and out the diner they went. The car was far off, but Ayale noticed the black sedan sitting out front. An extra few seconds might buy them a decent enough excuse. They knelt next to the back tire, grabbing their knife, and slashed open the first tire they made contact with. They went for the other back tire, but Osiris had already done the deed, bringing a short smile to their face. Ayale looked around and ran over to the elongated shrubbery beside the gas station to hide.

"Why here?" Osiris asked.

"Trust me." They mouthed, putting a finger to their mouth. He simply nodded, watching as the two men came out of the diner, one with blood running down his nose and the other trying to desperately take air into his lungs.

Osiris felt Ayale's hand still clutching onto his, tight and ready to act if need be. Their confidence was all he needed to feel safe in their hiding spot. From their distance, the two could hear the men speaking.

"They slashed the tires, probably drove off by now." The redhead kicked the one of the flats, still holding onto his broken nose.

"That's great. At least next time they might know to send more than just us. Fuck this, get Steven on the phone so we can catch a ride."

While the duo waited, the two Matxha men left Osiris just as tense and frightened as before. He told himself to keep it together, hoping they were soon to be gone. To their advantage, the darkness of the night allowed them to hide with a lot less worry. The idea of them looking around no longer mattered after the slashing of their tires.

But the wait was a long one. Ayale couldn't help the weariness. They tapped on Osiris' shoulder, signaling for him to take out his sketchbook. Hesitantly, he did so and handed it off to Ayale, who flipped to a new page and started writing.

*'Are you okay? I know this is taking a while and I'm about ready to fall asleep.'*

Osiris took the pen and paper, writing below them.

*'Fucking Steven.'*

Ayale covered their mouth, choking back their laughter. They scribbled beside him.

*'Steven needs to get his shit together.'*

Osiris felt a smile stretching across his face, looking up to Ayale who struggled to maintain their composure, writing again beside their last message.

'*Look up.*' Ayale met his confused expression before looking up at the night sky. Osiris followed suit, meeting with the dazzling clusters of stars. He found himself taken by surprise at the view, eyes wandering across the sky above them. But he found himself looking back to Ayale, whose expression shifted to a softer look. Truly breathtaking was all he thought.

Another hour passed by, leaving them exhausted while they waited for Steven to pick the men up. Ayale almost fell asleep sitting up against the building, surrounded by thick shrubbery. Their eyes glazed over, blinking every so often while they forced themself awake.

Osiris couldn't do much either but found solace in sketching the view from their spot. Quiet as could be, their only relief being each other's company.

The time finally came when the two could finally leave from their spot, sometime after midnight. Ayale yawned all the way to the car, barely able to settle into the driver's side. When Osiris went into the passenger side, he couldn't keep his worry quiet.

"Are you alright to drive?"

"Probably not. But what other choice is there?" They yawned again, this time tears coming down their cheeks. Osiris thought to himself, looking around, trying to find an alternative to the dangerous idea of them driving this way. While they couldn't stay here, further behind the gas station was flat enough land for them to park for the night, though other worries came after.

"What if we park behind the gas station for a few hours? The gas station obstructs the view of the car, and it wouldn't be for very long—"

"Yeah, alright." Ayale interrupted and parked the car a little bit further from the area Osiris initially pointed towards, in no state to argue while their eyes began to burn. They kicked the seat back and turned the car back off, eyes shutting immediately after.

He wondered if Ayale had fallen straight asleep.

"What time do you want me to wake you?" He asked in a soft voice.

"Doesn't matter. We get there when we get there."

Osiris blinked. "You sound excited for this trip."

"Sure am. I'm enjoying my last days of freedom before we enter Cxai territory and face what I left behind. Like I said, not in a rush. We get there when we get there. By the time we're out of Matxha territory, those assholes won't be a problem again. Old treaties state they aren't allowed to arrest anyone from another territory without extradition paperwork, which I guarantee they don't have." Ayale sighed, confident in their knowledge. They hiked up their charcoal hoodie over their short hair and frowned, regretting the idea of bringing up home while they tried to sleep.

Osiris felt his anxiety well up in his chest. The moments he slept were brief, streaming in and out of consciousness. The remainder of the night passed by without so much as a blink, but Ayale did not stir. He decided to keep trying, until sleep finally came at the first sight of dawn.

## VII

Driving was tedious to begin with, but now that Ayale was tasked to drive the two of them all the way to Cxai territory, their feelings on driving were more abhorrent during this journey than ever before. A part of them regretted learning to drive at all. They scowled at the feeling of being scrunched up in their seat, foot constantly on the accelerator, and upright against the uncomfortable seat. They occasionally found themself stretching forward and attempting to shift their stiff shoulders around. Of course, it didn't help that the two of them left at noon after a horribly long stop that should have been an hour at most, taking twelve instead. A combination of an ambush and the need to rest afterwards.

Osiris noticed them making various attempts to stretch while driving. He placed his sketchbook down on the dashboard, concern making itself evident on his strained expression.

Ayale made a note to stop squirming once they realized how odd they probably looked from afar.

"How do you draw in that thing while I'm going eighty miles an hour? I would have hurled by now." Ayale peered from the side.

"I consider myself lucky, I don't get motion sickness." He responded quietly. "Kind of sucks not being able to drive though, sorry I can't be more helpful."

"You're not missing out on much. Besides, it means I can stave off my motion sickness. A win-win if you ask me." Ayale said before squinting their eyes in the distance. "I know we had a slow start today, but want to stop off and grab some snacks?"

Osiris' chest tightened. "I'm worried about stopping off again. What if there's more of those guys from last night? And don't we have food?" Osiris pushed his hair back with the back of his hand, recalling Ayale's quick thinking from the night before. Part of him wanted to ask where they learned to fight, and everything else he had seen them do thus far, but held back his questions, assuming all of it had ties to their home clan.

"I think we're fine. Too far out from the capital for them to come this way now. Besides, we need to refill the snacks, and the driver appreciates something crunchy to snack on while driving." Ayale drove slower before pulling into a rest stop. Conveniently enough, they could top off the gas in the car, giving them the chance to drive through the night to make up for yesterday. The tiny store was nothing of note beside a large green sign on the roof.

As they both stepped out of the car, a collective sigh of relief as they were able to stretch out. They walked into the small building when they were greeted by a young man stocking to the side. The store was fully stocked otherwise, with only a few items missing from its shelves.

Ayale walked over to the snacks and picked up more than necessary. Osiris could hear their stomach grumble from across the way, trying not to laugh at the absurd amount of treats they piled into their arms. Everything from trail mix to spicy chips, bottles of tea and a few bigger liters of water they could stash in the back seat. They stared at Osiris, watching him struggle to pick out anything at all.

"Just grab anything you want. I'm already off the wall here, what's another to the pile?" They wandered over to the ice cream case, ready for their next mistake. "Oh my." Ayale's eyes widened, taking in all the options inside the freezer case. "Osiris, I think dinner should be ice cream tonight. Pick one of these, too. Mind grabbing me a cookies and cream bar while you're at it?" They staggered back a second, scrambling to hold all their items without dropping anything. Osiris came over and picked up their requested ice cream bar, grabbing a sherbet for himself.

Walking up to the register, the two took up most of the counter with their snacks, earning the attention of the stocker as he walked behind the register. His tag said Nis while his wrinkled face, dark eyes, and shaggy unkempt hair screamed tired.

"Damn, are you hungry or what?"

"What, I guess." Ayale answered with a straight face, gaining a chuckle from Nis and a stifled noise from Osiris. He stood to the side, finding his eyes leering out to the somewhat empty lot. He refused to be ambushed again like last night, feeling his stomach tighten from the memory. He urged himself to take a few deep breaths until he heard the clerk speak again.

"Ice cream for dinner sounds healthy." Nis commented as he handed over the ice treats to Ayale.

"I had a cigarette for dinner once. There's worse out there."

"Should think about quitting." Nis said with a warning tone. "While you're young, too. Don't wait until you're old like me." He finished ringing up all their snacks, padding through them to make sure he rang up everything. "Total is 28.10."

Ayale paid the man and headed out with two full plastic bags of snacks. Osiris tried to grab a bag, but they simply continued on before chucking them into the back seat of the car. When they shut the door and made their way to the driver's door, they stalled. They didn't want to get back on the road so soon.

Ayale shared a look with Osiris, whose exhaustion preceded their own, and he wasn't even the one driving.

"Let's get going." Ayale eventually sighed, both of them getting back into the car. They started up the car, listening to the gentle hum of the engine. They groaned at the idea of driving, so much so, they couldn't hold their mumbled complaints back. Ayale forced themself to exit the gas station, driving off towards the bright sunset ahead. It took less than a mile for them to cave and pull back over to the side of the road, the rest stop still in view behind them.

"Why are we stopping?" Osiris furrowed his brow, some of the worst thoughts bubbling up in his mind.

Ayale stared at the road ahead, putting the car back into park.

"Grab the snacks and ice cream, we are taking a break." They left the car after turning it off, settling themself on the hood of the sedan. Osiris hesitantly followed suit, putting the bag between them.

"I need some time to decompress. I don't think either of us want to go back to the road just yet." They looked to Osiris before busting open their ice cream from the wrapper. They rolled up the sleeves of their hoodie before biting into the bar, earning a horrified gasp from Osiris.

"You bite your ice cream?!" He exclaimed, parting his braids to the right in horror.

Ayale froze, eyes darting from the ice cream bar then to him. They nodded, unsure why that was so odd.

"Do you not?" They asked with their mouth full.

"No! I do not bite my ice cream!" He popped open the top of his frozen treat, taking the small spoon off the top. His treat swirled with the same colors as the sunset up ahead. When he took his first spoonful, he felt Ayale's stare on him. "What?"

"What's that taste like?"

"Like sugar and orange flavor. Want to try some?"

They nodded, leaning over the bag, and waiting for Osiris.

"Same spoon though, are you okay with that?"

"I truly don't care." They responded straight-faced, still expecting their sample. Osiris took a small spoonful and watched them stretch further, taking a quick bite of the spoon. They took a moment to think about the taste, unsure how to describe the flavor. They slowly nodded, pushing back the hair that fell forward.

"That's not bad at all. Want to try some of mine?" Ayale offered their bar over to Osiris, whose shocked face over the bite of his spoon was quickly overcome with intrigue. He took a small taste, getting mostly the outer cookie crumble with the smallest amount of actual ice cream. His eyes widened. Something about the flavor reminded him of Ayale. Crunchy outside with a hidden layer inside.

Ayale watched his reaction, awaiting a response.

When he looked up, he only had the thought in his head.

"It's good. I prefer this, but it's still good." He smiled, feeling a wave of warmth overcome him.

"Good. Means more for me." Ayale took a big bite, causing Osiris to choke up. He coughed back a laugh, adjusting his jacket and rolling up his sleeves. The sunset was nothing like he had seen before. Densriel was such an industry heavy city, sunsets like these seemed to be far and few between. There were no views of the mountains, no shifts of colors, where hues blended so perfectly together. The red sun barely glimpsed above the mountain tops, letting its last few moments of glow fall over the two of them.

It felt as if no one else existed, a show only meant for them while the two ate away at their ice cream. Osiris glanced over to Ayale, looking at the glow and the way the sunset shifted the color of their complexion. The way it shone made them seem far calmer and more collected, as if the nights prior never occurred.

Knowing he was the reason this expression wouldn't exist as often left him feeling disappointed.

He watched as they shifted, laying back against the windshield. Finished with their snack, they closed their eyes. Osiris imitated them, laying back after putting down his empty cup aside. He put his hands behind his head, taking in the scene and the tranquility it came with. He felt the warmth of the sun while it lowered bit by bit.

*Maybe this trip wasn't so fucked after all*, he thought. Not with such strange company.

The two of them sat around, silently watching the sky shift from orange to gentle lilac tones, bringing with it the darkness of the night.

Half an hour passed them by as though it were minutes. But it didn't stop Ayale from dozing off where they laid.

Osiris wouldn't be able to sleep even if he tried. He wondered if he should wake them, but decided a power nap would be better off. Driving around during the night would at least allow them to move without eyes on them. That was a better alternative than what they went through the night before. His tired eyes looked over at them after a while, watching the peaceful look take over the stoic face he grew used to. There was a part of him where his chest fluttered, almost enough that he wasn't sure if he wanted to wake them.

"Ayale?" Osiris whispered, poking at their shoulder. They didn't react. He put a hand on their shoulder, trying to wake them. "We have to get going soon. Being out here at night isn't the best idea." He stumbled as Ayale opened their eyes. They peered over their shoulder, eyes half closed.

"You're right, just give me a minute. Back is still a little sore," They sat up and groaned, feeling all the muscles in their back contract and release painfully.

"Do you want me to see if there's anything I can do for your back?" Osiris began to feel his own ache from sitting so much.

"No, don't even worry about it, this is just what being in your late twenties is like." Ayale stretched their arms out, trying to shift their back muscles around.

"Being twenty-nine, I can certainly relate."

"Wow, you're almost thirty?"

He frowned and nodded, a new ache of his own suddenly made itself known in his upper back.

"Brutal. I'm years away, but I feel like I'm already there. Once we're in my hometown, I'm sure I'll age an extra decade." Ayale slid off the hood of the car, landing on the ground in one motion.

The two of them left the side of the road, continuing the almost infinite highway with nothing but high beams and a simple crescent moon to guide them. The ride was quick but a lot less awkward. Both were wide awake for much of the night. Osiris sketched to the side using the light of the visor while Ayale attempted to pick up a radio signal on the radio. After a while of silent fiddling, they gave up, grumbling something about how a road trip could only be so lame. They placed their attention on fixing up their short hair, a small bun formed with their quick hands off the steering wheel.

Osiris peered up when they slammed their fist on top of the dashboard, both surprised when the percussive action caused it to pick up a signal.

"Oh, hell yeah!" Ayale exclaimed, excited to have a song or two, however long it lasted. They started to yell along to the next song, practically causing Osiris to mess up one of many fine lines on the page. He didn't show it, but he quietly watched Ayale have their moment, letting the night sky slowly drift above them.

The two drove until the moon slowly dipped back into the horizon.

# VIII

With the next day came nothing but an eerie silence and almost nonstop driving. Verbal affairs were seldom, save for when Osiris inquired about Ayale's condition as they drove through the deserted outskirts of the Matxha territory plains.

Hour after hour passed between them in silence. Trees became the new normal, passing by the car with thick trunks that bore down on the empty road. Greenery should have been refreshing but instead reminded Ayale of what they were leaving behind. Osiris had dozed off, leaning his seat back. The lull of the silent car ride doing nothing beneficial for his melancholy mood.

The trees of the forest allowed a great humidity to well within them. Whatever sun was evident before no longer shone through the clouds, bearing heavily against the sky. The highway felt more like an off beaten path than any real road. The density of the cedars and pines made it seem as though the winding road would break off any minute. As though the world could hear Ayale's silent complaints, the seemingly empty road began to empty out in a vast, uncertain desert, trees thinning out the further they drove.

As quiet as the last few hours had been, their first few days on the road flew by before either of them could realize it. The daylight had turned the sky from a sweet array of orange to a dusty rose. In less than a half hour, the sky had been taken by deep hues of indigo.

Osiris had awoken from his nap to a dark sky and unlit car. The only lights visible for miles being the moon above them and the gentle green glow of the dashboard. Ayale remained silent, brooding over the situation forcing them to go back home.

Just the switch of scenery was enough to send Osiris spiraling.

He felt everything hit him all at once. The Matxha clan coming after him, the days he spent wandering the streets of Densriel once he realized he was no longer safe going home. Only to be saved by some tea shoppe owner in what could have been his final moments of life.

He not only uprooted himself, but someone else.

Someone who had been actively trying to rebuild their life.

It wasn't long after that Ayale noticed him trying to hold back his overflow of tears in the passenger seat, swiping his shaky arm frequently over his face.

"You okay?" They asked, trying to keep back their own resentment.

"Fine." The slight stumble of his voice was all it took for them to completely switch their feelings off.

Osiris held his face to the side so Ayale wouldn't see him crying. But the sniffling noises were difficult to mask.

"Look, I know this is all a lot to take in, but this is our only option. Take us both to Nalira in Cxai territory, see what my family can do about this. Either that or be hunted down by the Matxha clan."

"What's going to happen to your friends?"

"Who? Lau and Rae?" Ayale asked, a little shocked at the question. "You kidding? Rae might not have magic left, but she's always looking for a reason to use that chair leg again. The Matxha will be lucky if Lau spares them at that point."

"What about if they—"

"Lau was part of this clan bullshit, too. Not related to one like me, thankfully, but trust me when I say they will both be fine. Why do you care anyways?"

"Why do you act as if I don't care about anything going on around us?" Osiris snapped, his muffled voice bursting through his sleeve.

"What are you going on about?"

"I didn't want any of this, I just wanted to get out," he pulled his arm down to his lap, fidgeting with the pen in hand. "Why couldn't you just leave me to die?" Osiris cried.

Ayale slowed the car down, pulling off to the side of the deserted road. The road went from smooth to bumpy before coming to a full stop. Ayale wasn't sure what to do while Osiris literally lost his breath while he wept.

"Osiris, let's take a breather outside of the car for a bit." They said in a much softer tone than before, exuding more patience than he expected after everything he had done to them.

"Why, so you can finally take me out of my misery?"

"If I wanted to do that, you wouldn't have made it outside of Densriel. Let alone out of Lau's apartment." Ayale pulled themself out of the car and slammed the door before moving around to the other side. Osiris hesitantly followed suit, walking behind them.

The road was lifted but once Ayale walked off and down the dip, there were small patches of soft but stringy green grass. They popped onto the grass, patting the area next to them. He sank down next to them, repeatedly wiping his face with his shirt sleeve.

"I prefer you alive, Osiris." Ayale said, reaching out to wipe away a stray stream from his lower cheek. He went from trying to catch his breath to frozen just by their mere contact. But once he remembered their situation again, it was harder than ever to hold back the panic attack that was heaving through his lungs.

Ayale looked out at the distant field and sat still, trying equally as hard to keep it together. They had to yet again escape their problems by running away, worse off by having to go back home again. They didn't want to leave behind their newfound family nor their beloved tea shoppe. They pulled their knees up to their chest, sinking their head into themself. The more they thought about it, their weariness coupled with the last week's course of events came crashing down. No emotion was spared; anger, doubt, anxiety.

How did they have to run away a second time?

The cool night air allowed for them both to take a moment and assess everything at once. To come up with some sort of plan in case going home ended up going awry early on.

They looked up, their serious face wandering up to the night sky. "I hope you know, I don't regret what I did."

"You made a bad choice. You should have chosen better." Osiris imitated Ayale and pulled his knees up to his face, concealing the fresh tears coming down. He felt a hand on his back seconds later, rubbing small circles over the fabric of his faded green hoodie. He found his ability to breathe again, taking in slow, meaningful breaths.

"I did though. I made the right choice." Ayale nodded with an odd sense of confidence.

Osiris felt his face warm up, if not from the comment, from the sting of the cold air. It reminded him of all the visits to the tea shoppe.

And the stark differences between the person from then and the one beside him now.

No matter their situation, he was relieved to be beside them overall. They did save his life, after all. It was a comfort to have a sort of friend in all of this.

A warm sensation traveled down to his hands, allowing him a moment to show off his tricks, as though they were in the tea shoppe again. Though this time, what he wanted to show them was something different entirely.

"Want to see something?" Osiris sheepishly peered up from his knees. Ayale hesitantly nodded, watching him hurriedly rise from the grassy patch as though he didn't just have a full-blown anxiety attack. He backed up a few steps for safety, allowing his affinity to take over soon after. A faded, pale green glow grew from his palm, and he slowly began pointing outward to the field behind them, letting out a small bolt of light unlike anything Ayale had ever seen.

They watched in wonder, analyzing the light glowing through his veins that lined his hands and down his wrist, even brightening his concentrative green eyes. The pale glow seeped with an aura of natural energy, bringing about a strange confidence for Osiris. The timing of each subtle breath seemingly swayed with the gentle breeze, until his next step began.

With the lift of his hand, the grassy patches in front of and behind him started to grow rapidly, with spring flowers coming out from it. Vines lingered and spread about the ground, creating beds of wild greens and flowering yellow and white daffodils sprinting forth.

Ayale was so taken aback, they almost didn't notice the messy circle of spring leaves beginning to surround him.

"I thought you only knew small magic tricks like at the tea shoppe! Is this your affinity?" They looked frantically all around them.

"Plants enjoy warmth, don't they?" Osiris beamed, happy to see them so pleasantly surprised.

Ayale nodded to themself. They supposed it made sense in some way.

"Osiris! Don't waste your energy like this!" Ayale scolded, investigating the wild red tulips that bloomed beside them. "Can you truly conjure nature in such a way?"

"Born with it. Though it's not an elemental, it is still my affinity." He smiled proudly in response.

Osiris pushed up his round glasses before allowing the remainder of his magic to dispel. As much fun as it was, there was a legitimate point made by Ayale, both should conserve their energy just in case either might need it in the future. But the moment brought up a lingering question in his mind.

"That reminds me, the other night in the alley... what kind of affinity was that? I honestly had some trouble figuring out what was happening, probably because we were being attacked." He walked back over and seated himself beside them. He could feel the tension coming from them at the sound of his question. Ayale didn't budge, staring out into the vast field as though nothing was asked.

"Don't worry about it." Ayale laid back onto the full grass that remained, avoiding the question entirely. They closed their eyes, allowing the gentle glow of the crescent moon to take them away from their current situation. Millions upon millions of stars twinkled above them, leaving a sense of peace if only temporary.

Osiris took the hint, lying beside Ayale, and taking in a view he had not seen in his lifetime. Such beauty he could not believe surrounded him tonight.

Yet, the moon and stars were just as breathtaking. It was only an hour before Osiris found himself lulled to sleep by the springtime breeze.

The morning light leaked through the edge of the vast field, awakening Osiris first. When he shifted to his side, he felt the weight of a jacket draped over him. Ayale had placed it on at some point during the night. As he awoke fully, the new morning light only reminded him of one thing, startling him back to reality. The two of them were runaways, escaping the wrath of one of the most powerful organizations in the land. It was almost immediate when his anxiety returned, wondering what the Matxha clan would do if they got ahold of them both.

As Osiris watched the sun rise, he could only wish that Ayale's family would find a way to help them both. As worried as he was for their predicament, he couldn't stop thinking what it was that forced Ayale to make a run for it to begin with. To leave behind an entire life, that meant something had to happen. But whatever it was, he stressed at the fact that Ayale was part of the Cxai bloodline. Such a thought had him uncertain what their intentions were.

Ayale woke up shortly after the full rise of the sun in the horizon, and both quietly resigned back to the car to continue their drive. According to their map, the nearest town was at least another two full days of driving, leaving them unsure why they suddenly saw a partially paved road forming up ahead.

# IX

The first sign of another town came in the form of a worn-out piece of wood, one which pointed up towards the mountains. The strange road tore through two incredible heights, winding around the back of the range.

The road was unsafe, bumpy and uneven, trickling anxiety into Ayale as they drove cautiously and in Osiris, who held his breath tight in his chest and clasped the bar above him, to the point where his hand became numb from clutching it so tight. It took a full hour just to get through before dual sighs of relief came from the two as the road smoothed out again beneath them.

Another sign, this time etched into a slab of white and grey granite, read *Istanza*.

The city was more regarded as a town to most, but with the region being less dense than most places, its population alone was considerably larger than others around it. As they entered the city, it was breathtaking to both Ayale and Osiris. Since it was midday, the air was warm and sweet, lacking the pollutants of the industrialized Matxha territory. Each building stood separate from one another, though were practically identical with the same grey tones making up the base except the rooftops, which were strengthened with off-red shale roofing.

If they were not on the run, Istanza would have been an ideal vacation getaway.

"What a place." Osiris said with awe, adjusting his glasses to see the details better.

"A whole city was hidden behind this mountain the entire time," Ayale drove until they found a small cafe a few more minutes down the road. "It's far more modern than I expected. Like it's been updated in the last couple of years." They became partly suspicious as to why a place in the middle of nowhere could be so up to date in infrastructure.

Before they could voice their concerns, Osiris was already out of the car and walking into the cafe. Ayale grumbled under their breath and hurried behind, hurrying past a line of wildflowers, and honestly looking forward to their first caffeinated beverage in days. The caffeine headache was ready to pry itself out of their skull.

The two of them sat in one of the booths to the side. Once they could smell breakfast food, all caution was thrown to the wind, neither thinking of what had happened to them only a handful of days ago. Ayale saw an espresso machine and suddenly couldn't think straight. Osiris' stomach grumbled violently and every moment without the waiter was more painful than the last.

A young blonde man came over and took their order, and soon enough both were full and caffeinated, something the two truly missed about Densriel. Osiris had his tea, relieved they had something that wasn't served in a mesh bag.

"I haven't had a coffee like this in so long." Ayale happily sighed, leaning back in the booth. The cup lingered an inch from their lips, with Ayale taking frequent sips.

Osiris looked at the beverage in their hand with intrigue. "What is that anyway?"

"Café au lait."

"Which is?"

"Ah, it is a hot coffee with milk. Well, steamed milk."

"Can I try some?"

Ayale stared at him. "What?"

"Is that too weird?"

"No, it's just—"

"What, do you think I have cooties? We already shared ice cream."

"Osiris, how old are you?" Ayale reprimanded, holding their cup tighter.

"Old enough to have old people cooties apparently."

Ayale shook their head and slid the cup over, hoping he would settle down after his sip. Osiris grinned at their excitable response. He tried the drink and saw the waiter move to the opposite end of the cafe, running down a set of stairs hidden behind the counter. He tapped the cup twice, warming their coffee up once more before handing it back to Ayale.

"Was that so bad?" Osiris asked, watching Ayale's face light up with the warm beverage back in hand. "Not as sweet as I'm used to," he said, looking out the window beside them. "This place is kind of charming, isn't it?" Osiris asked, earning a nod from Ayale.

The two of them watched the scenery outside, the cute patches of wildflowers in pre-bloom showing an organized nature of the city. They led in a line outside of a local field behind them, leading to a separate mountain path, presumably further up the mountain. The plains seemed to extend into another part of the small city, bringing with it a gorgeous greenery similar to the other night. Ayale lost themself in the views, thinking of the affinity that Osiris held so dear. The way he showcased it with such confidence reminded them of how they met in the tea shoppe.

They leaned further back, letting their legs kick up on the space beside Osiris. They knew they would have to come clean about their own affinity at some point. Though maybe later rather than sooner.

"I am glad you think my town is charming," A woman's voice interposed from behind the two, her smooth but distinguished accent taking their attention as they looked to her direction. Her dark skin shone with a deep chestnut tone against a poppy red suit, adorned with a spiked gold necklace, and a matching set of bangles, symmetrical on each of her wrists. Her black curly hair was pulled away from her serious face into a high ponytail, emphasizing her intimidating, inquisitive expression.

"May I ask what your business is in Istanza?" She stated rather than asked, as though it were an interrogation. Osiris couldn't move, his eyes darting to the person across from him with pure fear across his face. Recalling the incident at their first rest stop, Ayale responded in the same calm demeanor.

"Just passing through. Is there a problem?"

"Out of the way place to be passing by. It feels as though you may be here for a different reason." The woman shifted her hand to her coat pocket, before Ayale's tone changed.

"Is there a problem?" Ayale repeated.

It was right then that the woman's crimson eyes lit up, amused.

"Ayale, you truly have Diori's temperament." She chuckled, her straightened shoulders suddenly relaxing.

Ayale's eyes widened at the mere mention of the name. A look of familiarity that left Osiris confused and concerned all at once.

"Excuse me?" Their voice shifted as they turned to look up at the strange woman.

"Katari? No?" She stared back, waiting for some semblance of memory to strike Ayale.

Ayale furrowed their brow in response. A part of them was more bewildered than before, even if the name rang with a gentle familiarity.

"You don't remember me? Well, that breaks my heart," her amused expression fell. She reached into her pocket once more and took out cash to leave on the table. Osiris thought he saw his life flash before his eyes in those few seconds.

"Ayale, sweetheart, there is much to discuss. Come find me downstairs when you are done." She walked off to the back of the cafe through the same wooden door as the waiter, connected to a set of equally old stairs. Ayale and Osiris watched her go down and neither moved for a solid minute.

"Are we going to die?" He finally asked, beginning to tremble at the thought. Ayale looked calmly, thinking to themself about Katari's comment about Diori.

"Who is Diori?" Osiris asked as though he could share their thoughts. They did not dare respond, simply taking the cup of coffee with them as they slid out of the booth. Osiris followed suit but left his drink behind.

"Diori is someone I know." Ayale finally said, finishing their drink and left the cup behind on the flattened part of the railing, before its descent into the basement. They walked through the door and down the odd stairs, Osiris walking hesitantly behind them. At the end of the spiraling staircase, they were met with an unusual sight. The main area seemed to be regally decorated. The white marble floors had streaks of faded charcoal in no particular pattern. Much of the surface area had cream furniture to accompany the classical aesthetic. Every moment they looked around, Ayale considered the possibilities of who this woman was to the Cxai family. Nothing came conclusive to memory, but a bunch settled in its place.

They maintained their distance while Osiris peered around, wondering where they could possibly fit everything beneath a dinky cafe. To him, all the white furniture made her look more like a supervillain.

More stairs followed, the next set suddenly a white marble. The echo of their steps soon intensified as Katari led them deeper into the basement level of the cafe. Ayale who stopped abruptly.

"Why are you taking us into a clan compound? Are we in Rooiboux territory?" Ayale asked, their heart racing as they began to put everything together.

Osiris felt his heart stop for a moment. To drop the name of a notorious clan that fell off the face of the earth was far more than he could handle right now.

Since their last war, no one knew where the Rooiboux clan had gone, nor if any members remained. He recalled their history with the Matxha clan, as well as the legendary war tactics used to clear the Matxha from their borders at one point in the last century.

Borders that neither Ayale nor Osiris knew they had crossed, because they did not exist on a map, only left with a name.

The woman nodded to Ayale's question, her expression still and cold. "I'm in disbelief that you still do not remember me."

"Then why not tell me who you are already?" Ayale clutched their hidden knife in their pockets, their strained voice prompting Katari to stop and turn to her.

"Regardless of what you might be thinking right now, I am not going to hurt you. I would rather explain myself in a secluded area, to make sure no one can overhear us on these... sensitive matters." She spoke in a hushed voice. A brief crackle lifted the air around them, a strange flutter of energy making its way around Ayale. Katari's serious expression shifted as her eyes lit up a fiery red glow like her suit. Suddenly, Ayale's hand was no longer in their own control.

"Your mother told me she foresaw your return, and that you would stop here in a dream nights ago," she followed with a gentle voice. "I am only trying to guide you. To protect you." The tension in the air only thickened, just as the unseen force field stretched further around them. Osiris took a single look at Katari, feeling the energy that flowed out of her, and determined for himself she was no true danger. Her stance and the straight look in her eye were enough to tell him so.

"I think Katari is okay." Osiris muttered softly into their ear, trying to talk them down. He placed his hand on their wrist and into their pocket, taking their hand off the knife.

"Let us discuss this more in my office, we need not do this out here." Katari said in a hushed voice, hoping no one else saw her affinity at work. Ayale took hold of Osiris' hand and found their breath. Katari nodded at him before stalking off further down the hall that dipped towards a finely carved white door, the echo of her shoes clacking against the marble floor. The cream door, adorned with crimson flowers, was guarded by two men in black suits, red fabric sticking out from the edge of their collars. As Katari approached, they stepped out of their way.

When she opened the regal door in front of them, neither Ayale nor Osiris knew what to expect.

But the inside of the room looked like something out of a dream.

The first half of the office had been adorned in cream colored furniture, just as the other parts of the compound. However, the details that laid about similar swirls carved in each chair and table took Osiris by surprise. Her office was the most gracefully decorated by comparison. A chandelier made of poised gold and silver-tinged crystals had taken their breath away, curling at its edges high above her personal desk.

"The stones were found within this very mountain, you know." Katari commented as she made her way around the fine mahogany desk and sat in her chair. With the poise of a professional, she sat straight, her high chin and overall serious expression pointed to Ayale. She gestured to the pair of chairs in front of Osiris. "Sit. Let us talk." She adjusted her suit jacket.

"What was...all that?" Osiris gestured to the weird power that dwindled around them.

"Abjuration. My affinity allows me to temporarily control movement in certain spaces. I did so to ensure no one would be hurt." She smiled briefly. "Though hopefully it is unnecessary now." She shrugged, peering at Ayale.

"How do you know Ayale?" Osiris asked, protectively clutching Ayale's shaky hand while the pair sat down. Ayale's chest beat a million miles a minute at the thought of being trapped into the mountainside. Even more odd was how calm Osiris had managed to remain throughout the walk into the compound.

"I am Katari, leader of the surviving Rooiboux clan. Friend of their mother, Diori." Katari kept her careful gaze on Ayale, feeling their hazel eyes stare daggers at her in return. "And you?" She looked at Osiris.

"Osiris. Osiris Fyl." He smiled.

She nodded, her expression unchanged.

"A fine name. Your mother seemed to think such a name was foreboding though." Katari pointed the comment to Ayale, who said nothing but instead squeezed his hand tight.

"I am not your enemy, Ayale." Katari leaned back in her chair, bringing a sense of informality with the talk of their name. "And I am not here to intervene with your reasons for going home. I only want what is best for you. Now, looking at you as a growing adult, I realize I should have never worried." Katari's serious tone softened alongside her expression. "Your mothers foretelling, however, concerned me heavily. Your companion here, Osiris Fyl, yes?" She looked at him for affirmation.

Osiris hesitantly nodded.

"I want to ask you both what you know about each other, as well as your plans. Diori seems to believe one of you may be hiding something from the other."

# X

Osiris felt a pang of anxiety begin to make its way through his body. His grip on Ayale tightened before they retracted their hand. His heart began to beat almost faster than theirs.

Katari could tell her hunch was right, knowing her comment caused this reaction, before any actual questions were asked. Something told her Ayale's mother had the right sense to question the boy, but Katari did not want to cause more strife during such a trying time for them both.

"Is there something you would like to say before we begin?" Katari pointed her knowing stare at Osiris. His eyes widened, immediately meeting Ayale's equally conflicted gaze. They looked at him with uncertainty, hoping what he had to say was not as fearsome as the Rooiboux leader made it out to be.

"Osiris, tell me what you're hiding." Ayale said, their brow furrowing at the possibilities. Osiris moved forward in his seat, deep in thought. The look in his eyes was distraught, confirming Katari's suspicions.

"If you don't say it, I will. But they deserve to hear it from you." Her prominent stare came with a knowing look.

Ayale stared at him, expecting the worst to come out, patience being no virtue at this moment. As Osiris met their glare, the typically tiresome expression was replaced with disbelief.

"I was an errand runner for the Matxha clan. Learned a few things I wasn't supposed to know. Because I-I ran from them, they took it upon themselves to come finish the job. Please hear me out before—"

"Are you kidding me?" Ayale's disbelief ripped from their throat, hearing Lau's warnings ringing in their head.

"I didn't think it was…important."

"Osiris, why wouldn't you say anything? Why hide that from me?" They looked for something to grab from Katari's desk, ready to pick up the lamp or throw the nearest object at his face.

"Enough." The stern voice and strengthening force field of the Rooiboux leader shut down their bickering. Katari's stare was far beyond an intimidation tactic, until the next words to leave her mouth took them both off guard. She blinked away the subtle red glow coming from her eyes. "I am sure he had good reason to withhold this information." She said, looking for his defense. Osiris' eyes widened, unsure what to do now that he was given the floor. All he knew was he didn't want them to think the absolute worst of his choice. Clearly flustered, no words left his mouth, rendering him no excuses and no defense.

"Perhaps he wanted to protect you. Though it is quite the secret to keep. Your mother thought you should know your company, Ayale. She awaits to hear from you now that we have finally established contact." Katari's stern look made it seem otherwise. "It seems like you will be safest here for the time being, at least while a plan is made to bring you back home safely. Until then, stay the night."

"Wait, it's night?" Osiris asked, trying to account for the hours they spent on the road, as well as in Istanza.

"The Rooiboux will gladly grant you asylum." Katari took a set of keys out of a nearby drawer and tossed them in Ayale's direction, watching them catch the set midair. "There is a room above the café set up for your stay, though it is rather small. I will let you know when I hear back from her."

Ayale muttered their gratitude before leaving the office, Osiris following close behind. The gorgeous view of the starry night sky passed by Ayale and Osiris as they both silently retreated to the back room of the café and up the spiraling stairs. Katari was correct and the night sky was indeed here. Being so far from the city allowed for the stars to pop in the dark sky. While Ayale wanted to stargaze, they could not wait to sleep on a piece of furniture and not in a car or the ground. When they opened the door, Osiris and Ayale were met with the sight of a single bed and couch set.

Ayale audibly groaned and Osiris felt his face begin to flush.

"Whatever, I don't share beds with anyone." They said before walking over to the couch. The airy silence that followed filled with tension. There was certainly no getting through to Ayale, Osiris knew that much. Within the hour, both had their setups and spaces among the small room. Osiris kept to himself as he got into bed. The guilt ate at his conscience, but he didn't want to hide the identity that he knew for so long. He didn't really want to hide anything. Especially from the person who saved his life days ago.

Though, if he were to be honest, Osiris expected Katari to say something far worse. He felt a sense of relief wash over him when it was only his employer revealed.

Even with every light off in the room, Osiris struggled with sleeping.

"I'm sorry I hid something from you, Ayale." Osiris turned to face the window and simultaneously the couch. "I don't know if you're up. But if you are, I want you to know how much I appreciate you, for everything. It's been a rough couple of years." He held onto his pillow, his hand tightening on the fabric.

"The Matxha clan wanted someone to run their schemes and whatever bullshit they couldn't bring other members to do. I couldn't take it anymore. The pressure was too much. But when I cut off contact from my superiors, they put a hit out on me. They're not too keen on members with affinities up and leaving." Osiris confessed, speaking whatever came to mind. "I didn't mean for any of this to happen." He sighed, fed up with himself and life around him. A stifled yawn left him before he put an arm over his eyes.

Ayale shifted from the couch and made their way to the door, slamming it behind them. They pulled out their aluminum case, wondering how long they could make their cigarettes last, before lighting one up on the balcony and watching as the stars shift with the gentle glow of the filling moon.


The morning approached quickly, and Osiris felt himself far more exhausted than usual. There was no chance of him going back to sleep, so he threw on a random grey shirt from his bag and quietly made his way to the café downstairs. As soon as he entered the small storefront, he made eye contact with Katari, sitting in the booth across from the door. Her stoic expression instantly gave him anxiety. The only item on her table was a single white mug filled to the brim with fresh coffee.

"Good morning." Katari's solemn voice spoke directly to Osiris. Unsure what to do, he gave her a quick wave and awkwardly looked around the empty café for a spot to seat himself. "Or just sit here." She gestured to the empty seat across from her, less offering and more demanding. He quickly sat down, trying not to make eye contact.

"No need for formalities," Katari joked dryly, getting up from her seat to retrieve an identical mug of coffee from the coffee bar. She sat down once more, placing the mug in front of him. "You look tired." She stated.

"Wonder why." Osiris looked back at her with the most disdain he could summon, mildly irate with the comments pointed at him.

"Attitudes are not allowed in my city before ten o'clock." She said, raising the cup to her lips. "Are you upset at me or perhaps more with yourself?" Katari asked earnestly.

"Definitely upset with myself," He sighed and sank into his seat. She nodded along, watching the heightening sun rising in the distance.

"It's already a lot to deal with being on the run. Ayale left behind the new life they built for themself for me. How can I ever feel okay knowing I took them away from everything they loved?"

"What they choose to do is up to them. But instead of leaving you to deal with the consequences of your own actions, here they are. The two of you are birds of a feather who now need to deal with their problems together. Regardless, home would come to find them again whether you were involved or not." Katari wondered if things would end differently now that someone would accompany Ayale back home.

"What's going to happen to them when they go back?" Osiris couldn't help but think aloud.

"Anything is possible now," She looked down at her half empty coffee cup. "But I can promise that nothing will happen here. Not while I'm around." Her smile was genuine, something Osiris didn't expect.

"What you can do at this very moment is your best. Whatever that entails to you," Katari refilled her own cup. "Guilt is not necessary."

The honesty and advice given to Osiris helped put things into perspective, but he had more questions that needed answers. "How long are we safe for?"

"Diori is figuring that out as we speak. Neither of you can leave Istanza until we know what comes next." She answered, leaving no room for negotiation.

Osiris and Katari sat in silence afterwards, drinking their coffee together. The interaction was oddly comforting in the moment, as simply existing was hard enough during their time on the run. He parted ways with a quick wave before heading back up to the room above the café.

"Wait," Katari stopped him and headed behind the coffee bar, grabbing a new mug and a small plate with a muffin. She promptly handed the items to him. "If they're anything like their mother, bring them these."

Osiris nodded, keeping in the scoff that he felt in his throat. He took heed out of fear that they may still be upset after yesterday's events.

On the way back to the room, all he could feel was the impending anxiety building in him. His heart went crazy, flashes of heat working through his body. Though the walk was fairly scenic, the upper section of the café had a view like none other. Before he could reach the top of the stairs, he was met with the high mountains, prominent and strong as they protectively wrapped around Istanza, keeping it hidden away from the rest of the world. Trees grouped together in the distance, looking identical to a patch of moss if it were inches away. Dips and valleys devoid of anything but the harsh morning fog seemed to meet a ravine. Though he was sure it was a trick of the eyes, he swore for a brief moment that he saw a flash of green light. He ignored the passing vision as nothing.

As Osiris approached the top of the stairs, he was met with a different view altogether.

Ayale was hunched over the black guardrail, half a lit cigarette in their mouth, and a poised but half-asleep expression scrawled across their face. They only glanced in his direction for a second when he stopped beside them to hand over the goods from Katari. They balanced the cigarette on the guardrail, taking the mug first. Before he could speak, their face shifted and made an excited noise.

"Is the coffee okay?" Osiris broke the silence and Ayale couldn't help their strained expression.

"Tastes like the weird stuff my mother used to make for herself." They looked down at the plain mug, thinking briefly of the last time they were ever in the same room together before Ayale skipped town.

"I just want to say, I'm really sorry about all of this. In case you didn't hear me last night." Osiris fiddled with his hands, nervously looking around the railing.

Ayale stared at the distant horizon, overlooking the mountains. They thought of the concept of secrets, noting down that they held quite a few on their end.

"Secrets don't make friends." They finally commented.

He nodded, mimicking their posture on the guardrail beside them. The sun took its time rising, leaving distant shadows across the two-story building. Ayale placed the mug down on the ground beside them and absently messed with their hair. With a quick twirl, they placed both strands over their right shoulder, taking in the fresh mountain air into their lungs.

"No need to be sorry though," They finished, a calm demeanor finally pulling across their face. "This is a strange time for us both. No matter what, I stand by my actions. You should do the same. Maybe don't keep something like that a secret. It sounds like the Matxha clan is more of a problem to us than I expected. Especially if you handled something of theirs." Ayale nabbed the muffin off the plate, splitting it down the middle. They gave half to Osiris, and it felt like a sense of peace was attained, even if temporary. He felt relieved and worried all at once, thinking if anyone else would handle this situation better than him. No one, he thought, could ever be as calm as Ayale had been this past week. He only hoped things would stay this way throughout their journey across the territories.

"Did Katari send you up with all this?" They asked, eyeing the muffin.

"Mhm."

"Then she definitely knows my mother. This was her typical breakfast, down to the weird coffee from her homeland." Ayale snickered and picked up their mug, noting the odd combination they hadn't tasted in years. A brief smile fluttered across their face, a sight Osiris wished he saw more often. "Have you tried this yet? A bit strong, but pairs well with a muffin." They urged him to try the drink from his own cup. With a little hesitation, he drank the beverage with one far too confident gulp, as Ayale watched in mild horror.

Osiris coughed, his face twitching while he tried to process the bitterly thick coffee.

"Why, why would you drink it like that?" Ayale tried their best to hold back their amusement, stifling back a laugh with a series of coughs.

"This isn't funny, that coffee should be categorized as a hazard. Why is it thick?!" Osiris complained and ran to the room behind them for water. Ayale shrugged, drinking from their mug with no issue.

The view of the sun rising beyond the distant mountains took away their attention. A small part of them was able to push past their initial fear and felt relief. While they didn't want to go home, it felt a bit better knowing they wouldn't be alone.

As the thought passed them by, Osiris came back out with two water bottles in each hand.

"For when you're done drinking your acid." He rolled his eyes.

They shot him a glare in response. "You need to get it together, this is nothing."

"Only you would be okay drinking a liquid gas." He poked at their shoulder.

The sun's rays came out from above the mountain range, letting them both feel a bit of warmth before the cooling breeze took them aback and brought thin streams of clouds along with it. With one more sip, Ayale began to see the bottom of the cup, contemplating what could be said when their mother inevitably tried to contact them directly.

The remainder of the day was spent taking time to relax and to adjust to their newest location. Ayale paced around the building, awaiting to hear any news from Katari. But the majority of their time was spent outside, taking solace in the quiet town that supposedly made up the last remaining Rooiboux territory. They kept to themself, thinking and plotting about everything that ran through their mind.

How were they supposed to speak to an estranged parent and suddenly ask for help, after disappearing for three years?

What would they do if they asked where they had been hiding? How were they supposed to explain the incident with the Matxha clan and Osiris?

In fact, it begged a question they didn't consider.

Why did Ayale get involved in a clan argument?

Too many questions plagued them all at once, leaving them unsure where to begin. They simply took a cigarette and let the day run its course.

# XI

Their third day in Rooiboux territory was coming together as another day with everyone anxiously awaiting some sort of news from Diori to keep up to date on the situation at hand. Though Katari left Ayale and Osiris to their own doings, she had found herself equally, if not more restless than the two, awaiting to hear from her oldest friend and mother of her current guest. In her office, she stared at the never-ending pile of paperwork before her, all of which tended to official clan business. She sighed and settled her elbows on her desk, throwing off her reading glasses on the desk in a moment of irritation. How all of this happened so quickly was beyond her cognition.

As Katari recalled the events of a few nights prior, it was a simple phone call that began this chain of events. An old friend reached out, bearing the weight of both good and bad news, asking for help in return. When she received the initial call, she asked for the bad news first.

The bad news given to her was the Cxai clan's impending civil war on the brink of starting, the rift growing between Diori and the current Cxai leader she called her husband. Something like this did not entirely shock Katari, having known Ayale's parents for decades now. The attempt Diori made to take over in Ayale's absence clearly did not go well. A burden she knew all too well herself.

The consequences were the real problem. The Cxai were powerful, more so than any other, but if the coming collapse was true, what was going to happen to the surrounding clans, such as the Rooiboux?

To consider everything around her would cause a good headache the size of Istanza. This was not even close to the life she envisioned for herself. Perhaps it had been when she met someone at Ayale's age, already two decades long past.

That was when her quiet life turned into one of her worst nightmares.

A less than reserved man that had whisked her away with his genuine heart and charm was her first thought. She had been in love almost instantly but had to juggle both her emotions and her place in this world. Having come from a powerful family, she had her expectations from them as well as herself. She continued to be the perfect daughter, wife, and rising leader in the Rooiboux, never letting anything get in her way.

Katari would never allow herself to be viewed as anything less.

It was only months after her engagement, days prior to her wedding day, that everything went wrong. A surprise attack on the city that housed the heart of the Rooiboux territory rendered a massacre that she could never forget. The moment replayed in her head, day after day, a reminder of her past. An image she saw when she woke up in the morning and every night before she slept. The once peaceful Matxha clan, their neighbors to the west, had gone from friends to predators in a matter of days, expanding into the Rooiboux territory through the east.

A change in the leadership of the Matxha clan, after the sudden death of their beloved leader, rendered the Rooiboux clan less than half of their original population.

Another change in leadership occurred a year ago, bringing her same fear to life once more. Families of power typically passed their titles down to their own, but somehow, much of the original Matxha family had seemed to disappear seemingly overnight. Though recently, their bloodline had almost vanished entirely from the great nation, no trace left behind.

That should be grounds for increasing defense, she thought. Another silent regret that lived within her.

The attack was around the time she had met Diori, a kind soul with no greater motives, who lived alongside her for the first month after the massacre of the Rooiboux. In turn, helping a young, uncertain Katari. She had to rebuild, restructure, and grieve without ever being asked to do so. She had an idea of how to move but needed to maintain her strength through everything. That was the worst of it all, pretending nothing hurt, as though half of them were not just slaughtered by their allies without reason nor warning.

In those moments, Katari had a choice to make. Fight back and risk the lives of those who remained or build new life for herself and the remaining Rooiboux clan, away from the eyes of the other clans. With help from the wife of the Cxai leader, that idea came to reality. The Rooiboux had finally relocated to the mountains, remaining in an isolated part that remained of their territory, away from everyone and everything.

Katari put down her coffee cup in the middle of the marble plated coaster. All this reminiscing couldn't be good for her health. It was certainly not good for her coffee. Her rough exterior was the perfect front for hiding her vulnerability, but no match for the two that crashed into her lonesome hideaway. She only wished someone had protected her the same way.

Katari silently vowed she would do whatever it took to get Ayale home. For Osiris to find safety.

She picked up a nearby napkin and the gold pen from her white blouse pocket, clicking it open, ready to devise a plan.

Amid the early dawn, Ayale noticed their cigarette case begin to empty. To their dismay, only two little sticks remained. Already disgruntled this early in the morning, they set out with a few bills in their pocket to the nearest convenience store. Ayale made their way out of the room and down the stairs outside, walking down the steep road that whisked past the empty lot of the café. Lau's car sat dormant with the rest of their stuff strewn across the front seats. The long street dipped down the steady hill that overlooked the hidden city of oddly red rooftops. Ayale left the car behind their peripherals, looking ahead at the scarce buildings that made up steep inclines and declines of Istanza.

They tried to identify a nearby store but found they all looked as though they were occupied as residential buildings. With a grumble, they made their way down the hill, annoyed at how much effort it took to find a store around them. In their brief exhaustive state, they yawned and recalled Lau's voice, preaching as always to quit smoking.

Only when an older gentleman stood outside what looked like a home, did the pestering voice silence. The man was of a thin tall build, balding, and for some reason stood quietly beside his red motorcycle with aviators on though dawn had barely broken. He shifted in his worn brown leather jacket, not attempting to hide his blatant staring. "What are you looking for? You seem lost."

"What's it to you?" Ayale shot back.

"I might be able to help you if you tell me what it is you're looking for. Unless it's a hobby of yours to wander with that look on your face." He chuckled, taking out a cigarette from his upper jacket pocket and lit it up with a simple snap of his fingers.

Ayale's eyes widened, watching the stick light up with no effort. They blinked a few times, wondering if they were simply exhausted or had truly witnessed an elemental magic user light up their cigarette with magic.

"Pardon me, but I did just witness you using elemental fire?" Ayale emphasized, waiting for his denial of the accusatory statement. To their surprise, he shrugged.

"What else is it good for? We're born with these gifts to use them, after all. And fire is used for...well, nothing good now." He mumbled. Ayale looked to the buildings around them, checking if anyone else had been outside.

It was true what he said. Those born with a fire elemental typically had their lives written out for them. Every clan wanted to recruit as many fire elementals as possible, more than any of the other elementals. On the upside, those bearing fire were never without employment. They provided both defense and offense to whomever they served.

"So, you work for Katari?" Ayale wondered aloud.

The strange man's brow furrowed, but he persisted with a smile. "Retired now. Something not many clans allow. Call me Mit, since you're asking so many questions now."

"My name is Ayale. Nice to meet you." They hesitantly introduced themself.

"Now, can we solve whatever you're looking for since you made me monologue?" Mit tipped up his sunglasses to his forehead, revealing the lines beneath his tired eyes.

"Is there a convenience store around here?" They asked, casually staring at his pack of cigarettes hanging from his pocket. Mit followed their stare to his pocket and tried to hold in a laugh.

"You mean the one right behind us?"

Ayale huffed. "You're kidding me?"

"If I was, I wouldn't tell you I'm the one who runs it." Mit opened the front door, revealing a small shop of snacks, fridges, and other items behind the plastic countertop.

"Don't stand around, better to shop now before the gamblers wake up. Those active in the Rooiboux gamble heavily before their shifts." Mit slid his glasses back down and moved the countertop so he could enter, placing it back down behind him. Ayale hesitantly walked and looked around his store. The other end had wooden chairs stacked, aged with light scratches on the seats and legs. Something about the shop felt more as though it were someone's home rather than a storefront, which would explain why it was so difficult to locate.

"Is this whole town supposed to be elusive?"

"To outsiders, yes," He winked whilst he pulled up a chair towards the register. "But if you know about it, well, then you're not an outsider anymore, are you?" He said with a smile.

Ayale smirked in response. Part of them couldn't help but feel a sense of calm being in the store, feeling like they were an unspoken part of the Rooiboux clan. Mit had a way of making them feel like family.

"Now then, what were you looking for at the crack of dawn? That it couldn't wait until later." Mit commented, earning a snicker from Ayale.

"I'll take a whole carton if you can." They took out the colorful bills from their jacket pocket and placed them on the counter. Mit shot a glare from above his sunglasses.

"Only if you can explain to me why a child needs a whole box of cigarettes."

"Circumstantial." Ayale shot back. "I'm certainly no child either, I'm in my twenties."

"That is so much worse. But promise me one thing then." He reached for one of the full cartons on a shelf above him. "Quit before thirty. No need to keep doing this at that age." Ayale watched him place the carton on the counter, his tone serious.

"How about I quit if I'm alive by then?"

"Good enough for me." Mit nodded, pushing the carton to Ayale. When they went to turn towards the door, the older gentleman stopped them.

"Hold on, don't tell me breakfast is a goddamn cigarette, come back here." Mit flipped the plastic divider and grabbed a plastic bag beside him as he headed towards them. He picked up cheese puffs, wrapped croissants, drinks, and a few other items and tossed them into the bag. Mit placed the full bag on a nearby table, taking a single pastry from the case they were displayed on and used the same snap of his fingers to ignite a controlled flame below the treat. He snapped once more seconds later. He huffed, handing Ayale the warmed-up croissant in one hand and the bags of treats to the other.

"Being alive is your payment," He loudly protested, urging them to take back their money. "And share with your friend. It's nice to see young, new faces around here. Be safe, okay?" Mit walked them back to the entrance, earning a quick nod from Ayale. They waved at him as they left the hidden shop.

By the time they left the store, the sun had risen far higher above Istanza, illuminating the same rocky path Ayale took to descend to the main streets. They sighed as they realized they had to ascend the same awful road but happily ate their croissant. The treat bag was heavier than they expected, becoming unwanted extra weight as they trekked up the high hill.

As Ayale eventually made it to the top of the hill, they saw Osiris, leaning against the guardrail with the door open behind him. He gazed out at the never-ending hills of Istanza when he heard muffled footsteps, turning his attention to the stairs, watching Ayale carry the bag of snacks in one hand and a half-eaten croissant in the other.

"Got the munchies?"

"Nah." Ayale answered with their mouth full. "Might've been officially adopted by the Rooiboux clan though. The guy at the convenience store just fathered the crap out of me."

"Please explain, you sound kind of crazy—wait, is that a croissant?" Osiris couldn't hold back his disbelief, suddenly wanting every detail of this bizarre statement. Ayale nodded with a growing smile.

"Yeah, it is. The store owner gave it to me." They walked up beside him and offered a bite from the untouched side. He leaned in and took a quick bite.

"Can he adopt me, too?" He asked. Ayale shrugged, tossing Osiris a can of tea from the treat bag before going into the open room.

"I don't think you could handle being related to me, I come from a mentally ill family." They joked nonchalantly.

Osiris instantly choked on his food. "Ew, never mind, forget I asked."

"You could do worse!" They yelled from the room, placing the bag down before coming back out, settling next to Osiris. Ayale wanted to watch the sunrise this morning, but this would have to do. They looked over at Osiris struggling with the aluminum tab on his can of raspberry tea. Where one second, he struggled, the other he used his affinity to sneak beneath the tab and crack it open with ease. He could feel Ayale staring but pretended otherwise. A small tip of the drink to his mouth and his power was nowhere to be seen.

Ayale looked down at their half-eaten croissant, remembering Mit's words as he lit his cigarette.

*We are born with our gifts to use them.*

"Everything okay?" Osiris asked, genuinely concerned at Ayale's blank stare. They turned back to face the hidden city below them. Istanza had every rooftop covered in a clay red color. A tactic used to thwart any suspicion as well as represent the proud red that represented the Rooiboux clan. Such symbolism stood defiant yet defensive for the hidden city.

The sun rose just across from the two, having risen beyond the mountain range to the east. There was no greater beauty to witness than this, Ayale thought.

"Elemental magic probably created this hidden town," Ayale openly concluded.

Osiris kept his eyes forward. "Are you going to lecture me about opening the can with magic?"

"Not at all." They spoke softly, nowhere near as annoyed as Osiris thought they would be. "Do you think elementals should be hidden?" Ayale turned to him.

Osiris darted his eyes towards them, taken aback by the serious question. A few moments passed by with no words while he thought about his answer. At one point, he considered the same question when he was younger. Unfortunately for him, he had come to exploit his affinity for work and ended up wishing he never did. A regret that stretched into his whole time working for the Matxha clan.

"I think...we should be able to choose." He answered. "None of that hierarchy crap either. I wish I had more autonomy, a chance to understand myself, before everything hit the fan. But I needed to work. For me, for my parents." Osiris admitted.

"Wait. That's why you were in the Matxha clan?" Ayale interrupted, darting their eyes towards him. Osiris slowly nodded, clearly regretful. "Osiris, if I knew that, I wouldn't have ripped you a new one in front of a clan leader."

"You didn't know, it's fine."

"No, it's not, and I really mean it."

"Ayale, don't pity me please."

"I'm not, I just feel really bad now." They said, their expression shifting to one of embarrassment.

"That's the same thing." Osiris pointed out, only half serious.

Ayale looked up at Osiris, feeling as though they were looking at someone different. The same feeling they got at the tea shoppe washed over them, mixing in with their new context. They weren't sure what they were doing, but Ayale wrapped their arms around Osiris, pressing their forehead against his shoulder. "You did everything for the right reasons. Not many people can say that. Not even I could say that."

"Thank you." Osiris embraced them back, unsure what else to do.

"I left my mom behind without so much as a note. Nothing honorable behind it, even after everything we went through. I might be selfish, Osiris." They muttered.

"That's not selfish. Freedom isn't selfish. It's normal and human to yearn for something better."

"She probably hates me."

"If she did, she wouldn't be trying to help us." He squeezed them tighter, placing his chin atop their head. Ayale groaned, wishing family trauma wasn't the topic of the day. Though they didn't realize how badly they needed the comfort until Osiris' arms went around their back, holding them close.

"If both our moms end up hating us, we can ask Katari to take us in." Osiris chuckled, feeling Ayale groan louder. They pulled away, instantly bringing the croissant back to their face for another bite.

"Did you really hug me with a goddamn croissant in hand?" Osiris stole another bite, shaking his head in disappointment. Both went back to leaning on the metal guardrail, taking turns sharing Ayale's croissant.

Katari eventually wrote off on six napkins before deciding to take her business, and her coffee, back to her office from the cafe. As she walked through her compound, she reached the door to her office. The guard opening the door for her to enter remained quiet until they saw her coffee mug and doodled napkins in hand.

"Lady Katari?"

"Hmm?"

"Please bring the other mugs in your office back if the timing suits you. The shop owner has begun to send complaints."

Katari passed through the doorway and stared at her guard, her stoic expression unchanged. "Tell him he will get them when I am done with them. Unless he would like to come collect them himself." She emphasized, before softly closing the door behind her.

Katari sat at her desk, placing the mug and notes next to each other. She quickly unlocked her computer, clicking a few keys before looking back to the door. A part of her wanted to lock it before beginning to type up her proposed plan. But then she saw no reason for it. She continued clicking her keyboard, pressing a call button in the corner. A few rings passed through, but by the seventh is when the other line picked up.

"Is that Katari I see calling me?" Diori said with a tone of excitement in her hushed voice. Katari couldn't help but crack a smile at the sound of her friend's voice.

"Yes, how are you holding up in the new location? Why are you speaking so softly?"

"Better than expected. Though I expect opposition at any time. Sooner than later, I will be sending for support from those on the inside. When the excitement settles, I suppose." She said, clearly indicating the danger in her current situation. "How is Ayale?"

"Awaiting instruction, as am I." Katari bluntly stated. Diori grew quiet, trying to keep a handle on the stress in her mind. "May I suggest a safer route to get them to your new location? I spent the morning addressing routes, though longer in distance would ensure avoidance of the other main cities where the Matxha clan may lay in wait. We do not know their motives."

"Oh?"

Katari shuffled her napkins around to find the first part of the map she drew from memory and compared it to the one on her screen. She smiled as she stared at her work, proud to have come up with such a plan on such short notice. Katari began her spiel, explaining every stop, road, and city that would bring Ayale and Osiris to Cxai territory.

"However, I must advise that there is no avoiding the Oolonxg clan. They will need to be ready for anything. We don't know if the Matxha have spread northward."

"If that is to be done, then we will prepare them. I will do my best to reach out to the new clan head. See if you have any eyes on the inside as well." She stated.

"Of course."

A few moments of silence found its way in their conversation before Diori spoke up again. "Thank you for watching them, Katari. I owe you, as always." She said softly.

"Any time, dear friend. Until next time." Katari nodded before hanging up, wondering if she knew of anyone to contact within the Oolonxg clan.

# XII

Days into their journey, the anxiety of the situation had come to mix with the boredom of being stuck within the small borders of Istanza.

Osiris worked with his anxiety as best he could, meditating every sunrise and sunset respectively. These moments of tranquility helped him embrace a growing sense of peace, as well as loosen his grip on the fear of possibilities. There was no good that came from stressing about things out of their collective control. Besides, his trust in Katari helped repurpose his energy for the time being, helping her with remedial tasks around the compound when requested.

Ayale however, could not find that same sense of peace. Since Katari mentioned being in contact with their mother, they made it very clear that they object to the idea of speaking to family so soon, rejecting all requests to the idea. Osiris asked Ayale on multiple occasions if speaking to Diori was something they wanted, but Ayale reiterated their objection to the matter. Even when offered moral support on a separate occasion by a worried Katari, the answer remained a stern no.

While doing their best to rid themself of their disdain at the idea of speaking to family, Ayale joined Osiris in meditation every day. They tried to keep the smoking at bay for his sake, suddenly conscious at how often they did so. If Ayale had awoken earlier than Osiris, they simply went down to the convenience store to visit the man who quickly won over both Ayale and Osiris. That was about as much peace as Ayale could obtain during their time in Istanza.

Early in the morning, it was Ayale and Osiris who were awoken to the sound of knocking at their door. Ayale rolled off the bed to get the door, surprised when Katari stood before them in a sleeveless red suit. The fabric around her legs waved freely in the short breeze between the door and the outside, though her gold flower necklace stayed in place. They noted the Rooiboux emblem in the middle of the gorgeous necklace, fixating on it in their sleepy demeanor.

"Ayale, let us convene in my office as soon as possible." Katari stayed with her usual serious tone before leaving to prepare. Ayale sighed, feeling the tightness return in their chest, and yet, a sense of relief that their time here was coming to an end. They groaned sleepily back towards the bed, shoving Osiris who laid in a dead sleep on the couch.

"Wake up, Katari needs us."

No response.

"Seriously, wake up, let's go." They pushed harder on his shoulder, hoping to receive some sign he was even alive at this point. Osiris shifted to the other side, completing step one. Ayale was too tired to watch someone else sleep peacefully through the morning, yanking away the cover from over him and dropping the sheet onto the floor. Instantly, Osiris groaned in protest and Ayale stalked off to the bathroom. Their job was done.


Katari made the two of them meet with her in the main office. Her stern expression lingered on Ayale, unsure how to say what she wanted. In all honesty, she didn't want to send them away whatsoever. A part of her wanted the two of them to stay indefinitely in their little city, keep them under her watchful eye instead of trusting the plan she created alongside Diori. While their time here had been one of necessity, it was also one in which she enjoyed their company, giving her focus into something other than Rooiboux matters, though she would never openly admit that.

In one deep breath, she sighed heavily before coming out with the words stuck in her throat.

"A plan has been made. Instead of heading immediately home, you are to head north first to ask for the head of the Oolonxg clan. The young leader goes by the name Visu, and though he is fairly new to the title, he can provide protection for the two of you from the Matxha clan while more is being planned for your journey. Your mother believes this to be the best approach. Just in case either of you are being targeted by other parties at the same time." She finished hesitantly.

Both Katari and Ayale shared the same look of worry, wondering how the rest of their journey would play out.

"Katari." Ayale caught her stare. "Does the Oolonxg leader know we will be passing through?" They asked.

She shared an indifferent look. "We are not certain at this time. Your mother is currently trying to reach out to them."

"Oh, neat." They yawned, rolling their eyes.

Katari could sense hesitancy from both Ayale and Osiris. "We are going to do everything we can to contact them prior to your arrival." She started with a sense of confidence. "They're furthest north, past the forests. But on another topic of discussion, the route should be done in a particular way." She walked behind her desk, with both seated at the other side. She moved away a few of the items from her desk to an end table, stretching out a massive map of the region that covered the entirety of her desk.

Every inch of the map represented a once unified country under the name of Alqueris. The line between each clans' territory seemed to be drawn on, though professionally, with different colored markers to detail the many changes and landmarks that made up each border. Katari placed a firm hand on the current capital of the Rooiboux clan.

"Let us start from the beginning. Our territory is that which surrounds Istanza, our capital city. Nothing else. To the north sits a road that has been long blocked off since our arrival. While many believe there is only one road to enter and exit, we have long kept this one a secret, in case of another invasion. What this means is we have a direct connection to the northern forests. Now, do not believe because of this route that it won't take time to get to the capital." She pointed upward from their current placement.

"Bear in mind, the forest can be a touch dangerous, so get through it as quickly as you can manage. Odania, the capital city of the Oolonxg territory, will be on the other side, bordering the forest to the east." She finished, looking at the attentive duo taking notes. The hardest of all had yet to come. Her silence quickly subsided when she rolled up the map beneath her, handing it off to Ayale.

"Know that this map is older than most of our current clan families. Should you need it, the map may still be useful. But try not to rely on it when it comes to borders. Understood?" Katari stressed the importance of the map. Ayale nodded along with Osiris, both attesting they would only use the map when necessary.

It was then that Katari stood silently, straightening her back, and avoiding eye contact with the two. She struggled with what to say, now that they were both at the end of their stay.

Though Ayale didn't hesitate to get up and walk around the desk, pulling Katari in for a hug without warning. If it were anyone else, she would have recoiled instantly, but watching over Ayale these last few days had her feeling...different. She patted them on the back, a subtle curve of a smile showing on her face.

"Please be safe. Do not let anyone dictate your choices in life. You did well to fight for your freedom." Katari said.

"I'll come back when everything dies down. We both will." Ayale promised, Osiris perked up, surprised to hear the word 'both'.

He first thought the words to be an accident, a slipup of some sort. It didn't stop him from obsessively thinking about the possibilities. How far in the future could it be they were thinking about? Would they be alive at that point? Where would the two of them end up?

Osiris would proceed to overthink that statement for the rest of the day.

"We'll want the full tour, don't skip out on us next time." Ayale squeezed Katari tighter, eventually feeling her return the embrace. Osiris turned to look at one of the many glass book shelves behind Katari's desk, keeping to himself so they could have their moment. He heard 'us' and suddenly found himself thinking of their hug from a few days ago.

"Until next time, then." Katari released Ayale, wondering when the timing would come for them to visit once again.

The three of them left the office, with Osiris and Ayale going off to pack for the trip ahead. Lucky for them, they were set up with the money Lau had given them, something Ayale expected would have been their biggest worry. It wasn't long before the duo were back in Lau's car, preparing to leave the hidden Rooiboux city.

While the road ahead sounded as though it should be smoother than before, Ayale began the drive at the break of dawn, a heavy feeling lining their stomach, nervous of what was to come next.

Ayale followed the route Katari had written down for them to the exact road. The strange map led the two through odd, worn-out tunnels, not even known to any physical part of the map. At least for them, they had a plan.

The overbearing trees wrapped around the tightly packed road, evidence that the path had not been used in years. The red maples branches that bore down over the road forced them to drive with high caution. Though the view was like none other, Ayale felt their overly cautious nature on high alert for the next few hours. Even with Osiris trying to talk and start conversation during the drive, he couldn't help but note the clear overwhelm scrawled on their stoic face. When he opened the map gifted to them by Katari, he realized why.

It was going to be a long drive.

*One Year Earlier...*

The city of Densriel told a groggy tale of rain, one full of fatigue and heavy with clouds.

In the heart of the busy capital, tall buildings collecting at every street and corner, sat the most famed structure in Densriel; the Matxha clan compound, built at the very establishment of the clan system after the fall of the Alqueris Empire, to house the influential family that had once fought in the war to secure freedom, for magic and for all affinity users.

Now a tenth-generation family called the famous building home. The current Matxha leader Hied Umbra, his eldest son Belire, and youngest daughter Eines, whose birthday had come and gone a week ago.

Wandering the unlit halls of the fourth floor she called home, Eines found herself far more anxious than ever before. The incoming rain slid down the wide windows with a painfully slow rhythm, her gentle green eyes following a single drop down until it was no longer visible. She stared until she dozed off and blinked profusely. Her level of exhaustion was unbefitting of a spoiled clan daughter who had just turned thirteen years of age. Her pale blonde hair fell in lazy, thin streams over both shoulders, complimenting the equally pale complexion reflected back at her as she continued to stare at her reflection in the window.

Eines forced her feet forward, motivated once more as a short crackle swam between her fingertips as she rubbed them together.

A small creak came from a door a few feet away from her, a tall figure in a fine dark green suit leaving the office at the end of the grand hallway. The blond young man made eye contact with Eines, a smile curbing on his pleasantly surprised face. "Eines? What are you doing on this side of the compound?" He walked over before she ran the remaining distance between them and launched herself into his arms.

"I had to find you Belire, I-I need you to see this." She pulled away, stepping backwards to regain some lost space in the unlit hall.

Eines closed her eyes, stood herself straight, and pulled her hands out in front of her, clasping them flat together. She rubbed her hands slowly, her intent eyes shut tight just as the short crackle of electricity exposed itself to the two of them. The faster she put her hands together, the more electricity came from the friction. Illuminating like solid strikes of lightning, she created a gentle thread as she separated her hands, energy moving between them. With her last breath, she put her hands back down to her sides and let the energy dissipate into the air, as if they had never existed.

When Eines opened her eyes, the look on his face had been amused, if not a little bit proud. Until his expression shifted into surprise and immediately stern.

"Is that what I think it is?" An older man's voice sounded out from the other end of the hallway, slowly approaching Eines from behind. Her excitement died down, fear taking its place.

When she turned around, her straight face and stern posture found her father Hied, a middle-aged man with the complexion of cream, full of unruly white and grays blended together with blond strands barely visible, on a face with lines like a fallen tree, beneath both his widened brown eyes. Eines met his stare straight on, refusing to show any emotion. "I had been feeling strange and next thing I knew, my hands began to—"

"Enough." He raised his hand to stop her from speaking. "We will stop this before it becomes a problem."

Eines and Belire stood still and quiet, waiting for some kind of elaboration.

Hied only took out his phone, punching at the small screen in his hands, putting it up to his ear as the gentle dial noise echoed off his face. When the line clicked to voicemail, he stalked off to the other end of the dark hall, his voice loud but fading as he walked away. "Hello, this is Hied of the Matxha Clan, I need an opening as soon as possible for an affinity removal."

*Affinity removal.*

The words echoed in Eines mind, going from a sense of pride for her power to a sinking feeling in her chest, one that spoke of nothing but regret. The terror of affinity removal was known to everyone.

Every user of magic, everyone and anyone who had an affinity of any kind lived one of two ways. The first was to live in secrecy, hiding their power to keep away prying eyes. If caught with an affinity, many were easy targets for the clans. And those with elemental affinities were instantly drafted to their home clan's military.

And for most, that was not a choice. To live with an affinity was a risk in all manners of the word, in and of itself a fearful choice that was frowned upon in public spaces.

And because of that, the second was forceful removal.

Eines fidgeted nervously before quietly walking towards the other end of the hall, opposite of where her father had gone towards, and exited into the staircase.

Belire cautiously followed after Hied, knowing what was to come, yet all the more ready to defend her.

The way he wished someone had defended him.

# XIII

The drive through the forest towards the Oolonxg territory was nothing less than stressful. To do the constant drive from the early morning into the late afternoon left both Ayale and Osiris stir crazy in their seats. Before the road began to let up, the most either could do was think of the days to come.

The idea of being sent to another city left Osiris anxious. What awaited them in Odania was unknown. Even in his time in the Matxha clan, Osiris had never been sent so far away from home. He nervously parted his braids to the right, settling them over his shoulder. His hyper fixation led him to smooth down his hair. His thoughts raced with infinite possibilities.

"Are you alright?" Ayale asked, keeping their eyes on the road in front of them.

Osiris held his breath when he answered. "Never better."

"Sounds convincing, want to run that by me again?"

"It's nothing, everything is fine." He visibly scowled at Ayale's comment, who kept their knowing gaze averted.

"It isn't nothing if it's making you feel this way. I can feel your anxiety from here."

"Just let it go!" Osiris snapped, his voice much louder than he intended.

Ayale placed both hands on the steering wheel, exhaling as they adjusted their back against the seat. "Alright, you got it." They kept their attention to the thinning road. There was no use in pushing the matter if he was just going to get more upset.

Osiris found himself feeling immense guilt for his minor outburst, turning towards his window, and laying his head on the headrest behind him. It didn't help his case when he wasn't sure why he was upset in the first place. When he thought about his feelings, the last positive emotion he felt was safety in Istanza, a feeling he wished remained with him. The worst of his anxiety was finding no real reason behind his outburst.

If he had to admit something, he wished the two of them could have stayed longer. He enjoyed taking time to get to know Ayale. The city ran like a quiet village, but it had everything both of them needed; consistency, peace, and people they could trust.

Something the two wouldn't get back. They were on their way to who knows where.

Osiris realized the longer they drove, the shorter their time together remained before their arrival in Cxai territory, leaving a strange weight in his chest. For now, he would let the lull of the silent drive flow without a single word from him. There was no use in forcing himself to make conversation, waiting for the right words to come to mind before apologizing.

Hour after hour passed by, the sea of overgrown trees becoming a common scene on their newest route. The car dipped and rose with every bump in the unpaved road ahead.

Ayale slowed down the car at the sight of a small cottage-like building, before coming to a stop a few feet away from a small shop to their right side, embedded in an opening of its own between a multitude of low bearing trees. The sign was burnt in a large piece of wood and hanging off a roughly made post, hand carved by the rough markings. The shop itself was more of a log cabin but had its charm with all the flora growing uncontrollably around the front entrance, small white flowers growing around three flat stones that made up the path to the entryway.

They shifted into park and shut the car off, and without so much as a glance at Osiris, they left him alone in the passenger seat.

Osiris watched them in disbelief as they left him behind in the car to go inside the strange roadside shop. A part of him acted without thought, throwing down his sketchbook on the dashboard and fixing his hoodie before leaving the car. As much as he wanted to stay upset, he couldn't help the worry building in his throat by leaving them alone. With a roll of his eyes, he pulled himself from the safety of the car to follow them into the shop.

When he entered the shop, Osiris was instantly met with the strong scent of jasmine and lilac with a hint of smoke, a handful of pillar candles partially melted, dripping down from their own shelves beside him. The left side of the shop had a plethora of short, light wooden shelving units one on top of the other. Housing stones of every kind and texture, polished and raw, with mirrors on the wall behind them reflecting his anxious expression back at him. Towards the furthest shelf were huge pillars of polished stones, from rose quartz to malachite, obsidian, and a few others he couldn't recall the names for.

To his right was a more disorganized mess, but of the various items that lingered around, were somewhat settled in more or less of an order. One unsteady shelf had baskets of dried herbs and flowers strung together, wooden chimes hanging off other objects, and an unstable stack of small leather notebooks wobbling from the floor up to Ayale's shoulder.

He watched them standing beside it, their thoughtful gaze fixed closer to the bottom of the stack. When their eyes stopped moving, he knew that one of the notebooks had caught their eye. Unfortunately for them, they settled on one that was closer to the ground. They tried to slide it out as if it were a very intense game of building blocks, freezing when the pile started to wobble.

"Need some help with that?" Osiris chimed in, coming up from behind them to their side. Ayale didn't budge, not paying him any mind. Their focus was entirely on the stack of colorful notebooks and the neat pile they created.

"I can hold these and we can—"

"No need, I will figure it out." Ayale interrupted, keeping their fixed gaze on the notebooks. They attempted to slide it out and watched as the pile began to wobble again. The tower began to grow unstable, and Osiris couldn't help his open grimace, pulling Ayale by the waist and out of the way just before the notebooks tumbled over in their very spot.

The two looked down at the strewn notebooks, staring candidly at the mess they both made.

"I told you I didn't need your help." Ayale pulled away from his arms, kneeling over to grab the notebook they had their eye on, kneeling on the rough wood floor to grab one out of the pile. They began to wander off into another part of the shop, leaving Osiris dumbfounded where he stood beside the mess they made and left behind. As he began to stack the notebooks back together, Osiris swore to mind his own business from here on. He struggled to understand a lot as of late, but Ayale didn't make things much better. It felt like they were more reckless and airheaded than ever, a trait he didn't catch on to until well into their adventure. To wander into a strange shop on the side of the road, in the middle of nowhere, was probably pinnacle for the incautious human.

Osiris couldn't help his anxiety much of the time, but with or without it, he felt he would worry about Ayale regardless.

"Good evening!" Someone popped out from behind the checkout counter, their voice carrying drastically loud across the store. The woman stood tall and proud from her jack in the box entrance below the square shaped counter, her dirty blonde hair a touch frizzy up top. "My name is Mildred! What can I do for you?" The young girl leaned across her counter, eyes on Osiris, who almost jumped out of his skin while cleaning Ayale's mess.

Ayale thought the greeting had been for them and crossed towards the counter, hoping to ask her a question, but seemed to be missed by her eyes. They wondered how she couldn't see them standing in front of her, waiting patiently for her to notice them with the notebook in hand. Instead, they witnessed her longing eyes drink up Osiris' figure top to bottom, all subtlety out the door. She bit the corner of her lip as she watched Osiris stand back up, having rearranged the mess Ayale made of the notebooks into a neat stack again. He looked up from the stack, meeting her intent gaze with one of confusion.

"Question for you, Mildred," Ayale snuck up in front of her, breaking her intense eye contact with Osiris. "I'm looking for dried ginger root or lemon balm, do you carry either of those?"

"No." She answered, looking over Ayale's shoulder, making sure her emboldened eyes found Osiris again. He looked, at best, genuinely the most uncomfortable he had ever been since the two met in Densriel. Unsure what to do, he awkwardly looked away in the direction of the stones. In response, Ayale straightened their back and got in her way once more, doing their best to block her view.

"Mind scooching?"

Ayale narrowed their tired eyes at Mildred, an empty threat coming to mind before spilling out of their mouth without another second to think about it. "I do mind actually. Don't ogle my friend like that."

Osiris stood idly by, watching Ayale defend him without a second thought. The clear discomfort on his face was enough for them to speak up.

To Ayale, this was the least they could do after their sporadic argument earlier.

"Excuse me?"

"You're excused. Don't think you're immune from common decency living out this far in the forest. Osiris, let's go." Ayale placed their hands in their pocket, feeling the blade Lau left them as they walked back a few steps towards the door before feeling Mildred's eyes burn into theirs.

"Oh, you're not going anywhere after talking to me like that." Mildred said in a hushed tone, walking out from behind the glass counter, creeping slowly towards Ayale, who paused and kept their wary eyes steady on the strange shop keep.

"Shouldn't have tried your shit with my friend then." Ayale rolled up their sweater sleeves and Osiris' felt his face grow hot, even as he stood frozen in the middle of the shop. "Have some self-respect. Do you make every man you encounter uncomfortable?"

Mildred growled in response to the comment, and what once felt like a sure fight suddenly started to melt away when her fists began to turn red, glowing the same red of fire down to her wrist.

Ayale's eyes darted from her suddenly flaming knuckles tightened into a fist. Mildred's wild hair flew into a frenzy as she threw herself at Ayale, who promptly moved aside and tossed the notebook in hand at the shopkeeper's head before knocking over the rebuilt stack once more. That was not the day to test a fire elemental in the middle of a dense forest.

Both Ayale and Osiris ran out of the shop and to the car, hoping the mess would buy them enough time to start the car and speed off.

Mildred managed to run out of the shop just before they locked the car doors, fumbling with the passenger door when Ayale hit the accelerator with everything they had, escaping with their lives.

Ayale drove violently fast down the narrow road, not allowing themself to let up for even a moment in case Mildred was coming after them. The two tried to catch their breath, unsure what to make of the fire elemental's shop.

Osiris breathed heavily, trying to break the silence. "Ayale?"

"Yeah?"

"Pardon my language, but what the *fuck* was any of that?"

"I really need you to specify, a lot just happened." Ayale continued speeding down the suddenly winding roads, taking a sharp left up a steep curve.

"Let's start with why we stopped to begin with." Osiris felt his heart racing terribly fast, leaving him barely able to get air into his lungs.

"If I'm going to be honest, I just wanted to get you something as an apology. I'm not great at admitting when I'm wrong, but I felt bad for pushing you earlier. I don't want you to ever feel forced to talk to me about anything. I wanted to be supportive but pushing wasn't the way to do it, and I thought some stuff to maybe make tea at our next stop would be nice, but then—"

"Mildred." He finished for them.

"Mildred, the fire elemental who runs an apothecary in the middle of a forest. What a time to be alive." Ayale said, clearly exasperated.

"My life flashed before my eyes." Osiris sank back in his seat and looked out the window, watching the sea of muted green trees passing by the speeding car. No shapes were easily visible with how fast they were driving, but he chose not to comment on them to slow down. "Thank you for defending me. I certainly didn't deserve it after my outburst." His face heated up as he remembered their defensive stance and words as if they were seconds ago.

"Even if I'm huffy, I refuse to let you be sexualized, by some stranger in the middle of nowhere nonetheless."

"Ayale." He sank into his hoodie, embarrassed now more than ever.

"What? Honestly, the shop wasn't even worth the stop. Quality was looking a little subpar anyways." They waved their hand.

"Oh? You think everything in there was subpar?"

"Yeah, and there's no use supporting someone who chases handsome men the moment their eyes meet. Kind of gross." They started to slow down after a few more glances in their mirrors revealed no one following behind.

Osiris turned over in his seat, sliding a small rectangular object out of his pocket, placing it in between himself and Ayale on the top of the center console.

"So, you wouldn't want this notebook then? Or in your case, this gorgeous projectile?" He asked, their eyes darting from the road to the console for a brief second. He pushed the petite cream leather notebook closer to them, its floral design impressing even himself. The various flowers traced along the front through the spine, ending its intricate loops to the back cover. Ayale didn't take their eyes off the road, but put their hand out to grab the notebook, feeling the embossed designs in their hand, bringing it up to the dashboard for them to glance at.

"You stole this from the shop? Are you insane?" Ayale stifled back a laugh, unable to maintain their serious composure. The gesture was so outlandish, they didn't know the proper way to react. A part of them felt their heart melt. Even then, they wanted to stop driving and look at it up close.

Osiris didn't dare look up. "I don't know, I just felt bad. Then..."

"Fire fists, yeah."

"Yep." He chuckled, looking out at the road ahead.

"Well. I love it. Thank you, Osiris." Ayale slipped the miniature notebook into their pocket beside Lau's folded up blade. They hoped that after everything they went through today would lessen the gap between the two of them.

"That was the first time someone ever treated me that way. It was honestly the most off-putting thing I've experienced."

"Comes with the territory of being conventionally attractive." Ayale shrugged.

Osiris felt his heart jump a beat. "Are you saying you find me attractive?"

"I'm saying you fit the standard! Don't make this weird." They blinked profusely, but kept their eyes fixed on the tight road in front of them, feeling the sweat form in their palms.

"Apparently I fit her standard." He grumbled, looking at his reflection in the window.

The quiet settled in, the soft sounds of the car filling in the void.

Osiris was left with the ever-persistent feeling he could not quite place, swirling around his chest with no sign of stopping. With so much going on, it was difficult to discern the complex mess that made up his feelings. His eyes moved from his own reflection in the window to Ayale, whose diligent attention was slowly drifting as the bags beneath their eyes became more noticeable.

Before the overwhelming feeling could take its place, he took out his sketchbook to draw, attempting a steady hand while Ayale managed to drive over every bump on the road. He let flowers and vines take over the page, mimicking the design on the notebook he gifted them.

Ayale remained silent, looking in the rear-view mirror every now and again to make sure the elemental wasn't trailing behind them. The feeling of impending doom didn't seem to shake, keeping Ayale company for the rest of the ride. This feeling surely wasn't a first, though it had been years since they felt anxiety to this degree trying to settle into them again. Racing thoughts came soon after. The longer they spent driving this car, the worse the thoughts became.

Soon enough, their afternoon drive became an overnighter. Ayale, oddly enough, felt no sense of exhaustion after a while, surpassing the need for sleep hours ago. The sheer anxiety was enough to power them through a large portion of the drive, even as Osiris fell asleep a few hours past midnight.

The further away they were from the shop, slowly did their anxiety seem to decline.

As hour after hour passed them however, still no fatigue managed to slow them down. There was a single responsibility weighing on them, the adrenaline still running in their veins.

Once they made it out of the forest, then they would allow themself the chance to stop and sleep.

Ayale just needed to keep going and get them both to safety. If not for their own sake, then for Osiris sleeping beside them, uncertainty lying ahead of them.

## XIV

At the sight of the barely visible sky, Ayale watched as the sun reached its peak over the trees. They sighed, wondering how many hours passed by since they began to drive from the apothecary. Even Osiris, energetic and talkative as he's been lately, dozed off again soon after waking up in the passenger seat.

To Ayale's surprise, a strange settlement of small stone buildings appeared to grow closer from a short distance, leading them to slow down as the uneven roads turned to cobblestone beneath them.

"Where the hell did all of this come from?" Ayale wondered aloud, unable to take their eyes off the line of modern buildings approaching.

Osiris opened his eyes, and the thick settlement of trees gave way to what looked like a whole town. It was a surprise and a touch of awe for the stonework that made up each and every building. The way the town center was structured looked as though it were a large roundabout, with a massive flowering pink willow tree standing tall in the middle. The remaining buildings, never more than two stories tall, surrounded the almost thirty-foot-tall tree. Each building seemed to be made in similar design, built from the ground up with large pieces of stone. If it were not for the various shapes of each stone, the different residential buildings and shops would look identical to one another, save for the contrasting signs outside of each storefront.

The car came to a slow halt In front of a nearby building to their right. While there weren't many people out and about, the few who did collected around the center area, where benches surrounded a small fountain, with a small group crossing the road and entering a small café that sat just a few feet in front of their car.

The shop had a sign with the name Pink Willow Coffee, stealing Ayale's full attention.

Ayale and Osiris shared an understanding look before quickly exiting the vehicle. Both needed something to wake up. They entered the small café, immediately hit with the scent of fresh coffee and dim floating lights above them, surrounding the majority of the ceiling. The interior of the coffee shop gave off a comforting vibe with gentle music to accompany their aesthetic. But it didn't stop either of them from collapsing into the nearest booth.

From their seat, they could see a set of stone stairs on the side, leading up to a restricted area for employees only. There were seldom scattered tables and booths, a large stone counter stretched across the middle. Baristas sped around behind it, completing orders and leaving them in a designated pickup space to the left of the counter.

Ayale sat back in the cushioned booth. "Osiris?"

"Yeah?"

"I need caffeine before I pass out." They slumped forward, laying their head across the table.

"I'm on it." He yawned, getting up to join the small line of people forming before the front counter. Ayale sat patiently, hoping he would order them something half decent. They sat back up, feeling the miniature notebook shift in their pocket. They took it out to finally inspect it properly, not needing to focus on the road ahead anymore.

Each flower embossed around the front and back covers were native to every separate territory throughout the continent, with chamomile and ceylon tea flowers on the front representing nations that no longer existed anymore. Styled like an old plant encyclopedia, every flower represented the national symbol of every major clan. An odd choice of design, they flipped it over to see the ones on the back, sucking in a sharp breath when they saw the ceylon plant in fuller detail, its colorful hues undeniable.

Ayale felt the embossed design between their fingers before placing it down on the table, front facing up. Overall, they couldn't help but think of the gesture as a whole. It might be the fact that they were half asleep at a weird rest stop, but the thought of Osiris anxiously stealing from the fire elemental and running for dear life had them audibly giggling to themself. It seemed their olive branch worked out, just not the way they intended.

Ayale sat back into the booth and felt their eyes grow heavy, the back of the chair feeling oddly inviting. They threw on their hood over their short hair, wondering if they had time to nap for a minute or two.

"Aya?" Osiris came back holding two iced coffees, watching Ayale merely open an eye in response.

"You know, I only let my friends call me that." A yawn bubbled up in their throat. "Iced coffee, that's new."

He held onto both drinks in his hands, reluctant to share after their comment. "It's a lilac latte, it's supposed to be their specialty. Though if I'm not your friend, I guess I can drink both." He shrugged, unsure if he could do so even out of spite.

"Lilac? Is that really going to wake us up?" Ayale stared at the purple hued lattes in his hands, while he visibly struggled to come up with an answer, eyes sunken to the table.

"Maybe I can just..." Ayale yawned out loud mid-sentence. "Power nap in the car?"

"Might be for the best." He sat beside them, both taking their first sips of the strange drinks. Ayale nodded as they struggled to sit up but was pleasantly surprised with the result.

Upon his first few sips, Osiris found himself unable to pull away from his drink, surprised at how much he enjoyed his latte. The sweet taste of lilac delicately lingered on the espresso of the coffee, subtle enough not to overpower the drink but strong enough to give it a unique flavor. "Oh my god, that's incredible."

"Mhm." Ayale was more relieved to have some form of coffee than none at this point.

The two kept to themselves, watching as the line slowly grew, died down, repeating for well over a half hour. Neither wanted to move from the booth, enjoying their time outside of the car. Ayale and Osiris took in the adoring café and all the details within it. The standing blackboard sign beside the register showcased cursive handwriting, with cute flowers scrawled all over the phrase "lilac latte with oat milk". The calm lighting brought the two a sense of peace that could have easily made Ayale and Osiris fall asleep, if not for all the noise of people around them.

"So glad the Oolonxg don't come here anymore." Spoke a distant patron on their way into the long line.

Osiris choked on his latte, grabbing Ayale's immediate attention.

"Are you okay?" They awoke, alert from the sound.

"Yeah, just overheard something."

"What was it?"

"They're talking about the Oolonxg clan." He whispered, warily looking around the café.

"Shit, are we in their territory already?" They patted down their pockets, wondering where the map was. "We should really check Katari's map and see where we are."

"Hold on." He said, a distant look in his eye as he began to focus on the couple moving up slowly in line adjacent to them. He could make out a few words before they moved further up towards the register.

"The Matxha wouldn't dare, even if they want to expand north, and the Oolonxg wouldn't bother beyond their gates these days."

"...as long as they forgot about this place, we don't have to belong to a clan."

Osiris' eyes widened, a confused look expanding across his face, one that kept the mostly exhausted Ayale out of their half-asleep demeanor. He continued to listen in, silently reaching for a napkin to scribble down notes for Ayale to keep up. He wrote as fast as he could, making out the least coherent words as he struggled to keep up with the speed of the conversation near them.

Once the two left with their drinks, he let out a breath of relief before taking another sip of his latte. "Are you ready for what I'm about to say?"

"Spill the beans, what did you hear?"

"Ha, I get it." Osiris chuckled, pushing aside his already almost empty cup. "Do you have the map on you?"

"No, why?"

"Ah, alright give me a second to sort of doodle one." He mumbled, taking one napkin and drawing a crude outline of the continent, labeling with little accuracy where each major clan sat. Then, he circled a small section towards the middle.

"We are here." He tapped his pencil in the circled section. "In a rare, unclaimed section between old, prewar Rooiboux land and Oolonxg land. My theory is that when the Rooiboux were invaded, they left behind a good chunk of land, and this is what's left over from the Matxha invasion. Makes you wonder how much of it they really wanted when they left so much unattended. The Oolonxg has always been attentive to what they already own, being that their territory is already so massive." Osiris proudly said, happy to display his knowledge of history in any way he can.

"First off, you're a nerd. Second, the Oolonxg already staged an invasion of their own a long time ago. That's why they don't care about expanding their land; they already did and gained enough resources to be self-sufficient." Ayale pushed the notebook between them, pointing to the chamomile flower proudly displayed towards the spine. "Have you ever heard of the Chamoxile clan?"

"What?"

Ayale grimaced at his reaction.

"Not to out nerd you, but..." They slipped the pencil out his hand, drawing rough lines towards the northwest of the continental map Osiris drew earlier, labeling it Chamoxile with a sharp underline beneath it.

"Holy shit." Osiris took his latte back, bringing it up to his lips but remained attentive.

"Yeah. Rule number one about history; it is always written by the victor. All of this was taken in a coup, staged by the hierarchy of the Oolonxg family when the Chamoxile could not pick one single leader, leaving them on the brink of civil war. The Oolonxg had a history of struggling to survive without the help of neighboring nations, so this acquisition was thoroughly planned out. They had so many natural resources, it allowed the Oolonxg people to thrive in both industry and agriculture." They spoke knowledgeably, almost reciting the information as if it were a test. A moment later, they reached back for their drink.

Osiris couldn't lie, he was surprised and impressed all at once.

He stole a few of the napkins full of notes back, stuffing them into his pocket.

"Wait, what were those notes?"

"Local drama, location of a gas station, and maybe some information about our friend Mildred."

"Does she live around here?" Ayale nearly spit out their latte, holding back, but clear disgust displayed on their face.

"No, she lives in her shop, I think. However, she does frequent the area. Heard the woman in line mention a crazed woman with red hands and something about arson. Fits the description."

Ayale felt a shiver run up their spine. "We really shouldn't stick around, let's go back to the car." They started to get up from their seat, but felt Osiris place a hand to their shoulder, pulling them back to their seat.

"You haven't slept in a long time, I think we should stay the night. There's an inn next door, you could get some needed rest. We aren't really on a schedule anyways, right?"

"Not unless you count me not wanting to go home on schedule." Ayale blurted out, yawning shortly after.

Osiris stared at them, half surprised to hear them admit their disdain for Cxai territory a second time. A part of him felt the same guilt from their first night on the road creeping back, but shook it away and redirected his question into a statement.

"Then it sounds like we are staying. A nice break from family drama and fire hags." He said with a strange burst of confidence. Ayale could only nod, struggling to stay awake even in the busy café.

"Fine then. Ready when you are." They sighed, covering their exhaustion with a turn of their head.

The two headed out from the Pink Willow, walking along the cobblestone paths that surrounded the grand tree in the middle. Osiris walked beside Ayale, watching to make sure they wouldn't fall over.

The inn wasn't a far walk from the café, and almost identical in design, a gentle scent of flowers coming from every room, including the one they would end up in.

Ayale flopped backward onto the double bed, barely taking a moment to look around the room before allowing themself to sink into the mattress. Osiris took the chance to sit on the couch across from them and found himself just as exhausted.

It didn't take long for the two of them to fall asleep.

Ayale's eyes shot open hours later, blinking hard as they tried to shake off their sudden spike of anxiety. They lifted off the bed, but the weight of their exhaustion pulled them back down into the comfort of the plush mattress. They looked out the window, the only source of light being the various strings of beaded lights strung up on branches along the middle of the town square, a few shades of pink light coming from none other than the Pink Willow Café down the road. They illuminated the room with a subtle glow, but not enough to force them fully awake.

Just the barely lit up room left them wondering if this were a dream instead, until they saw Osiris curled up on the couch, his open sketchbook unattended at the edge of their bed. They peered over, curiosity getting the best of them. Ayale smiled, looking over the outline of the flowering pink willow tree that stood tall outside the window. Once the ache in their lower back and faint headache forming behind their eyes took over, the thought of getting up was no longer an option.

It only took them seconds before deciding to fall back asleep into the soft bed, leaving their issues for another time.

The next time they found consciousness, Ayale awoke in a frenzy, forcing themself to sit up. Drenched in sweat and their heart going a million miles a minute was enough to warrant a breathing exercise. A handful of shaky breaths in and out slowly brought them back down. They placed a warm hand through their hair, attempting to recall the fleeting dream from memory that had them in a chokehold, but to no avail. They simply reached over to the nightstand and plucked the room temperature remains of their latte and finished it off, hoping some form of relief would come from the floral drink.

"That was a trip and a half." Ayale's dry voice croaked, their weary eyes finding Osiris peer up from his lowered glasses. Hunched over his sketchbook on the couch, he unfurled and placed his various art supplies off his lap.

Osiris knew the answer but asked regardless. "How did you sleep?"

"Weird. Think I had a bad dream. All I remember is seeing my parents' faces. That's more than enough reason for a nightmare." Ayale moved off the bed, groaning and stretching out while seating themself at the edge, across from Osiris.

"I'm here if you need someone to listen."

"No need, I don't want to think about them until I'm closer and it's really my problem."

Osiris readied to say something, about how this was no longer just Ayale's problem, but both of theirs. He wanted to express that they didn't need to deal with it alone. But having watched their struggle with sleeping, he didn't want to push something they might not be ready to share with him.

Instead, he pursed his lips and nodded along. "Understood." Osiris took to a new idea instead, standing up from the couch to turn on a small lamp from across the room. "New question, what do you want to do from here? We can leave tonight, or we can stay and keep resting, we did pay for the full night. Maybe explore the town?"

"Why are you asking like that?" They groaned and rubbed their sensitive eyes.

Osiris sat beside them, a sense of excitement in his tone. "Can I admit something with no judgment?"

"Go for it."

"I'm scared every day that we are on this journey. Not just what awaits us at the end but the way there. We stopped in one place so far that didn't want our heads. You don't want to go home, I don't want to go to your home, let's do something fun tonight instead. So that way, when the time comes, when we are inevitably in deep shit again, we can look back and have some good memories."

Ayale turned to look at him, feeling the same exact way as Osiris. They were just as frightened but struggled to admit it, scared to allow that level of vulnerability to surface.

"I wish I knew what to say to all of that. It's easier to say it like this though: I would've had to go home eventually. For me, there is no avoiding whatever awaits me. At least with you, you might have a chance at a new start. Away from the Matxha clan." They said, letting out a long breath. "With that being said, I guess I should admit I'm scared, too."

Osiris felt something remnant of relief and endearment. "I appreciate your honesty." He smiled, though Ayale's sullen expression promptly took it away. Something about it left him wanting to change it, so he spoke his next words out of impulse. "Let's go to the bookshop down the road. That can be our venture for the night, maybe walk around a little after to take the edge off?"

Ayale lit up, the idea of leaving the small inn room being a godsend after their long drive.

"I think that's a great idea." They agreed, both getting up from the bed, and quickly sliding on their jackets before heading out the door.

# XV

Ayale and Osiris made their way out of the room, finding the cool night air to be refreshing after their naps in the hotel room. They walked down the stone sidewalk, taking in the sights of the humble little town between territories. Their section of town was less residential and gave more way to shops that lined the center, still teeming with people at the late hour.

Ayale's guard heightened, their shoulders stiff with every step, while Osiris did his best to remain in calm spirits. No clouds in the night sky, the only lights being the strings of bulbs around each establishment. The first few shops to their left were nothing of note, one with clothing, a restaurant, before the bookshop caught the attention of both Ayale and Osiris. A book on display had such a bizarre style of binding so ornate, neither could help themselves from approaching the window where it sat on display.

Ayale sighed longingly at the sight. "That's incredible."

"How long do you think that took to make?" Osiris adjusted his glasses, briefly wondering the level of talent he would need for him to learn such a craft.

"No idea. Depends on their abilities, I suppose."

He stole a glance of Ayale, his eyes lingering from the side of his glasses. "Want to go inside?"

"Do you?" They looked back with a raised brow. "I won't say no but it means we carry more, just remember that."

"Soooo, grab one big book or two small ones, got it." Osiris already made it to the door, holding it open for them both. The moment they walked in, the ambient gold lighting lit up the cherry red shelves surrounding the store, both sides of the walls and lined up

139

in the middle isles. The bookstore was full of people, but the organization of the books was unlike anything Ayale had ever seen before. Books strewn in piles along different corners of every room, making it so that most people could only move in a single file line throughout each corridor.

Osiris had already wandered to the other side, picking up various small books and inspecting the back covers. He cleaned his glasses with the edge of his shirt before picking up another. Two books would be perfect for stops like these or killing time in the car.

Ayale puttered awkwardly around the shop, finding their way to the farthest wall to the back. They picked up the first book to catch their attention, judging the book by its cover full of ornate lines similar to that of the one on display. The art style glittered with gold rings on a blank crimson hard binding, though to their surprise, lacked the title on the outermost cover. Upon further inspection, they didn't see the name on the equally decorative spine.

They looked around the shop, noting a handful of folks wandering around of various ages. An older couple to their left, holding hands and giggling to each other as if it were their first meeting. The group of girls to their right loudly scavenged the store in search of one author, pulling books off the pile on the ground in between them.

Osiris still struggled to choose one of the two moderately sized books in his hands. They watched the disdain in his eyes shift between the two colorful covers, clearly unsure which to put back.

They couldn't hold back the smile that crept on their face. Ayale looked down at their mass of a book before deciding to rejoin Osiris, throwing out their limitation altogether. As they stepped past the couple to their left, they felt a shiver run up their back and froze up. They scanned the shop and saw a familiar face, watching from the entrance of the shop. In an instant, Ayale thought their heart was about to pop out from their chest.

Mildred watched Osiris with a concentrated look in her eyes. He didn't seem to notice her, but Ayale narrowed their eyes, thinking quickly of what they should do. There was no telling what the unstable fire elemental was thinking, making the situation more nerve-wracking for Ayale. They decided to keep their distance and hid behind the dense shelf of fiction, not only for the sake of Osiris, but for the many others who innocently roamed around the store. They worried if they made any sudden movement towards him, Mildred might react and burn the whole place down.

Ayale clutched the giant book close to their chest. From their hiding spot, they saw Mildred slowly back away and leave the bookshop, walking backwards as she did until she found the sidewalk, walking out of sight. Ayale waited silently for a few minutes until they were sure she was gone, quickly approaching Osiris from behind and tapped his forearm.

They looked over their shoulder before speaking. "Hey, let's buy what we have and leave."

"Why, is everything okay?"

"I saw Mildred watching you from the door."

Osiris blinked. "W-Watching me?"

"Yeah, let's leave before she comes back and decides to make a bonfire out of us." Ayale grabbed his free hand to pull him along but felt resistance for a change.

"Are you sure it was her?"

"Absolutely." They retorted with a low voice. "Fire elemental, crazy lady, tried to jump into your pants? Or are we pretending that didn't happen now?"

Osiris placed his books under his arm. He couldn't help but wonder if maybe the stress of today had gotten to them. He was hesitant to believe them. The two of them had driven a decent distance between the apothecary and the town. Between their nightmares at the inn and their accusation that Mildred was outside the bookstore, his worry for Ayale's wellbeing grew exponentially.

"Maybe we need to go back and rest some more, I don't think she would try to come after us like that. Especially here."

"Osiris, I am telling you that I saw her, why are you acting like I'm crazy?" They let go of his hand and got into his face, unable to compose themself as anger bubbled up into their words.

"You're not crazy, but—"

"Don't say 'but' after that!" They interrupted, going from a hushed tone to a louder one, their eyes fixed on him. He placed his books on top of a shelf and put his hands on their shoulders and said his piece.

"I really do think we're safe here." He squeezed their shoulders reassuringly, his words soft. Osiris was adamant to prove there was no threat.

The two stared at one another, watching as the flutter of consideration became visible on their face. A deep sigh came out, their resolve rendered into hearsay for the past offender. They had no evidence she was even there to begin with, let alone enough to convince him they were in danger at all. It was surprising to them he could remain calm right now, but there was no convincing him.

"I appreciate you always looking out, but we are okay, I promise." Osiris reiterated with confidence, almost enough to be convincing had they not physically seen Mildred themself. He grabbed the two books back from the shelf, before looking down at Ayale's hands. "What in the hell is that?"

"I was thinking we forget the one book rule." Ayale placed the book behind them, forcing themself to disregard the conversation.

"And why is that?" Osiris looked over their shoulder, raising a brow but knowing the answer hid behind them.

"Very good reason actually."

"Is that reason behind you?"

"It might be." They lowered their voice and cleared their throat. Osiris held back his laugh, smiling at their reaction. He wouldn't question anything more, so long as it meant he could walk away with two books instead of one.

On the way back from the book shop, Ayale could not shake the feeling that someone was keeping an eye on them both. The feeling of foreboding never seemed to shake away, even when the two of them walked around the busy square.

As they made it back to the inn and up the stairs, Osiris could see the unspoken worry on their face, but didn't want to push the conversation of Mildred again. Instead, he stayed silent, only the muffled noise of the ground floor sounding out up the stairs.

When Osiris opened the door, the two were met with an empty room, except for their backpacks on the couch. Osiris felt a wave of exhaustion hit him once more, before solidifying his yearning for sleep again. What left him so comfortable about this town, he could not place. He held back a yawn as he went towards the lights to turn them on, watching Ayale drop their mass of a book on the bed with a light thud and a slight bounce before heading off into the bathroom. His cheeks flushed with warmth, tearing his eyes away from them to focus on anything else, instead looking to the large window beside him. The illuminated trees scattered shadows throughout the room. To think the two could have such a relaxing time after the earlier events of the day.

Another part of him wished their outing lasted longer. There was still so much he wanted to ask Ayale.

A brief rustle from the closet took Osiris' attention, focusing on the odd shaped closet door that creaked open, slightly more ajar than when they left. He leaned to the side, hoping to see if there was a reason for it to be opening further. He couldn't see the inside of the closet, forcefully ignoring the anxiety bubbling its way into his throat. His eyes came back to the book on the bed, reaching over and picking it up.

Osiris sat on the edge of the bed and flipped through the pages; its edges clad in a golden shimmer like the lace design on the front and back covers. When he opened it to a random page, the contents were surprisingly to say the least. "Are you into folklore, Ayale?"

"I guess so. Used to be an escape for me as a child, reading about ancient heroes, gods, and magic." They came out of the small bathroom, grabbing the book from his hands, and sitting on the bed beside him. They flipped it open to the glossary, Osiris leaning over to look at the breakdown of tales, a short smile on his face. Ayale flipped the pages gently towards one of their favorites, deciding to share a lonesome piece of their childhood with him.

When they went to speak, the creaking noise took both of their attention this time. The two of them froze and shared a concerned look.

Ayale closed their book and held it carefully, watching the terror grow on Osiris' face. They could only watch as he began to consider their earlier warning.

Osiris wasn't one for combat but rolled up his sleeves as Ayale had done in the apothecary. He stood from the bed and began approaching the creaking closet door at the other end of the room. He grabbed the handle and whipped the door open, the lamp light revealing a crouching figure in the back of it.

"Mildred!" Osiris practically screamed, jolting Ayale from their space on the bed.

Ayale didn't so much as flinch. "Are we sure someone is in there?" The feeling of Ayale's piercing stare remained intent on Osiris' back.

Mildred took a running start past Osiris, but he grabbed her by the arm and pulled her back to his chest. Her screams practically deafened the two of them as he attempted to restrain her.

"Let me go!" She screeched, flailing about in his arms.

"Why are you in our room?!"

Mildred went limp in his hands and looked up excitedly at him. "To see you! I missed you!"

"Ayale, help me!" He struggled to keep his arms around her, hearing Ayale's distant snickers from the other end, shooting a glare at them. "Is this funny to you?!"

Ayale simply shrugged. "I don't think she's really there. I don't see anyone, in fact."

"Are you serious? This is not the time!"

Mildred head-butt Osiris before swinging one of two red glowing fists into his gut.

He felt a warmth across his forehead then immense pressure in his chest, knocking the air out of his lungs. Mildred took the opportunity to escape from his arms, rushing towards Ayale next. Osiris crumbled onto the hardwood floor, motionless and unconscious.

Ayale barely comprehended anything beyond Osiris hitting the floor and Mildred's red fists making their way over to them.

Without hesitation, Ayale stood up from the bed and slammed their newest book right into her face. Her dirty blonde hair collected behind her as they dropped the book on the floor, swinging their fist into her gut, unwilling to give Mildred any time to attack them. A gentle shake moved through the room when Ayale stepped forward, each fist pouring into her gut with no remorse. When she fell over and collapsed on the floor, the spark of red color to her hands remained, writhing over in pain.

Ayale ran over to Osiris' side, placing their hands on his face and feeling the warmth emanating from the growing bruises on his forehead. "Osiris?" They propped him up onto the couch, struggling with his weight but managing to get him sitting up.

"Please wake up." They frantically lightly tapped his cheeks, earning a small stir, and a hesitant groan. He was alive and that was enough for Ayale.

They heard a rustle from behind them and watched as Mildred tried to drag herself out of their room. Ayale stood back up, swinging their leg back and then forward, kicking her from halfway out of the room to fully outside in the hall, slamming the door behind her and locking it with every mechanism attached to the door, praying the door could hold against a fire elemental.

"Aya?" Osiris' tired voice asked from the couch. They went back to his side, touching the newly created bruise beside the old one from the Matxha grunts, making its way from his forehead to his right cheek, a few lines of blood surprising them as it seeped down his face.

"Yeah, I know, crazy fire lady is gone now, just stay with me." Ayale said, scrambling for their backpack and the first aid kit within it. "T-Talk to me, tell me a weird story, just don't pass out on me." They said, dumping everything out of the bag and on their lap.

"A tale? Like from the tea shoppe?" He yawned, eyes barely opening to look at a heavily anxious Ayale.

"Sure, anything honestly." They felt their heart rate increase, trying to work as fast as they could on his face to check him for a concussion afterward. They dabbed the blood from his face, calculating whether he would need stitches. To their luck and dismay, the cut was small, but the bruise forming along a bump was not.

"You look so scared."

Their brow furrow shifted for a split second. "I'm not scared."

"You're always doing the best you can, and I appreciate you." Osiris touched their forearm, rubbing it softly back and forth as they tended to his face. They felt a small smile curve at the edge of their mouth before shaking it away, not allowing a single second of distraction.

Ayale tended to his face, avoiding his blatant, longing stare. "I'm sorry I made fun of you."

"No, no..." He started and tried to sit up but failed. "I should have believed you. And now you're here dealing with me. If anything, I should be sorry."

"It wasn't right, what I did."

He tried to replay the scene in his head, details suddenly becoming blurry as he tried to recall them. "Doesn't matter to me."

"What do you mean, it doesn't matter?" Ayale applied a sterilizing cream over the cut and placed a bandage.

Osiris forces his tired eyes fully open, staring longingly at Ayale for a moment too long. "I couldn't be happier."

"Fuck, you really might have a concussion." They intently shined a small flashlight from Lau's car keys into his eyes, checking to make sure his pupils receded under the intense light.

"That's not very nice." He blinked profusely.

"Neither is having a concussion." They grumbled. "We can't stay here. Are you alright to move?" Ayale leaned back to put everything back into their small pouch. They grabbed him before he could tumble off the bed. They began to hurriedly pack their bags up, shoveling their junk into their own bag before putting the remnants of their things into his.

"Dandy." Osiris kept his eyes shut, listening to the rustle of their bags and the sound of Ayale's frantic footsteps. "Am I going to die?" He forced his eyes open and stared off at the ceiling.

"Probably not, unless she comes back. But I doubt she could stop us from leaving with the way I left her in the hall." They sighed, grabbing their book and his off the floor to stuff into his backpack. They swung both bags over each shoulder. "Let's get out of here."

Ayale pulled Osiris from the bed, slowly leading him over to the door. They cracked the door open, peering out into the hallway in search of Mildred. They spotted her at the other end, her back facing them, attempting to open another door with a small lock pick in her hands.

Ayale shook their head and took Osiris' hand, leading him quietly down the opposite end of the hall and down the stairs. They situated the two of them into Lau's car, pulling their seatbelt over their chest before turning the key and speeding off from the inn.

"Why don't you start reading your book? What was it about?"

Osiris laid back in his seat, eyes ready to close again. "Contemporary short story collection. Kind of depressing, but in a good way."

Ayale pulled the book out of the backpack behind his seat and threw the book into his lap. "Sounds great, read it to me."

"The whole thing?" He turned his head to look at them as they drove, their serious expression unchanging. He shifted himself upright in the passenger seat, his head swimming.

"As much as you can."

Ayale found themself dozing off at the wheel soon after he began to read, barely driving an hour before they could feel the occasional glance from Osiris.

"What's wrong?" They yawned, keeping their eyes on the dark road in front of them.

"You shouldn't force yourself to be awake like this." He fidgeted with the book in hand. "I'm sorry about all of this." He said in a solemn voice, lowering his book. The apology was small, but his guilt was evident enough. He placed a folded piece of paper in between the pages before closing it completely.

"You were trying to warn me, and I couldn't look past spending our time together. To get to know you more."

Ayale felt inexplicably nervous by the words coming out of him, forcing their eyes to remain forward. "Our time together?" They repeated, losing their stoicism.

"I don't think we've had a chance to go out and have fun. But after everything today, I think we have a tale to bring back to the tea shoppe, like Rae." His sheepish smile showed there was thought put into his words.

"If. If we return to the tea shoppe." They corrected.

"We have a story to bring home." He reclined his seat back, holding the book tight in his hands.

"Way to look at the bright side, but we've had a story to tell since day zero. Fist fighting the Matxha clan at a diner, allying with the Rooiboux, and almost getting burned alive by a horny fire elemental." Ayale found themself grinning ear to ear, holding back a laugh from their little synopsis. The tender moment left Osiris smiling, too. He enjoyed every moment so far, more so when they made it out alive each time. If he had a choice in the matter, he wished their travels could last a lifetime. "I'm not sure how much longer I can drive, Osiris. Might just stop on the side of the road, if anything."

"I think we're far enough, Ayale." He yawned.

They stifled back a yawn of their own, pulling to the side of the road, taking care to park in a section with trees to hide behind. Ayale pulled the key out of the ignition, reclining back to the same level as Osiris. "Keep talking."

Osiris began to prattle on about the short story collection in hand to keep conscious. When Ayale didn't speak after a bit, Osiris looked to the side, seeing their tired eyes fully closed, their chest slowly rising and falling.

"Aya?" Osiris whispered, wondering if they had fallen asleep already.

They stirred with a short groan. "I'm awake."

"Whatever happens, we will find our way back to the tea shoppe someday."

Ayale felt their smile drop. They knew the promise he was making would never come to fruition. That was a simple fact to them. There was no way either could come out of Cxai territory once they entered. There was no going back. But Ayale kept silent, electing to say nothing.

Hoping Osiris would magically keep his word regardless, Ayale fell asleep, only stirring when they heard the center console lift. They felt a warm arm wrap around their back before leaning onto the warmth of his shoulder.

XVI

Ayale awoke in a panic a few times throughout the night, checking on Osiris to make sure he was okay. By the time the morning dawn broke, they awoke once more beside Osiris, both laying back in their seats, closest to the middle. They clutched his arm and rested against his shoulder. As soon as they realized their position, they scrambled away from his shoulder, leaning back against the middle seat. Unsure if he was okay enough to stay asleep, they leaned over and tapped his cheek to check if he was conscious, hearing him stir with a groan.

Still too close for comfort, Ayale moved back into the driver's seat and turned their back to him.

Osiris slowly opened his eyes, wondering where the weight on his shoulder had gone.

The two of them were back on the road by noontime, stopping at a gas station before leaving the remainder of the unmarked territory behind.

Going forward, they drove silently on a barely paved road, the path in front of them slowly turned back into a sea of green. Trees surrounded both sides of the car, leaving Ayale cautious and forcing them to a slower speed. They didn't want to risk hitting some unfortunate tree or wild animal that might be lingering in the middle of the road.

As impressed as they were with the sights, Ayale felt sluggish, having barely slept through the night prior. After what happened with Mildred and Osiris, it made sense to be worried. They were grateful

151

the swelling on his head began to diminish and his bout of fatigue had come and went by morning.

Ayale drove for only six hours before they began to feel exhaustion creeping over them. They struggled to maintain a proper breathing pattern, overheated where they sat, and felt a dull pain forming in their lower back, worse than it had when they began to drive. They gained Osiris' attention once they weakly pulled off their jacket and swerved for a split second.

"Maybe we should stop for the day, you don't look too well." Osiris narrowed his eyes, fixing his braids into a loose side bun. He practically jolted from his seat when he saw a clearing begin to come into view on the side of the road. "Oh! Perfect timing, we can even walk around a little." He pointed to the small section to the upcoming right.

Ayale felt the heaviness in their eyes, the burning that developed within the last hour of driving. They felt a yawn in their throat, too tired to ask questions. They quickly pulled the car over to the side of the tight path, squeezing the car as far in as they could get. As they shut the car off, Ayale instantly sank into the driver's seat, staring off at the opening in between the shady trees, leaving Osiris with a creeping sense of concern.

"Ayale?" Osiris asked, watching their eyes close in response. "Are you okay?" He placed the back of his hand against their forehead, instantly jolting them back to consciousness. He shifted it a bit further, pushing away their hair. There was certainly a little warmth, but nothing else to designate further concern.

"Don't mind me, I'm just a little tired." Ayale yawned, leaning forward in their seat. Osiris furrowed his brow, before reaching into the back seat for a plain black blanket and another with a double sided monstera plant design. He left the car, walking over to the other side, and opened Ayale's door.

"Let's take a breather. You certainly look like you need one." Osiris placed a hand over their shoulder to pull them up from the seat, feeling them lean against his chest.

"Sitting outside sounds great right now." Ayale muttered, lethargy making its home in the ache now forming in their head, getting out of the car and eventually standing. They sluggishly walked to the clearing, feeling Osiris' hand on their back keeping them steady.

The forest clearing had been that of a fever dream. Red maples surrounded the small opening of vast green grass, allowing the field to thrive whenever the sun would shine. Osiris left Ayale to run ahead with the blankets in hand, setting up a sitting area big enough for the both of them. Once he laid out everything carefully on the grass, he walked back for them, leading them over to his temporary setup. For a moment, Ayale had thought it looked like a picnic, only missing a basket. Osiris sat upward on the black blanket, but Ayale flopped over, laying their back flat on the ground.

The world swam around them, almost echoing In their ears. "My head feels weird." Ayale mumbled, their eyes shutting again.

"I can tell." Osiris responded by laying back on his side, half from solidarity and half from his own exhaustion. "Did you use an affinity on Mildred last night?" Osiris snuck his question in nonchalantly, recalling the floor shaking from beneath him after he was head-butted. While he fought for consciousness, he witnessed a few moments of Ayale's counterattack on Mildred, the irregular strength of their fists coupled with a rage he had never seen before. He couldn't help himself from curiosity, unsure if it were an affinity he had witnessed, not once but twice. It was a sight he couldn't forget, even if he tried.

Ayale laid still, thoughtful in their next words. "Forget what you saw." They eventually answered, barely able to open their eyes. The comfort of the fleece warmed them from beneath, stealing their attention once more. They were unsure how much longer they could stave his questions over their affinity.

To their surprise, the two of them were only able to briefly witness the sun above them, unlike the views they were spoiled with in Istanza. The sky shifted into a dusty lilac mixing in with the incoming night. The colors swirled overhead, causing Osiris to fall asleep first.

When Osiris dreamt, there had been a fog he could not cut through, one that surrounded everything entirely. He could sense the stir of trees, of nature in his veins, the scent of petrichor staining the air. He only knew to keep moving forward, cautious in every step. In a brief moment of clarity, Osiris sensed a familiar presence just before a hand reached through the fog. Without a second thought, he grabbed the hand with both of his, and felt himself being pulled away, walking in the thick cloud of grey and white. The fog disappeared as he moved forward, finding himself suddenly outside the tea shoppe. The air thickened with humidity and mist, familiar storm clouds surrounding the sky.

When he looked at the person who walked before him, Osiris wasn't sure what to feel.

Ayale held onto his hand and pulled him along to the entrance of the art alley, only a few streets away from the tea shoppe in Densriel, before loosening their grip. Osiris held onto their hand for dear life, wondering what prompted them to take his hand at all.

"When did we... Why are we here?" Osiris looked around at the familiar art on both walls, confused by the entire situation unraveling around him. Ayale averted their gaze and crossed an arm over their chest, looking at anywhere but him. It was visible that they were flustered, leaving him even more perplexed.

"I know this isn't ideal, and I'm sorry for dragging you out here. But I need to say something." Ayale looked over his shoulder, fumbling to get their words out. They leaned into his right shoulder, struggling to speak again. Osiris let go of their hand, instead placing his arm around their back. He instinctively pulled them close, feeling their weight press into his chest.

"Whatever you have to say won't scare me away, I promise." He smiled and rubbed their back reassuringly. When Ayale looked up at him, their flushed expression had rendered him weak. Never did he think such a vulnerable pout could cross their face. It wasn't something he thought could exist. He lived for it, biting his lower lip to keep his own flush from being visible.

"Promise you won't get mad at me?"

"On my life." Osiris had a strange feeling he knew what was going to come out next.

"After everything we've been through, I think... I think I should be honest with you. With myself, too." Their voice lowered.

Osiris sat perfectly still, barely letting a breath pass him. He wanted to hear the words so badly. He could read their face, his heart ready to stop entirely from beating so intensely, and somehow, he knew. And if they wouldn't say it first, he wouldn't let his fear hold him back.

"I love you, too." Osiris said in one fell breath. No other time did he feel he could speak so freely. He took their face into his hands, pressing his forehead against theirs. He felt Ayale press back before everything turned dark once more.

Ayale had a hard time staying asleep, being used to waking up in the middle of the night. They felt a warmth cover them, assuming that Osiris had covered them both with the plant themed blanket that fit his affinity aesthetic so well. They felt a small pang in their chest at the gesture and a smirk crept up in response. Ayale had a sense of gratitude for everyone and everything thus far. Even knowing what they were going back to, at least they got to experience love in so many ways they hadn't before. They were grateful. For the chance to know Lau, Rae, Katari, and the rest of the Rooiboux clan. To have Osiris with them along the way.

When Ayale drifted off, they felt the same warm arm from last night reach over and wrap around them protectively. For a moment, they wondered if they should shift away. Instead, sleep quickly followed.

The dream felt as real as the lilac sunset above them. Their eyes opened to the sounds of nature around them. There were no obstacles, nothing of note besides the cool air and the breeze that followed, likely stemming from the northern mountains, and the mild sway of the low hanging red maples branches that towered over them. The earth beneath them felt alive and warm, almost shifting at their presence.

When they looked beside them, they found Osiris seated upward over his sketchbook, staring in their direction with such intrigue, as though reacting to something. The gentle smile that turned up when they met his stare in return felt as though he could see right through them.

"Do you want to say that to me again?" Osiris grinned with a touch of mischief in his eyes. Ayale sat up and glared back at him, unsure what he was talking about.

"Excuse me?" They retorted. He scoffed, not daring to look away.

"Say that to my face, Ayale. I already heard it once in your sleep." He stretched out his arms behind his back, leaning back on his elbows. Ayale felt their heart quicken, trying so very hard to think of whatever it was they said in the last hour.

But gauging from Osiris' comments, their words were clearly embarrassing.

In their moment of intense thought, he sat upward, awaiting to hear a line they could not recall. The silence grew between them as the minutes passed by. When Osiris shifted closer to them, Ayale felt their cheeks flare up. He nudged them with his shoulder.

"Do you often dream of running away with me?" Osiris teased, leaning his chin on their shoulder. "We could always run off to Istanza and start another tea shoppe together. What do you think?"

"Wait, what?" They laughed briefly before feeling embarrassment flutter in their chest.

Ayale awoke in the night from the movement of Osiris beside them. They felt his arm surrounding them, wrapped around their shoulders. Part of them doubted for a moment that they were truly awake, feeling exhaustion fall over them once more. If they were this bad now, they only imagined how hard they had pushed themself the many nights prior, driving for hours without stopping once.

When they went to turn around, Osiris wrapped his arms around their waist, pulling them towards him in his sleep. If they weren't warm enough before, they certainly were now. Ayale hesitantly opened their eyes, struggling to wake up after being stationary for who knows how long. From what they could see, Osiris seemed so at peace, it was almost a crime to wake him. Their eyes fluttered up to the stars and the placement of the moon above them, the dark sky clear of clouds. There was no use waking him after all the driving the two had done in the recent days and nights.

It was not as though they wanted to continue, not so quickly anyways. Their arms raised around his back, surprised when he didn't shift away from them. Whether it was the physical exhaustion or the thought of going home, Ayale found their sleepy gaze drift down to his lips, his breathing a light pattern they memorized in a few seconds.

Ayale recalled their first meeting with Osiris in detail. They could still picture Osiris sitting nervously in their section, unsure what to order, and following a recommendation made by a stranger. His setup was for two, but his second never showed up.

They remembered Rae's encouragement to sit with him and get to know one another, while she offered to take on their shift tasks.

In that moment they wondered; was that his way of flirting?

Ayale's eyes widened amidst their exhaustion. They had never been in such a situation before, so it was difficult to gauge. It was easy to believe his friend never showed up. Why else would he invite them to sit down for tea?

Osiris shifted in his sleep, his hand moving down to their lower back, and managing to pull them closer against his chest. Ayale's cheeks flushed, recalling their dream in full detail at the perfectly wrong moment.

They realized that given the opportunity, if things were different, maybe they would have made bolder choices. To do things outside of their comfort zone. Maybe they would have leaned in and kissed him, if circumstances were not so dire.

Their eyes drifted back up to his sleeping face.

This wasn't something they should have found themself considering.

What were they thinking? After everything they went through so far, such a thought shouldn't have even crossed their mind. Osiris didn't need any more reasons to exasperate his already high anxiety. Let alone worsen the situation as the spawn of a high-ranking clan leader.

Ayale realized they were the perfectly wrong person for him.

If things were different, maybe. But the situation was anything but simple. Ayale knew better than to allow such a feeling to bloom. They knew it would never work in their favor when they eventually got Osiris into Cxai territory. Back to their home clan and the life they ran from.

Oh, *joy*.

Their last thought of the night was a silent vow to keep Osiris safe through their journey, wanting nothing more than to protect him from whatever danger lurked ahead. From the Matxha, the Cxai, and from themself.

They would do whatever it took to ensure the two of them would make it back to Cxai territory alive.

# XVII

The ambient light of early dawn left Osiris stirring in his sleep, unable to pull his arms away from Ayale. He wanted so badly to fall back asleep, at last giving up and letting his eyes drift open. When he looked down, Osiris found himself looking at Ayale, sound asleep. With Ayale sleeping against his chest, he felt a sense of peace like none other.

The last thing he wanted to do was wake them up, staying absolutely still where he laid. He feared any movement from him would disturb them. To be relied on was a wonderful feeling, even if it were brief and unconscious. Whether awake or asleep, Osiris yearned for moments like these more and more as their time together moved forward.

Like his dream last night.

In seconds, he recalled the events of his latest dream. The art alley, the almost instant confession, and the moments after that brought everything together. He dwelled on the dream before his anxiety and guilt had caught up with him.

However badly he wanted every part of that dream to come true, Osiris knew their chances for peace were slim. Even if he gained the courage to speak up, there was no guarantee they would feel the same way. It wasn't the thought of Ayale fighting for him that left him lovesick, but their energy and their personality. The way they smiled working at the tea shoppe and the subtle enjoyment of the world around them, even when so much was beyond their control.

Ayale cared far more than they let on, ready to protect everything they loved in an instant. They were noble, resilient, compassionate beyond what was necessary.

Osiris felt Ayale shift, trying to stay calm while their hand settled on his forearm. He watched them sleep quietly and took in the sight of them while he could, before daybreak would take it all away in an instant. When he pulled the blanket further up to cover them both, he felt his eyes grow heavy once more. The cool morning air drifted against his cheeks, softening the blush that crept onto them.

Maybe he would take the risk once everything settled down. Osiris planned to tell Ayale the truth once they arrived in Cxai territory; if they both lived.

Before anything, he wanted Ayale to be happy. There was no telling if he would live until the end.

Ayale stirred once more, barely opening their eyes in the process. The incoming sunrise made their weariness evident under its gentle light, the clear exhaustion in their eyes that yearned to go back to sleep. They mumbled unintelligibly, groaning before sinking further beneath the blanket. Osiris did his best not to laugh at them, instead choosing to take in the last few moments of Ayale laying across his arm. The weight lifted from his body, hearing a continued array of grumbles from Ayale.

Osiris sat up, keeping his numb arm around them for balance. Ayale yawned when they sat up and made no effort to remove themself from his embrace. Neither spoke a word to the other, only doing their collective best to wake up for the trip ahead. That was until he felt Ayale lean their forehead against his shoulder.

"How did you sleep?" Osiris questioned soothingly, gently rubbing circles on their back. Instead of responding, they groaned, trying their best to force themself wake up.

"Well, we could wait for the sun to rise fully before driving again. Do you want to keep sleeping?" Osiris asked without thinking twice, hoping to make the most of their time alone.

Ayale looked up at him, showing consideration for the offer. But their eyes shifted down to his outstretched arms around their back.

"I think I'm ready to go." They abruptly stood up from the makeshift spot on the grass and began to walk back towards Lau's parked car only a few feet away. Osiris picked up his glasses and followed suit, folding up everything in silence. He saw their rush towards the driver's side, fixing their hair while they waited. He didn't think twice about their time in the clearing, until he watched their expression turn stoic once more.

Ayale unintentionally recalled everything from the past two days, feeling their heart accelerate from the purest embarrassment possible. If the dream wasn't enough, waking up with Osiris as a human pillow was more than they could handle. They grabbed their cigarette case, pulled the window down, and started smoking as if they hadn't seen a cigarette in days. They took a long drag of their cigarette, exhaling a line of smoke out the window.

Osiris opened the passenger door and sat in the seat beside them with nothing to say.

Ayale continued their drive northward. They were soon forced to take their time just as they did before, the roads ahead becoming narrower and more difficult to maneuver through.

Minutes turned into hours, and part of Osiris wondered if he had done anything wrong suggesting the two of them to stop driving. The most he knew was that Ayale needed sleep. Stopping was not a luxury, but a necessity. There were no regrets in what he suggested, but rather he questioned what came after. But they were both exhausted, that much was certain.

If he were to be more honest, Osiris wished they could have stayed in hiding in Istanza. The thought of running amuck in the hidden mountain city compared to their long journey ahead looked more and more ideal the further they drove into the condensed forest.

Neither dared to speak up, both nervous for the reaction of the other. The air was slowly becoming more frigid, but to their relief, the road eventually widened, allowing the car more room to maneuver. The inclines were noticeable but of no real threat yet, though the red maples that once surrounded them began to thin out. While the secret road led them through a multitude of curves and rounded paths, the sea of trees was replaced with sporadic pines and oaks, no other flora in sight.

Ayale spent their silence heavy in thought. Between their family, the clan rivalries, and the ride home, they should have been more careful than to allow themself to get close to someone. The risk was taken as it was, bringing Osiris home and attempting to coordinate his safety from the Matxha clan.

It truly begged the question; why were they doing this? What are the odds they were being tricked into going back home?

Ayale peered over at Osiris from the corner of their eye, watching him fumble with his most used affinity trick on a bottled drink. Perhaps that theory was not entirely realistic.

Their main focus was his safety. They didn't even begin to consider why their estranged mother of all people offered to help without a single reason.

Ayale took a deep breath, reminding themself the plan at hand. Everything that needed to be done came as followed; they needed Osiris' safety guaranteed first, then maybe, if the chance arose, bargain their way back out of the clan permanently. But there was the possibility that their mother would tell their father. Though knowing their history and a gut feeling led them to hope she wouldn't. For now.

To make matters worse, Ayale knew very little about the Oolonxg clan. They could easily be driving into a trap. Their history of ruthlessness was supposedly from a time long gone, being ushered away by the new leader of only a year. His promise of peace and independence had been a refreshing touch to over a century of power.

But even that much did not sit well with them.

"Everything okay?" Osiris interrupted their thoughts. This was the first time he attempted to speak to them since this morning.

Without so much as a side eye, Ayale straightened their back, their eyes on the road. The trees began to thin out rapidly, previously fallen snow settling in thin layers on the ground. "If you're really wondering, I have a lot on my mind."

"Like what?"

They hesitated. "Everything."

Osiris wasn't sure what to say in response. Being someone with an anxiety disorder, he could heavily relate to the way doubt made its home in every thought. It wasn't too long ago that he thought his life was over, just as their adventure had begun. But as time went on, he gained a sense of trust, maybe something beyond that, every moment he spent with Ayale.

Part of him wanted to reach out and take their hand from the wheel. He wanted to say everything would be okay. As much as he wanted to comfort Ayale, words refused to leave his mouth, sitting stagnant in his seat while watching the snowy landscape begin to set in.

Within their collective silence, their exit from the forest was welcomed with a sight like none other. An extensive, snowy mountain range came into view, obstructing the smaller ones beside it. They saw the distant trees collect just below at the base. Snow collected near the edges of the road, primarily at the top. The crisp, cold air from their open window reflected as much. Ayale knew to prepare for the cold weather and had placed an extra jacket somewhere in the backseat prior to their trip.

The next few hours were the most silent In their tension filled drive. Ayale truly wanted to make it known they could use some noise but said nothing of their need. Osiris found himself dozing off, thoughts filled with what he wanted to do now. He thought of last night's dream again, a twinge of guilt filling his chest reminding him of where they were heading. Before he dozed off, he wondered what it would take for them to share a space like that again.

Ayale breathed out and let their tense shoulders fall forward, a little relief washing over them when they noticed Osiris was asleep. Truthfully, they struggled with the idea of driving into Oolonxg territory. They could only imagine what was awaiting them. There was no telling how the new leader would react to the spawn of the Cxai clan.

Just the thought of the interaction had Ayale stifling their breath.

How were they supposed to present themselves? Were they supposed to act like a Cxai member, even if they hadn't been a clan member in years?

What was expected of them?

Ayale twirled their loose hair over their shoulder, nervously bouncing their left knee. The moment their eyes wandered to Osiris, his peaceful expression reminding them of the clearing again.

They pried their eyes away and turned back to the road.

There were bigger problems at hand.

For a second, Ayale wished they were back in the tea shoppe, serving tea and pastries, listening to the newest tale Rae had ready for them after closing time. They missed Lau and her rough exterior, the front that everyone saw except for Ayale and Rae. Now, they had to deal with people coming after them and the clan system they ran from three years ago.

The idea of never seeing Lau and Rae again made their heart sink. The care and respect they received from both would never be felt again. Though the memories of their beloved tea shoppe would forever be the impact that made them into the person they were today.

The last few years had passed like the wind. They blinked away tears, trying their best not to let them fall, to no avail.

Everything felt one bad moment from falling apart.

The cold landscape of Oolonxg territory was serene; the only peace they would experience for their next hour on the uneven roads were sights of large trees losing their leaves and the pines that retained their greenery despite the declining temperatures. Mountains that felt so distant in view were hindered by the incoming grey stratus clouds that would bring about the fog soon after. The light fog was only a minor inconvenience, forcing Ayale to squint their eyes and drive slower than they would like. Between valleys and mountain sides, it was to be expected.

Osiris had awakened to the chill that befell the car. He watched through half opened eyes out the window as the sights passed him by. The dense sea of trees was now replaced by snowcapped mountains in the distance, barren hills with more sections of snow, as though it had fallen and partially melted in the same day. Whether it was a personal preference or aligned with his affinity for nature, he had a disdain for the cold all the same.

When he turned to Ayale, he saw streams of tears run down their face. He was completely unaware that Ayale was spiraling throughout the drive, surprised to see no change to their stoic expression.

Without thinking, he rummaged through his bag for tissues, pressing one lightly against their tear-stained cheek, all the way down to their chin. "Ayale, hold still for a second."

They tried to avoid him and ducked away from his hand. "What, why?"

"I know I'm not one to talk, but you're crying. Is everything okay?" He asked softly.

Ayale refused to acknowledge his concern and simply kept their eyes fixed on the road in front of them. "We have bigger things to worry about, I think we're getting close to the gates of the Oolonxg capital," They started to shift topics. "I'm wondering if they'll just ask us some questions and let us through. There is no telling whether my mother contacted anyone, and if she has, fuck only knows what she's told them. We need to be ready for anything."

"What do you think we should do?"

"I-I don't know. I'm worried, Osiris. I have a bad feeling about all of this."

"Diori sounds like she's trying to help, I couldn't imagine it would be so bad."

"You don't understand, my mother is..." Ayale lost their wording, unsure how to go about describing the woman who she called a mother.

Diori was the lesser of two evils, but when she was committed to an idea, she would do whatever it took to make it a reality. Dedicated, though not always in the best ways. She could be kind on the outside but tended to keep that sort of side for everyone...except her own children.

Ayale's father Mero, on the other hand, while always serious and short tempered, maintained most of his demands up front. Diori was nowhere near forward. For most of Ayale's childhood, she had been uncommunicative, ready to bail at any sign of inconvenience. Even if the inconvenience was a small child.

No matter how many times Ayale asked for her help, Diori never delivered. Nothing was ever deemed worthy enough to accrue a single moment of parental decency from either of their parents. But things had been a certain way for so long, Ayale couldn't even recall the last time they reached out to either under willing conditions. All they knew was it had been prior to their run from the Cxai compound.

It wasn't just them, either. Both Ayale's parents hated their own parents as well, and so on. Generation after generation.

"Your mother is...?" Osiris urged them to continue.

"She just can't be trusted." They blurted out.

His eyes widened, unsure how to react. "Diori is your mom, why else would she be trying to help you?"

"I haven't spoken to her in years, I don't know how to explain any of this right now, but please trust me when I say to keep your guard up."

He thought for a moment before commenting. "She can't be that bad."

Ayale hit the brakes a bit too hard, almost sending both of them through the windshield.

"Osiris," Ayale uttered, biting back every swear building up in their head. "You know what, tell me about your mom instead. I want to know what your childhood was like, if you would indulge my curiosity." Their voice strained, visibly struggling to maintain their composure.

Osiris thought for a second. "My mom is the reason I am who I am. She and my dad sacrificed for me, but never once made it my problem. She gave me everything she could. Even when I failed to do the same, she always believed in me. I love my mom to pieces, and my dad for that matter. I'd do anything for them...if they didn't disown me."

"Disowned?" Ayale looked at him, shocked to say the least.

"Disowned." Osiris reiterated, but didn't elaborate.

Ayale nodded, suddenly unsure what to say. They had so many questions, though one thing was for certain. Osiris loved his parents, regardless of how they felt about him.

They started to drive again, slower than before, and the two shifted into an uncomfortable silence. The point Ayale attempted to make was harder to do now, unsure how to paint the image that could sum up their childhood. But there was no way to make him feel the same distraught pain that swelled in their stomach every day for years of their life, for him to know uncertainty and fear as a child, stemming from the people that were supposed to take care of him.

Because Osiris wasn't failed by his parents.

The thought of reflecting back was enough to clench their hands on the steering wheel. "Trust no one, Osiris."

He kept his eyes pointed forward. "Maybe she changed. But I can understand your hesitation."

"That's a start." Their tone softened, slowly approaching a black, mechanical gate spanning the size of a three-story building, length and height wise.

The entrance was heavily guarded with more armed men than a prison. Their uniforms were black from top to bottom, militant styled, with bold sapphire shirts popping out from their coat collars. They watched the car slowly approach the gate, with only movement of their heads evidence that they were not statues.

As the two drove up to the city gates, guards came from both sides and swarmed the car, pointing firearms at them from all sides. In less than a minute, both Ayale and Osiris were thrown against the doors of Lau's sedan, cuffed up and fully restrained. Ayale could feel the remorse coming from Osiris as the two were promptly taken away inside the gate.

# XVIII



*Meanwhile, back in Densriel...*

Lau sighed with her whole chest, taking a long drag of her cigarette before letting it drop to the wet gravel and stomping it out. She exhaled the remaining smoke from her lungs and walked back into the less than busy Monday night crowd that made up the tea shoppe. The long lines creasing her brows were weeks of worry and concern that aged her at least a couple of years in mere days.

Every night since Ayale left Densriel, Lau had received questioning from various patrons as to their whereabouts. Figuring the questions would arise, the secretive bar owner came up with a simple answer, coupled with Rae's expertise in dramatization. Together, the two agreed to tell everyone Ayale went home to take care of some family issues. It allowed them the ability to be truthful, to an extent.

Just without any elaboration.

Lau cleared out the dishwasher and placed each tea set out on a mat before drying them with her hand towel, piece by piece. Busywork wouldn't keep her from thinking about the situation but allowed her moments to worry in peace. She watched over the bar scene, pointing her stoic gaze at Rae, who was in the middle of telling one of her tall tales.

Rae sat carefully in one of the bar stools, capturing the attention of a table in her corner section nearest the bar counter. Rae's latest tale happened to be about her most recent breakup, and how she single-handedly kicked a Matxha member out of her home with nothing but a copper iron pipe hidden between her bedframe and mattress.

Lau tried not to laugh, but she knew of the remaining details Rae elected to exclude from her story.

As impressive as it was to say she took out a Matxha member, the clan member in question was not entirely in shape to fight back nor was he anywhere near an important rank to his organization.

Lau respected Rae regardless. An especially dangerous situation for someone who lacked an affinity. There was nothing more frightening than having to kick out an ex-spouse who could easily call for backup, if he so chose. Rae knew of the possibilities and did not relent, understanding the risk she took for her freedom from her last relationship. It was a toss of a coin, depending on the person's temperament.

Lau thought of their individual pasts as Rae continued to go on about her valiant fight.

She had seen quite a bit in her lifetime. Events that could tear the heart and humanity out of any normal person. Different moments that changed her over and over, creating the person who stood behind the bar, who watched both exits carefully, a force of habit.

Once upon two decades past, Lau herself was one of few high-ranking officers in a thriving way of life, working for the Matxha clan. A time she did not look fondly back on. She was sought after for her incredible prowess, a well-known and powerful elemental water user. Lau could control, maneuver, and split apart water with no issue whatsoever. Her talents were rarely seen in common people, let alone in the small pool of elemental users that existed within the urban sectors of the Matxha territory. Her immediate recruitment to the Matxha clan was an attestment of that rarity among all affinity users, working her way up in a growing military empire. A hardworking woman who always tried her best.

A trait of hers that never changed, even as she came to question her place in the clan.

A mission arose one rainy night ten years ago. A sudden order that came from the Matxha leader themself. With only a handful of others involved, the details took everyone aback.

Lau had been ordered to be front and center of a Rooiboux raid of their capital city. Before then, the two clans lived in peace, longtime allies for over three hundred years. To be told to destroy it in a surprise attack three days from then, no one was sure what else to do except fulfill their orders.

The raid had planned to begin upriver, of course the advantage given to Lau's powerful water elemental. The orders were defied with a quick turnaround, Lau plotting to internally ambush the ship she oversaw prior to being sent out to battle. It wasn't much, but she flooded the engine of a second ship, before getting caught by her superiors.

Her time in the Matxha clan came to an abrupt end after that night.

Lau felt the thick faded lines that made up the back of her head, presently covered by her hair. She barely escaped with her life, though the scars remained. And yet, she was all the more thankful. Lau made an escape that should have never been possible. She changed everything about herself, from her name to her face, even her hair. Never captured, haunted for years by the thought someone would recognize her.

Lausen without the 'sen'.

Much of the Rooiboux was wiped out in that single raid. A day she soon learned was planned on the day of their newest leaders' wedding. A horrid plot that she wanted no part at all . She learned the outlying reason for the sudden attack had been for the sake of expanding the Matxha territory eastward. An attack pushed forward by the husband of the previous Matxha clan leader, who had died within the same year.

The last time Lau had used her water elemental was to take down the two ships, and never again. Lau felt like a war criminal for all its use and vowed to leave her affinity untouched.

She hid away for years before she started from the bottom to make something of herself. Beginning at a low-level job to keep a low profile, a feat that would be her only choice, so long as her luck remained, and no one came looking for her. Life began in a bar in the worst part of Densriel, finding serenity in her job as a bartender. While she was never much of the social type, it was her coworker Rae that brought out the best in her.

Their dynamic was day and night but attributed to the symbiosis that was their relationship.

The chance encounter with Ayale was the last of her restitution.

Lau worked alongside Rae for close to a decade by then, closing together one night when they met the twenty something year old, who was new in town with nowhere to go. Ayale told the two of them that they had recently escaped a bad situation in the Cxai capital, only learning the truth themself a year later.

A small investment later, and here was Lau. In that same place Ayale saw potential in, a dream that quickly came to fruition.

Lau watched as Rae had everyone huddled together hooting and hollering at her latest story, meeting her sunny gaze as she turned herself towards Lau.

"One more round before we lock up, Lau!" Rae exclaimed with a smile. Lau nodded and prepared six of her 'sunshine' shots. It was a mixture inspired by Rae herself. Orange juice, citrus vodka, and a touch of fresh lemon. She lined them up before Rae sauntered over with her tray and took them away.

The two discussed Ayale's sudden departure, but neither could do much except support them from afar. Both agreed it was best for them to go back to the Cxai, but they both felt the gap: the missing piece was gone, and Lau tried her hardest not to drown in it. Ayale had lived with Lau for so long, she almost forgot what it was like to live alone again.

Rae hid behind a smile but felt the gap in her own way.

As closing time quickly approached, Lau and Rae silently went about their nightly chore list before lockup. There wasn't much else to do, nothing to talk about, and the tea shoppe needed to be kept up with, cleaned and stocked for customers. It was the same scene every night for the last few weeks, and Lau was tired of it.

"Rae, lock up, but no cleaning just yet." Lau ordered, watching Rae hesitantly lock the door and pull down all the shades. She wandered over and sat at the bar, where Lau stood behind with a brooding expression.

Rae kept her careful gaze on Lau. "Is everything alright?"

Lau tried to grasp at the words, not sure how to phrase their intricate feelings. Her face must have contorted enough while trying to think because Rae spoke instead.

"I miss Ayale, too." She confessed with a heavy heart.

"Do you think the kid's okay? Should we have gone with them? Do you think they're in trouble?" Lau spilled out every thought in her head, leaving Rae's mind spinning.

"Calm down," Rae reached across the bar and grabbed her hands. "First things first, Ayale is smart. One of the brightest and they are going to be okay. Remember, they traveled here with no one and nothing but a single backpack. They have resources this time and most importantly, they have us here." Rae held onto Lau's hands tight, reassuring her with her remaining energy.

Lau nodded, holding her gaze with a tense stare. She put down the cup in her hands on the countertop.

"They know the number to the shoppe. And if they need us, we will go running. Right?" Rae wondered aloud.

Lau sighed at the morbid thought and nodded again.

"Good. So, let's keep our cool and make sure the tea shoppe is running. That's what Ayale would have wanted us to do." Rae said for her comfort as well as for Lau.

The two of them spent the night taking it easy and reminisced of days past. But they reiterated once more of answering the call to duty, should Ayale ever need them.

# XIX

The place where the two were confined was less like a prison cell and oddly enough, more like a minimalist room at a local inn. The closed off cell had the design of a bedroom, simply adding cement walls and barred windows to the equation. The bed was an unfortunate size meant for one, but the perk of all things considered was the well-kept bathroom attached to the left most side of the cell. Were it not for being arrested at the gates, this could be easily mistaken for a half decent motel room.

"I should have known better," Ayale muttered, sitting at the edge of said bed with their head in their hands. "This is ridiculous, I can't believe any of this is happening. We're prisoners! From mountain views to cement walls!" They raised their voice, feeling a wave of anger wash over them.

Osiris paced around the room in silence, looking at everything around them. When he approached the reinforced steel door, Ayale perked up, hoping maybe he noticed something they didn't. "Do you see anything?"

He finagled with the handle, noting the group of five locks cascading down the edge of the door, a single sliding block up top for guards to open whenever they pleased. With a focused breath, Osiris went as far as summoning a familiar vine, attempting to feel his way into the biggest of the locks. A focused look in his emblazoned eyes, his hand moved slowly with caution through the next one below it, feeling every notch inside the mechanism.

Every minute that passed, Ayale felt their chest tighten, thoughts that worsened as Osiris continued. "I need to get out of here before I lose my mind." Ayale let slip.

"I'll try my best." Osiris nodded once with confidence, careful to remain focused on the task at hand.

When minutes turned to an hour, both had found themselves losing hope of breaking out. Osiris felt his vines tire and quietly withdrew himself from the lock. With a heavy sigh, he moved to the bedside, seating himself near Ayale. His arm wrapped around their shoulder and pulled them against his side.

"We'll make it out of here eventually. They're just going to ask us questions and likely cut us loose when they figure out that we're just traveling through."

"You're too hopeful. You don't know how these clans' function if you think they'll let us walk as we are. Honesty won't get us anywhere."

"Let's try to stay positive. Katari said your mom would contact them and take care of this. We just need to be patient."

Ayale's fists tightened. "Screw them both! It was a trap, and we fell for it."

"Ayale—"

"No, I shouldn't have let you get into my head, going through the front gate was a rookie mistake. Trusting my mother was a mistake. I bet she's already got whatever she needed and left us to rot." They pulled away from Osiris and let his arm fall back to his side.

"All of this is stupid, you're right." Osiris agreed. "I wish I let the Matxha off me instead of putting you through this. I'm sorry." He put his hand back around their shoulder, pulling them back towards him.

Ayale felt his hands on their shoulder, turning them to face him once more. Their attention was taken when he bent forward, the gap between them mere inches. They were close enough to see the swirl of green in the brown of his eyes, having a far more serious look in his face than before. Unable to blink, they didn't dare to break away from his apologetic gaze. "I would have been found regardless." Ayale reassured him, unable to bring themself to pull away.

"But you chose to help me and now look where we are. All I've wanted to do this whole time was somehow make this all easier on you, but I keep failing." Osiris touched their face, and all Ayale felt was the gentle graze of his thumb across their cheek. "I want to ask you something and I want a serious answer, so please hear me out." He prefaced with an adamancy unknown to Ayale, whose cheeks burned by this point.

"When we get out of here, let's run away, Aya. Screw this whole world and everyone in it, we can put all of this behind us." Osiris stated his plan with a sense of confidence Ayale had never seen before.

The limited space between them had quickly filled with silence. He watched as consideration flashed across their face before it quickly turned into the disappointed exasperation that would haunt his dreams.

"Do you really think all it takes to fix our problems is to run from them?" Ayale met his gaze with a quick, fiery anger. "Or did you forget I tried that already?"

"You and I could start over somewhere, what if I ask Katari for us to stay in Istanza?"

"I've run already, started over only a handful of years back. I can't do that again." They pulled back, feeling his hand fall away. Ayale abruptly stood from the bedside, gesturing to the barred windows and white cement walls. "Look how well that worked out!"

"Katari wouldn't mind, we have so much potential for the Rooiboux clan. She couldn't say no."

"Osiris, just stop. You've said enough." They turned their back to him, hoping for him to back off before he saw the creeping flush across their face. This was no time to show any weakness to his indignant idea.

When Osiris thought of their time so far, he appreciated Ayale far beyond their withdrawn personality in the tea shoppe. What drew him in this moment versus in the shoppe were no longer the same concepts. The mysterious persona was exchanged with a wild card of a human, who existed with a sense of duty. He was enamored by everything they did, every move they made. Their strength, humor, care, and the way they handled their journey so far left him with a strange feeling that had once only been an inkling of affection. A feeling that had grown full size in his chest, just as the flowers did on the night in the fields.

His dream began to make much more sense. He truly could not fathom leaving Ayale's side, not after everything they had been through together.

Osiris didn't say anything more, having been certain of what he just saw in the last few minutes. The look of consideration, of the same desire to escape everything. He couldn't think of beginning a new life without Ayale next to him. Their absence would be too much.

Osiris was in love with Ayale; the mysterious runaway, the tea shoppe owner, descendent of the Cxai family.

Before he knew it, Ayale moved towards the bathroom in the corner of the room, slamming the door shut behind them. He shifted off the bed and leaned against the wall beside the door.

"Ayale." He knocked once on the door.

"I told you. I warned you and said it in the car, we cannot trust people like this. Here we are now, in some prison in the damn mountains!" They exclaimed, beyond irritated.

Osiris looked around the room, taking in the sights of the so-called prison. His eyes moved from the bed to the desk beside it. Sure, the walls gave off asylum energy, but the remainder looked like a minimalist bedroom.

"I'm sorry I doubted you." He leaned closer to the door, hoping the apology would be enough to get them to open the door, but there was no response. That was his sign to give them some much needed space.

His sign but not his strongpoint.

"There's nothing else to do besides wait it out at this point," He spoke again. "Though we could plan our next moves since Diori isn't exactly helping us from the sound of it."

"I'm not exactly thrilled with you right now, can we do this later?"

"No, we don't know how much time we have before we get any visits. Now is the time to think of something, while we still have that advantage." He pushed, trying to urge them out from isolation. The door slowly creaked open, Ayale's irritated glare hard on Osiris.

The dim light of the bathroom lit up the irritation scrawled across Ayale's face. It made sense to Osiris that Ayale came from a famous crime family now. Their eyes were part bloodshot and only seconds ago, stained with tears that remained evidence of their frustration on their cheeks.

"What did you have in mind, and don't say run away. This isn't some medieval play." They crossed their arms, disdain in their voice. Osiris wondered if their attitude was a front.

"Maybe we can pretend to be merchants."

"This isn't a tabletop game either. Try again, dungeon master."

"Okay, what if we tell them we are just traveling through?"

"Why are we traveling through? Where are we going?"

"For a...wedding?"

"Whose?"

"My sister's?"

Ayale pressed him, not blinking once. "Where?"

"Uhhh..." Osiris stumbled on his words, unable to form a coherent sentence while Ayale stared him down.

"Stuttering isn't an option. You need to be straight and to the point." Their eyes dropped to the concrete floor. "This isn't going to work."

There was no way Osiris could be convincing enough to be released by regular excuses. From what Ayale knew, there was a chance they would be left there for a few days as it was.

In a prison cell. Guarded by heavily armed Oolonxg soldiers. Food given through some weird hole in the door. Every freedom they took for granted was gone in minutes.

"Are you okay?" Osiris asked, concerned as he watched their scowl shift into a distinct melancholy, troubled with an exhaustion like their face in the forest.

"No. In fact, I'm tapped out." Ayale sulked from the bathroom door to the bed, landing face first, surprising Osiris. "I'm just going to lay here for a while."

Osiris sat to the side, trying his best to come up with some sort of comforting line. Instead, he reached to grab the dying vine plant wilting on the edge of the desk. He did what he knew best, using his power to bring back the plant from the brink of death. With the plant in hand, it slowly came back to life. Entangled with a certain thought, Osiris felt his heart beat a bit harder as he thought of a few more scenarios to get the two of them released.

What if he told the guards it was for their own wedding instead? A couple readying for their honeymoon would be easily believable.

Beyond flushed, he lost control of the plant, vines growing longer with each passing second. Once it reached the bedpost, Osiris realized what was happening and frantically pulled the vine back before he was noticed.

His only saving grace was Ayale's descent into sleep. He quietly placed the potted plant back on the desk, laying back on the bed to do the same. The whole day in its entirety was one problem after another.

Soon enough, sleep reluctantly found him.

Both slept dreamlessly. Though Ayale felt inclined to wake up when a blanket draped over them at some point during their nap. When they awoke, they felt Osiris' arm wrap around their waist. He was their only source of warmth in the bitter cold of the room.

Ayale looked at the barred window, surprised it was nighttime. They certainly didn't have time to be taking cat naps all day. They moved closer towards the edge of the bed but felt his arms pull around them, keeping them in place.

There they laid, in an oddly compromising position, wide awake and alone with their thoughts.

The foremost problem was the unshakable feeling of going home. Who would be there to meet them first? Depending on which parent found them first was detrimental to their plan entirely, even to some extent, their survival.

Particularly Osiris' survival. That led them to their next point of concern.

The sincerity in the way he asked Ayale to run away with him was unlike anything they had ever heard before. It was completely childish and demeaning to their entire cause, to the reason Ayale was returning home in the first place.

And yet, it shouldn't have been half as tempting as it was when it came out of his mouth. A part of them would have said yes in a heartbeat, if it were a viable option. But the dangers that lurk for the two right now were far too many. They had meant what they said, they would have had to go home eventually.

But that raised more questions.

What would the circumstances have to be for Ayale to say yes to his plan? Did Osiris mean something else entirely behind his words, or was it as simple as it sounded? Was this question raised out of concern for just them? Does he know he could be a target at the hands of not one but two clans?

Too many questions piled up, only to dissolve as Ayale felt Osiris shift in his sleep, pulling them further back into him. Warmth suddenly spread across their face. It didn't matter what they felt, all that mattered was that the two of them were alive.

Ayale's eyes widened. They figured out how to speed the process of their release. Speak to the head of the clan so similar in age to them, pretending as if leader to leader.

They gently pulled Osiris' hand off their waist and placed it on the bed, slipping out of his protective grasp. They went up to the metal door, giving it a light knock, only enough to get the attention of the night guard. When they caught his attention and the small slit in the door opened, they made their pleading statement.

"My name is Ayale Ceylonis and I am next in line for the Cxai clan. I request the presence of the Oolonxg leader immediately." The words flowed seamlessly from their lips. As the guard shut the door, they could hear the muffled sounds of his hand radio making noise. Ayale mentally prepared themself to play the role they had run from years ago.

The dread of morning started out as it always had; the cloudy, grey clouds of Densriel reflecting rain into the vastness of Eines' bedroom, its sounds barely registering in her ears. The gentle green of her eyes opened, sinking herself into the plethora of pillows behind her. She pulled her blanket over her face, a tiresome groan leaving her throat.

Only a handful of months since her birthday and the first signs of her affinity, Eines wished every day that she didn't show signs at all.

"Eines." A hard knock at the door and the harsh voice that accompanied it shook her momentarily. "Today is the day, come down to the basement and let's get this fucking thing removed already." Hied grumbled, his hard footsteps moving away from the door.

Eines shifted out of her bed, sitting at the edge with no more than a single, elongated sigh leaving her chest. She stretched out her hands in front of her, tightening them into fists. She quickly discovered days after the discovery of her affinity that if she focused hard enough, electricity could concentrate into one area.

It was only a week later she could aim.

Within the next hour, Eines was escorted into the basement of the Matxha clan compound, surrounded by random people she had never seen before. Within the barely lit room, sat a strange mechanism in the middle, intimidatingly covered with metal pillars and other technology she didn't recognize. Four odd contraptions shaped like massive vials surrounded, possibly even fueled, what looked like a magic circle filled with shapes and symbols that would remain in her memory the moment she laid eyes on them. Eines felt a fear like none other. She looked around the room, frantically looking for her brother, trying her hardest not to let the moisture in her eyes fall down her face.

With no one familiar in sight except her father, Eines stood silently by the door, the commotion of the strangers around her causing her chest to tighten. She nervously began to braid her blonde hair in small strands, doing anything she could to control her nerves.

Her nerves only worsened when the large, human sized vials began to fill with vibrant colors, each slowly filling to the top with elemental energy. The one closest to her, going around the mechanism was a glowing blue for water, a bold red for fire, a metallic silver for wind, and a reddish-brown remnant of the earth.

It was at that moment Eines completely resigned herself to the idea that the contraption before her, one that no soul in the room bothered to explain to her, was going to kill her as well as her affinity.

After her realization, she was left to the elevated circle in the middle, directed to stand still and not to move.

Eines felt her knees ready to buckle, unsure what to do with everyone's eyes on her.

The whirring sound of the machine began beneath her, every person suddenly silent as the circle beneath her glowed. Her heart in her throat, Eines let the smallest whimper slip, stopping absolutely no one.

The process involved drawing out her energy, using the symbols beneath her as a catalyst to start. The vials around her were there to draw out her affinity, keeping the user and their power bound to one place until the process was done.

The exhaustion hit Eines soon after beginning, leaving her struggling to keep her eyes open, and soon unable to stand. She felt sweaty as if she were with a fever, chills spanning her face and hands, but along all of that, one pain remained the most consistent; the knot in her stomach that seemed to grow.

The more the circle tried to take from Eines, the more intense this pain became.

Until, like an elastic band, the knot snapped.

Bursts of electricity filled the room, running over every person, every part of the machine keeping her in place, and taking out everyone and every living thing in the basement. Before she knew it, Eines had collapsed in the middle, unresponsive.

By the time she opened her eyes, she saw nothing but bodies on every part of the floor around the mechanism, every vial erupted and spilled over on the floor, coating the bodies in its strange liquid.

All except for the one vial filled with the earth elemental.

Sentenced to her room, Eines spent the next hour of her life barely alive, the screams of her father going into one ear and out the other. The only line she could recall from that night had been what he said before storming out. "Too bad you couldn't have died with the rest of the trash." He muttered one more thing under his breath before slamming her door behind him. "Bastard child." Eines heard before she passed out once more.

When she awoke, she felt a comforting hand on her forehead, and opened her eyes to Belire seated beside her in the dead of the night. The muffled sounds of a storm raged outside, but the concern in his voice frightened her more. "Eines, how do you feel?" He asked, her sleepy expression unresponsive.

"What happened in the basement?" Eines eventually croaked, her throat dry.

Belire sighed, drawing back his hand. "I don't..." He trailed off unsure how to go about the events of today. "Eines, no matter what I say to you right now, you know you are and always will be my sister. Do you understand?" He watched for her reaction, earning a nod. "Good, good." His vision shifted to the storm outside, the dull streetlights barely lighting her room.

"Elemental users are special. Down to their genetics. To get a removal done for those with elemental genetics, there needs to be special equipment. Even if you're only...related to one." Belire finished, his last words barely able to escape him.

Eines thought for a moment, her brow furrowing. "But mom wasn't—"

"No. Neither is Hied." He let out another deep breath. Belire instinctively reached for her forehead again, checking to see if her fever died down.

*Bastard child* echoed in her head until she fell back asleep.

# XX

Osiris stirred in his sleep, reaching for Ayale. His arms were met with nothing but the cold mattress beside him, quickly realizing they were no longer in bed. He frantically searched the room, noticing they were no longer in the cell at all.

The silence was deafening. All he knew was that he had to trust whatever they were up to, barely recollecting the muffled voices that stirred him from his sleep a few hours ago.

If it were anyone else, he would have simply gone back to sleep. Yet, there he laid, wide awake, painfully aware of the silence Ayale left behind.

The office of the clan leader sat at the top of the very same building as the prison cells on the basement floor of the Oolonxg compound. The light reflecting off the snowcapped mountains had allowed a small semblance of natural lighting inside the dark office. The black furniture was glossy, an untouched look on the couches in the corner, the standing lamps behind the desk, with bookshelves that made up the accent wall perfectly aligned with reference and history material. An ornate black desk blended in with the charcoal stripes on the other three walls.

Behind the desk sat the most exhausted thirty-year-old man, wondering to himself why he was awake at such an ungodly hour. His sapphire eyes were furnished with dark circles beneath them, clinging to a pale, ivory complexion. His worn face came with a five o'clock shadow, distinct raven black hair that fell symmetrically over both

189

shoulders. It was a rare day where he brushed it properly and didn't throw it up into a lazy bun above his head. A yawn ran through his body, forcing his eyes closed for a moment before his instincts kicked in and reached over for his iced coffee across from him.

The coffee looked more like an ice cream sundae, as it did every morning for the past year. His drink was decorated with whipped cream and caramel drizzle drenched over every inch of his clear cup.

An average morning for Visu Vindai, leader of the Oolonxg clan, whose tastes haven't changed since he was a child. Anyone who glanced at him immediately knew he was no morning person.

But as a newly appointed leader, he had to find ways to keep awake throughout the day.

His father, Wuyi Vindai, begrudgingly passing him this position was a common topic on his mind. Not only did he struggle with gaining respect of the Oolonxg clan with his new title, though his whole life revolved around preparing for leadership, but when the time came, Visu realized how little he wanted the position. He had been passed down an empire that drowned with old habits that were long gone in many other places. But any mention of change incurred Wuyi's anger, swearing that all traditions were necessary to uphold the clan.

Odania sat as the gated capital of the Oolonxg territory. High in the mountains, the territory had the advantage of isolation from many disputes and glaring eyes of other clans...or so would think anyone who passed through. Industrial design and development allowed the capital to thrive, even during its coldest seasons. A proud factor for the Vindai family and their centuries-long reign.

But Visu yearned for change, to improve their beloved capital of industrial innovation. He had so many ideas laying around to do so. Wuyi would hear none of it, no matter how many times he tried. To his unfortunate luck, Visu barely had any power, acting more as a face than anything else.

Over time, he started giving up altogether, bringing with it the decline of his mental health.

If Visu could start anywhere, his first change would be to open the gates to the capital once more. Wuyi's reason for closing the gates to begin with came with the goal of decreasing opposition forces. A product of the war he led on the long gone Chamoxile clan, whose name was no longer evident even in textbooks.

Visu had no certainty in how to institute new rules. Not many saw him as a leader, still viewing him only as the son of Wuyi. Many below him within the clan were from his father's era, with only a small circle chosen by Visu himself. So much of his ruling had been determined for him, a path already carved out for him to follow.

The thought left Visu in a perpetual state of dread he has not shaken since he took on his new role.

A few days ago, the line had been crossed when his father publicly announced an engagement in the family.

Visu's engagement.

One he learned of at the same time as everyone else.

He wanted so badly to speak up and reject the whole premise, finding himself in a nightmare he could not wake from.

Visu openly welcomed anything to distract him from his status of being a face forced into an arranged marriage.

And early that morning, during his daily workout, a distraction was exactly what he received.

Not even his morning coffee would wake him more than hearing of a potential clan leader being imprisoned within his own gates. Furthermore, luck had found him that day as it was one of his own personal guards to alert him of this information, giving Visu time to plan his next steps. He made sure to go into his office in silence as soon as he heard, bringing with him the guards who had detained two who tried to cross into the capital. Visu didn't dare consider what would have happened if Wuyi found out a Cxai descendent had entered their borders.

His request to them was to bring the supposed offspring of the Cxai clan to his office as quietly and quickly as possible. He sat behind his desk, feeling his mind race with thoughts. Visu awaited the initial meeting, hoping his fast reaction was not in vain.

Visu took out his cellphone and typed away at his phone, sending a handful of text messages with a small smile crossing his face before it sank back into a frown. The only happiness he held in his hands was quickly slipping away, soon to be nonexistent if he allowed his father to continue watching everything over Visu's shoulder.

A knock at the door brought him back to his current reality. He wasn't half sure how to speak to another clan's impending leader, contemplating ways to figure out and distinguish whether they were friend or foe. Visu silently hoped for the first.

"Enter." Visu stated loudly, straightening his back in his seat.

Ayale was escorted into the room by the two officers from earlier. They walked across the room as both guards went back to stand outside by the door. As they sat down across Visu, the apathetic look in their eyes added to the serious aura that emanated from their being.

Before Visu could say anything, he stopped himself, trying to come up with the best way to begin this conversation. Saying 'why are you here' was no way to introduce himself.

"So, you told my men you are a member of the Cxai clan family." Visu leaned back in his chair, maintaining eye contact.

"Yes. Ayale Ceylonis." They stated without so much as a blink. Already a great start.

Visu's eyes widened. "The runaway?"

Ayale sat still. "How did you know that?"

"The Oolonxg clan's last interactions had been with the Cxai clan three years ago. Within our first days in Nalira, you had gone missing, and all clan discussions were postponed indefinitely. If you're here now, clearly alive and well in front of me, what else am I to assume?"

Ayale recalled using the visit of the Oolonxg clan as their advantage to escape, utilizing the distraction in the creation of their escape plan.

"May I ask why you are here, Ayale?"

A thoughtful look crossed their face. They examined Visu, seeing the way the darkness under his eyes denoted he hadn't seen sleep in ages. The suit that sat over his chest without its Oolonxg emblem on the pocket. The coffee in the corner of the desk.

Ayale had a hunch and ran with it, speaking the first thing that came to mind. "From one potential leader to another, how are you doing in your new position?" They looked around the room.

Visu blinked, determined to hide his disdain for his position by straightening his back and pushing away his phone and coffee. "That is not what I expected to be asked today."

"You look like you haven't slept in days."

"Is that imperative to the conversation?"

Ayale shrugged. "Just an observation."

Visu adjusted his seat, pulling himself forward towards the desk, shaking off the comment altogether. "May I ask what you are doing in Odania?"

Ayale thought to themself for a moment, quietly trying to gauge if Diori had managed to contact anyone within the Oolonxg clan. They quickly shook off the idea.

"I have someone with me who has been targeted by the Matxha clan and I...got involved, so to speak. My new life no longer existed once I made that choice, and I am currently on my way home to hopefully grant him asylum. We need help keeping away from the Matxha clan, and anyone else they may be sending to find us." Ayale let out every detail they could. There was no telling Visu's reaction but there was no use in hiding their intentions either. Whether shot down by the Oolonxg clan leader or back home, it was all the same to them.

Visu couldn't help but stare. The minute that passed between them took Ayale for a spin, trying their best to keep a straight face as they awaited to hear a response.

"Who else is in danger, other than the two of you? Or do you care so much of the one with you?" Visu placed a hand under his chin, his questioning stare trying to piece together the unusual turn of events that came from the outsider before him.

After an uncomfortable silence, Ayale finally cleared their throat to speak. "I care enough to be here."

"Defensive, are we?"

"More concerned with the off-topic question."

"Is it so off-topic? Why else would..." Visu trailed off before leaning over the desk to whisper. "Why else travel all the way home and not leave the other to die? Why come out of hiding?"

"The Matxha clan is out of control. They were probably going to kill him, I did what I thought was right. Any more questions?"

"Ayale—" Visu's phone began to go off, the high-pitched ringing completely interrupting him. As he picked up the phone, he turned his chair around, speaking quietly into the mic. There was a subtle voice on the other end, though Ayale could not quite make out any details throughout the short conversation. *Let's talk later, please* was the only detail that stuck out before Visu turned back around with a softer expression.

"To think you would give up your new life so willingly." Visu shook his head. "I cannot sit here and say I am not envious of your ability to drop the whole Cxai clan and run towards amnesty." He held his phone, briefly glancing down to it. "And all the same, I cannot help but feel bad that you are returning to this way of life. You may not be met with open arms."

Ayale's heart sank at the reminder of going home. From freedom back into the tight grasp of the Cxai clan.

Straying from their plan was far more tempting. Thoughts of how and where worked through their mind. Katari would likely take them if they asked. The idea of waking up to tea, muffins from the store in Istanza, and a view of the mountain tops every day was a far-off dream.

With Osiris beside them each time.

They swallowed hard, pushing the thought aside. Going back to Cxai territory was the only way to ensure both were safe from the Matxha clan.

"What is it that you need from the Oolonxg clan?"

They thought about Diori and her promise to contact the Oolonxg clan on their behalf. They decided to change their request. "I don't know what awaits me at home and I want to ask for your support."

Visu braced himself for his next question. "Are you going to take over for your father once you arrive home?"

"I don't know, I also don't want to. But if I must, it's better to be prepared."

"I had heard rumors of dissonance among the Cxai clan. Perhaps that would be a point of advantage."

"Why does that sound like you won't help me if the endeavor arises?"

Visu leaned back in his seat. He thought to himself briefly before rewarding their honesty with his own. "I barely hold any power beyond my face to the people. My father still has a hold on all major points of government. Old ways reign supreme around here."

"Do they though? Or are you too scared to speak up and step away from his shadow?"

He shot a glare at them, stolid words leaving his mouth in a warning. "For a runaway asking for my assistance, you do not seem to realize where you stand in this situation. You do not have the upper hand here, Ayale Ceylonis."

"Don't you want more from this role than sitting here, rotting away? Isn't there anything that makes you want to fight this?"

The office door opened with a slow creak, revealing a tall, inquisitive young man before he snuck into the room, closing the door behind him. He looked to be around the same age as Visu, standing cautiously in front of the door. His outfit consisted of a cropped black leather jacket and loose-fitting black jeans held up by a matching belt, a jade tee shirt adorned with white daisies. His pale complexion complimented his bold grey eyes, his wispy, light brown hair bouncing as he slowly walked towards the desk with a subtle smile on his face. The sides of his hair were close shaven, clean and aligned on both sides of his head. A surprised expression crossed his face when he made eye contact with Ayale seated across from Visu.

Ayale met his confused stare with one of their own, equally surprised by his entrance. When they peered at Visu, his stoic look melted away into the gentle smile that crossed his lips.

"Hello dear, this won't be long, I promise." The stranger's voice sounded with a sweetness tinged with intimidation in Ayale's direction. They simply nodded and sat still as the kind voice shifted to Visu. "I just wanted to say congratulations on your very recent engagement," His smile grew with insincerity. "May your happiness last you both for eternity."

"Teryn, we can discuss this later."

"No need, I have plans after here that involve a nice bottle of wine and a few sad movies. Is this the lovely spouse to be?" Teryn smiled at Ayale, who openly cringed at the question.

"Absolutely not." They corrected, noticing something shiny trapped in one of Teryn's hands.

"Correct, they are taken by another." Visu interjected.

Ayale's face shifted with disgust. "Not that either."

Teryn closed his eyes and took a deep breath, trying to keep his calm collected expression from retreating and his blood pressure from rising. "I'm not sure what's happening, but I am only here to tell you as nicely as possible that I am done. I have dealt with more than enough, being patient as can be for years at your side. Arranged marriage is where I draw the line. Have a good life, Visu." Teryn placed a simple gold chain with a matching star charm on the desk and made way for the door. Visu stared at the necklace while Teryn left with a subtle slam following his exit.

Ayale had seen a lot of shows and movies in their lifetime, and yet, had never witnessed a breakup. They darted their eyes to the man across from them, who stared diligently at the edge of the desk where the gold chain sat.

"What just...was that a breakup?" Ayale asked, his eyes unmoving and distant. "I'm sorry." Ayale said softly.

He shifted uncomfortably in his seat before taking the chain off the desk and placing it in his inner chest pocket within his coat. There were no words, the only thing left for him to do from here was move forward.

Visu cleared his throat. "Where were we?" He spoke as if nothing happened.

"Are you okay? I feel like that should be addressed first."

"No need."

"I can't ignore that whole debacle, did he say engagement?"

"Father had spoken of it, but I didn't think he would go as far as he did." He sank down into his seat, the color draining from his face.

"Your dad is out of control, you need to tell him to back down."

Visu shot a glare in Ayale's direction. "Do you really believe I haven't tried?"

"You are the head of the clan, Visu." Ayale emphasized their words, almost forgetting it was them imprisoned and asking for favors. "Start acting like it."

Another phone call interrupted their conversation, prompting a heavy sigh from his lips.

There was no more fearful look than Visu's expression as he looked down at his phone. He answered after the third ring, placing it up to his ear, and turning his chair around once more. The conversation is far more abrupt, mechanically spoken 'yes' and 'no' coming out interchangeable. He turned partly to the door, worried it could open any second. The voice on the other line was gruff and louder than the one before. Tension thickened as the conversation went on, until he finally placed the phone back down.

When he turned back around, his tired eyes rang with a deep-rooted exhaustion, before the slight of envy ran through him. Though his words were anything but envious.

"My father is on his way here. You will have to stay in the holding cell until he leaves again."

Ayale's chest tightened at the thought of being stuck in such a small room. "Is there anywhere else we can go that isn't a prison?"

"For now, it is safest. Neither of us want him to know you are here." Visu had already begun to call over a guard to escort them back.

"Don't let him push you around. And maybe try to think of somewhere else to throw us."

"I will do my best. But before anything happens, he needs to leave."

They nodded along, preferring not to interact with Wuyi. "Alright."

Ayale was quickly escorted back down the dark hallway and down a large flight of stairs, though treated less like a prisoner when they noticed no one went to cuff them. As the guard led them back into the room, his soft expression took them by surprise while the large metal door shut behind them.

What exactly was going on in Odania? The last thing they expected was for the guards knowing face and the allyship with the Oolonxg's newest leader.

When Ayale took their eyes off the door, they turned and met with Osiris' worried glare from where he sat at the edge of the bed.

# XXI

Ayale ignored the scowl making itself apparent on Osiris and seated themself at the edge of the bed, contemplating their initial meeting with Visu. The horrific realization that he was everything they almost became would haunt them for a long time to come. But it also made them thankful for leaving Cxai territory when they did, however long they could. It was a sight to behold another person in the same situation, though more comparable to a nightmare. Still deep in thought, they wondered what kind of hell that would transpire when they finally reached home.

Osiris had taken up the spot beside Ayale, shoulders touching, as the barebones sunlight began to settle into the room. His glare settled back into only worry and curiosity. "How did you get the leader to grant an audience with you?"

"Why do you care?" Ayale flopped back onto the bed with a deep exhale.

"You know, I'm getting tired of you giving me so much attitude."

"Get used to it. We're here for the long run." They said, exasperated by the fact they must wait multiple days before being able to leave their quite literal prison. Visu's strange comment of 'being taken by another' from earlier ran through their head, momentarily pulling them away from the drama of the breakup they witnessed during their meeting.

But they shook away the thought. It wasn't the time to think about trivial things.

"Are you okay?" Osiris asked, apologetic and quiet.

They moved an arm over their eyes, unable to look at him while thoughts of their time in the forest arose into memory. The feel of his arms wrapped tightly around their body, the warm aura that imbued them as they slept. It was the first time they trusted Osiris to be so close to them, even as everything fell apart around them.

While isolation seemed like their only option, Ayale was intent on coming up with a plan to convince Visu for his support. They could use all the help they could get, for both the Matxha and the Cxai, depending on the outcome of their plan.

They wondered if Visu's freedom from Wuyi was possible, first and foremost. The man seemed to be a step short of a hostage in his own territory. Beyond the exhaustion so evident in his eyes and tense features, he had the audacity to make a comment on their journey home. The word 'amnesty' killed them inside, drowned in the envy he held for Ayale's freedom, even if it were a brief three-year period.

They wondered if he ever had the chance to breathe outside of the Oolonxg clan.

Visu deserved a semblance of that feeling.

"Ayale?"

"Yeah?"

"You didn't give him the same greeting as you tried to with Katari, right?" Osiris fiddled with his hands, a sure sign of his anxiety rising.

"Not this time since we ended up imprisoned first." Ayale snickered, recalling what he was referencing. Hopefully, Katari would find it equally amusing someday.

He breathed out a sigh of relief, half expecting their strange ways to get them both in more trouble.

"Visu needs our help, Osiris. He is exactly where I would have been had I stayed." Ayale moved their arm away, an adamant look in their eyes.

"What do you mean? Don't we need his help?"

"His father is controlling every part of his life from behind the curtain. If we help him break out of that, he might be more willing to agree to help us after. Better us asking before my mother, we can maintain a higher hand in the case we need it."

"What did you have in mind?" He asked, nervous for the answer.

"Revolution. Shifting the scales in his favor."

Osiris nodded to himself. "You're insane."

"Is it sane to allow some old man to keep his own son in a chokehold to control the masses?"

Osiris didn't know what to say from there on. As unfortunate as it was, Ayale made a point. Projected, but a point, nonetheless. "It isn't possible to try and start a revolution from a prison cell, Ayale."

"It's the safest bet for us. We could be okay, but if we have Visu's support, that's two full clans behind us before approaching the Cxai territory. We could be ambushed by either of my parents or the Matxha clan, this could secure our path against whoever turns against us first." Ayale stopped before saying anything more. Take it all and shift the scales of power.

Osiris nodded along. It wouldn't hurt to have that sort of support just in case.

"Can I ask you something sort of strange?" Osiris's timid voice caught them off guard.

"Hm?" Ayale broke out of their train of thought, waiting patiently for Osiris to come forward with his inquiry.

"Is your affinity an elemental?"

Ayale only blinked, not daring to react to the sudden question. "Funny. We have bigger things to focus on."

He looked at the plant across the room and the far extending vines with thriving leaves. Perhaps he should trust their judgement. He considered the possibilities that were Ayale's affinity, thinking which might suit them best. Because of his affinity to nature, he hoped it was something to do with water.

A water or earth elemental would perfectly match his own affinity.

His cheeks warmed up at the thought. He didn't want to let his face shift so drastically, so he did his best Katari impression, straightening his back and placing a horribly stoic look across his face.

"What's wrong with your face?" Ayale choked back a laugh. "Kind of reminds me of Katari. God, I miss Istanza." They felt their heart drop, thinking back to their time in the quiet territory. The small capital deep in the hillside mountains felt far more tempting than the snowy region of the Oolonxg territory. They could feel Osiris' stare on them, knowing he was trying to come up with some comforting phrase, because that seemed to be what he did best. Instead, he remained quiet, keeping his serious expression fixed on them.

He wondered how much he could say without making them more uncomfortable.

"I miss being there, too." He murmured before staring off at the door to the cell.

The next few hours were spent doing next to nothing productive. First, the two spoke of what they noted in the room. Ayale investigated the strange cell thoroughly, partly impressed with how much it looked like a formal room. Beyond the bed was a fully functional bathroom, a miniature coffee maker, and a desk. It was odd for a prison cell to be so decent, but once they figured out the cells were created with long-term capture in mind, both fell silent again.

Once the night set in and they were both tired of moping, that was when they began talking about their next moves. Being imprisoned wouldn't stop them from being ready for the best and worst to come.

Their discussion led them down a 'what if' rabbit hole. Ayale put together what they thought of when it came to shifting everything into Visu's favor.

The first step was to take control of the guard. There was little loyalty as it was with the civilians living in Odania at all, survival being the primary thought. The focus should remain on those who did trust Visu to begin with during his rise to power. Allyship from age was another. To bring in the younger generation would leave more to question the older one.

There was only one other problem.

"What kind of affinity did you say Visu had?" Osiris chimed in, but as Ayale thought about it, they realized they had no idea. As if he could tell, he sighed. "You didn't ask?"

"Why would I ask him that? His affinity isn't my priority, getting us out of here is. Besides, we got cut off, someone barged in."

"Who?"

"I guess his now ex-boyfriend, Teryn. Guy came in to break up with Visu while I was there. Allegedly, Visu's father arranged a marriage behind his back." Ayale huffed, annoyed at themself for forgetting to ask.

Osiris shifted his hair over his right shoulder, wondering if this was the fate for everyone involved in these crime families. There was little chance at freedom for Ayale if they went home, he realized. But on a far-reaching thought, he remained hopeful. Maybe there was a chance everything would work out. He wouldn't want asylum if it meant losing Ayale to the Cxai clan.

"Teryn. I think he's the key here." Ayale sat up from the bed as though they were a reanimated corpse rising from the grave, grabbing Osiris' horrified attention. "Teryn ties everything together. To be brutally honest, Visu's life sounds awful right now. What else does he have left to fight for? I think the guard works under Visu only, we can let him know we need to talk sooner than later. What do you think?" They grinned with excitement.

In turn, he couldn't hide his own smile.

"I think this might just work, Aya."

The hours passed and before either knew it, the time had been midnight, only evident by the placement of the moon through the barred window. Ayale and Osiris took turns for the shower, still discussing their plans for Visu when the time came. There was no discussion on sleeping arrangements, a thought that eluded Ayale due to the other thoughts at hand, but plagued Osiris even more. He wasn't sure if it would be weird to them to share the space, since his recent realization and their night in the forest clearing.

All he knew to do was sit at the edge of the bed pretending to sketch in his book, while Ayale laid in bed and wrote down their plans in the floral notebook Osiris had stolen from Mildred's shop. The shuffle of notes was all he could hear, the rush of writing on each page, and the turn of each page. Ayale worked hard with the momentum in them, until yawns began to spill from their mouth. They tried to fight the temptation of sleep, dozing off only a half hour or so later. They fell asleep halfway through their last thought of the night.

Osiris peered up from his sketchbook, the sound of paper and scribbling no longer taking up space. He took the notes from their hands and placed them on the nightstand beside Ayale. He turned off the light before inevitably deciding to get into bed beside them. When he settled in, he felt his heartbeat far harder and quicker than before. The flushed feeling left him weak and too awake.

It was...sort of awful. He just wanted to do what he normally did and now, he feared the act altogether.

Osiris leaned on the pillow, monitoring their sleeping face. He inched closer, wishing with everything that he had the ability to close the gap between them. Since the dream in the forest, he lost all ability to be subtle. He thought so often of how or when he could tell them about everything he felt, enough that it drove him a little crazy. His feelings were a lot stronger than when he first noticed them.

They seemed so at peace. How could he try to take away the dynamic that took so long to build?

In that instant, Osiris wrapped his arms around them and pulled them into his embrace. They shifted a bit in their sleep but relaxed instantly after a few moments passed. The initial relief of their comfort had him realize this dynamic was nothing new either, having shared the small space of a car for a few weeks. So why was sleeping next to Ayale so nerve wracking?

Osiris felt his anxiety begin to spike, the air around him no longer breathable and stagnant, his body temperature rising a degree for each racing thought. They were both essentially imprisoned, at the will of those around them. Their luck began to rise at the initial encounter of Katari, but he knew it wouldn't always be this way. It was evident in fact, considering they were sleeping in a fancy prison cell.

A prison cell meant for entrapment, for long-term holding.

Before he knew it, Osiris struggled to keep it together. He didn't want to awaken Ayale after working up the courage to hold them as they slept, but he could no longer take their warmth, nor that of the comforter atop them both. He snuck out of the bed as quickly as possible, doing his best not to wake them. He settled at the edge of the bed. Next thing he knew, he was trying to catch his breath and control the hyperventilating breaths trying to rip from his throat.

Ayale felt the warmth around them disappear, followed by shuffling. They had been somewhat awake before Osiris pulled them into his arms. Unsure how to react, they froze and pretended they were fully asleep. It was the sound of his choked back breath that had their eyes snap open. They recognized an anxiety attack when they heard one.

"Hey. Are you okay?" Ayale slid out from the comforter, placing a hand on his shoulder. The uneven breathing turned into a held back sob, meeting their words with incoherent sentences. That was their sign to get up and do something. They went into the bathroom and grabbed a small towel, dousing it in cold water before wringing it out. Their next move was stealing a water bottle from the odd mini-fridge in the corner. In mere moments, they were back by his side.

"I didn't want to wake you." Osiris furled into himself, head in his hands, unable to hold back crying.

Ayale placed the water between them and the cold towel at the base of his neck, knowing there wasn't much else they could do except support him. They kept the water bottle to the back of his neck and moved the towel up to his forehead.

"I couldn't sleep anyways. I can't seem to stop thinking either. I'm sorry if I haven't kept my cool and caused this." They apologized softly. When he leaned back, a heavy look of distress crossed his face, accompanied by a steady stream of tears running down both cheeks. All they could do from here was to talk him down from his attack before it worsened. They used the towel to dab away some of the tears at his eyes, wiping away the remaining lines on his face. When they finished, they placed it back behind his neck.

"Let's do some breathing exercises together." Ayale picked up his hand in theirs, making sure to keep his attention. They led him into short, guided breathing exercises, inhaling a deep breath into their lungs and squeezing his hand. They held it for a short time before letting it out, simultaneously loosening their hold. They repeated the process a handful of times, until the strained look began to fade away from his face. He was slowly coming to, so they kept going, never once letting go.

After what felt like forever, Osiris finally found himself breathing steadily.

Ayale drew back the towel, patting away tears once more before meeting his tired gaze.

"Are you feeling a little bit better?" They asked, taking up his remaining hand into theirs.

He nodded, still a bit shaky in his breathing.

"What triggered an attack tonight? Is it being stuck in the room?" He nodded again.

"Fair, I'm sick of being here, too." They fixed his hair, pulling it back from his face and behind his ear. "I will get us out of here tomorrow. At the least, I'll try my best. That's the plan." They smiled at him, confident and ready to make their plea to Visu once more. Even in the dark, the two had been close enough together that he could see the faint smile.

"Maybe if we talk about it, we could get some concerns out of the way. Is that okay with you?" Ayale asked, seeing his hesitant nod.

They stood from their spot on the ground to the bed, bringing Osiris with them. They understood the nonverbal composure that held Osiris all too well. It was as much a part of them in moments like this.

Ayale spoke of the plan that plagued them earlier, allowing Osiris to lay his head in their lap while they softly went on about their conversation with Visu. Neither could tell how much time had passed but knew it had been enough to steal away hours of sleep from them.

In the darkness of their room, Osiris focused on the voice above him. And when he thought all was said and done, Ayale found new things to talk about. The one-sided conversation became less formal and focused, filled with initial judgements and comments of their journey so far. They wandered into previously unspoken territory, allowing Osiris to hear of every thought that went through their head, beginning from when they left Densriel. A sense of honesty that neither expected to come out.

Osiris tried to force himself to remain awake, so he could listen to the things he knew wouldn't be repeated after tonight. He struggled against the exhaustion settling in his eyes.

"When we get out of here, let's explore the city. If everything works out for us." Ayale yawned, quickly losing their momentum to continue speaking.

"If everything works out for us." Osiris eventually responded, repeating their line back as if it were an important promise.

## XXII

Three days had passed since the initial meeting between Visu Vindai and the Cxai family runaway, Ayale Ceylonis. It felt as though weeks had gone by, considering the long stay of his father Wuyi, who dreaded the city and everyone in it.

In Visu's office, the tired leader's eyes wandered to the window across from him. The cloudy overcast over the mountainous city was a welcome sight.

To Visu's relief, the visit was temporary. This meant he could take his time and ask Ayale more questions, maybe answer a few in return. His main concerns were in their goals and the odd defiance that coursed through their last conversation.

*You are the head of the clan, Visu. Start acting like it.*

The envy of being able to speak freely with confidence behind their words was everything he wanted and wished for.

Visu ran his fingers through his dark hair, agitated. His mind sat heavy with thoughts of the past few days. The stress was enough to send him to the grave.

He disappointed Teryn. He hid their relationship, worrying for the safety of his beloved since the two confessed to one another. Visu told him he would come out about their relationship once he took his father's place as leader of the Oolonxg clan, asking for Teryn's patience until the day came.

In the meantime, years had gone by with both hiding their love from everyone.

After taking the role, Wuyi managed to remain in power. Visu found himself asking for more and more patience from Teryn as he navigated the new role, hoping his father would see his initiative and step back.

But that day never came.

Instead, his father arranged a marriage for him. News of the engagement was, understandably, the last straw.

The moment Teryn threw the chain onto the desk, Visu could not find the will to fight him. He was right to leave. He asked too much of him.

Visu wanted so badly to speak up, to tell him to stay.

But there was no way he could ask any more of him.

He sat back in his seat, the chain still clutched between his fingers. The necklace was a gift to his beloved on the event of their first anniversary.

Teryn was everything to him. He was the only one without lopsided expectations, nor did he ever need to pretend to be someone else. There was always understanding and love in their relationship.

He wanted to throw down everything and run to him, plead and apologize for everything he had done. In that brief instance, he wondered if this was how Ayale felt. If this was the feeling that drove them to take Osiris and get him to safety, Visu felt a sense of deeper understanding for their situation.

He truly wondered if the words that came from Ayale were achievable. Surely, it couldn't be so simple.

Visu waited patiently for the moment his father would leave to call on his newest ally.

Ayale and Osiris sat in the room, bored well into the night. The lack of noise was enough to drive anyone to lunacy, though Ayale constantly claimed 'it could be worse'. They laid at the edge of the bed, swinging their legs off the edge in boredom.

Osiris sat in a stillness he struggled with, unsure what to do. There was nothing he could do about it. Keep his feelings to himself and focus on staying calm. There was no way he could speak his thoughts aloud, not at a time like this.

"I need to get out of here before I lose my mind." Ayale groaned, putting the longer strands of hair in a lazy braid down their shoulder to keep themself busy. Osiris nodded in agreement, already mostly dozed off. His thoughts still burdened with matters of the heart, though still the two shared frustrations.

"I'm pretty sure I screwed this up, do you mind fixing it?" Ayale pulled apart the braid.

Osiris hesitantly moved from the desk to their side, taking their hair into his hands, and quietly working the same small section of hair into a simple braid. He smoothed back their hair, attempting to keep the stray strands on both sides in check.

"How long do you think we have to sit here for?" Osiris asked, finishing the first braid.

"If we don't hear anything by nightfall, I'm going to try sending another message."

"Don't be too pushy, we need him in our good graces." He finished off the end of the other braid. "Have an elastic for these?"

"Borrowing yours, if that's okay." Ayale handed off one of his own to him from their wrist, a quick scoff leaving his mouth. He tied it off and secured the piece without any issue. "I'll get us out of here, I can promise that much." They turned to Osiris, a serious look crossing their face.

"I know you will." He couldn't help the smile from coming back, earning one back. A few other thoughts weighed heavily on his mind.

The further from Densriel, the closer they came to their destination. "Can I ask a serious question?" Osiris moved over to their side.

Their arrest at the border cut their conversation on Ayale's parents abruptly. His curiosity mixed with his boredom, figuring now was a good a time as any to know more about what to expect. He squeezed his eyes shut before blurting out his inquiry.

"What are your parents like?"

Ayale's eyes widened, a multitude of emotions crossing their face, until they settled on a timid expression. They stopped swinging their legs as the thought of home bore down on them. "Valid question, what would you like to know?"

"Whatever you're okay to tell me. You don't need to tell me anything if you're not ready." Osiris bumped his shoulder into theirs, lingering as a means of comfort. Ayale took a hard breath and thought to themself.

There were more than a handful of ways for them to describe their parents. The issues that laid forth the catalyst of their need for freedom were events and people far beyond their time.

That was the simplest way to describe the problem that was the Cxai clan family.

Ayale bumped into him but left their shoulder against his. There was nothing they wanted less than to mess around with family history like a lecturing professor.

Osiris picked up the notebook and inched closer to them, waiting for Ayale to start.

"My parents are complicated people. My father's background was...one of struggle. He was of Cxai origin, at least that's what he said. He wasn't given anything to start with in clan life and I know this, I've always known this. But as I grew older, it wasn't used for understanding but as an excuse. 'I dealt with this, you have it easy', you know? Every day, it was something. Anything he could scream about, he would. If you didn't immediately understand something, you had no chance to learn it. You were expected to be the best with no room for error because he didn't have that chance himself. From age five, up until the day I left, living there was a game of survival." Ayale looked down at their hands. They raised a hand to their throat, swallowing hard. "I feel like I never left."

Osiris placed an arm around them, pulling them against his side. They settled into the half embrace, the tight feeling in their throat slow to dissipate.

"My mother never brought up her bad upbringing, but we knew. She never used the excuse of a bad childhood for anything, either. The issues that accompanied her were nothing like my father's. She was originally from the Ceyxlon clan, you know. There was never a moment of peace between either of them, the extremes went in both directions. She was barely coherent as a parent. My father's voice yelled and demanded, but my mother was always silent. She never defended us, nor anyone. I understand why. But that didn't make anything easier.

"Once I realized that I was a prisoner in my own home, I needed to leave. I couldn't let myself live a life chosen for me. They wanted me to take over and continue my father's legacy, but I couldn't stomach the idea of leading the Cxai clan." Ayale met Osiris' thoughtful expression, nervous to have their entire life spilled out all at once. "I didn't want to be miserable like the rest of them. I deserved a chance to be happy, so I ran away in the pursuit of happiness." Their voice softened, holding back the emotion begging to let loose.

Osiris rubbed their arm, a fleeting thought of his own parents passing by. "I'm sorry you went through all of that."

"It could be worse, it could be better. My biggest worry is whether my grudge bearing father welcomes us or imprisons us."

While they both silently contemplated their situation, Ayale worried for the next questions to come. The topic of family was difficult enough, but to delve into more might give them a heart attack from the sheer stress.

Osiris didn't know what to say. To learn so much in a day was enough to send his own heart on a marathon. "Are you alright?" He whispered, leaning against their head. He could sense the tension settling over their collective exhaustion, ready to tell Ayale they don't need to speak any more about their past.

"I'm fine. But you know, this room we've been stuck in? This is more freedom than when I was back home."

The line left an ominous feeling in his stomach. The still air came out cold from the vents above them, a brief noise filling the gap of words.

"You impress me, Ayale. I don't know anyone else who could have run away to build a better life for themselves." He kept them close, unwilling to move.

"I don't want to go home." To his surprise, he felt Ayale's arms slowly work their way around his lower back. "Osiris, aren't you scared about all of this?"

"Not as much as before if I have to admit." He hugged them back, letting out a held breath. "You've survived so much. I wouldn't see us this far otherwise."

"You give me too much credit." They settled their forehead against his shoulder, wondering when Osiris had become such a source of comfort.

"I don't give you enough. To me, you're amazing for your courage." Osiris squeezed them, earning a short scoff, as well as an unseen smile. They settled against him, comfortable for the first time since the forest clearing. The moment would have lasted had it not been for a knock at the door to disrupt them.

The knock was followed with the creak of the metal door. Visu slipped by the small opening and entered the room, with the bodyguard beside him just as Ayale pulled away.

"My apologies for barging in so late. We only have so much time alone, and my father is gone for the next few days. Teryn agreed to house you both under the radar, per your very forward request. However, we need to move you both tonight. Your things have been brought but your vehicle will remain here, lest we raise suspicion."

The ride across town was everything they missed. The cool night air was the most refreshing part, but the city lights glazing passed the car were a sight the two wished they could focus on. A lively nightlife for a chilly city known for its cold seasons.

In the back seat sat the unspoken Ayale, head filled with worry as to what else could go wrong now that they were out of their prison.

Osiris sat in equal silence. The possibilities were endless. While their newfound freedom had been sought after for so long, he was barely ready for anything to come their way. That didn't stop him from stealing a glance every now and again, wondering what else he could do to comfort them, until he felt a cold hand slide into his. He didn't dare look down but tightened his hand around theirs.

Soon after stopping in front of one of many identical apartment buildings, the two were escorted into a tiny, third floor apartment with only their backpacks in hand, one somehow smaller than the cell they were just released from.

It was the strangest of times, the most questionable of their whole journey.



Eines would have preferred the call of death than to wake up. Last night's tears stained her cheek, crying before and while she slept, too.

The next attempt at removing her affinity had been scheduled for the evening. Her hands crackled at the memory of the last try, the bodies scattered around her burned into her mind. In her flashback, Eines felt a stronghold in her veins, one that wanted to cling to her affinity. Since the initial attempt, she had found herself questioning why she should allow this. Perspective had changed her once Belire had told her what she needed to hear.

After all, why should she lay down and die just because their father asked her to?

Eines sat up in her bed and wiped her face with her palms, feeling the salty residue linger on her hands before patting them clean on her comforter. Her head pounded with a headache, eyes burning in their sockets. The day had come and gone, time itself no more a concept than the ever-shifting clouds. But the pulse in her head propelled her forward, and against her better judgement, Eines followed the feeling. She left her room in her bed clothes, clad in a matching set of green with little red flowers.

Barely awake, she shuffled down the long, dark hallway, passing by closed doors that had once belonged to each family member of the founding Matxha family. One had been her mother's, the next belonged to Hied, the last one being Belire's. The simple hall had only a dark green on its walls, a minimalist painting of grey lily flowers on the wall between doors. The floor had been hard and cold, but the bare hardwood didn't bother her after her first few steps. The large, antique casement windows that passed her by showed the inclement weather outside hadn't been opened in years, the gold trim covered in dust.

When she reached Belire's door, every one of her knocks were received with silence. She sighed a few swears to herself, her voice muddled with frustration. Eines left the hall, proceeding towards the elevators at the other end of the hall. Her goal was the highest floor, one she didn't dare go to unless she truly needed to find her brother. If he was anywhere, he was likely in one of the offices on the top floor, where the functions of the Matxha clan occurred.

At her exit, Eines looked around the new hall, noting the silence around her. Odd for the operational floor of an entire clan. No guards had been around, nor soldiers. While strange, she carried herself forward, her eyes on the office all the way to the end. Almost identical to the housing floor of her family, she carried forward, only peering at the heavy clouds outside the windows for a small glance. Just before she could get to the door, a familiar voice yelled out, a sudden slam following her father's muffled words.

The next few minutes were a blur to Eines.

As far as she could recall, she entered the room, saw blood splattering the floor from the entrance of the clan leader's office towards his desk. Her eyes darted up, her brother's body crumpled in the corner of the room, him being the source of blood. The claw marks on the carpet matched his bloodied fingertips, his green collared shirt laden with red.

Eines looked up at Hied, only seeing a target.

The next thing she knew, it was on her, too.

She ran towards Hied, jumping up and grabbing his neck from behind while he was distracted with Belire. With his neck in her hands, she tightened her grip on his throat, twisted, and let the energy in her chest spill over, mixing in with her adrenaline. She let her electric currents split into his neck, spreading into every part of his body as if it were blood in his veins.

The body of the Matxha clan leader convulsed, until he no longer struggled against her hands.

Hied would be the first of many bodies surrounding Eines.

Eines dropped Hied to the ground, letting her hands fall to her sides. Her sleepwear covered in his blood, her disappointed expression remained unchanged before kicking him, just to ensure he was truly dead.

She heard a shuffle from the corner of the room, running over to Belire's side. "Why did he try to kill you?"

Belire forced himself to sit up and pulled Eines into his arms, his hands unable to stop shaking.

Eines hugged her brother back, never once regretful of her actions. "He won't hurt you, I-I made sure." Her voice quaked, feeling Belire crying on her shoulder. "That's what matters, he's gone now."

"I tried to talk him out of the removal." He muttered, sniffling and trying to desperately control his tears. "I can't run this clan, I can't do this, Eines. These people will eat me alive. What the fuck are we going to do?" He began to hyperventilate, panic in his voice.

Eines let out a shaky breath, the drive to live hitting her once more. Relief was the first emotion to wash over her, more prominent than nonexistent guilt telling her what she had done laid behind her. "If that's all you're worried for, I will run the Matxha clan." She said in a quiet voice, pulling back to face her brother. She wiped his tears with a bloodied sleeve, a solemn look in her glowing eyes, colored a muddled yellow. "May the gods have mercy on our enemies, Belire, because I will not." Eines pulled her brother back in her arms, a new resolve flowing in her veins.

Eines soon called for a meeting in the very same room where she murdered Hied, leaving the Matxha clan leader's body in the middle of the floor, and announced her new role. Anyone who opposed was promptly disposed of in the same manner, while others were welcome to join the rest of the bodies in the basement.

# XXIII

By the time the group arrived at the apartment building, Ayale hesitated before walking into the lobby, surprised to make eye contact with Teryn, of all people. Osiris, having tasted freedom for the first time in days, didn't mind for the most part and simply waved at Teryn. The idea of being outside the prison was enough for him.

But Ayale couldn't say the same. The two walked through the lobby, making their way up the winding marble stairs behind two of the most awkward men they had ever seen before.

Visu walked beside Teryn, struggling with maintaining his composure.

Teryn made sure to keep his distance, even going as far as to walk slightly faster to stay ahead. It was clear he wasn't entirely enthused with the situation. The look of conjured silence left everyone quiet and unwilling to break the airy tension.

Everyone except for Osiris. "These stairs seem to go on forever." He huffed as he walked up closer to Ayale, who was too busy surveying the old apartment building as they went.

"Elevator breaks a lot, and I would prefer not getting stuck in one tonight," Teryn joked, though his pointed words were not meant for humor. "Here we are!" He said, arriving to the middlemost door of the third floor. He fumbled for his keys, but when Visu moved forward to help him look, he stepped away in the same breath. Once the door was unlocked, the two led them into what felt like a micro apartment. A single bedroom to the left, a living room across from them with a short couch against the wall that separated the remaining tiny kitchen behind it. The bathroom to their right, and that was it for their tour. To some relief, a small balcony area stretched just a bit beyond the kitchen and connected with the living room. Though space was limited, Teryn made use of every inch.

Plants made up most of the corners and shelves that lined the walls, some towering over while others were fresh propagations.

Neither Visu nor Teryn tried to interact with one another unless necessary, a sign to Ayale that they were still barely on speaking terms since the breakup at the Oolonxg compound.

Osiris on the other hand remained oblivious, enamored by the plants and overall, having the time of his life. Ayale wished they could be half as carefree.

"I know it isn't much, but the couch is a pull-out." Teryn walked over to the living room, pulling off one of the many succulent plant shaped pillows.

Osiris gazed in awe. "I want ten of these, I love them so much." He picked them up and held them in his arms, before Ayale moved to his side and plucked it out of his hands, lightly squishing it with their fingertips.

Teryn perked up. "I'm glad you like them! I said the same thing, then I realized I was an adult who could make his own choices and bought a few!" Teryn smiled brightly, handing Osiris another couple of the plant pillows. Osiris tried to hold onto them, but struggled and let one tumble off the couch, which Visu promptly picked up.

Visu held the plush in one hand, recalling the day Teryn spotted the plant pillows. He remembered watching Teryn struggle to carry them all, and how willing he himself was to carry the massive bag up the stairs afterwards. All while Teryn gave him words of encouragement for the daunting task.

Ayale looked over at Visu, watching him freeze up like a statue. They stepped over to him as the other two messed with the couch-bed mechanism and talked amongst themselves.

"You okay?" They mouthed, not letting more than a tinge of voice spill out.

"No." Visu muttered his reply. There was no way he could be after the scene that was made in his office just days ago. "I'm grateful he responded to any of my texts. This wasn't easy to pull. I was sure he was going to tell me to rot in hell. But he somewhat accepted the idea of this temporary placement."

Ayale stared at Visu. "Are we safe here?"

"Teryn would never endanger a soul. Leverage, however, may be a problem for me in the future."

"You're making the prison cell sound safer." They raised their brow, suddenly wondering if this was a bad idea. "Do you mind if we talk tomorrow, one on one? I have some stuff I want to go over with you."

"Likewise." Visu nodded. "We can meet at Teryn's job in the late afternoon. It's the only restaurant down the road, not very far from here."

"Ayale, come see the goldfish tank!" Osiris excitedly said, eyes wandering to every fish in the tank nearest the border wall that separated the kitchen from the living room. Many of the fishes were small, colored in neon primary colors, with a few handfuls of black and gold goldfish made the rest of the fish population. Teryn peered over from behind Osiris, his eyes piercing into Visu. The tension was clear as day, leaving Ayale to wonder why Teryn would agree to hide them at all. The faster they learned why, the better they would feel about the two of them being there.

By the time Visu left, it was far past midnight.

Teryn left both Ayale and Osiris to themselves, giving them the usual 'my home is your home' line.

Ayale turned on the stained-glass lamp that sat on the adjacent side table, its dim light still emanating warmth. The bulb from it likely meant for the ferns and oddly tall snake plant in the corner that adorned the wood floor.

"Are you alright?" Osiris asked, placing an arm across their shoulders so casually, Ayale stared at his hand on the other side, wondering if this was the first time this occurred, or if their adventure was so hectic, they just never registered his behavior before now. Their reaction must have been far too obvious because he shifted back, patting their shoulder before his arm went back to his side.

"A lot's happened to us the last few days so let me know if you need someone to listen or talk to. Or someone to point out the cute fish again." He smiled at them, looking at the tank to the right wall. Ayale nodded, watching his vision bounce from the fish to the flora that thrived inside the tank. They knew better than to be fooled, he was more interested in those plants than the fish.

They sat at the edge of the bed, suddenly more awake and nervous than before. They looked at the space on the bed, and for both to share that space was nothing less than terrifying to them. They grabbed and held onto the pastel green succulent plush, occasionally squeezing it with all their strength. It wouldn't be their first time sharing a space like this, so why were they so nervous? They had shared a sleeping space together since they left Densriel.

Osiris walked into the tiny bathroom, giving Ayale a moment to pull themself from whatever was causing their heart to beat so hard. They tried to focus on steadying their breathing, on the pillow in their hands, on every plant that seemed to fill the space in the living room.

Until Osiris walked out and seated himself far too close once more. "Are you sure everything is okay? You're spacing out a lot."

"I'm tired, I think." They excused, thinking maybe their struggle stemmed from being stuck in the cell the last few days. "Or I need something to keep me occupied. One of those." They groaned. By now, the clock struck well past 1 am, making their sudden anxiety that much worse.

"Do you want to go out with me tomorrow? Maybe take a day to explore the neighborhood?" He asked, laying back in the bed.

"I have a meeting with Visu in the afternoon at Teryn's job. Besides, I'm not too sure he would appreciate us wandering around during a time like this." Ayale slowly mimicked his movements and laid back as well, hugging their edge of the bed. Their arm still brushed up against his, though he didn't seem bothered in the slightest as they both stared up at the apartment ceiling.

"Where do you want me during your fun trauma bonding session?"

"Don't call it that!" They slapped his arm, hearing him snicker. "We might be descendants of clan leaders but give us some dignity. If anything, he's far worse off than me. I got away, even if it wasn't forever. Visu didn't get that chance."

"Do you feel bad for him?" He asked, stretching an arm under the back of the pillow he laid on.

"I guess running off might've been both for me. But still…" They trailed off.

Osiris brushed his hand next to theirs, taking their attention away. "Want to practice your pitch with me first?" He turned his head to look at them.

"What?"

"Aren't you going to convince Visu to overthrow his father?" His hand moved away but his arm remained beside their own, feeling their skin prickling where their contact remained. They tried to move theirs away but felt no more room for them to take up without contact of some sort.

"I-I don't know, I'm really confused, Osiris. I'm sorry." Their words flooded out like a river, overstimulated by the cramped space.

"Aya, you're worrying me." Osiris said in a soft voice. "I don't think I've heard you talk that fast before."

Ayale breathed heavily, squeezing the plush in their hands, struggling to get their thoughts in order. They weren't sure where the words came from, nor could they distinguish any one thought from another. From the moment they met Visu, there had been an internal dialogue inside of them, of what was supposed to be right and wrong, of regrets and a mixture of feelings from all sides. From Osiris and Visu to their parents, feelings and emotions were more than abundant; uncertainty, guilt, and fear being the most prominent.

"It was like looking in a mirror of what could've been. Well, of what can be. If I stay, both of our lives are at risk. If we go back to Cxai territory, it's instant death to everything I ever built. Of everything and everyone I've ever cared about, of everything I am now. I'll never see anyone again, I'll never be able to be myself again. This is a lot to accept." They breathed out, feeling their chest tighten. "What if Visu is just as scared of his father, how can I convince him to overthrow a clan leader when I can barely convince myself to go home?"

"I think you're getting a bit too overwhelmed by all of this. Why don't we take a few deep breaths together?" He suggested.

Ayale's eyes snapped shut, their voice lowering. "What if Teryn is the one to kill us?"

"Alright, conspiracy theory time is over, we don't have enough information to continue thinking like this."

"Osiris, I can't even think straight, let alone control it," They felt stuffy in the tiny apartment, squeezing the ever-loving life out of the plush in their arms, audibly unable to catch their breath. "My head feels funny."

"You're having a panic attack," Osiris quickly stood from the bed and took their hand, pulling them away from the bed. He led them over to the balcony area and sat them down carefully in a plastic white chair. Osiris let go of their hand and rushed back inside to grab a water bottle from the fridge to bring outside with him. He kneeled in front of them, rubbing their back for comfort.

Ayale breathed unevenly, trying to hold back the burning feeling in their eyes. They hated crying and worked hard to make sure they didn't let their tears fall. Every time they cried as a child, they always remembered the look of disappointment in both their parents' eyes. Their father once distinctly said to them it was a sign of weakness, something no self-respecting Cxai should ever do.

"He was right, I am fucking weak." Ayale whimpered between breaths, their attempt to hold back tears futile from here on.

"That's a lie and you know it. Whoever told you that isn't here right now, it's just you and me." Osiris whispered, wiping stray tears away with the back of his hand. "You're one of the strongest people I know." He took their hand into his, their choked back tears turning into full sobbing.

"You're lying, I'm sitting here bawling my brains out like some baby."

"I swore I would tell you the truth, remember?" He half smiled, recalling the time he was called out by Katari in her office beneath Istanza. He shook off the memory, focusing back on Ayale.

They pressed the pillow into their face. "How the hell did we get into this mess?"

"You saved a stranger's life." He felt a semblance of warmth return to his face.

"Osiris, I'm sorry, you don't deserve any of this."

"Yeah? I don't think I deserve someone like you." He chuckled weakly.

"No! You were better off and-and you were right, I should have left you in Istanza. You would have been safer there than going home with me. Happier, too." They wept further into the oversized plant plush.

Osiris bit the inside of his cheek, wondering if what he said in the prison had been misconstrued.

"I'm glad we kept going. I wouldn't want to be in Istanza without you. There is so much left for us to see and I don't want to see any of it without you. I..." Osiris trailed off, feeling his heart pound a little harder. Words were ready to slip out, but he sat still, putting his thoughts together. Every place they ever went together, every glance, every drink, every moment they shared together played in his mind.

Osiris almost said something he shouldn't have.

"I'm glad you're still here." They said, peering up from the pillow, tears fizzling out into lesser sniffles.

Osiris glanced up into their glistening eyes, losing himself in the way they looked at him over the pillow. He felt the words string together again in his mouth, threatening to spill out over and over. While he forced the words back down his throat, his focus remained on the current moment, where his only goal was to comfort them. In a way, he was so proud of them. He knew firsthand how difficult it was to share everything, especially for someone like Ayale to show vulnerability so contradictory to their typically stoic nature.

Osiris was happy to be their safe space.

Ayale frantically swiped at their eyes. "I'm sorry for dumping all this on you. That was probably weird to say."

"Not at all." Osiris smiled faintly, wiping away the last tear dripped down to their chin. His thumb lingered, stroking part of their cheek afterward. Their soft skin was warm from crying, even as the cool air hit the two of them. He watched their sad expression fade, the melancholic look barely evident. It was replaced with intrigue, a different thought taking its place instead.

Before he realized it, Osiris had leaned in and pressed his forehead against theirs, finding himself entranced by the look they gave him. At that moment, he wanted to close what little space remained between them. He held their cheek in one hand and their hand in the other, feeling their fingers thread through his own.

"Is everything okay?" Teryn walked out onto the balcony with his plant themed pajamas, ruffled hair, and a yawn. "I heard crying from my room—" His grey eyes widened as he met with quite the scene, with both Ayale and Osiris suspended in place, unable to find words.

Osiris pulled away and stood back up, moving to the edge of the balcony, embarrassed as much as one could be caught in such an intimate act.

Ayale shrunk into the chair, their hands tightening around the pillow as they promptly apologized. "Just a bit of nerves here. I'm sorry if I woke you."

"Don't be sorry, Visu told me about your situation. Clan life can be overwhelming, I've seen plenty of it firsthand." Teryn yawned again, trying to be affirming while ready to fall back asleep. "I hope this isn't too forward, but I think we should all get to know each other better. Let's go on a walk tomorrow, get some coffee before my shift?"

"I would like that a lot, actually." Ayale quietly agreed.

"Osiris?" He looked at the embarrassed man leaning awkwardly against the railing.

He nodded along, barely able to meet his eyes. "Sure, sounds like a plan."

"Perfect. I'm going to go back to bed, but please don't hesitate to wake me if you need anything, alright?" Teryn's gentle smile brought a sense of comfort to the both of them, before turning to go back inside and leaving Ayale and Osiris alone once more.

"We should go to bed, too." Ayale struggled to meet Osiris' eyes, standing and shuffling back towards the pull-out couch. Osiris agreed, quietly making way back to their side.

The two hesitantly laid down in the bed, feeling one another's arms brush up against each other, even as they both tried to give the other some semblance of space.

Ayale fell asleep first, exhausted from their minor breakdown on the balcony. Osiris struggled to find sleep, shifting around uncomfortably until he finally turned inwards. He met with their sleeping face, watching their gentle breathing and the soft rise and sink of their chest. Without a second thought, he moved closer and leaned in, taking the chance he missed earlier. He left a light kiss to their cheek before enclosing an arm around their waist. They only stirred for a moment before settling into his embrace.

Osiris finally fell asleep, dreaming of nothing, but yearning for many more nights with Ayale fast asleep in his arms.

## XXIV

The early morning sun brought Ayale back to the land of the living, unfortunately with only five or so hours of sleep under their belt. They shifted around, noticing they were far over on Osiris's side. Their leg was over his, their head rested against his chest, and their hand flat on his stomach.

They could barely place when all of this started. When they felt him stir beneath them, his hold on their lower back kept them secure on the small bed. While they were certainly comfortable, there was a small part of them that wondered if the two of them should really be this close.

The glimmer of the early morning sun left a view in the room that last night did not do justice. The furthermost wall that lined with plants had sunshine directly on them all sat in the back of the line, closer towards the corner. A large philodendron sat most prominent, at an eye catching six foot tall. Every plant there had clearly been well cared for, a sight that showed Teryn's dedication to his greenery.

Ayale felt their weary eyes roam to Osiris beneath them. He looked so at peace. Looking at him, they couldn't help their wandering eyes on the scars that laid on his face from the night the Matxha clan attacked him. A few scratches healed over close to his collarbone, leaving Ayale wondering if they were from the night of the attack in Densriel or if they were older. His hair had never been disheveled since they met, garnering a touch of jealousy from Ayale, who had to brush their finer hair in the car in order to be somewhat presentable.

Osiris was self-sufficient in most ways, if not all the time, his hair being a prime example. His lochs were always maintained, just like the rest of him, and even if he had an anxiety attack, he managed to look as if nothing happened shortly after.

Ayale felt a small tinge of pain behind their eyes. They spent much of last night crying in front of him. A breakdown in front of someone who certainly didn't need to see it. A feeling of guilt made its way out knowing they unloaded their problems on Osiris. They couldn't take back any of the time wasted on crying, the damage was done.

But their frustration dissolved, recalling how Osiris took care of them throughout their panic attack. They thought about how he spoke to them, his hand on theirs, his kindness and understanding every second.

The moment Teryn came out as Osiris drew closer to them took up space in their thoughts.

Though it was embarrassing for not one, but two people saw them cry in the same night.

But Ayale knew they wouldn't have pulled away had Teryn not come out to check on them.

Ayale suddenly wondered more about Teryn. They were glad to get the chance to know him, anticipating what they could learn, both about him and Visu from a separate perspective. But for the time being, their eyes grew heavy with exhaustion. They placed their head back down on Osiris before letting sleep take them once more. They drifted off again, the lingering feeling of anxiety ringing in their stomach, reminding them of a time long gone.

Ayale felt the tight embrace of Osiris' arms surrounding their whole body. His hands laid flat on their lower back, keeping them both close together. There was no movement or noise, nothing outside of the gentle rise of his chest beneath them.

Ayale shifted onto their side. They were met with his face inches away from theirs, the peaceful expression on him leaving them with a racing heart. While everything was suddenly becoming more complicated as the days passed on, the only thing that brought them peace was no longer being imprisoned behind cement walls. A step forward.

Osiris interrupted their thoughts, running his hands up their back, with one making its way into their hair.

Ayale froze up, unsure what to do with Osiris and his lingering closeness. They ran the back of their hand over the scars that lined his cheek, feeling the warmth emanate from his face. They investigated the fresh scars from Mildred, making sure they were healing properly. As they did so, they felt his face lean into their touch. Though his eyes remained shut, a part of them wondered if he was awake or not.

They pulled their hand back, relieved to see the evidence of that night slowly recovering.

Their goal, first and foremost, was to get him to safety.

Get him to Cxai territory and tackle whatever awaits them at home.

Give up their new life.

Give up their friends and adventures.

Give up Osiris so he couldn't be used as leverage.

Ayale looked at the clock against the wall of the room and squinted, seeing the few minutes after noon. "Son of a bitch." They groaned, stirring Osiris from his sleep. His eyes gradually opened, feeling as Ayale pulled out of his arms and hopped off the bed.

"What's wrong?" His sleepy words came out in a half yawn.

"We were supposed to meet with Teryn this morning."

Osiris struggled to sit up in the small bed, looking over at Ayale, whose groggy but anxious stance left him worried. He tapped the spot beside him to try and get them to sit back down. They hesitantly sat down but rubbed their eyes profusely, anything to force themself to wake up. "We can talk with him later."

"Yes and no, my meeting with Visu is coming up. Which reminds me," They yawned and reached for a hair elastic from the side table beside them, handing it over to Osiris. "Don't bring up Visu to Teryn if you can help it. They're not exactly on great terms, if you didn't notice already."

"Yeah, it's hard not to when the two of them only managed to stare at each other last night."

Ayale recounted the breakup in full detail, managing to wake up Osiris with their tale. To have witnessed the last surviving part of Visu's personal life fall apart was dramatic enough as it was, especially for a runaway from another clan family with their own problems.

As if they summoned him, Teryn entered the apartment, clad in his leather jacket and jade shirt, carrying in a canvas bag and a tray of iced coffees like some ethereal caffeinating deity to the groggy duo on the couch bed. "Good morning, you two. How was the couch, hopefully not terrible?" He grimaced a little before handing off a coffee to each of them. He worried over the two of them having to share such a small space, partially embarrassed over the apartment. Not aware they were used to those circumstances.

"I slept fine." Osiris' sleepy gaze looked to Ayale, who in turn focused on the coffee in their hands.

They felt his stare and decidedly ignored it. "No complaints." Ayale answered quickly.

"I'm glad. I feel like I should apologize, Visu asked me to house the two of you at the last minute and I didn't have much time to prepare. Bet it's still better than that prison cell though." Teryn joked, stifling back a yawn of his own.

"Oh, have you been inside that part of the compound before?" Osiris sat up, asking out of curiosity, Ayale sipping their coffee with equal intrigue.

"You know, can't say I have." Teryn shrugged the question off, heading into the kitchen with the tote bag in hand. Osiris and Ayale shared a look before drinking their coffees in silence.

Some time had passed with the three of them left alone, with no word nor visit from Visu or otherwise. Teryn decided to head into the living room, the warmth of the sun illuminating the apartment, every plant basking in as much of the light as they could get.

"So, a nature affinity, I see." Teryn pointed out, keeping his attention directed on the plants in front of him.

Osiris did a double take, eyes wide with worry. "How the hell did you know that?"

Teryn shrugged, his shoulders settling back with a subtle sigh. "A hunch." Was all he managed to say, a short smile gracing his face. "Takes one to know one, after all." He admitted.

He thought to himself for a moment. "D-Do you have a nature affinity?" He stuttered, too surprised to keep his voice down.

Teryn took the question more as a challenge, the gentle green glow lining his eyes as he took a closer look at the plant in his hands. He shared a glance with Osiris, a knowing smile shared between the two. "I suppose I do."

The feeling Osiris had entering Teryn's home had come to make more sense, knowing the two shared the same abilities. He felt a sense of comfort he couldn't quite place with a stranger he barely knew.

Osiris tried to busy himself with helping Teryn water plants, listening to the multitude of small, conversational stories about his knowledge on gardening and his affinity, limited to what he could accomplish in his apartment. Teryn had explained to him how he discovered the affinity for nature, and how he found his peace in gardening early on in life. After about an hour, instead of listening to Teryn, Osiris occasionally veered off, more than a few times in Ayale's direction, who focused intently on their tiny notebook.

Osiris didn't mean to steal glances so often, but he couldn't help it the times it happened. It was far more than concern that had him sneaking looks, but the wonder of last night. He thought of how close the two of them came to kissing, how they shared a small couch together, letting his mind wander and his heart think for him. For all the times they maintained a strong outward appearance, he couldn't help but be grateful to have seen the other side. After all the time that had passed since the beginning of their adventure, the intimidating stoicism known to be the basis of Ayale's outward look became distant from their real demeanor.

To him, it was an honor to see the complexity that made Ayale so interesting. From their kindness to their strength, and everything in between.

"Still with me or did I finally bore you to death?" Teryn asked, picking up a small bonsai from the kitchen into the living room.

"I'm listening. I take my job as an active listener very seriously." Osiris perked back up from his trance, placing the glass spray bottle in his hands onto a shelf. When he looked over at Ayale on the couch, they didn't so much as move an inch from the last time he checked on them. Their unmoving stare to the page beneath them, they seemed frustrated and perplexed all at once.

Teryn watered his miniature plant with care, watching Osiris' concerned stare unmoving from Ayale. He shook his head, for a moment thinking to himself about where he was at their age, reminiscing about days past. Sneaking around to Visu's, stealing him away after college classes to adventure around the city at night, spending whatever time he could with him.

As of February, Teryn was thirty-four, and unsure how he ended up where was at that moment. Housing two random people on behalf of his ex-fiancé, without so much as a reason outside of 'Wuyi can't know they're here'.

Ayale and Osiris shared some similarities with him and Visu, he thought. Teryn saw a part of himself in Osiris especially. A knowing smirk wrapped around his face before he decided what to do with his newfound assumptions based on the interactions he witnessed occur between the two of them within the last twelve hours.

"Ayale, what are you up to?" Teryn asked, picking up a jade plant into his hands.

"Taking notes, making sure I write down what I want to ask later." They responded, blank faced and still, eyes never looking up.

"I see," Teryn said, having his own uncertainty as to what questions they'll be asking later, wondering if any of their queries will be pointed in his direction. "Want to take a break and help us out over here?"

"I'm all set, and you have Osiris, after all. I think you have enough help to cover three people with the nature affinity beside you." They looked up at Osiris, a barely evident smile crossing their face. He returned it, before tearing his eyes back to focus on the line of philodendron propagations in front of him, a touch embarrassed. "Has he told you about his particular talent for plants?"

"We share the same affinity." Teryn chimed in, Osiris' small smile turning into a glowing one.

Ayale turned back to their notes, an unusual sense of amity taking over the apartment. A day in which no one seemed to focus on the situation surrounding Ayale and the Oolonxg clan leader, but of the company they held. Both Ayale and Osiris felt a sense of belonging for the first time since they arrived in Odania.

For Ayale, it had been worth bargaining with Visu to see Osiris thrive on their first day free from the prison cell.

Teryn and Osiris spent the remainder of the day before nightfall talking amongst themselves. A shared affinity was the best thing that could happen for either of them during such trying times. Among their conversations, one question in particular prompted by Osiris left both Ayale and Teryn frozen.

"How do you know Visu?"

Teryn shifted about, carefully thinking about his next words before they finally left his lips. "I met Visu in middle school. It wasn't until high school that we became friends. In our senior year, I realized I cared more for him than a friend should." He hesitated, a stifled breath leaving him.

"You don't have to talk about this if you don't want to." Osiris said quietly.

"Well," Teryn shrugged his burdened shoulders forward and met his eyes once more. "It would be a shame to leave you on a cliffhanger. One of the reasons Visu and I reconnected is the same reason you were brought here now. Once upon a time, during my time in college, I worked security for the Oolonxg clan."

Ayale didn't move their face from their notebook but intently listened to every detail.

"It was a weird time in my life, working for the clan system. But I made good money, especially when I was placed as one of the personal bodyguards for the son of the Oolonxg clan leader. We spent quite a bit of time together and one thing led to another..." Teryn trailed off, unsure how to finish his story.

For the history that Teryn divulged, Osiris and Ayale learned a good amount of information, including a little bit of background on Visu Vindai, the current standing leader of the Oolonxg clan.

And from the sound of it, where their relationship had started.

"And how did you and Ayale meet?" Teryn didn't dare continue his story after that, instead turning questions towards him, making it clear to everyone in the room that he wanted desperately to change the subject.

"Oh." Osiris thought to himself, trying to figure out the best way to sum up their first meeting. His heart was in his throat, just as it had been that very night in the tea shoppe. The sort of feeling that left him thinking about the night prior. "I met Ayale in their tea shoppe in Densriel. Days later, they would end up saving my life." He said solemnly, feeling Ayale's eyes briefly find him before pulling themself back to their notebook.

As the evening began to settle into the gated city, Teryn walked off to his room to prepare for his shift, the three of them eventually leaving the small apartment together. On the way there, Ayale struggled with more than enough thoughts and worries in their head, wondering if they were truly anxious, if the foreboding sense of being watched was anywhere near real. So much had been going on all at once, they struggled to prioritize or organize their thoughts.

Teryn was more worried for Visu than he was willing to let on, and for some reason, that bothered them more than they wished to admit. Ayale wasn't one to get involved in other people's lives, but they had been the one to offer Visu help in exchange for his assistance in going back home.

After everything they experienced so far in Odania, Ayale had more questions than answers.

How long had Visu been hiding his relationship with Teryn? How long had the two of them tortured themselves existing in Oolonxg society, with the images that others placed upon them?

All of these theories begged a fearful question to Ayale; Can any clan leader have a decent relationship, or are all of them doomed to suffer in some way? Between Katari losing her husband the day they married, Visu losing Teryn just a few days ago, and their own parents' marriage, the statistics for a clan leader's happiness weren't looking so great.

When Osiris' hand brushed up against theirs, Ayale pulled away and placed their hand in their sweater pocket. Neither could so much as look at each other, not until they had arrived at the high scale restaurant where Teryn worked, surprised to see the place with a small line going out the door.

# XV

When the trio arrived at Teryn's job, they were met with a familiar face.

Visu sat in the back corner booth, dressed far more formal than usual. His midnight suit looked freshly pressed, his hair up in a smooth hair bun, not a single strand astray. Ayale wondered if he put that extra effort for their meeting or perhaps for Teryn, whom his eyes followed as he made his way into the back kitchen area.

Before Ayale could walk over to the back of the restaurant, Osiris grabbed their wrist to stop them.

"Everything okay?"

"Yeah. I mean, kind of? Are you sure you want to talk to him alone?"

"I have my notes. I won't freak out like I did last night, if that's what you're worried about. Since I'm unsure where my mother stands with these people, we have to make our own impressions. I decided I would stick to the plan and ask for support in getting back."

"Makes sense." Osiris took his hand back, suddenly embarrassed by the act altogether.

Ayale walked over with Osiris in tow, sitting across from Visu. Ayale felt their own shade of embarrassment, having shown up with puffy, tired eyes and a random maroon hoodie they stole from Lau from their backpack. But if they looked tired, Visu looked exhausted, a similar look in his eyes. He looked far worse off than when they met him a few days ago, his cool demeanor startling and far more depressed.

"Have you slept recently?" Ayale asked, taking the notebook from their pocket onto their lap for reference. Osiris looked over at them, horrified at the question, wondering how they could say such a thing before asking Visu for help.

"We need not go into trivial matters. Let's discuss what we came here for."

"Of course." They nodded, looking at Osiris. "Do you mind sitting at the bar for a bit? Get whatever you want." They handed over a small wallet from the same pocket.

He watched them carefully, a concerning stare meant for only them. "If you need me, please come get me, okay?"

They nodded again, giving him a short smile in response. He held back his respite for the situation, leaving the two alone in the secluded booth, and seating himself at the black marble countertop, its resemblance strikingly similar to the tea shoppe.

"Alright. Let's talk freely now. How miserable are you?" They shot the question directly at Visu, who nearly spit out his drink.

"Excuse me?" He patted his mouth dry with a napkin. "What kind of question is that?"

"A simple one, really." Ayale interrupted. "Clan matters can wait." They didn't show any particular care for how or when they got home. What they wanted to ask was the priority they chose. They felt a strange relatability to Visu, knowing their fates were similar. While their question was far beyond their jurisdiction and absolutely overstepping a boundary of someone they barely knew, it was better than watching Visu suffer the way he did. His family and his job pulling him apart was like seeing what could have easily been their future.

Visu watched Osiris seat himself at the bar. "Why did you send your partner away?"

Ayale leaned in over the table, not allowing any of his words to phase them. "Fuck all this clan bullshit for a minute and be honest with me. What is your personal life looking like right now? How much of your life is really in your hands?" They pulled back, fixing their aching back, genuinely wondering what was left of his life that was within his control.

"This is entirely out of line."

"Would you rather be anywhere else?" They continued. "This can't be what you wanted, right?"

"Ceylonis," Visu said in a low warning.

"Vindai, how much do you think I want to go back home?" Ignoring the blatant threat that came out of him upon hearing their last name, they persisted and matched his energy. "I care so little that I'd rather let the Matxha finish me off, right here and now. Do you know why I'm still going back? Do you think it's because I oh so look forward to being in your shoes, to be someone's punching bag again?"

"I truly don't know." His glare softened, unsure what to make of their mildly suicidal joke.

"You had it right the other day, when we first met." They took out their floral notebook and placed it on the table, maintaining eye contact with the Oolonxg leader. Visu's hesitant gaze shifted to the bar with Ayale's.

Both of them took a glance of Osiris, watching him order from Teryn, with both happily speaking amongst themselves as if they had all the time in the world.

Visu breathed out a long, heavy exhale, solely watching Teryn as he made the other man's drink with no hesitation.

Ayale briefly glimpsed at Osiris.

"I think we both have our reasons to keep going. The reasons to fight for something better. This is no life to live, Visu. I'm sure this isn't what you wanted for yourself."

A heavy sigh escaped his throat, far beyond melancholic as he looked at Teryn once more. He was truly at his wits end.

"What did you have in mind?" Visu asked in a low voice, his eyes remaining fixed on Teryn leaning over the bar, wiping the countertop in front of him.

"A lot. I want a list of everyone you have hired since the start of your leadership, without any chance of your father's influence on their employment. Next, we figure out who still has more allegiance to Wuyi, and those who straddle the line, we can navigate separately, maybe convince them to join Team Visu instead. When a good group of people within the compound are secured, that you are absolutely confident would back you up, you go up and tell your father to step down. Make yourself known as the true leader of the Oolonxg clan."

Visu could already feel a headache forming, and a particular ache behind both eyes. "How are you so confident this would work?"

"I'm not." Ayale closed the notebook, having already memorized their next part of the bargain. "It's a risk for us both. If this falls through, your father doesn't even take you seriously enough to run a country so nothing should come of it."

"But there would still be consequences for me."

"I know. But would you rather be under his thumb and placed into an arranged marriage, where every part of your life is planned out for you? Or maybe you would prefer your fiancé in the hands of someone else?" They tapped the table, watching his face tighten with angst. The gears turned in his head, all the possibilities and considerations playing carefully in his thoughts.

Visu thought of everything put together, thinking if he would be willing to risk turning the tide of leadership all onto himself. Beyond the extra work he would have to put in, there was so much more on the line, but the risk existed whether or not he tried and failed. The plan at hand offered a glimmer of hope, of a future in which he could find some sort of middle ground between leadership and control over his life. To be content would be a step in the right direction.

All he had left to do was reach out and try.

Visu sat back in his seat, receding back into his typical stoic expression as he thought of everything this would mean for him. "Is there any particular reason for doing this? Are you expecting something if this works out?"

"Just an ally, from one hesitant up and coming leader to the other, and some resources to get back home. And one other, very small favor if this all works out." Ayale trailed off, fiddling with the small cream notebook on the table between them. "I want you to keep Osiris here. Give him permanent asylum." They looked up at Visu's surprised stare, nervously tapping the cover.

"Why not take him back with you? I thought you—"

"I have a bad feeling about taking him home. At least here, he would be in a gated capital city, guards everywhere, I don't think the Matxha clan would come for him here. Are you willing to let him stay here or not?"

Visu thought long and hard about this request. Feeling a sense of similarity to their situations, it left him more concerned than before about their collective fates.

"If he agrees to these terms, then yes. Absolutely." Visu nodded, hoping he would not be present for said conversation between the two of them.

"Then it's settled." Ayale reached their hand out, feeling Visu take hold of it, both shaking hands before letting go.

The duo chatted amongst themselves, plotting and planning for the discussion with Wuyi to come. Their collective hope remained on the idea of finding those already loyal to Visu, thinking back from the beginning of his leadership. Ayale knew what groups to focus on for the sway of leadership; their age group. The younger generation greatly outpopulated the older ones, giving the best advantage for Visu to pull together a following.

As the two brainstormed together, they began tossing ideas back and forth on how to collect citizens from all over Odania, should his father decide Visu was unworthy of the role.

At the end of it all, Visu had to confront Wuyi, the most fearsome task to pull everything together. He thought of his father, the man who always made control a top priority in his line of work. There was never a moment in which anything else could come close to the same importance. He had seldom memories where his father was anywhere near pleasant as a human being. While he overworked, Visu took the few free moments he had to see life outside the Oolonxg compound. His time on the outside of the compound left him appreciating so many simple aspects of their city. He was lucky to have made a handful of friends, one of which stayed by his side through everything and more, fated to be far more than a confidant soon after reconnecting.

Visu sat quietly as Ayale went through each component of collecting people within their age range. They wanted Visu to be the change he wanted to see, from a shift in economic structure to a lightened political stronghold on the people within the Oolonxg territory.

During their conversation, Visu found his eyes flutter back to Teryn, watching him run across both ends of the suddenly busy bar, placing down full glasses wherever he stopped. Teryn had never seemed so frantic before at work, leaving a bad feeling in Visu's stomach.

"Hey, I feel really bad, but I need to interrupt you guys for a second," Osiris rushed to the table, sounding a bit panicked. "We kind of need a huge favor." He looked nervously at the two of them, who shared a concerned stare before looking back at Osiris.

"Is someone here for us?" Ayale asked quietly, earning a wide-eyed stare from Visu.

"No, but Teryn's working alone right now, the bar is slammed, and two people just walked out of their shifts."

"And why is that an emergency?" Visu chimed in.

"Teryn needs our help. He can't work both sides alone." Ayale emphasized, staring knowingly at Visu. He silently thought to himself before he realized what they meant.

"What can we do to help?" Visu asked abruptly.

"Teryn said aprons are in the back if the three of us can help him run food and drinks. I know you're more than ready," He looked at Ayale, then to Visu. "But have you ever worked this kind of job before? Know how to take orders?"

"Unfortunately, I have taken orders all my life." Visu grumbled, getting up and heading to the back, taking his midnight blue suit jacket off and tossing it on a back table. They each grabbed a bright blue apron and strapped in for a busy night at Teryn's job.

"Ready to be coworkers for a night?" Osiris joked, nudging both Ayale and Visu.

"As about ready as I am to jump off a bridge." Visu sighed, intimidated by the growing number of full tables. The three agreed to which sections they would take, with Ayale ready to take control as if it were their beloved tea shoppe.

# XXVI

Ayale, Osiris, and somehow Visu, all ran around the restaurant as if it were on fire. It may as well have been, considering the turns the busy night took.

They began by dividing up each part of the dining room into thirds, giving Ayale the bigger portion due to experience, leaving Osiris and Visu to split the rest. The square shape of the general restaurant did allow them to divide sections as evenly as possible, excluding the extended corner by Teryn's bar.

Visu, having never worked retail a day in his life, stood before his first table petrified, overheating, and unsure how to start. He quickly cleared his throat to grab the couple's attention. All he could do was think of the many times he ordered food and work backwards from there.

"Hello. How can I help you?" Visu asked gruffly. His stoic face shrouded over his confusion, speaking lines he had only ever been asked. The couple didn't seem to pay much mind to his awkward interaction as they told him their order, with Visu scribbling it down quickly. He walked by Ayale and Osiris, watching them to see what he could be doing better. He forced himself to the kitchen, trying to keep his eyes off Teryn, but the sound of his voice from across the bar quickly motivated him to keep going.

Ayale hustled as best they could, excitement finding its way in their veins. Once the bright blue apron hit their torso, it was as though they were back at the tea shoppe.

There was no hesitation on their part to help Teryn. They ran around every occupied table, taking orders, running back to the kitchen to drop off food orders first, then to the bar for drinks. Ayale maintained a sense of organization unlike the other two, their renowned retail personality coming out for the first time since Densriel, briefly catching Osiris' attention.

As Ayale dropped off another batch of orders to the kitchen, they watched the only two cooks who showed up for their shift run around stove top coils, ovens, and pans as though their lives depended on it. One man was tall, gruff, and easily the most intimidating of their staff, but also the most careful as he tossed dough into the air. They could have sworn a smile crossed his face when they looked at him. The other man rushing around looked tired, small shadows beneath his eyes. He was thinner, shorter, but sharp and precise in every movement as he cut up various vegetables and tossed them into one of the many frying pans. The sizzle that came after left him with a victorious nod and a small toss of the handle.

Towards the other end of the bar was Osiris grabbing a small circular tray and slowly placing a large order of drinks from the bar onto its grooved surface. He moved just as carefully towards the center of the dining room, going to each table from memory, until he blanked in front of the last one. To his surprise, he was received with patience, something he didn't quite expect. All he knew to do was his best and that's all anyone expected of him tonight. His ability to learn so quickly and the aptitude in which he learned allowed him to go faster than when he started his rounds.

The smile on his face told Ayale he was going to be okay, giving them a sense of relief before they carried a table's worth of drinks from the bar to their back section. Ayale had more than an idea of what they were doing, their only struggle was bringing over large quantities of food orders. For one particular table, they had to walk over an immense amount that they were unsure if two trips were needed. They attempted it alone, almost tipping themself over in the process. The look of struggle scrawled across their face followed with a frustrating groan when they couldn't put everything in their arms.

The bigger of the men in the kitchen put down their work, running around the entryway to help them out. He picked up and stacked plate after plate in his arms. They took the remaining dishes into their hands and hurried behind him. Relief washed over them as they made their way to the bar counter, barely paying any attention to the incoming Visu, until they realized he rushed by them with at least six drinks in his arms and no tray to carry them.

Glass after glass wobbled as Ayale ran after him with a tray, helping him place them down safely before taking the order of the table that was beside him. Visu struggled to keep his balance regardless of the tray, a few of the drinks spilling over the edge of their glasses.

Osiris walked by and saw the impending accident ready to happen, grabbing Ayale from behind, pulling them out of the way of the incoming crash of glass onto the ground where they stood only seconds ago.

Visu looked down at the mess, his face flushed in horror.

Osiris kept Ayale in his arms for a few seconds too long before quickly backing up and rushing off to find something to pick up the glass shards with, hoping he wasn't out of line.

Ayale stared at the glass on the floor but felt a strange panging feeling in their chest, one they chose not to give the time of day. They hurried back towards the kitchen, running past Osiris.

"Are you okay?" Osiris asked as they rushed away.

Ayale refused to look back and continued forward. "Just fine, thank you!"

The night progressed, drawing in more crowds, as nighttime on a weekend tended to do.

Ayale, having fully adjusted to the dynamics of this restaurant, thrived and sped around as if they worked there full time.

Visu tried his best and did everything asked of him. He worked tirelessly, wanting to offset any unnecessary stress for Teryn if time allowed him. But Teryn never seemed to show any sign of overwhelm, and if he did, he certainly hid it well, maintaining a cordial expression on his face.

Visu couldn't help the softness he felt as he watched him work.

Osiris held a similar awe for Ayale, who ran around as a professional in a strange place. He pushed forward, trying to help them as much as possible whenever he had a minute to spare.

By the end of the night, closing time was a saving grace for all the temporary and permanent staff. Everyone collected by the bar counter after locking up the doors. The remaining tasks were quickly accomplished with a pushing group effort.

The most exhausted he had ever been since running away from the Matxha clan in Densriel, Osiris felt his thoughts begin to catch up with him. He wondered what Ayale and Visu spoke about earlier before having to interrupt them, recalling the tense expressions the two shared from where he watched at the bar. He slumped over the bar counter, a small wave of exhaustion washing over him.

"Osiris?" Ayale bumped into his shoulder, prompting a startled uplift from the counter.

"Sorry, I think I dozed off." He yawned halfway, stretching his arms over his head.

Ayale leaned against the bar chair. "Teryn, do you want us to stay to help you close up for the night?"

"You have done more than enough tonight. Feel free to head back to the apartment with my keys." He swept a hand over his warm forehead, pushing his sandy hair back before shooting a knowing stare at Visu that had everyone worried. "Visu can help out with the rest." His eyes poised and pointed all at once. Visu himself simply nodded from his seat at the bar, meeting the knowing gaze back with his own.

Ayale and Osiris stood from their seats, sharing a brief look before saying their goodbyes and heading out the door.

The two were instantly met with the cold night air, refreshing against the heat they experienced throughout the night from their impromptu shift. Ayale didn't bother putting on their jacket, still overheating from all their running earlier. They would be lying if they said the sudden shift wasn't a thrilling distraction from the impending conversation they needed to have with Osiris.

They walked by a fluorescent streetlamp, seeing the infinite apartment buildings, standing almost identical to every other on the block, quickly come into view. Further out in the distant background sat the dark mountains of the gated city, grand and miniscule all at once. From the apartment to the restaurant was barely considered a long walk. A bit relieving considering how tired they were.

Osiris yawned behind them, reminding them of the situation at hand and the topic of conversation they began rehearsing in their mind.

Ayale turned to peer over at him, slowing down to match his groggy pace. The most they knew was he worked retail at some point but had never mentioned working at a restaurant in his work history. A part of them felt bad at how he was thrown in, but another was impressed at how willing he was to help Teryn, someone that neither of them knew for longer than a day.

"How are you holding up?" Ayale moved to his side, looking Osiris up and down, who only groaned in response. "If this was your first time serving, you did really well." They continued, feeling the uneven sidewalk crumble partly beneath them before steadying themself.

He sighed, no verbal response given otherwise.

Ayale placed a hand on his back, encouraging him to keep walking. He looked at their arm and instinctively moved away. They blinked but kept their eyes forward and continued to move down the sidewalk, surprised he shifted away from them. They lowered their hand back to their side before suddenly feeling his hand slip into theirs.

"Do you remember that celebration at your tea shoppe the night we met? It was so much more packed and louder than what we saw tonight." Osiris commented, his eyes falling to the sidewalk, not daring to look at Ayale nor their hands together in between the two of them. "I feel like I'm on the brink of death. Meanwhile, you walk around looking perfect, like nothing happened to you." He laughed off his compliment to them, not daring to look in their direction.

"I can only do my best. Some days are better than others. You haven't seen me in zombie mode."

"I doubt I would change my mind." He retorted as they reached the front door to the complex.

Ayale hesitated in their response, letting the words slip out anyways. "You don't look too bad for someone who just worked their first restaurant shift." They took their hand back as they made it to Teryn's apartment complex and unlocked the main door, letting them both into the dusty foyer and up the old spiraling marble staircase, his heart beginning to beat harder than ever before.

Back at the restaurant, an apathetic Teryn stood idly behind the bar, unsure why he kept Visu, besides for his own selfish reasoning of company. "Rarely do I imbibe on the job, but I think we both deserve a little something after these last few nights." Teryn set up two shots on the empty bar top, sliding one glass in front of Visu, who watched the clear liquid within settle with intrigue. The moment he took the shot in hand was the second it disappeared down his throat.

Teryn observed the other man, his bright eyes dim with unease. It was hard to tell what he felt outside of disappointment and anger, but didn't dare speak up just yet as he thought his next words carefully. He only leaned over the bar, taking down his own drink, refilling both glasses quickly after.

The pair took their second shots in silence, then their third. The nighttime bar held nothing but the muffled noises of the street outside the windows and the distant radio on in the back kitchen. So much weighed on both of them that neither seemed to know where to begin.

All Visu knew was he wanted to be there, even if it meant withstanding Teryn's ire.

Before any words of the sort could leave him, Visu was promptly interrupted. "Let's get out of here, before we get into trouble." Teryn sighed, quickly clearing the counter with Visu in tow, locking up the restaurant for the night.

The walk back was familiar, and yet, all too strange for Visu. Out of habit, he stood far too close to Teryn, reaching for his hand before retracting it back into his coat pocket. His eyes remained on Teryn, except when he turned to meet his eyes, quickly bringing his eyes down to the shoddy work of the sidewalk beneath them.

The tinge of the cold air wasn't enough to cool Visu down. Unsure what came over him, he took off his suit jacket, draping it over

Teryn's shoulders. He walked further forward, trying harder than ever not to look at him as his cheeks flushed with warmth, leaving Teryn on the quiet sidewalk behind him.

## XXVII

The time was far past midnight, though no one took notice.

Ayale stood from the bed setup in Teryn's living room, glad to have the couch bed ready before any more waves of exhaustion could hit them. They wandered over to the tiny balcony area where Osiris stood, leaning over the old metal railing. He took in the sight of the city streets below them, the empty sidewalks lit up only by the faint streetlights and a barely visible moon above them. He was so engrossed in the landscape, he almost didn't notice when Ayale moved beside him, leaning over on the same railing. "I can't believe we got through that shift alive. I thought the night would never end."

"It was fun, in its own way. I've worked in retail before, but never in a restaurant." Osiris felt a smile cross his weary face before taking off his glasses to clean them with his shirt.

"The cooks saved us a few times, too. We should bring them something before we leave here." Ayale yawned.

The moment he heard the last of their comment, his chest tightened. To leave yet another cheerful oblivion to continue towards their final goal was nothing less than frightful. Osiris would have never found a job like serving fun in any other context.

But working with Ayale made the night exciting, thrilling to be alive.

Working beside Teryn, watching Visu hustle harder than he ever did to gain an ounce of his once fiancés' attention. The two cooks that came to their rescue without being asked.

How many more moments like this would they have together before the two of them met their fates?

The chilling mountain breeze brought his attention back to Ayale, whom he didn't dare face with the disappointed expression stretching across his face. Ayale was doing all of this for him. After everything was said and done, would a life of freedom in a completely new place be worthy when he wouldn't have the one person he cared for there to navigate it with?

Osiris bit the inside of his cheek. He knew he wanted to explore these new territories with only one person by his side. At the end of the day, the concept of freedom from the Matxha clan would mean nothing to him if Ayale had to sacrifice their own life for his.

A life beside one another was all he could think about, since asking Ayale to stay in Istanza. His mind wandered, thinking how they could likely afford one of the small apartments if they kept working at Teryn's job. Life in Oolonxg territory wasn't bad, though it would take some getting used to the cold mountain weather. Visu was trustworthy so far, the gates were constantly guarded. The Matxha would never think to look for them so far away, in Odania of all places.

"Do you like it here?" Ayale absent-mindedly asked aloud.

"It took me a while, but it isn't bad. Weird people and perpetual cold weather has me reminded of Densriel. What about you?"

"Good way to put it. I don't entirely mind it here."

"Why do you ask?"

They froze up, shifting their hair to the side while they thought of their response.

"Osiris," Ayale cleared their throat, unsure how to bring up their end of the agreement from earlier. Visu made it very clear that Osiris had to agree to stay before he would let him stay in Oolonxg territory. "Do you want to stay here?"

Osiris turned to look over at them, eyes wide with shock. He almost wondered if he had hallucinated the question, relieved to hear the words. "With you, of course." The answer slipped from his quiet voice in a single breath.

Ayale stood still, blinking from the chill breeze coming from the night sky. They felt his intent eyes on them, his body shifting closer to their own, not wanting to clarify their true meaning. They thought his exhaustion must be speaking for him, convincing themself as much with his quick agreement.

"I meant... without me here. Instead of dragging you back to my territory to deal with my family, you can stay here and start over. Visu is willing to help you settle here and would keep you safe under his asylum. What do you think?" They were straight and to the point, too tired to beat around the bush.

Osiris remained silent, what was a hopeful expression on his face fell into distress. No words left his mouth, no movement, both of which left Ayale terrified of his reaction.

Ayale felt the urge to reach for a cigarette. Instead, they redirected their focus on the street below them, leaning further over the railing and hoping something would catch their attention. Enough thoughts raced through them to power a small town from stress alone.

Osiris went through every emotion in the book. He was startled, terrified, anxious, angry, then sad. Before a sudden calm painted his face when they found his eyes again.

"How about I ask you something and if you can answer me honestly, I will genuinely consider your offer. But I want to know something first." Osiris began, breathing in deeply before continuing. "Do you want me to go home with you, or would it be easier on you if I stayed here?"

Ayale thought for a solid minute about their answer. Whether from the sheer exhaustion of the day or their poor decision making, they knew there was a difference in what they wanted to say and what should be said. The difference between what was necessary and what they truly felt were far too different and required more focus than they had at the moment. Afraid for what fight this conversation could evolve into, they instead shifted away from the topic entirely.

"I should've saved this conversation for another day, why don't we get some sleep? It's probably two in the morning at this point." Ayale placed their hand on his forearm, ignoring every questioning thought making its way into their head. "At least we can sleep in tomorrow, right?"

Osiris pulled away his arm from their hand and straightened his back, taking the moment to think of his next words. He had a small feeling their answer wasn't as straightforward as their question. His gaze never left theirs, their hand awkwardly receding back to their side.

Ayale felt their chest tighten from the silence. They felt instant regret bringing the conversation up after their eventful day. His tired eyes studied them carefully, leaving them feeling as though for a brief moment, he could hear their thoughts. They stood silently, almost as nervous as the night before, trying to find something to say.

"Come on, let's leave this for the morning." Ayale resigned while they tried to lead him into the living room area, but he didn't move.

"Not yet." Osiris said quietly, a half-smile crossing his face. Not once did he look away.

"What are you waiting for?" Ayale asked, matching his quiet tone. The words left them oddly embarrassed, though their stoic face refused to divulge as much.

Osiris carefully took their hand, holding them carefully. He half expected them to pull back, surprised that he was able to hold it again. Before he knew it, he brought the back of their hand up to his lips.

Ayale felt their heart in their throat. "Osiris, you're clearly not thinking straight." Their voice quivered. So much of their being screamed to stop him, to run, to do anything except stand still and let him tear at the walls they lived so comfortably behind.

There was no going back if either of them acted outside of their sensitive dynamic.

"Why do you suppose that is?" He left a gentle kiss to the top of their hand, his heavy-lidded eyes no longer conveying the soft, anxious aura they were used to.

"That is because..." Ayale trailed off, losing the words at the tip of their tongue. They shook their head, regaining a moment of clarity before their flushed face could give away their feelings. "You're making a mistake. You should stay in Odania, it would be what's best for you. You need sleep." They stuttered out multiple excuses.

That would have been more effective had they pulled their hand away.

Ayale turned to pull him towards the living room again, though he did not budge, pulling them back towards him. Both held on to the others' hand, Osiris standing firm on the balcony.

Ayale swallowed hard. "Osiris. Please." They averted their gaze and looked down at the cracked tile beneath them. "Taking you back with me will only make everything harder for us both. At least here, you have a chance to start over. I can deal with the rest alone. There, that's my answer. No need to wait."

Osiris shook his head. "That's a dumb fucking excuse of an answer, if I ever heard any." He retorted softly.

"Excuse me? I'm sorry that I want you to be safe from the Matxha clan and from the psychopaths I call family!" They raised their voice.

"Then why can't you stay here, too? Make it make sense to me! Whether we're in Istanza, Odania, uncharted territories," He squeezed their hand, wishing they would turn to look at him. "I want to be wherever you are, experiencing new things together. You have made all of this exciting and wonderful, all because you're there with me. I need you, far more than any of these clans could scare me."

"Osiris, you don't mean that. We can't—you can't just say something like that." Ayale struggled to keep themself together. In an instant, they let go of him and pulled their hands away. They hesitantly turned and met his knowing gaze, maintaining what little stoicism they had left, their fists tight by their sides.

Osiris stepped closer, adamant against their argument. "Who says?"

"I do!" They spoke defiantly.

Before they could continue, Osiris reached out to touch their face, holding one cheek in his hand. The warmth of his palm was almost the same as their flushed cheeks.

Ayale continued to struggle to maintain their composure. "This isn't a game, this is dangerous for both of us. I can't just...we came all this way. There's no going back. I need to keep going until I get back to Cxai territory. But you, you can't pass up a chance to start over." Their expression fell before they continued, soft spoken. "You can't do this, Osiris."

"Then tell me off." His calm voice was suddenly closer than before. His thumb brushed against their cheek, waiting patiently for words that both knew would never come. "Tell me to go away once and for all, and I'll stay. I'll tell Visu myself in the morning, if that's what you want."

They touched his arm, feeling the soft fabric of his sweater beneath their hand. A part of them could feel their heartbeat in their throat. "All I want is for you to be happy. Safe, unbothered, somewhere to thrive as you are with your affinity and not hide a single part of yourself. That's what I want."

"I am already. I'm happy just to be by your side."

"You don't understand how difficult this journey is going to be. This is nothing compared to what's waiting for me at home."

"It doesn't have to be difficult." He pressed his forehead against theirs. "Let's stay here together, forget going back, and we can start over together."

"Osiris." They pressed in return, no longer able to resist the burning feeling that raced in tandem with their mind and heart. "Please."

"I care too much, Aya." Osiris pulled Ayale forward by their waist, pressing his lips gently against theirs in a lingering kiss, one he never wanted to end.

"I care, too." The quiet words bared against his lips. He leaned in and kissed Ayale with a feverish need, but remained sweet and gentle. His arm wrapped tightly around their lower back, while the other sank to the back of their head, threading through their hair. To his surprise, Ayale cupped his face, kissing him back with such softness, no dream could compare. Every part of him yearned to keep them close, wanting to take in every moment before it was taken from him. His hand traveled up their back and remained there, refusing to part for any reason.

"I can't stay here." Ayale pulled back, their hands less than steady on his warm cheeks.

"Give me one good reason." Osiris kissed their cheek, making his way towards their neck. Ayale struggled to think for a brief moment while he pressed his lips along their collarbone. They felt their breath elevate, every kiss lighting their skin with warmth against the cold night.

"Because everyone is at risk if I stay. Visu is barely functional as a leader as it is, no territory could handle a civil disagreement and invasion, if the Cxai clan decide to come crashing in to look for me. I don't know what my mother is doing, or if she's told anyone I'm on my way back. I could probably keep going."

Osiris stifled back a groan, pulling away from their neck but keeping his hands on their back.

"Didn't expect you to make an actual point when I said that." Osiris grumbled, looking out to the sleeping city streets before looking back to Ayale. He couldn't help the dumb grin painted in exhaustion on his face, one that left Ayale visibly flustered and mildly annoyed.

They dropped their eyes to the ground beneath them. "You're not allowed to make that face."

"Hard not to when you just admitted you care about me." He tilted their chin up, forcing them to meet his eyes.

"I take it back," Ayale's shoulders stiffened. "I hope your next sketch comes out weird and you can't quite figure out how to fix it."

He leaned in and closed the gap between them with a gentle brush of his lips against theirs, watching their annoyed expression dissipate. Though the two were easily giving in to temptation simply from exhaustion, Osiris only wished the night would never end. The curve of their lips brushing softly against his was everything he could have wanted.

A rustle of leaves from the living room caught both of their attention, their heads turning to the source. Ayale and Osiris' eyes widened when they met with not only Teryn's attentive stare as he handled a large philodendron plant, but Visu's as well as he stood by his side, equally invested in the scene happening on the balcony.

With all four parties frozen in place, no one was certain what to do.

Osiris took a moment to wave at Teryn, receiving an awkward wave back with his free hand.

"How was the shift? Was it alright, do either of you need anything, maybe some water?" Teryn broke the silence first, spilling out with words and offers.

"Not bad, it was my first time working in a restaurant." Osiris answered before feeling Ayale slip out of his hands.

"How long were you both standing there?" Ayale asked.

"Not very long at all!" Teryn answered quickly.

"Ten minutes." Visu corrected, earning a scornful stare from Ayale, Teryn beside him, and one of surprise from Osiris. "What?" He asked everyone.

Without so much as a word, Ayale crossed their arms over their chest and moved into the living room, pushing past Teryn and Visu towards the bathroom. Osiris watched as the door shut behind them and held his breath, the reality of his actions finally setting in.

"Do what you need to, we'll be back here if you need us." Teryn watched as everything went down with far more intrigue than before, placing the massive philodendron down, quickly grabbing a nearby teal can to briefly water the plant before he took Visu by the arm, and dragged them both into his bedroom.

"Aya?" Osiris approached the bathroom and lightly knocked on the door. When nothing happened, he knocked again.

A short click followed, Ayale peering out of the thin opening of the door. "That was embarrassing. Did you see Teryn and Visu at any point?"

"I wasn't exactly paying attention to anything else." He admitted, a goofy grin painted on his face until Ayale slammed the door in his face.

Osiris profusely apologized at the door until they reluctantly left the bathroom, walking back to the couch area with their arms crossed, for the two of them to sit down.

"I'm sorry." Osiris apologized again, much more meaningful in his quiet voice. "I really didn't know they were watching." His vision glanced over to the closed bedroom door before finding Ayale.

"Those two need to talk to each other. Clear a few things up." His arm moved to their side, pulling them close. He placed his head on their shoulder and yawned. "I still think we should stay."

"I know you do." Was all they could say, too tired to retort with anything else. They would fight against everything another time. For the night, they leaned against his head, unsure if everything unfolding was a dream or a nightmare. Ayale placed their hand on his arm, which only led him to wrap it tighter around their lower back.

If tonight was all they had left, Osiris felt no sense of regret for his feelings. While he maintained himself alongside a mood disorder, there was no denial for the feelings he harbored for Ayale from the very first night in the tea shoppe. The real reason for his visit being a secret he hoped to never divulge.

All he knew was that he didn't want to lose Ayale. Not now, not when they made it to Cxai territory, not ever. He wasn't sure how, but he held onto that resolve until the two fell asleep during the silence that embedded itself between them.

# XXVIII

Ayale awoke in the midmorning, hoping to avoid all thoughts of the events from the night prior. As much as they wanted to pretend nothing happened, they had trouble trying to pull off such a feat. The once stoic tea shoppe owner was anything but, struggling with their thoughts as they slipped out of Osiris' arms.

They wandered quietly over to the balcony, witnessing the morning rush of folks making their way to work in the chilly daylight. Ayale leaned over the low bearing balcony, arms crossed on the edge of the concrete.

The urge to reach into their bag and take out their cigarette case was quickly overshadowed by everyone's warnings throughout their journey. As much as they struggled to keep their thoughts in line, Lau's own scolding loomed over them, similarly warning them of the dangers if they kept going down this path.

So, there they were. Groggy, stressed, anxious, and worst of all, unable to control replaying the same scene from last night.

And how much they wanted the same feeling again, to render their situation with the clans as nonexistent again, even if just for a second.

Ayale watched a pair of pigeons settle along the electrical lines, sitting close enough to where their wings brushed against one another. The birds reminded them of their time so far, of every moment they spent together with Osiris. From being barely able to be in the same vehicle to sharing even the smallest spaces with one another, no questions asked. Their time together seemed to have lasted forever, as though the two had known each other a lifetime.

They laid their chin on the flat of the concrete and closed their eyes, feeling more the warmth of the sun than the cold breeze prickling their face. The idea of separation once they arrived in the Cxai territory was becoming harder to come to terms with. The words from last night stood true, a mistake having come out of their mouth at all.

The creak of a door behind them inside the tiny apartment had their eyes snap open. They turned their head and saw the unsure and fairly disheveled Oolonxg leader sneaking out quietly from Teryn's bedroom. His navy-blue suit undone, he had a soft look sprawled across his face, fixing his raven black hair thrown to one side. Truly a sight to see.

Ayale and Visu made eye contact from across the silent apartment. In that instant, surprise and instant indifference. A slow nod from Ayale and a flustered stare from Visu was all that made up their quick interaction.

Teryn appeared behind Visu, tired and yawning as he drifted out of the room half-awake towards the kitchen in a pale blue satin robe.

"Did I miss something?" Ayale asked with as much poise as they could muster. Visu's sharp stare pointed at them did not help as Ayale held back the scoff coming up their throat, stifling it into a quick cough.

"No." Visu grumbled, shuffling into the bathroom nearby.

They snickered, but knew better than to say anything that could affect whatever progress occurred between Teryn and Visu last night, if any at all.

They turned back to the crowds of people below them. The noise of the city reminded them how much they missed Densriel. The rushing of tires on paved roads, the overwhelming scent of diesel and bread mixed together and drifting up to the balcony, all of it almost felt like their beloved city, only with a much more dense population. The tea shoppe was nowhere near this close to the capital or downtown as Teryn's apartment. It was unlikely that they could grow used to such an urgent and serious place, only bringing brief relief before the dread set in. The two would leave soon, Cxai territory bound, and in turn, leave another place in the dust of the past.

"Morning." Osiris rolled over on the pullout bed, facing the balcony area where they stood. "How did you sleep?"

"Could have been worse. Better than Visu and Teryn, I bet." They said, looking warily over their shoulder for either of them.

"Did I miss something?" Osiris sat up carefully, trying to follow their line of vision, unsure what they were looking at.

They sat still, barely able to face Osiris after last night. "You wouldn't believe me if I said it."

"Try me." He yawned.

"So," Ayale turned around fully, leaning their back against the balcony. They made sure to speak quietly. "I caught Visu sneaking out of Teryn's bedroom, made eye contact, now I'm half sure he's hiding in the bathroom."

"How are you so sure?" He retorted, but a smile crossed his face regardless.

The sound of the bathroom door opening took their collective attention, revealing a much more kempt Visu sneaking away to the small kitchen area.

Osiris blinked once before readying an apology. "I—"

"Was wrong to doubt me, yes." Ayale whispered quietly while walking over and sat in the small gap of the bed beside Osiris, trying to get a better look into the kitchen. His eyes floated to them as though by instinct. He felt his chest tighten but fought against the all-knowing feeling that tried to take up space. He didn't want to lose the dynamic of trust the two shared together. Yet he still silently hoped their feelings from the night before remained mutual.

On the other hand, Ayale began to actively avoid him after pointing out Teryn and Visu, beginning their search for their bag somewhere beneath the fold out.

"Want to go get coffee somewhere nearby?" Osiris managed to ask, wondering if he could catch their attention.

"Not today. I have to cover some ground I missed yesterday." They said in quick succession, before grabbing their bag and abruptly standing back up.

"Anything you want to ask about last night?" He asked, watching them gather their sweater.

"Nope!" Ayale decidedly walked away towards the kitchen, disregarding his question.

They wanted to do something to push forward, to distract themself from Osiris. Today was not the day they were going to talk about the events of last night. What was supposed to be a serious discussion between two prospective clan leaders cascaded into a sporadic work shift and an unintentional moment of honesty.

Visu and Teryn turned to them, pausing their conversation.

"Let's go down to the restaurant and talk, one on one, no distractions." Ayale directed their request to Visu and before he could get a single word out, they threw on their jacket from the coat rack behind them. They rushed towards the door, and soon enough, was out in the hall by the broken elevator.

Visu stuttered to himself before simply following behind, shrugging to Teryn on his way out.

Both Ayale and Visu sat in the same booth as the night before, with far less people crowding the restaurant so early in the morning. The noise was no less distracting but easier to ignore this time around, with daylight shining through the large, rectangular windows. Ayale looked out their window, watching people pass by on the sidewalk attached. They waited as Visu looked through the menu, only coming to when he placed it down abruptly on the table. "Why did you want to leave so suddenly?"

"I wanted to discuss once more the possibility of backup, in case things go awry at home, in Nalira." They answered quietly.

Visu clutched the side of his head and watched Ayale carefully. "What happened up there?"

"Can we focus on the plan that we have yet to discuss?" They shot a glare at him, prompting him to sink a little against the high-rise red leather on his back.

"Well, as much as I agree, I am equally confused about last night."

"What about last night?"

"Osiris."

The mere mention of his name was enough to leave Ayale visibly frustrated, clear with a blush to boot.

"After the events of yesterday, I'm not sure either." Ayale reluctantly answered.

"Do you wish to talk about it?" While emotions were not his strong suit, Visu had the patience to listen. He owed it to them after the events of the last few nights.

"It was inappropriate and that's all there is to it. I can't kiss the person I'm trying to help," They said, a heavy sigh lifting from their chest. "He keeps looking at me and I don't know what to say to him. Visu, how did you do all of this while you had feelings for Teryn?"

Without so much as a moment's hesitation, he answered. "I did it because I love him." Visu stated confidently, looking down at the near empty table. The words were no less thought than that of waking up in the morning. It was a habit, it was instinct. To Visu, it was love at first sight. "And last night, I took a moment to remind him that those feelings never changed."

"Visu," Ayale couldn't help but smile, knowing after last night that Teryn felt the same. "I hope you find your strength to do what you need to do. It sounds like Teryn is worth the fight."

"I think he is, too. I wish I had known this before he broke up with me."

Ayale leaned in, anxious to hear an update on the two. "What happened with you two last night?"

"I do not think that is appropriate conversation, we are talking about you." He excused in an instant.

"Oh, please. Boy troubles are mutual between us right now."

Visu sharply inhaled at the comment before clearing his throat and composing himself. "I suppose there is truth to that."

"So, what happened last night?" Ayale pushed the topic.

Visu shifted in his seat. It was difficult to get the words out of his mouth, feeling his palms warm up with the growing silence. He wanted to be honest, but to speak of Teryn and him so openly was not a concept he was used to.

"If you are adamant on making this about personal issues, I can say that we had a few drinks before leaving and subsequently, spent the night together. When we came back to the apartment and saw the two of you, I can only speak for myself when I say it reminded me of when we were young, hopeful, and thinking nothing of the future, but always of one another. At that moment, we were those same people once more. Anything that happened in between those realizations is...personal." He finagled the last word before drinking up one of the teacups set down on the table. The two collectively agreed to order a plain black tea, one very popular in their region. Ayale's eyes widened as they read the inner context of his words, the furrowed brows and avoidance lining his pale complexion, slowly realizing what he meant.

Ayale pulled their hair out of their maroon sweater and over their shoulder. "Wow."

Visu's eyes flickered up. "I didn't expect for us to speak of personal matters at the meeting you called for, but here we are."

Between the few minutes of silence, they drank their tea, watching as people passed by outside the window beside them.

"It's nice to know you're in a similar situation." Ayale looked up at Visu, feeling a similar sense of comfort. "I've never had someone who could understand the clan upbringing and everything that came with it. The expectations that are set for us the second we're born. Talking to you gives me anxiety but it also makes me more relieved than I've been in a long time." Ayale took the two menus from the table and set them at the edge. "Don't get me wrong, I would absolutely prefer not to go home."

"Why go home at all?"

"I can't keep running. Inner sense of responsibility. It's no longer just my life on the line." Ayale played with the spoon in their drink, thinking not only of Osiris, but of Lau and Rae back in Densriel. Had they not left, the Matxha clan could have easily taken the others, accusing them of being accomplices for their own crime.

"Does Osiris see the situation the same way?"

"I would imagine so. We went on the run so he wouldn't die, after all. Why else would he just let some random person drag him across the continent? For fun?"

"Perhaps not at first, but to him, maybe the severity of the situation has dulled." Visu slid his phone out from his pocket, checking the lock screen before placing it back. "I think with that, something grew in its place. Clearly for both of you." His brow rose at the last comment, averting his eyes as he brought his teacup to his lips.

Ayale's frustration grew. They wanted to fight and question his theory but remained quiet. Visu didn't lie, there was certainly something there. Something that shouldn't be but nonetheless persisted.

They stared back out the window once more and tapped their fingers on the linoleum lined table, annoyed that their clouded judgment left them in another unusual predicament. "What do you suggest I do from here?"

"I don't know. I am still learning that for myself." Visu answered. While confusion was not something he would typically admit to, his confidence in Ayale was well founded. "Plans change, life isn't always linear. There is no shame in learning new things about yourself, no matter your age. Take that however you will."

"Did I do something wrong?" Osiris held tightly to the massive fern plant in his hands, barely able to see Teryn between its thick leaves.

"That depends. Feelings are fickle, kind of like our plant brethren here. Give it too much water and you'll drown it. Give it too little, it'll dry up and crumble." Teryn shifted his collection of colorful clay pots around, making space for Osiris to place down one of the larger plants. "You asked a lot of Ayale, staying in Odania is not an easy task. Not after everything they risked keeping you safe."

Osiris sucked in a sharp breath, realizing Teryn and Visu witnessed the scene from the start. The words weighed heavily in his chest, guilt panging in tune with his heart.

"I thought it would make things easier for them."

"More like it dismissed the work they put in so far." Teryn grabbed a glass spray bottle from a high up shelf, pointing it at the small collective of various plants. He carefully watered each plant, feeling the soil for moisture levels. Even after the harsh truth that came out of Teryn's mouth, he maintained a tempered smile across his face. "Your heart was in the right place. But don't forget that their mission isn't just to take you home. They have lots to confront when they get there." Teryn said, the knowledge having been clearly informed to him by Visu.

Osiris felt the weight of his words in a different light. One much more unsure. "What if I say something wrong again?"

Teryn turned his back to the plant, going towards one of the shelves full of smaller scale vials of propagations. "Give them some space. I believe that both of you have some thinking to do." Teryn said quietly, the comment taking space in Osiris' thoughts. He felt worse than before but knew it needed to be said.

Osiris needed to make things right, though he wasn't sure how.



Day turned into night, the four of them in the apartment once more. Under the soft lights that scattered about the apartment, Ayale and Osiris prepared for bed once more, neither entirely sure what to say to one another. And so, neither said anything, tending to their own personal things as the night wore on, side by side on the pullout couch. Ayale wrote in their small notebook, while Osiris sketched silently to himself.

His eyes wandered over to them when they seemed Ingrained enough in their notes, wanting to cease the collective partition of silence between the two of them. He stole a handful of glances, thinking to himself how to approach the topic that he and Teryn spoke of earlier.

Teryn and Visu took to cleaning up the kitchen together, though their silence was anything but uncomfortable. Their mutual stolen glances from the heart, occasionally exchanging memories, reminiscing of their younger days. Teryn had always held up their conversations, just as he did now, while Visu patiently listened to every word to come out of his mouth, losing himself to the soft voice he missed more than he realized.

Visu missed far more than just his voice. He missed everything.

In that split second, a decision was made for him.

No longer did he want a life made out for him, but one he led himself, with Teryn by his side every step of the way.

As Visu peered down at his suit pocket, the glimmer of the gold chain took his attention, before returning to Teryn's newest hyper fixation.

In the other room, Ayale and Osiris went to bed, without so much as a word to each other.

The next morning rolled around, the silence between Ayale and Osiris thick with tension. After what happened on Teryn's balcony, so much was still left unsaid, emotions running high. Every time Ayale so much as glanced at Osiris, he served as a constant weight in their stomach that they had done something wrong. There was no regret in their words. Yet, they could not get it out of their head that they had acted selfishly.

Before Osiris could awaken, Ayale promptly left the bed, relieved to see Visu had spent the night again as well. They quickly pulled him outside onto the balcony with coffee in hand, ready to discuss their journey home. The two of them sat down in the plastic chairs, leaving Ayale semi excited to talk about clan drama.

Until Visu had come out with his plan to confront Wuyi, calling him for a one-on-one meeting as soon as possible.

"You did what?" Ayale asked in a low whisper, lowering their voice when Visu worriedly looked around the apartment, hoping no one else was listening in.

"I set up a time to meet my father. It is highly overdue, I need to take responsibility and assume my role, take full control as leader of the whole Oolonxg territory from his hands. This way of life as it stands now will not and cannot keep going this way," Visu leaned into his hands, elbows propped onto the arms of the chair. It felt as though speaking the words alone put into motion the next set of events for him. "It's now or never, Ayale." He exhaled, shifting uncomfortably in his chair. The thought of confrontation was a stressful concept, one he didn't particularly want to deal with, let alone put his words into action.

The two drank their coffee side by side, watching the Incoming, thick grey clouds appear over the other hillside apartments all along the street around them. The air was certainly warmer than the days prior, but the sudden humidity had the city in a chokehold of moisture and a slow decline in sunlight.

As the two watched the morning light dim from the tiny balcony, Teryn's subtle yawn had caught their collective attention, causing both Ayale and Visu to turn around.

"Morning, you two. Want me to make anything?"

"No need," Visu put his hand up, waving off the suggestion. "I made coffee already." He peered over his shoulder, a softened look crossing his face when seeing Teryn's tired smile pointed at him before he walked off into the kitchen.

Ayale stood up from their chair and leaned on the concrete balcony wall, letting the warm breeze distract them for however long they could achieve. They felt a short smile grace their tired face, a sense of pride giving way to hope for the first time since they began their journey back to Cxai territory. "If anyone can do this, it's you." They yawned, taking a sip of their coffee, no longer bothered by the heat of it. Their confidence wasn't based on much, but they felt it to be fact. They were confident in his abilities to be the next Oolonxg clan leader.

Visu kept his tired sapphire eyes over the incoming stormy horizon, a simple but oddly genuine smile making itself known. "As do I." He muttered under his breath, taking in the warm air into his lungs.

Visu's phone began to vibrate in his pocket, causing him to stiffen up before taking it from his pocket to glance at the small screen. "If I do not return, take Teryn with you to Cxai territory. But if I do not try to take control of my position, then I am unworthy as a leader altogether." He placed the phone back in his pants pocket, he rose from his seat with a steady yawn. "I hope we speak again soon, Ayale." Visu motioned past Ayale without any regard for their dumbfounded reaction to his request and made his way over to the kitchen, standing behind Teryn, who had been pouring himself coffee. He pulled him in by his waist and rested his chin on his shoulder, closing his eyes with a long exhale.

"I am truly sorry for everything I put you through the last ten years. I could never ask for your forgiveness, but...know that I would do anything to keep you safe." Visu tightly embraced Teryn, as if it were going to be the last. "You make all of this worth it. You always have, Teryn." Visu's arms tightened around him, breathing deeply before letting go. He walked over to the door, feeling Teryn's gaze on him. He looked back and flashed a quick smile at him as Ayale joined Teryn in the kitchen, only partly confused as to what was going on.

"Ayale, remember our deal." Visu pointed to Ayale, his expression looming ominously before leaving the tiny apartment, closing the door softly behind him.

"Soon." They nodded as they repeated his words, more to themself than anyone in particular, silently retreating outside once more.

The wind coming in from the balcony whipped wildly through the stems and leaves of all the plants outside, the rustle of shifting flora and a soft howl between buildings grabbing their attention back to the darkening sky.

Teryn's line of vision wandered back to Osiris, who slept almost too soundly on the couch. He didn't want to think about Visu and his apology, nor the abrupt goodbye he left him with, nor even the strange 'deal' he spoke of in Ayale's direction.

In fact, the mere seconds of remembering those things were overwhelming, the worry instant and measuring out a far distance. He stood still with his plain black mug in hand, feeling the quick acceleration of thoughts and heartbeats take over. Teryn didn't like letting these sorts of things show, and so, straightened his back, taking a mere sip of coffee as if nothing were bothering him.

He breathed in, watching the rain begin to drip gently onto his plants outside. At least he didn't have to water them today, he thought.

Ayale moved back inside, meeting Teryn's tiresome gaze. They knew better than to try and bother him after Visu's mild dramatics, so they bee-lined for the living room instead, taking their coffee with them to the couch next to a very groggy Osiris, who struggled to open his eyes on the low bearing couch as they sat down. He peered over to where his glasses sat, noticing Ayale's troublesome expression, unnerved from events he slept through. It was easy for him to assume they were upset at him, having slept through the majority of the morning's events.

Osiris wanted to reach out and touch their arm but found himself unable to move without second guessing everything. "Can we talk for a minute?" He struggled to ask, feeling himself become shifty with unease.

Ayale's line of sight remained on the windows as they nodded, silently agreeing to his request. Osiris fidgeted with his glasses, making sure to leave space between him and Ayale as he sat upright. He wondered if they had any lasting regrets about the night before, a part of him unsure if he could handle hearing as much if they did.

Ayale sat at the very edge of the bed couch, almost risking falling off if they moved any further away.

"What did you want to discuss?" Ayale shifted their eyes towards the bright fish tank across from them.

"Nothing, actually. It isn't really a discussion, but more of an apology. It seems like I keep doing the same thing, over and over again." Osiris replied in a timid way, looking down at his hands. Ayale's glazed over eyes took to one of the chubbier goldfish, allured with the tank itself now that they truly stared at it.

"It's not easy going back home to confront everything you left behind. And it probably doesn't help every time I make a comment about us settling somewhere...permanently." He hesitantly added. "I want to support you properly since you've done so much for me, and that wasn't the way to do it. Running away from our problems isn't the answer." Osiris looked out at the balcony, watching the thick clouds begin to pour rain over the city.

"I want to ask something, if you would amuse me for a second." Ayale placed their hands into their grey sweater pocket. "Would you want to stay here if given the option?"

"No." He immediately responded, a tense, if not mildly appalled look stretching on his face. "Absolutely not, not without you here." He reiterated, making sure his point was properly made.

"Just in case. I want you to know that it's an option for you if you change your mind."

"Then if it isn't clear enough, I refuse to let you go home alone. We started this together, we will end this together." He said, adamant to make sure they knew he wasn't willing to leave them to go back home by themself.

Teryn walked out of the kitchen, eyes fixed on his cellphone before looking up to the pair on the bed. "Very touching, but for now, neither of you are going anywhere." Teryn turned his screen over to Osiris and Ayale, both sharing a worried look.

"Is everything okay?" Osiris got up from the couch and looked down at Teryn's outreached phone. When he locked eyes on it and scanned the screen quickly, it seemed like he had to read it a few times before realizing what he was reading.

Osiris couldn't bring himself to say anything for a few minutes, his worry so honest and apparent that even Ayale was beginning to feel their stomach turn.

Ayale darted back between both men, impatiently waiting for someone to speak up. The only response that came out was Teryn's tired voice. "Visu went to meet with his father and two Matxha clan representatives were there. He isn't sure why they showed up, nor if there are any others roaming Odania," His eyes narrowed and his hand swept over his tired face, yawning a gentle obscenity beneath his breath. "We need to stay put for some time, meaning no work for me and no moving for either of you. Visu says he will come by when the dust settles and or if they leave." His voice strained, clearly concerned for Visu over everything else. "If either of you need me, I will be in my room." Teryn gingerly made way over to his room, inadvertently slamming the door behind him, and leaving Ayale and Osiris to process everything on their own.

The uncertainty surrounding the Matxha clan's sudden appearance in the Oolonxg territory settled within them both, the airy silence bringing nothing but possibilities and fear. The muffled noise of the thunderstorm outside was all that was left, with rain violently hitting the glass windows.

Osiris sat quietly beside Ayale, wanting to bring any form of comfort for their overactive brain. There was nothing either of them could do to change this waiting period.

Ayale spent the better part of a half hour drifting off, their eyes glazed over at the storm outside. Osiris opted for his sketchbook, letting the storm pass over the two of them.

The only way anyone could spend their time during lockdown.

# XXX

The moment finally came for Visu and Wuyi to talk, readying himself to take a step forward in the role that he had been preparing for all his life. During the walk over to the Oolonxg clan compound from Teryn's apartment complex, Visu found himself scrolling through photos of himself and Teryn that made up his entire phone gallery.

While he wasn't one to be particularly sentimental of physical value outside of his necklace, Visu enjoyed taking photos. He made sure to always snap a picture or two, regardless of the time of day, so long as he was with Teryn. These moments were tangible evidence of his affections, memories he could reflect on whenever he needed. Every photo instantly replayed a different memory in his mind, bringing him back to a moment where he experienced peace or joy, existing outside of the clan he had been born and raised within.

The pressure of meeting with his father held nothing to the risk of losing Teryn forever.

As he wandered the streets of Odania, Visu found a sense of necessity, of confidence in himself long overdue. Nothing had empowered him more than the clarity surrounding his need to take back control of his life.

Crossing the busy street, Visu through a small crowd of folks, making his way towards the large compound he called both home and work. He didn't feel as much hesitation surrounding his upcoming demands, straightening his back as he made sure to look the part of a leader. Just as he made it into the building, the rain began to lighten from its ferocity, turning into a drizzle instead.

Visu had shown up into his father's office assertive, ready to make his case to become head of the Oolonxg clan, without his constant hovering. It was overdue for him to take the full role of leadership from his father.

Wuyi awaited him inside Visu's office, across from his desk in a midnight blue suit that rivaled Visu's, his focused black eyes on his son. Though the suit had been far older than Visu himself, the ensemble remained in pristine condition. Neither regarded the small setup of pastries on the otherwise empty desk, a small peace offering between both parties.

Visu crossed over to his desk, a confident look on his face as he regarded his father. "Wuyi."

"Visu," He nodded briefly before taking his seat on the black leather chair. "What is the urgency to call me back into the city so abruptly?"

"Quite a bit, father." Visu stated, seating himself last. "There is much to discuss. I believe there are conversations between us long overdue." He said, maintaining his impassive expression on his father.

Wuyi nodded, cautious but ready to listen.

While talking between the two had begun slow, conversation started to slowly pick up. Awkward stares at one another were no longer, and words flowed easier between the two of them.

But Visu barely began his first few points in obtaining full control of the Oolonxg clan before an unexpected interruption found its way into his office. One of Wuyi's guards had come into the room, his expression crossed with confusion and more than enough worry to cause alarm to both Visu and Wuyi. He leaned in close, informing the two of guests from the Matxha territory.

Not an hour into their meeting, two men were brought in, by direct order from the head of the Matxha clan to meet with none other than Wuyi. The two who suddenly entered the office in were of the Matxha clan, clad in black suits with spearmint green shirts beneath.

Wuyi had shifted over to Visu's side, two extra chairs brought over for their unannounced guests to sit down across from them.

"An honor to meet the one and only Wuyi of the Oolonxg clan. My name is Belire of the Matxha clan, sent on a direct mission by our leader." Belire looked ready to put out his hand to shake Wuyi's, but instead, his pale hand reached over across the table, his intent eyes openly yearning for the donuts within reach. He grabbed a bismark donut from the tray of welcoming treats on display. Nothing grabbed his heart more than something sweet. To his dismay, he had to keep his attention on the visibly irritated Wuyi before him, whose icy eyes tore through the partly disheveled blond man.

Belire wasn't one to feel intimidated, though. He giggled to himself at the attempt, unsettling everyone in the room as he adjusted one leg over the other. He swept a free hand over his short cut hair, pulled back by a matte gel with darker blond highlights against natural pale-yellow strands, clearly a man who had all but a care in the world.

When Visu watched these men make themselves comfortable in his office, the second one hesitantly reaching for a donut as well, mimicking Belire's movements.

Visu looked towards Wuyi, who met him with the disinterested gaze he knew too well, an affirming nod being all the evidence that he was just as confused as he was. So, at least it was not an ambush created on his father's part.

Visu shifted in his seat, steeling himself for whatever troubles the meeting would bring.

"Wuyi, you never mentioned you had a son. I would say congratulations but, you don't seem very...anyways." Belire said, stuffing the remainder of the donut fully into his mouth, stretching his cheeks out like an overstuffed squirrel preparing for winter.

Both Wuyi and Visu shared a look once more, nothing to do with the comment of fatherhood, but with the odd nature of their Matxha clan guests.

"Let us speak for what you came here for." Wuyi cleared his throat, already tired of this abrupt disruption of a meeting. "What is the reason behind your visit? What does the head of the Matxha clan need with the Oolonxg that they send two officers unannounced?" Wuyi asked, keeping his eyes steady on the two Matxha men across the empty desk.

Belire switched legs, while the other Matxha clansman shifted uncomfortably. "As you may know, the Matxha and Oolonxg clans have always had close ties together. This relationship has spanned since the very beginning of clanship, from the days following the fall of the Great Monarch. Now, not to quiz you," Belire shot his stare at Visu. "Do you know of the battle in which the Oolonxg clan took over the Chamoxile clan?"

Visu's plain expression searched Belire's, trying to figure out the hidden meaning behind his question before answering.

"The Battle of Wuyi." He hesitantly answered to which Belire's eyes swung back to Wuyi. "A grand victory for your father. So much so, he named you after the war? How remarkable, and all the same; depressing." He exclaimed with a smile, as though he were a participant in the war himself. "But also, no need for me to be giving a history lecture to the current and prospective leaders of this great land." Belire wiped his mouth with the back of his hand, looking at his reflection on his phone to make sure he cleaned everything from his mouth.

Wuyi didn't move, nor did his pointed gaze leave their guests.

It wasn't clear if the comment was considered offensive or an observation, but Visu felt his guard heighten, knowing there was more to the visit than a history lesson from the Matxha clans finest.

Belire noticed the intent stares of both the son and the father, certainly trying their collective best to maintain an intimidating air to them both. "Who helped the Oolonxg in their time of need during said battle?"

"What does the Matxha clan want with the Oolonxg?" Once he realized the topic of conversation, Wuyi closed his eyes, painfully, as his expression immediately tightened.

"An invasion." Belire smiled brightly. "Of the Cxai territory. Just as your clan sought to expand for the needs of your people, our time has come to do the same."

"On what grounds? Are the Matxha struggling so much that they must threaten the order in which the world sits now?"

Was the Rooiboux clan not enough of an expansion for the Matxha clan? Visu wondered to himself.

"No. But sources tell us the Cxai family are struggling. Their leader has been dealing with quite a bit back home, sources tell us. And this poses a civil threat to the peace of the land we all love and know so well. However, it also presents two sets of opportunities for us."

"And what might that be?" Visu maintained his composure, settling into his seat as if nothing happened.

"First, to uphold the old treaties with our dearest and closest ally, the Oolonxg clan. Second, to take advantage of civil unrest in an unstable clan and take their land, resources, and the like. Just as the Oolonxg did almost a century passed." Belire looked out longingly out the window of the office.

The room grew silent, the request seemingly so simple for Belire to say, but the weight, the severity of it falling onto the shoulders of both Wuyi and Visu.

Wuyi sat quietly, his closed eyes open, barely processing the worst thing he could have heard today, possibly his entire time in leadership. For the first time during their meeting, he looked to his son, his salt swept hair lightly pushed back to meet his equally uncertain gaze.

Visu's own heart raced as he thought of the request. It wasn't only that Belire had asked on behalf of the Matxha clan to gain the assistance of the Oolonxg, but to note the civil unrest in Cxai territory. He wondered what the reason could be and unfortunately, he found himself asking aloud.

"What is happening in the Cxai territory to cause such severe civil disagreement?"

"Supposed divorce between the leader and his wife." Belire spoke so quickly, as if he had been waiting to be asked.

Visu nodded, knowing that's likely all he could get out of him. There was too much to think about, so much he needed to tell Ayale, but when he looked to his father once more, he saw something he didn't expect.

Wuyi looked utterly tired. The conversation aged him a decade alone.

And in light of everything, Visu acted in a way that surprised himself.

He placed a hand into his perfectly pressed coat pocket, doing something he wasn't sure of, for his own sense of security. Visu slipped one of his own personal business cards between his fingers, focusing his remaining pool of energy heavily into the same hand that fished for it, and imbuing the tiny card with a gentle stream of his energy, a cold aura temporarily washing over it. When the chill dissipated and the business card was warm from the touch of his hand, he pulled it out of the tight pocket and handed it off to Belire, meeting his wandering eyes with an unphased expression.

"We would like some time to discuss this beforehand. For the time being, here is my contact information so that way we can remain in touch." He said, taking over control of the situation.

"Wait too long and our offer may expire. From then, I don't know what could happen. Out of my hands, you know?" Belire responded, taking the card and depositing it into his chest pocket.

"I would imagine you need us more than you need to make empty threats." Visu snapped back with a subtle tone he didn't break from, earning a sneer from Belire and a similar glare from Wuyi. "Do not forget whose territory you are seated in." He continued, motioning for the Oolonxg guards to escort them from the room. Just as they did so, Belire's scoff and sudden giggle engulfed the room followed by a single wave as he walked out.

As the door closed behind them, Wuyi's unbroken expression shifted drastically at the sight of his son.

"When did I raise a son who did not know how to keep his mouth shut?" Wuyi pointed his comment sharply at Visu.

"I was led by example." Visu retorted without hesitation and straightened his back. He dreaded any and all interaction with his father, even a few minutes at a time being too many.

The two grew quiet as the weight of the meeting settled into the two of them.

Wuyi looked far more solemn at his son, watching a tinge of red settle into the white of Visu's eyes.

"Did you...?" Wuyi trailed off, inspecting his son as a concerned father would. Visu only nodded.

Wuyi leaned over and tilted his son's head to the left and pushed away his black hair, watching a visible but thin blue blood vessel stretch across the side of his head.

"Stop staring, what's done is done." Visu pulled his head back. "How are you doing with all this information?" He hesitated heavily.

Wuyi took a sharp breath and nodded. "I am too old for this, Visu. For the head of the Matxha clan to send people here, to be asked such ridiculous things this late in my lifetime." He didn't finish his statement, only waving his hand.

Visu saw this as his chance, turning to face his father.

"Then maybe it is time to step down and let someone else take charge. Perhaps a son who just used his affinity to spy on the opposing clan." Visu commented, looking almost expectantly at his father.

# XXXI

After a night of seldom sleep on night one of lockdown, Ayale tossed and turned, only to be met with the barest form of light from the morning sun. Their eyes slowly opened, unsure how much longer they could take the uncertainty surrounding their current situation, and decided a distraction was far overdue.

Their back flat against Osiris' back, they shimmied out of his space, moving slowly towards the edge of the bed before his hand reached out to grab theirs. They wouldn't say it if asked, but as they sat still, the two of them with their hands clasped together, they felt wrong leaving the bed. Something about holding his hand brought them a sense of calm in the chaos.

Ayale couldn't help from overthinking their situation. They had the audacity to ask for help from the Oolonxg clan in getting home, and still, they thought more of where they stood with Osiris. Their leg bounced nervously at the edge of the bed, pushing the thought out of their head.

Ayale stood up and took their hand back, going into the bathroom to clean up the exhaustive expression almost permanently embedded on their face. When they came back out, Osiris was seated upward, both hands covering his face, struggling to fully awaken. "Did I wake you?" Ayale wandered back over to his side and brushed out their hair.

He didn't know if it was frowned upon to speak to them after the last few days of silence. A part of him missed their company, wondering if that made him so weak as to be excited when they spoke to him without disdain in their voice. "No, I think I'm just restless at this point."

They nodded, knowing exactly how he felt firsthand. "Ah. I'm going to call this good timing then."

"Why?" He muttered, a ray of light from the morning sun beginning to warm his shoulder.

"Get ready and grab your jacket, we're busting out of this place for a bit."

"Ayale, that's a bad idea." Osiris moved his hands away, his eyes finally open, and ready to retort.

"Lower your voice," They hushed and sat back beside him. "I can't sit here another day waiting for Visu to tell us it's safe to leave here, we need air that doesn't smell like Teryn's balcony! Besides, when I open that door, I smell pastries and coffee. There's a café around here and we need to see it."

Osiris watched them plead their case but was less than convinced. "Please don't get us in any more trouble."

"Osiris, don't you miss fresh coffee? Cappuccinos? Lattes? All made with those fancy machines that you can't operate?" They leaned in and placed their hands on both his shoulders, adamant to convince him to break lockdown with them. "Who knows how many more of these places we'll get to see? How much longer can we explore territories on our own accord?" A sense of sadness flickered at the end of their statement. They didn't mean for their words to come out the way they did, and the unbroken eye contact may have added too much emphasis.

Osiris saw the flash of melancholy, wondering to himself if he was reading into their demand a bit too much. Their time together was growing shorter by the day, something that quickly became more real as the two of them made their way across the continent.

Ayale leaned in close, almost bringing him back to the temptation to close the gap that he felt a few nights ago. "Not to add insult to injury but, you did say when we got out of prison, we could go out into Odania and look around. I'm cashing that in now."

Osiris looked at them far too seriously, keeping their eye contact. "Is this what you want?"

"Yes." They answered instantly.

A timid smile crossed his face, holding back the growing warmth in his chest. "Then it sounds like we need to get ready to go before Teryn wakes up." Osiris lifted himself from the bed, unable to convince Ayale to stay put. And somehow, he felt happier for it.

Ayale and Osiris decided to break the rule of lockdown and snuck out of the apartment in the guise of the early morning light. Osiris simply took it as a sign they were getting agitated at being stuck inside all day until they eventually heard from Visu. The two of them yanked the spare keys to the apartment hanging up by the entrance and shut the door with a gentle click.

They both hurried down the spiral white marble stairs, eager to taste freedom.

As they both stepped out the door, the warmth of the sun hit their faces and suddenly, Ayale and Osiris felt like they could do anything.

"Finally, we get to be outside!" Ayale stretched their arms forward, Osiris snickering beside them.

"Settle down captain, where should we go first?" He asked, more excited for their outing than he thought he would be.

"Where there are pastries, coffee follows, so let's go this way." Ayale started walking off to the left, following the faint scent of pastries in the air.

A collection of heavy clouds threatening rain flourished above them, but with or without the sun, Ayale and Osiris walked down the sidewalk with no worry for the weather. Being able to walk around again without someone watching them was a pleasant start to the day.

Soon, apartment buildings turned into shops, the first being a small convenience store that descended into a sublevel area inside. After that came a confection shop that stole Ayale's attention, leaving them to almost walk into a pole had Osiris not pulled them out of the way.

"Watch where you're going, please." He said in a low warning tone. His hand remained tight over theirs, his concern for their safety even more evident.

"Sorry, I'll be more careful." Ayale sincerely apologized, though Osiris expected a snarky comment. "Remind me to stop in here before we go back."

"Sure thing." He smiled, carrying on beside them.

Down the remaining block, the two of them waited to cross the street, and Ayale looked down at their hand still entwined with his. They looked back up at the lights, taking in the sights of other shops in the distance. For a moment, Ayale wondered if they were supposed to take their hand back by now or if it was too strange to do so.

Meanwhile, despite Osiris keeping a cool demeanor, he was unsure what to do. As if he didn't just confess a fraction of his feelings for them a couple of days ago, share a bed every night, secretly admit his love for them to Teryn the night before, stealing glances at them every chance he got. Osiris felt like a conflicted high school student. In a spur of confidence, he squeezed their hand and looked over at them until they met his oddly serious gaze.

"So you don't walk into any more poles." Osiris lifted their conjoined hands, his eyes going from that back to Ayale. His subtle smile remained as he looked at the changing light, and the two began to walk again.

"Smart." Ayale agreed, scratching the back of their head as their vision wandered off again. They saw the back of Teryn's apartment building as they crossed the road, before looking ahead once more. A small boutique came up next, made up of a stone exterior and a large blue and grey sign, with unimpressive clothing that barely caught Ayale's eye. In between the boutique and the shop after it sat a door leading to a small set of apartments in between store fronts, before giving way to a brightly lit jewelry shop.

The shop had a small sign in the window stating it accepted antique and vintage pieces as trade-ins. Osiris looked at the matching jewelry sets in the window, spotting his favorite shade of green in an amass of a solid-colored band. The shade of green was reminiscent of Teryn's philodendron, a piece of raw stone wrapped around a set of two rings and two necklaces.

The two of them continued to walk away from the shop, and Osiris did not allow the next few thoughts in his head to flower. Ayale slowed down soon after they passed over to the next shop.

Everything seemed familiar to them, down to the streetlights that towered every block or so. They narrowed their eyes on one spot in particular as they investigated their surroundings, coming to a stop in the middle of the cracked sidewalk. Osiris felt them slow down, worry lining his expression. "Everything okay?"

"Café across the street." Ayale spotted a place, eyes pointed at a small hole in the wall across their location, discreet with a small chalkboard outside their storefront as the only indication they were a coffee shop. Osiris and Ayale moved across the crumbling sidewalk and took a closer look at their colorful specials board, with the name *La Lune* written up top.

From the top of the board in red chalk paint, a red eye coffee. In orange was a soy chai latte, in yellow was a honey vanilla macchiato, in green a matcha latte, in blue an oolong tea with blueberry milk.

"This is definitely a place with one of those machines I can't operate." Osiris mumbled, peering at the cute purple handwriting at the very bottom that said lilac lattes. His newfound love affair for lattes was only going to get worse at this rate. He felt a violent yank on his hand and followed Ayale's pull inside the shop.

"We can read them inside, I need a bagel." Ayale led Osiris into the small shop, hearing the sounds of the espresso machine and various chatter among the groups of people inside. They both walked on creaking wood and went to sit down in an unsuspecting corner. Osiris let go of their hand and took a menu for each of them to look over, while Ayale's eyes wandered around the café. They noticed the shoddy muted color of the stain below them, probably having once been covered by carpet from the look of the staple marks scattered around. The walls were simplistic and rustic in a way, with the upper half made of exposed brick and the lower of wood paneling. The décor was somewhat vintage, a mixture of black metal chairs and tables with wooden tops scattered around close to the walls and windows. They saw a small bar area on a raised platform, with bar stools lined up alongside the bar side that displayed their espresso machine on the back wall, below a set of three large boards with the menu spilled over them.

A tired man around their age swept along the empty parts of the café, leaving Ayale reminiscing of their tea shoppe.

"Everything okay?" Osiris asked, noticing their distant yet longing gaze.

"Yeah. See anything you like yet?" They shifted the conversation.

"A few things, but I'm still thinking. You?"

"Same." They yawned.

As Osiris looked back down at the menu, he bit back his smile. This was beginning to feel a lot like the night they met, leaving him oddly nostalgic.

Ayale noticed his behavior and elected to ignore it for his own dignity. They continued to investigate the café, their gaze fluttering around like a child in a candy store. A single, thick wooden pole stood strong in the middle of the shop from the floor to the ceiling, yet decorated as though it were a design choice, with colorful fliers and business cards corked onto it from all sides. The café's condiment bar was across from the bar against the other wall, on top of a reused metal cabinet that stood out more than the pole. Ayale couldn't help but be impressed with the place.

The two walked up to order and Ayale got a chance to see the extra seating towards the entrance. A few seating spots were indented at the sapphire painted wainscot framing that laid thick around the windows, where worn out cushions sat with enough space for two to sit down and watch the street. They nudged Osiris and pointed it out to him while they stood in line, and he nodded, an unspoken agreement for them to go sit there after they both ordered.

The shorter the line became, the closer the two of them got to the front. By the counter was a busy collection of items, from various syrups to fliers and a glass display case full of treats, including bagels.

"I'm not sure if I want that chai or a macchiato." Ayale squinted at the menu in hand.

"I was thinking of trying the oolong latte they have, it sounds strange. But I bet it's good."

"That's new, I figured you were more of a coffee kind of person."

"Well, I'm starting to appreciate fine tea these days." Osiris looked at them with a lingering smirk before returning his eyes to the front of the line.

Ayale froze, the comment sounding an awful lot like flirting. First, they wondered if they were looking too much into the simple words, but the smile on his face said otherwise. They could only stand immobile, unsure how to flirt back. Recalling Rae's words to be themself, they took in a sharp breath and said the first thing on their mind.

"Did you know that the sun could explode and kill us at any time?" Ayale said, keeping their eyes on the board up front.

Osiris didn't know what to say, instead finding himself laughing. "That's quite the fun fact." He responded, nervous to say anything else to their fun fact.

By the time the two got to the front, Ayale ordered a macchiato with a bagel and Osiris his oolong tea latte. Even quicker did they retrieve their beverages and retreat to the spot Ayale pointed at earlier.

Ayale and Osiris sat beside one another and sipped their drinks, watching people walk in and out of the coffee shop.

Osiris peered over, looking at Ayale who clutched their drink tightly in both hands. They took a small sip before placing it down behind them on the window sill.

"Is it good?" He asked softly, almost tempted to reach in and taste it for himself.

"It's perfect." They sighed, pleased with the caffeine pumping into their veins. "Yours? It looks very...blue." They eventually concluded, taking a bite of their buttered bagel.

"It's definitely strong with the blueberry but it adds a sort of intensity to the tea. Do you want to try some?" He placed it in front of them, watching them lean over and quickly take a sip from his straw. Ayale looked visibly puzzled in the first few seconds, then pleasantly surprised, bringing some relief to him.

"That's actually really good." Ayale said.

Osiris smiled, happy to see them enjoying something new. "See what I mean?"

"I do. Want to try your luck on this? It's hazard free."

"Sure," he giggled, taking a sip from their cup. "A lot sweeter than I expected."

"If I'm going to be honest, I tend to enjoy sweeter choices. I just don't let myself order them often."

The thought of Ayale enjoying little sweets was one fact he didn't expect to learn about them. "Why don't you order sweet drinks?"

"Easiest way to answer this is that... it was frowned upon. I'm just happy to be able to have a treat in my hands now."

Osiris was surprised to hear that response. He felt bad, first and foremost, knowing Ayale had to hide one of the most miniscule pleasures to keep up a façade in front of others. He handed back their drink, drawing a bit closer to them until they met in the middle, his leg brushing up against theirs.

Ayale focused their attention on their macchiato, inhaling the scent of coffee and the scenery around them. It was the ultimate peace.

"Thank you for convincing me to go out. This is nice." Osiris peered out from the side of his glasses, a smile growing on his expression when they returned his glance.

"Agreed." They said, a less than subtle smile remaining on their face. "It's nice to be outside again."

"Helps to have good company." Osiris said, his soft gaze fluttering back to them, their cautious expression imminent. His free hand found Ayale's, carefully taking their hand into his, half expecting them to pull away.

But to his surprise, Ayale leaned against his shoulder, feeling Osiris tighten his hand around theirs. They stayed close to one another for some time, while they finished their coffee and bagel, the two quietly watching people come in and out of La Lune.

Ayale and Osiris walked back to the apartment, the once bright sun diminished by the incoming set of clouds. When the building came back into view, Ayale felt their chest tighten. There was a strong chance Teryn would be awake by now and ready to scold them. They only hoped the chocolate in hand would help convince him not to snitch to Visu.

But, what the two of them walked into was far more frightening.

Standing in the living room were Visu and Teryn, the most serious looks painted on their faces.

And suddenly, it was as if the beginning to their day didn't exist for Ayale and Osiris anymore.

## XXXII

"Ayale, Osiris, please sit down." Visu requested in a tone far more pensive than usual. As he did so, a repressed groan left his lips, clutching his forehead in one of his hands. Teryn moved to his side, holding his shoulder and free hand for support.

Ayale and Osiris sat on the kitchen chairs placed in the living room across from them. Both readied themselves to make excuses for their excursion.

"This entire outing was my idea, I'm sorry I broke lockdown." Ayale lowered their head in guilt.

Neither man looked in their direction, almost ignoring the confession altogether. "That's no issue right now, we have a bigger problem at hand. But I think it would be best heard from Visu." Teryn said, still looking over his partner while he decided what to do. "I'm going to get a cold compress ready, don't move." He whispered, a caring statement and a threat all at once. Visu hesitantly nodded, unable to lift his head just yet.

When Teryn hurried off to the bathroom, the three were left alone.

Ayale motioned toward the couch. "What happened to you?" They watched him forcefully straighten his back onto the pillow behind him.

"Ayale." Visu cleared his throat, moving his hand away from his face. His left eye was fully bloodshot with no white left to surround his sapphire iris, a sight that had Ayale and Osiris audibly gasp.

"Holy fuck, Visu!" Ayale exclaimed.

"Did your father do this to you?" Osiris asked quietly, horror and intrigue painted on his face.

Teryn came back out, placing the compress on the back of his neck, feeling him wince from the cold. "Both of you settle down and use your inside voices, Visu is a bit sensitive to sounds right now."

"As I was saying." Visu started, struggling to keep his shifting vision on them. "Ayale, please listen closely." The pain in his eye interrupted, leaving him inhaling a sharp breath. "There were two Matxha clansmen, and to our luck, they were not looking for either of you. No mention of a hunt to us, at least."

Visu leaned back with the cold compress against his eye and forehead, groaning from the cooling sensation.

"What they asked for instead was for Visu and Wuyi to support the Matxha clan." Teryn continued for him, bringing the compress slowly over his bad eye. Visu's hand took hold of his, a tight hold on one another.

"They wish to invade Cxai territory in the following weeks, to expand westward. They see an opportunity because your parents are getting divorced." Visu completed, struggling to hold his head upward.

The room grew immediately silent. Osiris couldn't help but look to Ayale, waiting for a reaction of some kind. Teryn did his best to focus on Visu, not daring to look anywhere else.

Ayale stared blankly at Visu, the words barely hanging onto anything. They sat in the stillness, a mixture of emotions flooding through them.

An invasion of their homeland.

A divorce between their parents.

Diori's sudden involvement in bringing Ayale back made less sense than ever. Did she know about the invasion like she knew they were coming home? Did she just make Ayale do the dirty work of bringing other clans in for help?

Beyond the unsure thoughts and possibilities laid one major fact; Ayale's home and everything they left behind was suddenly in danger.

"Aya?" Osiris whispered, reaching out to grab their hand into both of his.

"Did...did one of them do this to you?" Ayale looked up at Visu.

He shook his head. "I am both blessed and cursed with an affinity unlike any other recorded in our territory; enchantment. I can do but a few things with it. Tracking and dispelling of other affinities. However, as all things do, a hefty price to pay." He said, weary and far beyond exhausted.

"Every time he does anything, to place or dispel magic in any way, he gets this way. Exhaustion sets in, temporary blindness, and pain concentrated in his head, among other parts of his body. We never know where until after the use of his affinity." Teryn explained, keeping the ice pack on his eye.

"I haven't heard of someone getting ill after the use of an affinity." Osiris whispered, a mix of sympathy with his intrigue.

"He isn't the first to be disabled by his own body and he won't be the last. Regardless, he persists as he always does." Teryn rubbed circles on Visu's left temple above his eye, while still holding up the compress.

"What did you end up doing to get this way?" Ayale muttered their question.

Visu kept his head down, but his eyes peered up to answer Ayale. "I placed a tracking spell onto a business card of mine and handed it off to the Matxha representatives. To keep an eye on the clan, and perhaps, buy us time. They expect a response from us soon, but I will try to stretch out a response for as long as I can. If I cannot convince them to leave quietly, then we will be forced to openly violate a treaty, one far older than any of us combined." Visu finished, wiping away the tear-like discharge coming from his bad eye. "But we need a plan, sooner than later."

"I need a cigarette." Ayale breathed out before forcing away the numbness collecting in their legs and walking out to the balcony area.

Osiris and Teryn looked at one another before Teryn mouthed '*go*' at Osiris.

While he followed behind Ayale, Teryn took Visu into his bedroom, setting up the bed for him to rest.

Osiris hurried to Ayale's side, watching them take the longest drag of a cigarette since their first days on the road. The lingering smell of smoke took over the balcony entirely, leaving him choking back a cough. When he turned to face them, the dissociative stare out at the afternoon sky was replaced with watery eyes, threatening to spill over.

"Everything is going to be okay." He tried to put an arm around them but they shrugged it off, keeping their distant look at the city below. They didn't know what to say, what to feel, an assortment of anxiety flooding them from the inside out.

The two of them stood by the balcony railing, side by side, doing only what they knew, and watched the citizens of Odania go about their daily lives. Sometimes in groups, sometimes alone, some on their phones, and others searching for something. People moved about with their sense of peace in these moments, indifference plated over every single person.

But no one, Ayale thought, was aware of the war to come.



Ayale and Osiris rested for the remainder of the day, Teryn leaving them alone to go work a few hours at the restaurant. He entrusted

Visu's supervision to the duo, leaving a small list of instructions as to where to locate Visu's medications. He warned the two not to let him move around too much, as he was partially blind for the time being.

By the time night arrived, Visu was still in Teryn's room, sleeping on his fourth or so hour.

Ayale rotted on the couch while Osiris tended to all the plants and herbs around the apartment. There was no telling what Ayale was thinking, leaving him even more unsure what to say. But identically, he knew silence was not an option either.

"So, the Matxha. And the Oolonxg. And the Cxai." Osiris started, casually swinging the empty watering can in his hands.

"What of it?" Ayale took a succulent pillow from the couch and placed it directly on their face.

"Well," Osiris thought for a second. "There is, apparently, a lot to it. We know they invaded the Rooiboux clan during Katari's wedding, to start. Now they want to do the same with your clan, while civil unrest unfolds. And that is information we are better off knowing, I think." He spoke carefully, putting down the watering can beside the massive philodendron beside him. He took a clip to his lochs, placing them in a quick updo. "Or would you rather go home not knowing about the invading army?"

Ayale groaned in response, knowing he made a good point.

"I would rather go home and face my parents and my parents alone, not an impending fucking war." They groaned, muffled by the pillow in their face.

"Aya," He sat by their side at the arm of the couch. "Can I tell you something?" He put his hands together, bringing them up to his mouth as he stared at the fish tank across from the two of them.

They took their pillow out from their face and shifted it lower to expose their wary eyes and pointed stare at Osiris.

"I am a defector from the Matxha clan, I know you know this because well, here we are, right? Found me about to die at the hands of two of my own superiors. People I used to talk to and see every day." Osiris watched one fish in particular, his eyes following it into its cartoonish looking home in the tank.

"Did I ever tell you what uh, what caused them to go after me?" His brow lowered, suddenly losing a bit of his nerve.

Ayale sat up straight, clutching the plush tighter than before.

"The talk of invasion has been there since I joined. Never said where but always made a heavy point of our territory's 'need to expand'. I was given this list with names and places, told to go investigate possible locations of elemental affinity users. Anyone who could control a major element on that list was to be brought to the attention of the Matxha clan immediately. One of the places was the tea shoppe in the southern district of Densriel. And I couldn't..." Osiris took in a sharp breath. "I couldn't bring myself to expose any of you. Affinities and magic in this world should be more sacred than this. You know my stance on the autonomy of magic, how little of it there is, to the point where we know better than to use it in public. It's asking for trouble. I took that lovely list they gave me, a few others to boot, and destroyed all the names I could get my hands on. And then they came after me." Osiris took off his glasses and folded them into his hands, reaching for one of the many plushies on the couch to hold for himself. He shifted his head to look at them, a mixture of relief and uncertainty in his expression.

Ayale put the pillow down, their wide eyes pointed directly at Osiris. Their stare left him frightened, wondering if they were about to finish the job of the Matxha clan.

They stood up from the couch and moved in front of him, towering over Osiris with the same pointed stare of their hazel eyes.

"Why?" Ayale asked.

"Because affinity users should be free to choose their own path." Osiris answered with no hesitation, looking up at them with fierce belief. "No matter their powers. Everyone deserves the choice."

Ayale took his face into their hands and pressed their forehead against his. "I have no words except that of gratitude. How many names did you see on the list?" They asked, watching his eyes tighten.

"I don't remember. It was compiled via rumors and the like."

Ayale sat still. "Does anyone in the Matxha clan know about the tea shoppe being on the list? How many hands did it pass through?" They quietly interrogated.

"Just one other before me, as far as I know. And every list ended with me." He whispered, willing himself to stay calm despite the close proximity and his heavy beating heart.

Ayale breathed out a breath of mild relief. They suspected they knew whose names were on that list and to know of both its existence and its destruction was a lot in a five-minute range. They froze, but a sense of relief washed over them like nothing else.

Their promise to protect the tea shoppe had been upheld by someone none of them knew of. By someone who didn't have to do what he did, but did so out of his own sense of justice.

Ayale felt a warm hand reach for their cheek, touching them softly.

"Was that too much to drop at once? I figured I should tell you before someone else might. Are you upset with me?" Osiris asked. They shook their head. Before taking a step back, they kissed his cheek gently, muttering a quick thank you before pulling back.

The creak of Teryn's door took them back to reality again.

Visu shuffled over to the seats across the couch in a black tank top and borrowed sweatpants. He groaned at the first sight of light, prompting Ayale to dim down the lights and for Osiris to go get the medicine Teryn had made earlier in the day. Visu collapsed onto the couch with a loud thud.

"Teryn gave us some pointers on how to help out." Ayale spoke deliberately softer than before, prompting a smile to cross his exhausted face.

"Thank you." Visu muttered.

"I should be thanking you, Visu. You're the one who put a tracker on the Matxha clan." They sat across from him in the chairs that were left there from earlier.

"I'm afraid it was for a purely selfish purpose. As is my next request to you." He took in a passive breath. "Take my fiancé with you to Cxai territory." Visu said, less asking and more requesting.

"I think the phase of tossing people at one another has come and passed." Ayale shook their head, spotting Osiris from the corner of their eye, watching him choke back a reactionary cough on his way to the kitchen. A conversation for later, they thought.

"In fact, I would rather cover a different topic, one you never mentioned once since you left. When were you going to mention you convinced him to back off and officially took the role of the Oolonxg clan leader?"

"I am barely a leader but I thought mentioning it now would do us no good. How intuitive of you, Ayale. How did you know?"

"The way you spoke earlier. Don't mind my attention to detail." They waved, a small smile creeping onto their face. Visu nodded, attempting to open his bad eye with a sharp groan.

"Time to discuss a plan?" Visu asked, before Osiris handed him pills and a cold water bottle.

"Of course, leader of the Oolonxg clan. I figured I would run home, let everyone know of the invading army coming, maybe take advantage of the time you give up to prepare. How much can you slow them down?"

"Slow them how?"

"Exactly how they expect a newbie leader to act; unorganized. When they decide not to take you seriously, they'll go back to Wuyi, who will pretend to work with them. Lastly, give them a path through the Cxai territory mountains so that way most of them lose their way." Ayale said, recalling an old tale about a much older invasion of Cxai territory.

"You want me to feign irresponsibility to the Matxha clan." Visu clarified.

"Yes."

"Ayale, this plan is incredibly questionable, at best. Where do I begin?"

"Wear that to the next meeting." They gestured to his borrowed outfit of a tank top and sweatpants. "But on a more serious note, Osiris and I need a clear path to leave Odania. Can you secure that for tomorrow morning and get my car back?"

"Certainly, I should be able to get everything together and avoid questioning since I have this." He pointed at his eye. "We are lucky there are only two for now, but more are coming I suspect."

"Nothing you won't be able to handle." Ayale said, a confident smile tugging at their lips. Visu dutifully nodded but looked ready to pass out again.

Osiris stole a glance between the two of them, his own confidence cementing his faith in their plan.

## XXXIII

History had a way of repeating itself. Only weeks after they first scrambled out of Densriel, Ayale and Osiris gathered their things from around the apartment, rushing around to prepare for their escape from Odania. Teryn had insisted on helping the two of them pack and prepare, leaving the others working around a groggy man, who struggled to sit up straight at six am, having worked a shift until midnight. Visu stopped midway in the small living room, putting his hands around Teryn's waist and pulling him towards the couch for him to sit down, telling him to stand down and leave the two to prepare on their own.

"Relax, they can handle themselves." Visu whispered in Teryn's ear before sitting him down on the couch and kissing the top of his head, walking towards the kitchen to make coffee. He missed being able to spoil Teryn, taking every opportunity to show him how much he cared, no matter the state of his eye.

Ayale changed into a much more obscure outfit than they were used to, sporting a suit of bold blue and black, to keep up with appearances in case they were stopped at the border. Osiris agreed to wear the same, doing a bit of extra work in the bathroom mirror to add his own flare. He yawned, clipping back his hair like last night and messing with the odd suit that was reminiscent of the men who arrested him and Ayale not too long ago. Funny to think how quickly things changed around. He rolled up the sleeves, the blue fabric stopping halfway up his wrists. He wondered if an accessory would give him a bit more of a modern look.

Of all the things that have happened to Osiris thus far, he was torn between whether being arrested at the gates of the Oolonxg capital was worse than being stalked by Mildred in unclaimed territory. A shiver ran down his spine at the thought of Mildred.

"Move over." Ayale pushed him to the side with their shoulder, wanting to grab some mirror space. They began fixing their short hair, trying to fluff it from the back. They parted their bangs to one side and held it down with a single black clip, shifting their own uniform and turned to multiple angles to adjust accordingly.

"Dapper." Osiris complimented but fluttered his sight to other parts of the small bathroom. By the time they were both done messing around with their outfits, the two of them looked far more professional, and easily convincing low-level Oolonxg clan grunts.

"Thanks, you are too." They said, still messing with their hair in the mirror. "Ready to sneak out of Oolonxg territory? Maybe get into a few fights along the way?" Ayale brushed out the back of their hair.

"I'm not sure I'm ready to fight, but hopefully this goes better than when we snuck in." He moved to the side to let Ayale take over the whole mirror.

With the matching suits gifted from Visu, the two made quick attempts to modify their outfits to their liking until the very last minute.

"Here's hoping we do well today, or else we end up in prison again." Ayale joked before strolling out of the room, leaving Osiris alone in the bathroom, his anxiety rising at the thought of being arrested again.

Once everyone was fully caffeinated and ready to make their next escape, Ayale and Osiris waited patiently with Teryn in the dusty foyer of his apartment building for Visu to show up with their car. A few yawns left his mouth as he struggled to keep up small conversation and keep his eyes open. Teryn wanted to comfort the two, to tell them everything would work out in the end.

As he watched them interact with one another, spilling the details of their secret outing with him, he quietly hoped their ending would be a happy one.

Visu pulled up to the front of the building and left it running, coming to the foyer to grab their bags. In his typical suit once again, he flashed a subtle smile to Teryn, a glimmer of gold showing itself on his neckline. The surprise subsided when Osiris approached him.

"Teryn?" Osiris stood before him, hands in his pockets, sort of boyish in his stance for someone in a full suit. "I um," He took a short breath to keep himself together. "I just want to say how grateful I am that you let us stay in your home. Not even that, but it means a lot to me to know someone else is sort of like me. Sounds weird, but—" Osiris was interrupted by Teryn's arms thrown around him, embracing him with all the power he could muster.

"You're a good man, Osiris. Never forget that." Teryn pulled back, looking at Osiris' Oolonxg suit up and down. "Very convincing. Reminds me of a younger version of myself when I worked for the clan."

Osiris blinked, staring back at him. "You *spied* for the Oolonxg clan? I thought you only did security!"

"It's not like I lied to you, I worked security for quite some time. But soon after that, I was sent on a few missions to spy on behalf of the Vindai family. Learned a lot about myself, picked up a few skills on my very last one, and here I am." He pat Osiris on the shoulder, a strange smile gracing his features.

A part of him was nervous to ask the question lingering on his mind. "Do you miss working for the Oolonxg clan?"

"Not particularly." Teryn said quickly, clear disdain on his face on the thought of ever returning.

Meanwhile, Visu and Ayale stood side by side in the small doorway, glancing over at one another with a shared uncertainty.

"Ayale." Visu greeted quietly.

"Visu," Ayale nodded back, matching his energy before inevitably bumping their shoulder into his. "I really appreciate everything you've done, are doing, and will do. All of it. You could have easily let us rot in prison. If they had figured out who I was before you, I don't want to imagine what could have happened." They clasped their hands together, watching Teryn and Osiris get irreversibly emotional. "You've done a lot for us. So, thank you." Ayale turned abruptly to hug Visu, the surprise in his face slowly lessening. He placed an arm over them, letting go of his uncertainty for a moment. "I'm sorry this was how you got it, but I think you're going to make a great leader, Visu Vindai." They reassured him, letting go to stand beside him again.

Visu battled back a sudden flurry of emotions, but his bad eye occasionally reminded him of his affinity.

The two stood together for a bit before Visu and Ayale separated again, returning to their individually reserved nature.

"As far as I know, you shouldn't encounter any issues when leaving. If anyone stops you, remember what we discussed." Visu gave both Ayale and Osiris knowing look to which they collectively nodded. "One more thing, take this with you and keep us both updated. One of us will always have the phone on them so if there is any problem, call. Don't hesitate to reach out if things are good, too." Visu said, hoping to hear good news rather than bad as they continued towards Cxai territory. He took out a small box from his pocket and handed off a cellphone to Osiris. He fell back to Teryn's side, remaining close to him as the two of them left the foyer.

Ayale and Osiris waved to Teryn and Visu before leaving behind the silent city. The two of them made their way into Lau's car and began their drive once more, with Teryn and Visu looking on while they made their way down the small street. The two men silently clutched each other's hand tightly, watching as the two turned the corner and out of sight.

"Ter." Visu said rather quietly. "Are you free the rest of the day?"

"For you, I can be." Teryn held back the smile threatening to spill on his lips. Visu promptly led the two of them out of the foyer as they both were and towards La Lune down the street, leaving the impending doom of a war on the horizon for another day.

The early morning sun glowed with a red hue, illuminating an orange sky. Ayale sat straightened up at the wheel, keeping their apprehensive eyes in the road in front of them. Osiris kept an eye out from every side he could, making sure no one would follow them around or out of Odania. His weary self could not rest until they were alone on the road once more.

As they approached the gate of the city, the two were met by two guards dressed similarly, but not quite identically. Upon simply looking at the emblem on Ayale and Osiris's suits, they were waved through and allowed to leave without a single word exchanged with those who watched the gate.

When they hit the open road, Ayale visibly unfurled, slowly pulling off the tight jacket from their body, with one hand tight on the steering wheel. Osiris simply removed the clip from his hair and attached it to the handle above him instead. He sank into his seat, the stress of the what ifs and possible confrontation with Oolonxg troops melting off him entirely.

"That was easier than I thought." He sighed, taking out the phone from the box, and turning it on.

"Can you let them know we made it out of the city without any issues?" Ayale asked Osiris, making sure to flop their hair back into place, going back and forth between the mirror and the road.

"Don't kill us by changing at the wheel, please." Osiris looked ready to clutch the bar above him.

"We'll be on the road awhile, gas tank is full from our new friends, and I refuse to drive in that dumb suit jacket longer than I need to." Ayale unbuttoned the collared shirt with one hand. "We need to move faster than before, meaning less breaks and a lot more driving." They exhaled, stressed out at the thought.

Osiris nodded, looking out at the distant, mountainous road ahead of them. "It feels like everything is happening so much faster than when we started. Are you ready for any of this?" He asked thoughtfully.

"Honestly? No." Ayale shook their head, pulling off the collared shirt and tossing it in the back seat, on top of their backpack. "All I know, and this includes everything, is that I want my parents alive. That's it. And the sooner I get there, the sooner I can explain that the Matxha clan is coming, maybe get them to put their differences aside and get ready for the invasion. Rest is arbitrary." They stretched their shoulders back, relieved to be in their undershirt instead of a heavy suit. They pressed their foot down on the accelerator, resolve settled within them along with the tense worry of being home and bringing someone with them.

Osiris shifted uncomfortably, wondering if the 'rest' they spoke of meant something he should have looked more into. Instead, he flashed them a swift smile before he began to text Visu, letting him know they were safe, and to ask if the plants in Teryn's apartment were watered yet.

# XXXIV

The road to Cxai territory was a long path, endowed with worry and nerves from both Ayale and Osiris.

Ayale remained heavily focused on the road in front of them, driving fast and silently to keep consistent on the road. The last time they had driven in such a way was when the two of them escaped the shop in the remote forest, making their escape from Mildred, the fire elemental. The mountain passages passed them by in a sort of blur, no amount of majesty nor beauty enough to gain even a fraction of their attention. Hyper focused and shaken with thoughts and possibilities as to what might be awaiting them back at the Cxai compound, Ayale's hands remaining on the worn steering wheel.

Osiris's eyes widened at every sight they drove by, enamored by everything from the distant mountainside to the thick clouds hanging over the noisy sedan. When he wasn't using the phone to take photos, he was attempting to add to a larger piece in his sketchbook. Activities were limited in a moving car, and he knew better than to distract Ayale while they drove.

On the long road back to their home city of Nalira, Ayale settled their eyes on the road. Hands tight on the steering wheel, with the occasional grasp at their coffee in the cup holder beside them. They didn't take to any of Osiris' attempts at small talk, the lull of the drive slowly draining them, until they noticed they had reached an area where the snow could no longer reach them. When the first yawn rumbled through them, Osiris threw a glance in their direction, worry settling into his thoughts. He went through a few ideas as to how he could convince them to pull over and rest, playing out a few scenarios in his head. He expected pushback regardless but chose the least confrontational.

Deep in thought, he subconsciously smoothed out his hair and parted it to one side before beginning to draw once more, the small act catching Ayale's attention.

Ayale's nerves spiked when they saw his anxious fiddling, wondering if their silent demeanor wasn't the best for either of them. They narrowed their eyes down the distant road, the partial pools of melted snow settling along the sides of the open road, where grass began to spring out along the expanse of land. Within those few minutes, Ayale pulled off into a grassy patch with the least amount of snow near it.

"Are you okay?" They pointed their question at Osiris, putting the car in park and turning it off.

He instantly perked up from his sketchbook. Their worried expression was a bit more severe than he could have expected. "I was just about to ask you the same."

Amused by the thought of one another's worry, the two of them relaxed a bit, stretching out and unfurling from the strained car ride.

"Sorry for being so weird." Ayale slid back against the seat, closing their eyes and giving themself a moment to rest.

"Don't be, I know a lot must be going through your head. And I don't want to say the wrong thing to you." Osiris admitted, looking from the dashboard to the field-like expanse beyond them. "What do I say when I can't even drive?" He let out a stressed sigh, mirroring Ayale and leaning back against his seat. While he had always felt bad about not being able to drive, he felt it more as time went on. It was clear they had a lot on their mind and driving through it all was a lot for one person.

Ayale turned to face him, genuine curiosity in their eyes. "Have you ever driven before?"

He thought to himself for a moment before responding. "Once or twice with my parents before I joined the Matxha clan."

"Do you..." They struggled for a moment, speaking without fully thinking of their next words. "Do you want to learn how to drive?"

Osiris turned to them with a strained expression on his face, but the gradual smile that came with the thought smoothed out his nerves.

"If you taught me, I might be okay with that. Maybe when everything settles back down, and war isn't on the horizon?" He said nonchalantly, unbuckling his seat belt. Osiris was more than ready to get out after sitting around for so long.

"Why not now? We have time." Ayale began to unbuckle their own seatbelt, opening the car door without a confirmation from Osiris first. They left the key in the ignition, passing by the front of the car, and waiting outside the passenger door. "It's a large, open highway, no rain or anything. Conditions are perfect."

Osiris hesitantly opened his door, fear clear as day on his face.

"I promise, it isn't as bad as it seems." Ayale reassured him as he got up from his seat. "We won't drive far. Just a few miles and that's it."

"I-I don't know about this." He said, eyes bouncing between Ayale and the dashboard. "You know the last time I drove, I was an actual teenager, right?"

"I did not." They said, pulling him up by the hand to get him around to the driver's side.

Osiris sat himself down in the driver's seat, frozen in fear by the thought of making the vehicle move. Before he adjusted anything in the car, he placed his hands on the steering wheel, a blank stare pointed at Ayale. Their adamancy wasn't typical without some underlying reason beneath it. "Why the sudden interest in teaching me to drive?" He wondered.

Ayale looked around the passenger side, peering at the dashboard full of small pencils and a closed-up sketchbook. "It's a good skill to have. In case of an emergency."

"Ayale." Osiris said flatly, feeling something off about their words.

"You should know how to drive anyways. What is the big deal?" They adjusted the seat back, almost breaking the lever beside them. "God, this car is old."

"Ayale." Osiris repeated, pulling their attention away from the window.

They hesitantly met his eyes. "What?"

He sighed, frustrated at trying to get an answer out of them.

Ayale leaned forward onto the dashboard, placing their arms beneath their chin. "What if something goes wrong and you need to escape?"

"I am not leaving you behind, no matter what happens in Cxai territory or wherever. I told you that already."

Their eyes found him, somber and almost expectant. "And if I die?"

Osiris sat still, readying his retort until Ayale reached over and took Osiris' hand into theirs.

"Please, just hear me out. I would rather you know how to drive, if not for some drastic possibility, then for the smaller, more likely ones. If I can't keep you safe, I need you to leave. Find Katari or text Visu and get out." They squeezed his hand, feeling his tighten around theirs.

Osiris pulled up the center console and shifted closer to them. "How long have you been thinking about this scenario for?"

"Since I started driving this morning," They admitted. "We haven't heard from Diori in a while, either. The whole point of going back is for me to confront what I left behind and to keep you safe from the Matxha clan. Imagine if we couldn't manage that much." Ayale pulled back and leaned against the seat. "What if this was all for nothing?"

He almost smiled at the thought of them worrying over him, but the tensity in their eyes kept him straight-faced. "I wouldn't say it was for nothing. At least I have you."

Ayale turned their face to the side, a small flush creeping forward. "That's not as great as you think it is."

He pulled them forward, the space between them smaller than before. "I think it's more than enough. It's why I asked you to stay with me in not one but two territories."

"Rose colored glasses, Osiris."

"Let me ask you this before anything else," Osiris pushed their hair back behind their ear, his hands lingering on their cheek, his expression both curious and uncertain. "What do you think of me?"

Ayale snickered, unsure where the question came from.

"I'm serious. Sometimes you're up front with me, other times I can't tell." Osiris let his hand trail down the side of their face. "Even now, I can't begin to explain how nervous I am to ask this outloud. Do you think I'm weak, Ayale?"

"Not even for a second." They said, watching his chest visibly decompress.

Osiris watched their eyes closely, nodding once when he felt they were being truthful. "That's a bigger relief to hear than you might think."

"Good. Because I mean it. None of my worries are because I think you're weak." They said, placing their hand on his shoulder, reaching around his back. "I just want you to be safe. And if that means teaching you to drive, even just to make sure you know the pedals, that would be enough to calm those thoughts down a bit."

"Only a bit?" He teased, his eyes looking over their shoulder and down their arm. "I better get started then. Buckle up."

Ayale smiled, pulling back into the passenger seat and putting their seatbelt on. They watched Osiris settle into the driver's side, fix the mirrors up, and turned on the car once more. Hesitant, he looked to Ayale for support, earning some minor instruction to get him started.

When Osiris started to hit the accelerator, he took his time down the highway, barely reaching a drivable speed. But neither seemed to mind. Every moment was spent helping him gain some confidence behind the wheel, thankful only one other car had come up to pass them. Ayale reassured him that if he needed to stop, he could pull over at any time.

And for a bit, Osiris found his consistency.

Ayale didn't move, the only difference between them and a statue being that they visibly breathed, even as their eyes settled on the sights they didn't get a chance to take in earlier.

The covered sun, lingering in the afternoon glow, began its descent behind the distant mountain to their west, the same one which stood proudly and concealed the capital city of the Oolonxg territory.

The two switched seats an hour after, leaving Ayale back to driving through the late afternoon before they stopped again to take a break for themself.

"Do you need help getting out?" Osiris asked, hand hovering on the door handle.

Ayale shook their head. "I'm too tired, I might not even make it out of this car."

"Oh, don't say it like that. You make it sound like if you move, you'll die."

"I just might." Ayale groaned, sinking into the seat some more.

Osiris left from his side and walked over to their door, opening it with a small click. "Come on, no life contemplation until we breathe some outside air." He said, taking their hand from the steering wheel into his, tugging them up towards him. Ayale decidedly let him lead them out of the car, though unwilling to admit he was right. He walked the two of them a few steps forward before Ayale tightened their hand around his.

"Osiris?" Ayale's eyes dropped to their hands held together. "Do you miss your parents?" They asked, causing him to stop in his tracks.

"I do. Always did."

"That's sort of nice. In a way." They responded, looking around them and focusing on a patch of grass beneath them.

"What about you?"

"I don't have a real answer for that. Just that I would rather they not die. I want to miss them and let go of being angry, but if I let go of everything they've done to me and my brother, it feels like an injustice." Ayale watched the lingering cumulus clouds ahead cover the setting sun, its warm rays no longer reaching the land around them. "Someone needs to be angry, or else those kids went through hell for nothing."

"Then I'll be angry." He squeezed reassuringly. "I can just be extra angry."

"What?" Their serious face splintered into a forced back snicker.

"I won't let it go. I'll be mad, upset, and I'll be grateful, too."

"Grateful for what?"

Osiris watched the gentle sunset with a soft admiration, thankful for the view after their long day. "Grateful you somehow ended up in Densriel at the same time as me. Grateful our paths crossed even in the strangest of times." Osiris stopped their walk together. He turned to face them, stepping close to Ayale, a sort of longing in his eyes. He placed a hand on their cheek, rubbing gently. "If it wasn't for their transgressions, I probably would have never met you."

Ayale recalled the night the two of them spent on Teryn's tiny balcony, side by side. The way he stood far too close, his hand on their cheek, speaking reassurance just the same. Some of the time shared together had managed to make them feel a certain way, reminiscent heavily of their kiss. They tried to push the memory out of their head, focusing on the moment at hand. "Bit of a stretch, don't you think?"

"Not really, if you ask me." Osiris' eyes dropped to their lips for a mere moment, pulling his hand down and continuing forward, trying to clear his mind.

"I'm sure." They shook off his strange comment, at least feeling a bit unburdened. "I think as an artist, you have this flare for the dramatic. But even so, I'm glad I met you, too." Ayale met his eyes, a timid but clear smile lingering on their expression.

Osiris struggled to keep himself from spilling over with his feelings. He wanted to say everything he was feeling, let every emotion he's kept within him to let loose.

But all the same, he knew that if he did, it wouldn't help anyone or anything.

For now, he would enjoy their presence, the real version of the person beside him that had only recently come visible, before Ayale would lock it away when they arrived in Cxai territory.

With a swift movement, Osiris left a gentle kiss to their cheek, lingering for a few seconds before moving himself back and continuing to lead them off on their little sunset excursion. Anything to get the two of them out and about before going back to the small sedan they would call home for another long haul of a drive. Every so often, their steps would go over a patch of crunchy melting snow, but the occasional settlement of grass would pop up from within it.

The two would walk a bit further into the expanse of land, where trees barely settled into the field. When they finally turned, the smaller the car seemed in the distance.

Osiris could feel their eyes without having to look back. "Are you scared?" Ayale casually inquired.

"Yeah." He answered without slowing down and tightened his hand over theirs. "But I won't leave you to deal with this shitshow alone."

The line alone reminded Ayale of their deal with Visu. It was strange to think how the two of them had treated Osiris and Teryn. Ayale wanted Osiris to stay in Odania to keep him safe from the impending doom that began to take up space in their plan to go home. Visu wanted to send Teryn out of the territory in order to keep him safe. Odd how the two of them treated the idea of safekeeping the people they cared for.

After Ayale was told what Visu learned from the Matxha clan representatives, something didn't sit right. Finding out about their parents' unsurprising split made things even more complicated.

But an invasion of Cxai territory, of their home, was too much to think about on top of everything.

And now, a possible war was something they had to consider in all of this.

Ayale and Osiris walked quietly alongside one another, taking time to themselves before their peace would come to run out.

# XXXV

Just as their walk together had been quiet, the next few hours of driving were full of silence and ruminating. Osiris took to his sketchbook, letting the remnant of the day light his pages. The sunset turned from its shades of red into deep purple, falling behind distant mountains. The road was unassuming and straight-forward as Ayale drove for another four or so hours until they couldn't control their yawning.

The constant driving on an almost infinite looking highway, Ayale found, was far beyond tedious. Somewhere in between anxiety inducing because it felt like a nightmare and exhaustive because the only thing that changed was the distant mountain range and the position of the sun and moon. Something about sitting still in a car they had to maneuver alone was already too much, but letting their hands and part of their right leg go numb was a lot for a day of driving.

Ayale yawned, long, and with a bare stretch of their arms over their head. The night sky was illuminated by the mere glow of the almost full moon, almost positioned directly above the car.

In the passenger seat, Osiris simply watched the world move from the window, with nothing left to do except scout the scenery; the mountains turning into small hills, the snowy landscape turning less like a tundra by the hour. The ever shifting highway became less intimidating as time went on.

Exhaustion washed over the two of them. There were more than enough reasons to stop driving, and if they were lucky enough to find a place to stay rather than sleep in the car again, Ayale wouldn't hesitate on settling for the night.

Yet, they let themself go numb from driving, to gain however many extra miles to get home as fast as possible.

It was both a blessing and curse when they spotted a small sign for an inn while still within Oolonxg territory borders, slightly off their path but still close enough to be worth the stop. Fighting exhaustion with anxious energy was a battle that left no winners, so they took the turn down the rocky off-road path covered on both sides by a thin layer of tall but thin pine trees, stopping directly in front of a place that looked like someone's average house put in the middle of nowhere, bordering a section of woods that scatters behind the building.

In their collective yawns, Ayale and Osiris grabbed their bags, and dragged themselves inside, taking whatever room was available without hesitation.

The moment they both opened the door, the two collapsed side by side, face first into the full-sized bed. Minutes of full silence and no movement followed, until Ayale forced themself with all their remaining power to reach the bathroom attached to their room at the other end.

Osiris rotted in the bed for the entire duration of their time in the bathroom, not even daring to look at the time on the phone in his pocket. The phone vibrated with notifications every so often since their arrival, leaving him to assume Visu had utilized some kind of tracker that knew they stopped off somewhere. He decided he would respond eventually, instead drifting off to sleep until Ayale placed a hand on his shoulder, gently trying to rouse him.

"Come on, lay down properly at least." They encouraged him in a soft voice.

Osiris groaned, shifting further into the bed, and onto his back. He took off his jacket and sweater, tossing both to a chair beside them, pulling the phone out of his back pocket and handed it over to Ayale, adjusting his pillow further beneath his head.

They unlocked the phone, staring at the last message sent. "What am I looking at?"

"Visu wants to know how you're doing. Think he knows we stopped." He stretched his hands behind his head, eyes closed against the dim lamplight beside him.

"Of course he has a tracker in this thing. What should I say to him?" Ayale squinted at the small phone.

"That we stopped for the night. Anything after that is up to you."

Ayale shrugged, hesitantly tapping the phone, and hitting send before plugging it into the wall nearby. They looked at the sleek phone, something about it making their chest tighten just before their next thought.

*If you have a moment, let me know that you are safe.*

Ayale grabbed the phone again, scrambling for the number scrawled on a piece of paper somewhere in their bag. They found it to their relief, then mindlessly began to type again, typing quickly a similar means that they were getting close to home.

With pause for thought, Ayale tapped their chin, trying to condense the adventures they've had so far, in as little words as possible.

Instead, they typed for what felt like forever, tapping at the screen nonstop. When they finally sent the shortened version of their adventure thus far, a sense of relief washed over them. They felt a small smirk tug at their mouth, a little bit of normalcy settling into them.

Ayale put the phone back onto its charger, noting it was nearly midnight compared to almost four am in Densriel, and that Lau would likely not see their message until far later in the day.

They turned off the lights and laid back on the bed, feeling an arm reach around their shoulders. They shifted further into the bed, and subsequently into Osiris, letting him become their comfort before drifting off to sleep.

Ayale dreamt of a distant, familiar sunshine illuminating their eyes, awakening them in their old bedroom in Nalira. It was decorated still as if it were a teenager's room, with beloved posters from shows, books, and art prints from various favored media. The fog of exhaustion painted the familiar room, one they realized was from home. They looked down at their comforter, looking at its dark fabric absorbing the early morning sunlight. When they tried to climb out of bed, a familiar panic settled into their stomach, a pain that was common when they started each day.

They reached out to the wood nightstand beside them, grabbing the cellphone off of it with its glittery casing and sword charm hanging from the bottom. When they turned the phone to the screen, they did not see their own face, but saw the reflection of their father instead. A judging face, one far beyond their own age, stared back at them in a brown eyed resentment, with a thick mustache made up of white and grey, and lines for every terror he ever witnessed, from every story he ever told them as a child.

The sudden noise of the phone vibrating on the table jostled Ayale from their sleep, awaking them with a jolt. Ayale touched their face, feeling for those lines from their dream, but feeling their own familiar complexion instead. They breathed out a sigh of relief before getting up from bed to reach for the phone. They recognized the incoming call instantly.

They placed the phone against their ear. "Lau?"

"Ayale?" Lau's surprised, saddened, and relieved voice asked all at once. "Are you okay? Where are you?" Lau rapidly fired queries of concern, leaving Ayale half smiling in the dark, touching the side of their face to make sure they were still themself.

"I was asleep, we are alive, and border between Oolonxg and Cxai territories. It'll be a few more days before we land in the first town there, maybe another after that before I'm back at the compound." They said with a soft mumble of words. Lau sighed, silence taking over the other line before she spoke again.

"Do you already know?" She asked in a hushed voice.

"About?" Ayale genuinely wasn't sure what she insinuated.

"The invasion. I heard some intel in the clan. They haven't left yet, but they're getting ready."

Ayale held back the groan simmering in their throat. "Yeah, I'm aware."

"Okay. That's good to know."

"I'll let my folks know and we'll go from there. If they believe me."

"Well, they better. They're going to send an initial group, a small one, but they're not to be fucked with. I'll keep trying to learn more, but for now, make sure you get home safe. And let your clan know." Lau emphasized. "This is a fucking mess, Ayale."

"I know, Lau." Ayale said, now fully awake from the anxiety pounding away at their stomach. "Let me know, if you can, when the Matxha clan are about to send their first group. Any information helps."

"You know I'll try my best, kid. Just," Lau cleared her throat, holding back more than just that. "Just be safe."

"I will. Talk to you later, tell Rae I said hi." Ayale hung up the phone, sitting at the edge of the bed, letting memories of home and what was to come overwhelm them into silent tears.

With no idea what to expect going home, Ayale could only hold onto the memories that made them who they were in that moment, and keep moving forward.

Warm arms enclosed their waist, the rustle of sheets filling the soundless void of the inn room. Osiris pressed his head on their back, feeling the exhale that escaped their lungs in response. The sound of a quickening heartbeat thumped violently against their chest, loud enough that he could feel it.

"Lau?" Osiris muttered in a low voice.

"Mhm."

"You alright?" He continued, his voice a groggy mumble, tightening his arms around them.

"Fine."

Osiris felt a yawn creep out of him, but forced himself to sit beside them at the edge of the bed, side by side. "It's okay not to be okay. Was it something she said to you?" He persisted, watching them wipe away whatever stray tears remained in their eyes.

Ayale met his tired gaze, unsure what they could possibly say that he didn't know already. All they knew was the warmth coming from Osiris left them a little less worse for wear, relieved that they weren't alone in this endeavor, especially as they approached their territory.

The mere thought of being home, an invasion on their tail, and handling family matters they once ran from was enough to leave Ayale ready to openly weep. They didn't want to give up their freedom, they didn't want to deal with an invasion, and they absolutely refused to take the path made out for them.

And yet, at least for now, they had Osiris. Whatever was to come, they were relieved to have him by their side.

Ayale leaned into his shoulder, the groan almost enough of an answer for him. "It's everything." They exhaled.

Osiris moved an arm around their shoulders, making sure not to disturb the place they laid their head. His arms remained tight around them, his hand petting the back of their head. A small source of comfort among every thought raging in Ayale's mind.

Ayale laid against Osiris, suppressing every urge to cry. They wanted to feel like nothing existed, while everything remained distant for the time being.

How many more moments did the two of them have left? Home being on the horizon, they wondered if this was the last night they would spend curled up with one another. They could no longer hold onto the idea of leaving him to some assumptive safety.

All they knew was that once they were in Cxai territory, they couldn't be with Osiris anymore. For his own safety, they would need to keep their distance. Otherwise, taking him back home with them would have been for nothing. The thought alone was enough to leave them melting into Osiris more. Their arms wrapped over his stomach and around his lower back, not wanting to separate from him.

Unaware of their thoughts, Osiris only wanted to bring a sense of comfort to them. His hand fell from their hair, rubbing small circles into their back, pressing his lips to their forehead.

Ayale moved back and looked up to Osiris. Even in the absence of light, the hazel green in his eyes were soft, gazing at Ayale in a way that had become far too familiar to them. The steady glimpses to their lips and back, as if they wouldn't catch him if he had done so quick enough. A gentle look that was only meant for them.

Ayale looked briefly at his lips, almost mimicking the glance but in a far less subtle movement. The look on his face was inviting, as it always was. But the telltale sign of his curiosity was the way he slid his hands down to their sides, almost out of fear that they would move away from him.

They acted on the feeling of warmth growing within them, reaching up to kiss Osiris, surprised to feel him reciprocate with such ease.

They were both unsure when they would be able to feel a moment like this again, letting what might be their last night be spent in each other's company. The gap between them closed, the sound of rain beginning to fall outside the single window beside them. The noise was of little distraction for either of them, certainly not enough to move away.

Osiris softly grasped at their hips, leaving no space between their bodies. When their delicate hands enveloped his flushed cheeks to pull him closer, he felt like nothing could get in between them. His tongue brushed softly against theirs, daring to see how far he could go.

Ayale was equally ambitious. Their hands roamed away from his face, one making its way to the back of their neck while the other traveled down to his chest, feeling whatever skin exposed itself in his tank top before gripping tightly onto one of the straps and beckoning him closer.

Blindly obliging to anything and everything they wanted, Osiris went from a half-asleep daze to fully conscious, where every feeling he ever felt towards Ayale opened like floodgates that burst the moment they touched him. In seconds, he turned and pinned them onto the bed, never letting Ayale out of his grasp, not even for air. He tried not to put his full weight on them, but let their bodies collide together in a flurry of repressed feelings and fear for the days to come.

Ayale felt his need becoming evident, leaning into Osiris as he threaded a hand into the back of their hair. They nipped playfully at his lower lip, a suppressed groan rumbling in his throat, ready to spill out. His hand slid from their hip, rubbing gently up and down their side. With another yank on his shirt, Osiris was barely hovering over them, gripping the pillow above them as if some form of control could be had if he held on tight enough.

Ayale's heart pounded much harder than ever, in a similar, furious tune to Osiris's. The idea of separation no longer existed, so long as they felt each other writhe in one another's arms, neither needed anything else. They barely noticed him move down, his lips leaving fervent kisses tinged with the warmth of his breath going down the side of their neck. They were left breathless and sensitive to everything he did to them. Ayale pulled him back up to them, crushing their lips against his, a startled moan leaving his overtaken lips.

Osiris brushed his hips against them, hoping and praying he could hear it again. He felt as though he lived and breathed only to hear the sweet noise he could elicit from them in response to his contact.

"Aya," Osiris groaned against their lips, forcing himself away. "I-I need to tell you something." The sound of his voice was low and needy. They played with the hem of his shirt, ready to lift it over his head, until a strange sound came from the door and stopped them.

They froze up, the hem of his tank top still in their hands as he feverishly kissed the side of their neck.

Osiris stopped immediately, hearing the sound of scraping against the wood door. He looked at Ayale, the horrified look on their face being burned into his mind. The both of them laid flustered and breathing heavily while they struggled to catch their breath. Their heavy lidded eyes stared at the door, trying to come up with a plan.

"What is that noise?" Osiris asked out loud, lifting himself off the bed to go investigate the scraping. When he opened the door, he was met with a kneeling man, staring up at Osiris from the ground. In his gloved hands were a small set of tools, his goal clear.

While not his proudest moment, the next few minutes were completely unlike the last two anxiety ridden decades of Osiris's life. He might not have learned much from the Matxha clan, but enough to get him through this situation.

"Were you trying to break into our room?" Osiris mustered the most serious expression he could while straightening his back and crossing his arms over his chest. His eyes darted down to the older gentleman's hands; a lock pick tool as clear as day.

Before he could say anything, Osiris swung his knee into his face, letting him tumble to the ground. He slammed the door in his face and locked it behind him, leaning his back against the wooden door.

"Is that what you were like in the Matxha clan?" Ayale watched from the bed.

"Kind of, at least when people were watching." He felt his voice grow quiet, struggling to move from his spot at the entrance.

The two of them were visibly unsure what to do from there, a moment that came in the night, and left when someone tried to break into their room.

"We don't have to...go back to what we were doing, if you don't want to." Osiris breathed, his words coming out without thought.

"I'm sorry." Ayale mumbled, sinking their face into one of the pillows. Embarrassed wasn't a strong enough word to describe how they felt, though mortifying may have been.

"Don't be, I-I could have easily said no, if I wanted to." He stuttered.

They groaned in response. "This doesn't feel fine."

"You didn't do anything wrong." Osiris sat beside them, putting his arm around their waist. "Let's get a bit more sleep and head out in the morning, alright? I'm going to check on the car, make sure our stuff is still there." He reassured Ayale with a quick nuzzle to their cheek, tossing on his jacket and shoes before hurrying out of the room.

The cool night air was everything Osiris needed after the turn of events tonight. From everything he had done, and almost done. Relief washed over him when he saw the car had not been tampered with, but the constant replay in his head would take up his thoughts for a long time to come. He leaned his back on the driver side door, wondering if he should have let the words slip from him in the throes of passion.

And yet, he was all the more relieved he didn't.

Osiris was a bit too old fashioned for his own good, an unfortunate trait he's had all his life. As willing as he was to keep going, he wished to make himself clear about his intentions.

To tell someone he loved them was a big deal, and he wanted to do it right.

He breathed in the humid air, taking his breathing exercises seriously as the rain became a subtle drizzle. When he felt he was calm once more, he made his way back into the inn, and towards their shared room.

Osiris laid beside Ayale again, putting his arm around them as if tomorrow would never come.

## XXXVI

The late morning sun awoke Ayale, Osiris rising shortly after.

Moving around the room to collect their bags before leaving, he put on a sage green shirt he took from Teryn's, crossing in front of a mirror that reflected two semi rested young adults. He watched Ayale slide on their jacket before debating whether to keep it on or not.

By the time the two of them were ready to hit the road again, Osiris had decided to reach into the backseat and take out two small cans of tea. He tossed one over to Ayale, who caught and opened in in a single movement.

"Probably should have asked, what is this?" They took a small sniff of it, questioning its contents even more.

"I think it's like a mix of tea. Chai, matcha, I'm not even super sure."

They took a sip, unsure how they felt about the strange beverage.

As Ayale and Osiris hit the road, the sun brought with it enough warmth to render long sleeves useless. A tentative few hours passed by, the two sharing occasional tales of their homes of both the impactful and the miniscule events throughout their lives. Some things that changed them as people, while others passed on as nothing.

With his sketchbook in hand, Osiris felt nostalgic for a different time. The days when he struggled as an artist but prevailed with the support of his parents. He sought out something to make money on the side and quickly found himself taken up by an entry level guard job for the Matxha clan. A job he never thought too much about, present only for the pay, as many did. His only want in life was to be happy and the rest would follow so long as he could continue his art, or so he believed. Such sentiment sounded simple. Yet as time went on, there was a growing danger to his plan. One he didn't notice until it was too late.

Desperate to keep the conversation flowing and his mind away from a time long gone, Osiris brought up a piece of his history, as a sort of exchange for Ayale having told him so much about themself recently. "Have I ever told you about how I started off as an artist before I joined the Matxha clan?" He took the sketchbook from his hands and placed it on the dashboard in front of him.

Ayale raised a brow and threw a curious glance in his direction. "I think you mentioned it once or twice before. Why?" They asked a bit too seriously.

"Well, it's embarrassing and clearly did not work out for me. Sort of became the reason I joined the Matxha clan not too long after. Art doesn't make money."

Curiosity remained on their face, prompting Osiris to continue.

"I loved what I did. Though I don't think anyone really gives artists a chance these days, unless you're already a big name. You need to know someone who knows someone, or something like that. Already have connections established."

"Did you study art?"

Osiris shook his head. "Not in school. All self-taught. Or whatever I learned from the internet."

Ayale snorted on accident, their smile too evident to hide.

"Is that funny?" He asked.

"No, just the way you said it, I imagined a much different side of you."

"Hopefully nothing negative," He poked at their shoulder, worried his image in their mind might be worse for wear. Osiris knew it was too late to take any of it back, so he kept going. "I can do more than sketch, you know."

"You paint as well, right?" They asked nonchalantly.

Osiris narrowed his eyes in their direction. "How did you know?"

"Your hand strokes in sketching, they're reminiscent of a painter."

"That had to be a lucky guess, there is no way you just knew that. Unless..." His mind wandered before his eyes lit up. "Oh my god, you paint, don't you?"

Ayale did not dare meet his excited expression, refusing to answer.

"That is adorable, you're so embarrassed right now." He teased heavily, their straight face unchanging.

"It was a long time ago, when I still lived at home. I needed something to find peace. My brother told me to pick up art and lent me his paints to try his preferred medium."

Osiris grew quiet, feeling a stream of guilt creeping into his conscience.

"Spoiler alert, it did not work. As you can clearly see." They gestured their hand in a circle, hoping to earn at least a chuckle from their dark humor. "I ran off a year or so after that. When I think back to the paint set, I wonder if Ateno knew I was reaching my breaking point."

"Your brother?"

Ayale nodded. "The only sane person in that entire house. He always tried his best to support me, especially once our parents hit their worst selves. But he couldn't be there for everything, no matter how hard he tried. I tried just as hard to hide my own pain, in order to protect him. We aren't given a choice to the circumstances we're born in. I never knew how to comfort him when I couldn't even comfort myself."

"Ateno knew you cared." Osiris reached out to Ayale's free hand on their lap, placing his hand over theirs.

"Happiness is such a loaded concept sometimes." Ayale described their own meaning, knowing their own stemmed from the biggest heartbreak they ever committed. "I barely gave him a heads up. A couple of days before, he told me to leave and go make something of myself. Never contacted him again after I left. The thought of leaving him behind still haunts me to this day."

Osiris wanted to know more than anything how they ran away. Since the two met each other, that mysterious air about them had slowly dissipated in his eyes. The more tales they shared with one another, the less of that fog he experienced.

Learning something that defined their existence would mean knowing almost everything there was about Ayale.

"How did you leave the Cxai compound, Ayale?" Osiris asked quietly, letting the subtle question linger in the air while they seemed to figure out how to answer him.

Ayale thought for a couple of minutes, spanning a mile or two with Lau's sedan before speaking again. "I had thought about it on and off for a long time. But after one...incident in particular, I needed to leave. The idea of staying put my life on the line. I couldn't leave my room without feeling dread. One night, I played with the thought of leaving a little too much. Went into so much detail as to how I would do it, where I would stash my things, what bus I would take and to where. I knew how to get access to Cxai clan money without raising any red flags towards myself." They detailed to Osiris, recalling how they planned their escape and how long it took them.

"I don't regret what I did. I ran to survive." Ayale reassured, both for themself and Osiris, who watched them intently.

"I'm glad you were able to get out." Osiris managed to say, threading his fingers through theirs.

"I went to the Cxai clan meetings with my father as I always did. I knew better than to act out of turn and raise suspicions. He trusted me too much and I took advantage of that. Clan matters have and always will be every man for themselves. He taught me to never rely on others from a young age." Ayale recounted, a sour look flashing on their face. "On my last night, I had everything I needed and put everything in motion." Thinking back to their very last day they spent in Cxai territory, detailing as if it happened yesterday. From attending meetings, accompanied by their parents, hiding away the bag they had prepared on the side. They described the fight they heard that night, over money as it always was. Mero's accusatory screams always pointed at Diori. Though in the last few nights, it had been Ayale taking money at a slow rate to prepare for their exit. They fell asleep soon after, no feeling enough to keep them home any longer.

"I watched the sun rise over the coastline for the very last time, and I walked out the front door." They recalled the early morning glow as if it were the most beautiful thing in the world. How the gentle orange hue greeted their last morning in Nalira, and how they took their backpack, and simply walked away from everything they knew, towards the rising sun in the west.

"I boarded a bus and went as far as it could take me, then another, and a few switch offs later, I landed in Densriel. With the money I stole, I changed my last name, rented a room, met Lau, and the rest is history."

Osiris listened to their story, a heavy weight in his chest replaced with sympathy. He never imagined disliking his parents so much he would plan so heavily how to run from them. One reason becoming two, three, four, five more.

Letting the truth settle between them, Ayale felt as if they told Osiris too much.

"Do you think I'm awful for leaving?" They found themself asking.

"Never. You did what not many could." A gentle glance shot over in their direction. "If anything, I envy your strength."

"I wanted to see things I've never seen before. To add to my reasons." Ayale recanted the advice their older brother gave them days before their plan; leave and go make something of yourself.

"Why have I never heard about this brother until recently?" Osiris interrupted their train of thought.

Ayale only shrugged. "Why not?"

"Wouldn't mind hearing more about your normal family once in a while."

"If I wasn't driving, I'd throw something at you for that comment." They darted a defensive glare in his direction, secretly going through what was in their pockets for a possible projectile, eventually settling on a pen, and tossing it at Osiris. He flinched, choked back an awful noise, and Ayale struggled not to laugh at him. They picked up their tea from the cup holder, taking a long sip of the strange chai mixture when he grabbed it out from under them.

"Tea is for the kind, not you." Osiris leaned in and stole a sip for himself.

"Don't make me pull over," Ayale threatened, their hand outstretched, waiting for the can to return to their hands. "Give it."

"Apologize. Maybe I'll consider it." Osiris demanded, a playful smirk stretched across his face.

"I'm sorry that you're bad at dodging." They finished.

"Then I'm sorry you won't be caffeinated." He stole another, much more drawn-out gulp of their tea. Ayale smacked him in the arm, Osiris laughing as he tried not to spill anything on himself. The two of them cracked up, losing whatever composure was left over from their serious conversation, bursting into uncontrollable chuckles and giggles. Neither of them could hold onto a straight face longer than a few seconds.

Osiris eventually handed them back their drink, stealing one more spiteful sip before returning it back. The brush of their hand against his lingered, bringing an odd bout of embarrassment to the car ride once more.

*

The distant noise of clattering metal, the sound of people indistinctly speaking to one another, and the overall overwhelming effort of random Matxha officials trying to get the attention of a particularly disinterested thirteen-year-old teenager, who sat at the very back of a warehouse on her phone. The seemingly distant look in her eyes accentuated her pale complexion, and the thin blonde strands that fell around her shoulders, but not quite past them. She was small in stature, but to everyone in that large work room, a finite terror on bad days, and a nuisance on her better ones.

When one particularly loud thud took her attention away from her phone, her unblinking stare met with that of the perpetrator, who dared to continue his work as she approached him, to ask if the noises were necessary.

She stood there beside him, waiting in a stone silence for him to notice her presence.

The rest of the warehouse fell silent, but the metal worker before her failed to put his torch down. When he realized she was there, he did not bother to look at her, only pointing a question in her direction, the last one he would ever ask. "What are you looking at?" He pulled up his welding mask, not quite sure for himself who she was.

In a split second, the young girl reached a hand onto his shoulder, her pale eyes and piercing smile the last vision he would have as he jerked and fell to the floor, an electric current running through him, stealing the light from his eyes, and leaving a charred, lifeless worker on the dirty concrete.

"My name is Eines. And I am your superior." Her soft voice answered the lifeless corpse. She looked back to her seat, walking back over to sit with her phone, ignoring the collective looks of horror as she did. "Keep the noise down, please." Eines said, looking back down at her phone. The two men beside her straightened their backs and nodded.

The gradual sounds of machinery took over again, though with a slower rate of completion to their dismay.

The young girl sat patiently in her seat, overseeing the completion of the warehouse's latest projects. The bustle of people around her worked on various weaponry, by her orders as of recent. She put her phone onto her lap and looked to the older gentleman on her right. She waved her petite hand, signaling for him to lean in close to her.

"Let that be my one and final warning. Insubordination, any sign of it from anyone, will not be tolerated." Eines whispered, as though she were at a slumber party telling the soldier a school yard rumor. At the edge of her small voice came another warning, one she considered thoughtful. "Unless anyone here would like to end up with the same fate as my father." She smiled, unsettling the soldier she spoke to as well as the one to her left who overheard her.

Eines wanted to make it clear who was in charge. And as of a year ago, under circumstances kept within the closest of the Matxha clan, it was her now.

As she went to pick up her phone, she crossed one leg over the other and smiled.

Eines, leader of the Matxha Clan, had a certain ring to it. One that never failed to put a smile on her face.

# XXXVII

Ayale and Osiris stopped once more for the night on the side of the highway until morning again. They continued to drive after the sun rose further into the horizon, going well into the afternoon without any issues, stopping for gas at one point.

After everything they had done in the last twenty-four hours, the drive was a welcome distraction. Between their actions at the inn and telling Osiris everything from the time they ran from Cxai territory, Ayale almost didn't recognize the person they had become.

Why Ayale had kissed Osiris after their call with Lau was far beyond their comprehension. They wanted to shut all their feelings down, but every so often, under the subtle rumble of the road beneath the car, and the radio in the background, they recalled a multitude of events, all shared with Osiris throughout their adventure, one by one. Their tales were far more than they could have initially expected from day zero.

They stole a small glance at Osiris in the passenger seat, his eyes on the phone in his lap. Ayale looked back to the road, trying to shake off the discomfort in their chest that came after. With a feeling they couldn't quite place, it began to feel like something was weighing them down every time they so much as looked at Osiris, outside of the threat of invasions and going back home to Cxai territory.

"Everything okay?" Osiris shifted in his seat to face them, putting the phone back into his pocket.

"Yeah." Ayale muttered, shifting their legs and straightening their back, unable to settle that weight in their chest. Unwilling to acknowledge its source, they needed a subject change. "How are

Teryn and Visu?" They almost asked about Lau, but decidedly didn't want to know after their last conversation.

"As good as they can be. Visu made his recovery and can see out of his eye again, but the tracker diminishes with his symptoms. Teryn offered to spy in his stead and return to the Oolonxg clan, they got into a heated argument, so for now, they are both texting me separately. I think talks of an invasion have everyone on edge though. Being in love can do that to a person, let alone a war." He covered his eyes with his arm before pulling down the visor to shade him from the sun. Osiris straightened himself in the passenger seat, his eyes wandered out at the sunny expanse of fields, majestic foggy mountains no longer capped with snow rolling out, reaching the clouds in the distance. It was one of many new sights on their journey eastward that left Osiris full of wonder and awe. He pulled the window down, the warm dry breeze blowing back his sleeves, causing him to roll the long fabric up his arms. A part of him wished he had bought sunglasses at some point during their trip.

Ayale tensed as the familiarly warm breeze hit their cheeks. What was supposed to bring warmth and sunshine had only managed to bring up memories of the past, and soon enough, their latest nightmare. Nothing woke them up more than the sight of their father's face reflecting in their own.

The idea of being home, under the same roof once more made them want to turn the car around, change their names, and settle somewhere far from the Cxai clan. Let the clans battle it out for whatever territory they went after next.

They tapped idly at the straight pointed steering wheel, having no need to move it even slightly in the last hour.

There was one memory that led them down the rabbit hole. A single reminder of who he was to them within his actions; when they were a child, alongside their older brother Ateno, and their father opted to use force at any minor inconvenience. They had been kicked in public, shoved into furniture, and in later years as his movement and health deteriorated, a verbal punching bag. An onslaught of derogatory language always pointed at them or some other family member.

Ayale couldn't sit there and say there was one issue to have pushed them to run off. Even if he was around, it felt like no one was there at all.

It wasn't the times he said he owned his family members like cattle in front of strangers, that they were property before people, nor the times they were left to fend for themselves because asking him for help had been a fate worse than suffering. But if they had to choose one reason, it was when their father said, with an utmost sense of pride, how well he raised his children.

Ayale slowed the car down, pulling off to the side of the open road highway. They parked the car and promptly turned it off, all music from the radio cutting off, and left Osiris looking at them, thoroughly confused.

"Can we sit here for a bit before we get to the border?" Ayale looked down at the dashboard, straight-faced, serious, and unwilling to look Osiris in the eye.

"A break wouldn't hurt. Are you okay?" He asked, leaning over the center console, flipping down Ayale's visor to block part of the sun from their eyes.

"Yeah." They lied. "Just need a small break to stretch my legs." They slowly left the car, motioning towards the back seat to take off and store their sweater in their backpack.

"I have an idea." A warm hand settled on their shoulder, the noise from their shuffling through their bag all they wanted to focus on. "Want to grab the snack bag for me?" He requested with a childlike excitement to his soft voice, to which they obliged. Osiris led them over to the back of the sedan, sliding over the trunk before settling himself on the other side. He took the bag from their grasp and placed it beside him, taking Ayale's hand to help them climb up.

Hesitantly, they hopped up, sitting up against the back of the window.

The view of the glowing sky, the dry air around them, and the mountains aligned with the skyline was unlike any other for Osiris. To him, the contrast between the mountain range in front of him and the one he saw in Odania were day and night. But Ayale found the scenery too familiar, in a way that hurt their stomach just looking at it. They unknowingly leaned over and crossed their arms over their abdomen.

"Are you sure you're feeling okay?" Osiris asked, stretching a hand into the snack bag and producing a bag of chips for the two of them to share. "You keep staring off a lot. Kind of reminds me of when I met you."

"I'm fine, just a little jittery." They said gazing off at the long road in front of them.

"In that case, I just want to remind you that you're not alone in this, no matter what happens. That's a promise." Osiris moved the bag behind him. "But I did want to bring up what that...means to me versus what that might mean to you, just to see if we—you and I, sorry—are on the same wavelength." He shook off his stutter, the thoughts of last night, and forced himself to continue.

Ayale seemed unphased by him, but a part of them couldn't help thinking this was the result of them going too far the night prior. They unknowingly tapped their fingers impatiently on the sedan, an unsteady rhythm against the warm metal.

"I-I think it might be good for us to discuss...this..." Osiris lost his momentum, trailing off as his cheeks burned with embarrassment. He gave himself a second to breathe, before letting his heart guide the next few words out of his mouth.

He took Ayale's hand, one over theirs and one beneath, letting his fingertips lace between theirs. "You mean more to me than the fear of what's to come. And if I don't tell you how I feel—"

The crackle of a rough, rumbling engine in the distance increased, in both sound and speed, leaving Osiris paused mid-sentence and staring at the source further down the eerily but otherwise abandoned road.

"What the hell is that?" Ayale narrowed their eyes at the speeding car coming down towards them from the east.

"Probably just a nutjob who can't help but go fast on the highway. We can ignore them." Osiris reasoned, hoping the odd car would be out of their way and leave them both be. There wasn't much daylight left, but he wanted to say his piece before they crossed over the borders, needing to know how or if Ayale felt the same way about him, especially after their moment together at the inn.

Osiris wasn't one to be lucky. He knew this all too well. But even so, he held on to hope. For mutual feelings and for the moment of peace to speak to one another about it.

The incoming car slammed on their brakes, a handful of meters away from where the two sat.

Ayale tore their hand away and slid off Lau's car, their tired eyes wide and alert as the odd car sped towards their direction, straightening their back and ready for anything. Whoever was about to approach, they stood in front of the car, more than ready to handle it.

With the odd vehicle still on, a woman left the car, almost tripping over herself as she fled from the car towards the two of them.

Ayale's confident stance crumbled into confusion, then terror, their brow pulling together like a scared child, all a series of looks Osiris had never experienced seeing on their face before. When his eyes drifted to the woman running across the road, a part of him wondered why she looked so familiar.

"Ayale!" She screamed from the top of her lungs, leaving her throat like a screech. She threw her arms around Ayale, who stood frozen like a statue in the middle of winter, their face stuck in their terrified but confused look. Their eyes seemed to scream for help when they found Osiris again.

"I had a feeling you were close by!" The woman exclaimed, squeezing the life out of Ayale, and subsequently, turning their face a different hue. Osiris wasn't sure if they were going to cry, faint, scream, hurl, or all four at once.

They tried to move, but the woman refused to let go or stop fussing with them, as if she were Ayale's—

"Hello mom." Ayale's strained voice grumbled, hoping she would take the hint and let go.

Diori turned around with Ayale still in her arms, barely attentive to Osiris and his blank stare. In that moment, he saw the resemblance. It was in the eyes more than anything, their shared skin tone, but stood with equally drastic differences.

For Diori, she had a plethora of platinum grey hair amongst rare instance of black that sat straight and stretched far over her left shoulder and parted to the side. Barely the same height, she was a bit shorter, a strong touch of wrinkles beneath both dark eyes. A light bronze colored shawl covered her shoulders with a lace black tank top beneath it and simple but loose black pants to match.

What stood out the most was her strange scar, placed in the middle of her forehead, oddly prominent with what seemed like wrinkled skin just above it. Not to say it was weird, but it certainly caught his eye.

"I can't believe it's really you." Diori squished her face against the side of their head before leaning back, grabbing their face tight in her hands. "She told me I should have waited but I couldn't do it."

The noise of the car across came to a stop, the engine cutting as another body left the passenger side. With a set of keys in hand, a woman emerged, carefully crossing the road. She wore a pale red shawl, her dark curls pulled by a clip to the back of her head.

"Reuniting in the middle of the road, Diori?" Katari approached the group, her smile subtle but noticeable.

"Is that Katari?" Ayale attempted to turn around but was held back by their mother.

Osiris became highly overwhelmed by everything going on at once. One minute, he was readying to tell Ayale how he felt, how he was in love with them, the next the two thought they were about to be ambushed. Instead of a romantic moment of confessions, he was in front of Ayale's mother, with Katari coming up to his side as if it were a planned reunion.

"Osiris." A glint of a smile crossed her face. "How have your travels been? How was Odania? Has everything been smooth?" She asked, a touch of hesitation in her question, leaving Osiris to believe she already had a few ideas of just how much Ayale and him had gone through.

"We're alive. That's all that really matters when you think about it."

Katari grabbed Osiris in a hug, cutting the conversation short.

He didn't know how to react, but returned the hug with his own, glad in his own way that she was there.

"I'm glad you are okay." Katari said, voice solemn with her own worry. When she let go, she turned to Diori, unsure how to get the older woman to let go of Ayale, who struggled to leave her arms. "Let Ayale go. Come on now, just as we practiced." Katari tried to reason.

"This is my child, I just need one more minute." Diori mumbled.

"Time is not on our side, Diori. We are not supposed to be here to begin with." She warned.

"Wait, why?" Ayale tried to shimmy their way out of her tight grasp.

Diori let them leave her arms, a bit hesitant to speak about the situation at hand.

"I have been formally kicked out of the territory. A few have followed, but we have been quick to resettle elsewhere. Maybe you could come with us?" She struggled to ask, hopeful as she waited for an answer.

"Mero is a piece of work," Katari said, looking at Osiris with an uncertain look, and placed a hand on his shoulder. "If you choose to go to the main house, please be careful." Her tone forewarned.

"I am not letting them go alone." Osiris said, a finality in his voice with no hesitation.

Diori shifted her gaze up at him, with a gentle nod in his direction. She was at least glad Ayale had someone beside them for what was to come.

"I need to talk to Mero, there's a lot I have to bring to his attention, whether I want to or not. Lives are on the line now, and not just ours. I can't just ignore what I came here to do." Ayale put their hands in their pants pocket, feeling awkward to turn down yet another chance to get out of this heavy feeling of responsibility.

"I understand." Diori said in a hushed sadness. "Just be safe, please. I can't help again once you cross that border."

"And that's to say you did at all beforehand? Like when we were arrested in the Oolonxg territory?" They emphasized, the words spilling out before they could stop them.

Diori didn't move an inch before lowering her head, unable to come up with anything more than an apology. "I'm sorry."

"I'm sure you are," Ayale told themself and everyone around them out loud. "But I need to get back to the house and tell him about an invasion, and eventually ask for a favor on top of that."

Diori nor Katari seemed to budge, already confirming to Ayale what they had suspected before. Nothing really gets past their mother, after all. Katari herself looked down at the phone in Osiris' hand, an idea crossing her mind.

"Here, let me see your phone so we can give you our numbers." Katari took the phone and input both of their contact information. "While we can't be there in person, we can still communicate. Just let us know if you need anything." She handed the phone back, a stifled breath coming back out.

"I won't call this goodbye. More of 'see you soon', okay?" Diori met Ayale with a hesitant, careful smile. They only met her eyes for a second and nodded briefly, straight faced and unwilling to open their mouth again.

Both women made their way back to their car, getting back in the vehicle before driving away.

Ayale and Osiris watched them leave, silence filling the unattended highway.

"Ready to go?" Osiris asked, rolling the stress off his shoulders before he felt a weight on him as Ayale placed their head on his right shoulder.

"Not yet. I need some time to prepare myself mentally."

His arm snuck around their shoulders, pulling them in for a tight hug, even as the afternoon sun beat down on the two of them.

Osiris didn't mind taking some time before moving again. He could have sat there forever if they asked him to.

Part of him would soon wish they did.

# XXXVIII

Just as the two finished with Diori's ominous forthcoming, Ayale and Osiris soon found themselves at the border that divided the eastern span of the Oolonxg territory and the northwestern Cxai territory. No real border existed, save for a single, worn-out sign made half a century ago in the style of the boxed Cxai lines, with something along the lines of Welcome to Cxai faded on a piece of weathered limestone.

Ayale drove slower than before, quickly becoming aware of their surroundings. Everything from the sign they had not seen since their escape to the upcoming farmland they recalled the first bus driving through. They suddenly felt the sweat cling to their forehead and palms, gripping the steering wheel a little tighter, as if the act could do anything to avoid the fate they were driving towards.

Their stomach, their thoughts, everything In their body screamed at them to turn back and let the invasion happen. What good would telling Mero do? Why should they put their life on the line a second time so soon?

Osiris could see the stress grow across their features, visibly increasing the longer they drove. He placed a hand on their shoulder, feeling them jump before unfurling their back against his hand. "I'm sorry." They muttered, letting their shoulders fall back. "Every time I think about Cxai territory, I can feel the dread settle into me."

"Come on, let's pull over for a bit." Osiris said, looking for a place for the two of them to stop off.

Ayale swallowed hard and nodded.

The two found themselves on a narrow road, bated breath barely able to escape their tight lips. They forced the car to a much slower speed, particularly on the road that barely fit a single vehicle to begin with. Ayale spotted a small lot of gravel, overlooking the remnants of the town from about thirty feet up, where the sun had peaked through bare amounts of clouds across the horizon.

The exhale that left their chest only partially lifted the weight from their body.

"It feels strange to be in a place that I know next to nothing about," Osiris pulled them close, his arm encircling both shoulders, his hand on their forearm. "Why don't you tell me something about your territory?"

Ayale snickered, tempted to place their head on his shoulder. "Why would you want to know about Cxai territory now?"

"I want to know about the place you came from, is that so funny?"

"A little bit." They sighed. "What do you want to know?"

"Everything." Osiris rubbed their arm, hoping this would distract the two of them from their journey, if only for a moment.

Ayale took a minute to think about their territory's history before beginning. "Let's start from about three hundred years ago. The Cxai family was one of six to rise from the ashes of a burned down monarchy. Out of the six areas that claimed their independence, they rose to become individual territories, creating these finite borders that were more spoken rather than agreed upon. It was necessary to make these changes, there would have been far more unrest if left to the ruins of an old world. Among the Cxai family's rise in the northeast was a neighboring territory called the Ceyxlon clan, who had taken the southern coast and islands. The Matxha clan claimed the southwest, the Rooiboux took the central plains, the Chamoxile to the northwest, and the Oolonxg in the central north. I mean, we knew that last one already." Ayale shrugged, looking around the car for their notebook and pen, drawing on a random page against their thigh.

A crude but basic sketch of the continent was born, with awful, dotted lines depicting borders from over three hundred years ago from memory.

"Alright." Ayale stared at the bad drawing and placed it between themself and Osiris. "Tell your artist brain I tried, I can see you cringing." They shot a glare in his direction. "The history of these clans isn't black and white. Everyone has problems with everyone, that's politics in a nutshell. Typically, there is at least one clan that gets along with another. For the Rooiboux, once upon a time, it was the Matxha. Until about twenty or so years ago. The Oolonxg had the Chamoxile until about a hundred years ago, and the Cxai had the lesser known Ceyxlon."

Osiris peered up at Ayale with a knowing look. Before he could ask, they continued speaking.

"Before you ask, the Cxai ate up that territory after my parents wed about thirty years ago. Not to say they were well known before that, but the Cxai had their eyes on expansion for a long enough time and waited for the Ceyxlon to show some sort of weakness. That's what all clans do. They take over, conquer, expand, and tell everyone a lie to cover it up. Do you know why clans absorb the weak, Osiris?"

He blinked twice, wondering If that was a real question. "To expand and conquer?"

"There is no good reason behind a well-off clan to take another. To eat up and colonize land that was never meant to have monetary value to begin with." Ayale put their hands to their lap, exhausted from talking about clan politics. They found the horizon, looking over the small town. "Look at all of this. All these buildings, these roads. Everything in this town was made by the people who live here.

The clans had nothing to do with it. Why should they have a say in whose land this is when it belongs to the people who built it?"

Osiris' hand slid up to the side of their head, pulling Ayale to his shoulder. They settled against him for a moment, his eyes never leaving the scene in front of them. A breath left his lungs, solemn but not regretful for stopping, even if temporary.

In a fleeting thought, Osiris wondered if Ayale knew their own potential as a leader.

He would follow them anywhere.

Ayale and Osiris began their drive once more, following the sole road through the small town eastward.

At one point, they had to stop the car entirely in the middle of what they assumed had been an abandoned town. A row of goats followed by an older gentleman crossed the narrow path through a village, coming from a settlement of small houses built into rock and wood alike. Ayale waved him through, watching him cross the road while struggling to keep his livestock from straying. Unfortunately for him, one had turned towards the car and walked decisively on its own, the bell around its neck clanking gently as it approached Osiris' open window.

Osiris sank into his seat, clearly startled by the goat approaching the car. He turned to Ayale, whose strained expression softened, placing the car in park. "He looks friendly, no need to be frightened." Ayale got out of the car, heading over to the other end of the car to pet the goat and gently herd the stray animal back to its owner.

Osiris placed his head out the window to watch, a part of him surprised how well Ayale handled themself around animals. He watched Ayale wave to the farmer who waved his hand back as they made it back into the driver's side of the car.

"That was impressive." Osiris complimented them, giving him another reason for his feelings to flourish. "How did you stay so calm?"

"Don't be too impressed. Ateno showed me how to handle animals when we were kids." Ayale responded, putting the car back in drive when the road eventually cleared up.

While the sun slowly set behind them, Ayale could see the tall buildings in the distance, remnant of Densriel without the dense population. Homes and residencies made up the path towards the capital. They drove past farms, tentative fields growing young fruit trees in semi organized lines, all ready to bear the incoming summers' fruit. Roads were bumpy, uneven and made up of primarily dirt paths, places Ayale passed by on their escape from Cxai territory, having once thought they were never to return again.

That prickle of anxiety made its appearance on their bare arms, leaving goosebumps in its wake, even when they were overheating. They straightened their back in response. The last thing they wanted was to allow that feeling to return.

Ayale took a deep breath, doing what they could to calm themself. They promised and swore when they returned, that they would be stronger than the naïve version of themself who ran away.

They wanted to defend the child they were when they walked away from the Cxai clan.

And with their return, they would be bringing someone with them. Someone who needed their strength and defense just as much, if not more.

Osiris' voice suddenly cut through their introspection. "Where is the nearest café?"

"Are you really thinking about coffee right now?" Ayale shot a short glare towards Osiris.

"Isn't this territory known for that weird coffee you had me try in Istanza?"

"First off, not weird, you just can't handle real coffee. I've seen the lattes you order, they are more like ice cream sundaes. Second, don't start a fight you can't win." They waved their hand, resigning from the conversation.

Osiris shrugged, smiling to himself as the sights stole his wandering eyes again. A fight he couldn't win was when they became stuck in their head. 'Arguments' like these were the easiest way to force Ayale to think of something other than, well, everything else.

And so, he tucked away his mischievous smile and persisted with the topic with a new comeback, to annoy them like no one else could. "Do the Cxai not know to put milk in coffee?"

"Do the Matxha not know when to quiet down?" Ayale responded too quickly, driving over a rough patch in the road. They tightened their grip on the steering wheel in an attempt to keep control the car on the awful road. Even the occasional swerves did little to avoid the persistent holes in the paths around the unsteady farmland.

"What's with the roads?" Osiris clutched onto the handle above his head.

"Not sure, they aren't usually this bad."

The road eventually stabilized, the potholes soon behind them. The midday sun wrested beyond the cliffside buildings in the distance, the scenery changing before their collective eyes. The further into the groggy city, the closer they came towards the capital city of Nalira. The roads thinned and paved, Ayale had to force the car to slow down.

Osiris' eyes widened, never having seen a city sitting at the edge of so much water, let alone traveled this far from where he once called home. Soon, the two of them were met with a view that signaled the end. The ocean glimmered farther ahead, miles beyond where they were, a picturesque view like none other. The sun soon settled at the edge of the water, filling the sky with orange hues for all to see.

Ayale stopped the car on the side of the dense city street, part of the car settling over the sidewalk lined up behind others in front of them. They parked in front of an unmarked building, the residential look leaving Osiris wondering if they were in front of someone's home, barely convincing for an inn of some kind. A common occurrence in Cxai territory, especially during the height of their tourism season.

When they turned off the car, Ayale inhaled another deep breath before trying to take off their seatbelt.

Osiris' warm hand settled over their own, unwilling to let go. "One more night before the big conversation?"

"Yeah. Just need to get my bearings together." Ayale let out a frustrated breath. Admitting they needed more time was almost as bad as needing it to begin with.

But Osiris never seemed to mind it in the least. That alone was enough to justify the stop.

The two of them left the car, the air singing with the warmth of the descending sun, along with the vaguely salty air from the sea miles away. A coastal city, to be expected.

Osiris was overwhelmed in his senses, between the seascape, the cluster of residential and shopping buildings, the close proximity of bakeries, to banks, to restaurants, to everything. While he waited for Ayale to walk over to him, his eyes drifted over to a sign, one with an arrow pointing towards a set of white painted stairs. His curiosity grew, unknowingly walking towards it.

"Where are you going?" Ayale stopped in front of the car, watching Osiris slowly walk up the winding stairs, his shadow disappearing behind him when he turned the corner. As much as Ayale wanted to rot and sleep the remainder of the evening away, they groaned and followed behind him, sprinting up the unfamiliar staircase.

At the top of the rooftop, Ayale and Osiris were among a small handful of people, a tucked away café with scattered white metal tables and matching set of chairs around them.

Osiris took Ayale's hand and led the two of them to the nearest table, pulling a chair out for them before seating himself across.

The salted ocean breeze brought little relief to their flushed cheeks when it came to the way Osiris went out of his way for the small things. They shifted their eyes away, towards the view from the rooftop that looked like that out of a dream. Swirls of cream and orange, hues of distinct shades of red lingered in the distant skyline, where the sun met the ocean. Neither needed to fill the silence, the swish of crashing waves and cars on the street filling the gap of conversation for the two of them.

Ayale turned forward and found Osiris' hazel eyes drift off at the horizon. They looked out to where he stared off, looking at the sunset before their eyes. "You ever see the ocean before?"

"No." Osiris said with a gentle, dreamlike grin across his face. "This is unreal. You see it in movies, books, photos but they don't do this any justice. Up close, it's different. For a minute, I thought I was dead." He laughed but his eyes never faltered. "And I..." He trailed off, a short glance shot across the table and back out at the view. "I'm glad you brought us here. I'm happy we can see this together."

"I'm glad it was you." Ayale said unexpectedly, even surprising themself. "I couldn't imagine dragging anyone else cross-continent.

You are good company, Osiris." The sides of their lips lifted just slightly, barely allowing the reasons that brought them to Nalira in the first place to cloud their moment.

All they knew was Osiris, the sounds of the city, heart pounding in their chest as they shifted in their chair, the thick air no longer sticking to their bare arms.

The detour lasted up until the night sky took over. Some food and light conversation between them, and soon after came the coffee. Osiris was worried when Ayale seemingly ordered for both of them, at first understanding what they said before they briefly switched over to a language he had never heard come out of their mouth. But the look in their light eyes and smirk on their mouth pointed to him, saying quietly, trust me.

Without question, Osiris nodded and smiled back.

Ten minutes later came out identical iced drinks, both with a light layer of foam at the top. Beneath the small table, Osiris reached a hand to their own, holding it carefully without truly looking at Ayale, eyes out on the darkening horizon. They didn't dare comment on the act, nor really acknowledged him at first, until they squeezed his hand.

And just like the tea shoppe, it was love for Osiris.

Nothing could seemingly get in the way of the time Ayale and Osiris spent together on the rooftop café. One of many shared ventures and moments together that brought Osiris to where he felt so comfortable and understood.

From the first sip, he had remembered every day they spent since the start, as if it all happened in the last week. Every moment felt fresh in his memory.

At the last sip, Osiris understood a simple truth, one cared for and nurtured since his great escape from the clutches of the Matxha clan. One that he saw clearly in every smile, at the bottom of every cup he had drank from since the tea shoppe.

He didn't want to leave Ayale's side.

Osiris readied himself to fight for those feelings, placing down the empty coffee cup, and biding his time for the right moment to confess everything to Ayale.

# XXXIX

After staying at one of the many tourist houses in the city, the two awoke, knowing what was to come. The day to confront Mero had arrived. No more running away.

It was time to face what they left behind.

Ayale stood in front of the redwood double doors to their old house, sitting on top of the famed Cxai compound. Around the main house had been stone walls, most of which began to crumble far before Ayale's lifetime. Unusually contorted pine trees sat overgrown and hung over the walls, some bearing citrus fruits while others had thin green leaves, casting shadows onto the stones. The sounds of birds and cicadas filled the air around Ayale and Osiris, tension thick enough to cut through.

Osiris found himself distracted, staring at the wild flora scattered around the front yard, his eyes clearly trying to assess each flower and overgrown shrub.

Ayale's hands remained in fists at their sides. Face straighter than the intricate faded grey columns at both sides of the front entrance. Neither said a word, no one moved. The humid air was thicker than coffee with a tension Osiris never felt emanate from Ayale before. He brushed the back of his hand against theirs, a reminder to them he was there and present.

They took the deepest breath possible, puffed out their chest, and raised their shoulders back before forcing their hand up to the door to knock.

A few minutes later, a roughly thirty-year-old man opened the door, his tired eyes and unkempt hair reminiscent of Ayale's, sharing both color and almost similar length. If he had squinted hard enough, he would have looked somewhat like Visu, Osiris noted.

But as the stranger's eyes widened, a stare of uncertainty followed with frantic blinks as if forcing himself awake. He quickly settled on a saddened but relieved look, pulling Ayale into his arms without a second to lose.

"Ayale, why?" He managed to breathe out, before tears forcefully streamed down his eyes. Ayale threw their arms around the mystery man, putting their face on his shoulder, muttering their own brief apologies.

"I'm back, Ateno." Ayale choked back, voice barely sounding. "I'm sorry."

"Why did you come back, what did I say to you?" Ateno mumbled, frustration lacing every word.

"Leave and go make something of yourself." Ayale answered. "I had to come back, I had no choice." They pulled away, wiping away their own tears.

"Nothing could be so important to come back to this hellhole." Ateno scolded them thoroughly, his voice rough.

"I pissed off the Matxha clan and attacked their men. I also kind of stole someone away before they could kill him." Ayale threw a brief glance at Osiris. "While we made our way back, we heard from another clan leader that the Matxha clan are days away from invading us. I am here to tell Mero."

Ateno thought for a moment before placing a hand over his forehead, almost at a loss for words, but surprisingly calm. "You think that old man is going to believe you?"

"He's going to have to." Osiris chimed in.

"Who the fuck is this?" Ateno pointed a permanent glare at Osiris, every bit of disdain obvious in his body language.

"That's Osiris, and I am telling you, we don't have time to get into it, I need to see him right now."

"Shit out of luck, he went north for the day." Ateno scratched the back of his head and yawned. "Get inside, I'd rather no Cxai guard see us right now. The apartment should be safe." He moved to the side, pulling the two into the house, surveying the surrounding courtyard.

Osiris first took in all the details of Ayale's childhood home. Discolored parts of the cream walls left marks of long past wall décor, having left behind the once original color of the walls. The remainder of the long walls were barren, until the three of them crossed through a short hallway, full of dusty black photo frames, of pictures that reflected better memories. Osiris couldn't help his wandering eyes, landing on a photo of what looked like Ayale and Ateno side by side at a beach, adolescent and teenager respectively. The hint of a smile on both their faces was the only clue he had of their enjoyment, wherever they were.

At the end of the hallway came a set of wooden stairs, an odd shade of orange and red that he couldn't quite place. As the three of them went up, Osiris could feel the stiff tension within the silence of Ayale and Ateno. He would have spoken up but found himself distracted by the lapses around the house Ayale had once called home. Thin layers of dust settled on everything, from the items decorating the almost abandoned halls down to the overpainted hand railing. Disheveled was barely the word to describe the state of the Cxai compound.

Nearing the top of the stairs sat a door, leading into a living room area, with multiple doors sectioning off other places in the apartment.

"When did you end up here?" Ayale asked, curiosity piqued while they poked around the place.

"Sometime after you left. A lot happened after you went missing."

"Missing?" They stopped by the large triangular table in the middle, confused by the word. Ateno stopped at the opposite end of the table, keeping his stare on them.

"Everyone thought you were taken. No one believed me when I said you left of your own volition."

Ayale pulled out one of the high-top wood chairs, seating themself with a tired groan. "Of course not. Why would I want to leave this place after all?" They looked at Osiris, pulling the chair beside them out for him. As he did, he couldn't help but feel intrusive to their conversation.

Ateno began to fill up three different mugs with instant coffee and sugar, with no regard to ask either of them their preference. He simply made up three frothed iced coffees, setting a pair of black mugs down in front of them. He shifted some miniscule clutter to the side and placed oddly blue beaded coasters beneath each drink.

Ayale's cup wrote 'Always Weird' in block letters, while Osiris' said 'Thank the Gods it's Friday', in huge white cursive letters.

Ateno settled across from them, his harsh eyes set on Osiris.

As Osiris took a cautious sip of his coffee, he was pleasantly surprised it wasn't the bitter liquid he drank from Istanza.

"Who is this guy anyways?" Ateno asked, never taking his tired gaze from Osirus, half expecting a response from him.

"This is Osiris, I thought we already established that." Ayale chimed in, a brow raised with their mug to their lips.

"No, I mean what is he doing here?" Ateno clarified. "Why is he here with you?"

Ayale choked and hit their mug by accident, some of their iced coffee spilling on the table beneath them.

Osiris stifled his laughter, taking a handful of napkins from the neat part of the table and helped them clean up. Though not without a partial smile on his lips. He didn't dare look at them longer than the lapse of a second before retreating back to his seat.

Ayale cleared their throat from the last drops of coffee and looked idly down at the dark expanse of the table. They tried to find the best way to go about their explanation.

As if knowing their struggle with finding the words, Ateno nodded. "Just start from the beginning." He leaned back in his chair, bracing himself for what he was about to hear.

Ayale tapped their fingertips on the black wood top of the table, a thoughtful stare making its way to the surface of their tired eyes. "Let me see your phone." They asked Ateno.

He shrugged and handed over a large screen phone, to which they started to type frantically. Using the search engine, they brought up a result that had Osiris leering over their shoulder.

"L'Ayale's Tea Shoppe?" Ateno slid the phone back to himself, scrolling through reviews and photos. "Ayale, what is all this?"

"That's my tea shoppe. I left here and built that shoppe from the ground up with two friends I made in Densriel. Took a bit to take off, but we did it day by day. It was ours, after all. Three years and I wouldn't take a single minute of the experience away." They said, wistful but confident.

Osiris felt the warmth of those words to a different extent, nonetheless just as much.

Ateno smiled, but quickly felt it slip away before he asked. "Do you miss it there?"

The question brought a sharp pain back in their abdomen. "I would miss it more if the Matxha clan weren't about to invade our home."

"I'm guessing you two met in Densriel?" Ateno pointed his question to Osiris, who silently nodded. "You still never said why the anxious one is with you?" He asked, looking back to Ayale.

"We had to leave Densriel." Ayale spoke quickly, taking a sip of their coffee as Osiris froze on his seat, eyes fixed on the mug below him.

"Because?" Ateno urged them to continue. He yawned, blinking a few times in an attempt to keep himself awake.

Ayale thought for a brief second before deciding how to bring up the original reason for their arrival. "I'm going to be very honest with you. And before I do, I am going to need you not to overreact to this." They pulled their nervous face up from the cup to look at Ateno, who was already bracing himself.

"Osiris came into my tea shoppe. What I didn't learn until recently was that he was scouting for elemental and affinity users, and our names were on some list meant to recruit affinity users to Matxha clan. He destroyed the list, along with all information on elemental users in our part of Densriel." Ayale's voice turned soft, slowly trying to pull together the story of how the two of them got here. Ateno's sharp expression didn't help either of their nerves. "When they learned he destroyed the list of names, Matxha clansmen were sent to kill him." They recalled the horrific moment they discovered Osiris close to death in such detail.

"Ayale saved my life by confronting these men, but that left us wanted by the Matxha clan." Osiris blurted out in one breath. "If it wasn't for Ayale, I would have been left without an affinity, or even dead. I think I set the Matxha clan back by getting rid of the list."

Ateno didn't blink with his next question. "Do you work for the Matxha clan, Osiris?"

"I did. Until that night." Osiris met his gaze with feigned confidence, combatting the pulsing fear that told him to keep his head down. "Before you accuse me of being a spy, know that my loyalty is to the person who saved my life and no one else."

Ateno's line of sight settled back on his sibling. "Did you use your affinity on those men?"

Ayale could feel Osiris' eyes shift on them. "I had to. There was no other way for us to make it here in one piece. We were ambushed a few times, and I tried not to use it, but there were moments where it was life or death."

"Are you serious?"

"There was no other way, Ateno." They reiterated with emphasis, maintaining eye contact.

"Did you...kill anyone?" He whispered.

"No. I don't think so, at least."

Ateno raised his voice. "How are you not sure if you killed someone, Ayale?"

"They didn't kill anyone, why would you ask that?" Osiris watched Ateno go from careful to an accusatory glare, pointed towards him.

"You are not involved in this conversation. You don't know what that affinity can do."

Osiris crossed his arms over his chest. "You act as if they're a criminal from being an affinity user."

"Ayale, does he know what your affinity is?" Ateno's harsh eyes dictated more than words could ever describe. "Or should I say, affinities?" He corrected.

Ayale quickly shook their head, unable to look up.

"Tell him before I say something mean to him."

Osiris awaited Ayale's answer with a defensive but worried stare, one that was genuinely unsure what was going to come out of their mouth.

They shied away and looked down at their half empty cup. "I'm a dual elemental user. Though I can seldom control which comes out when I use my affinities. I struggle to keep them both in check when they're used." They admitted quietly.

Osiris nodded, unsure what to make of their confession. A dual affinity user was unheard of, but such a statement did explain their disregard for his questions over their affinity. Still, he didn't hesitate on his defense. "Being an elemental user doesn't make you a killer," He reiterated before continuing. "It's a blessing, if anything."

"Curse, more like. With both our parents' worst genetics. A shame we couldn't get them removed before adulthood. To take out one is already too much work, with two elementals, no one would dare attempt removal." Ateno chimed in, bringing his bright blue ceramic cup to his lips.

"They controlled their affinity, er, *affinities*, just fine. How could you say something like that, to your own family of all people?" Osiris asked Ateno, much angrier than he intended on showing.

Ayale drank the remainder of their coffee, letting the gentle chill of the remaining ice cool down their warm face.

"I'm not justifying your stupidity with a response." Ateno responded, another yawn rumbling through him as he found Ayale once more. "Do you want to stop by when the old man comes back? I know you don't want to stay, I can see it in your face."

"Call him and tell him I need to talk. The longer we wait, the less time we have to prepare for whatever is coming our way." Ayale said with a straight face before picking themself up from the chair and heading back towards the descending staircase, Osiris following behind.

"Ayale." Ateno yelled from the table, causing them to pause. "I'm glad you're okay."

A short smile graced Ayale's face before the two of them reached the bottom of the staircase and out the front door, towards the front gates.

On their walk back to the outer edge of Nalira, Osiris couldn't help but notice the stationary expression that graced Ayale. After so long, he finally understood why and where it came from. For a while, he struggled to differentiate when Ateno was worried and when he simply pressed too hard on them.

And from the look of it, this dynamic wasn't anything new to them.

"You okay?" Osiris asked, partly wanting to reach out and grab their hand reassuringly.

"I..." They wanted to come up with an excuse, but as their face fell, so did their guard beyond the Cxai compound building they once called home. Their eyes shut tight while the words fell out of them.

"No," Ayale answered truthfully. "I am embarrassed. Among other things."

"Why?" Osiris felt bad but pressed on, not even allowing the overgrown gardens to take his attention away from Ayale.

"Why wouldn't I be? I didn't think his royal asshat would call my elemental issues a curse. With both our parents' worst genetics. That was uncalled for, and it reminded me why I ran to Densriel. Words like that stay with me. Mero, I expect to talk to me like that, but when Ateno says them, it hurts more." They walked out of the unkempt greenery and into the adjacent street, a silent sigh of relief leaving them both when the compound was left behind.

"I've never been conscious enough to distinguish which affinity it was," Osiris wondered, not mentioning how much Ayale didn't like talking about their affinity to begin with. "But whatever you hold, I don't think you're cursed."

Ayale looked up ahead, the distant ocean coming into view at the top of the crumbling road. They stopped on the side of the road, beside a neighboring house's black metal fence.

"It's wind and earth." Ayale muttered their confession, shooting a nervous look in Osiris' direction before rocking back on their heels. But Osiris didn't say anything in return. He only smiled, coming up beside them to take their hand into his, and walked the two of them back to the inn.

# XL

Having to unpack everything that had happened at the Cxai compound, Ayale and Osiris headed back to the inn. The remainder of the evening had come and gone, giving way to a new day.

Ayale and Osiris forced themselves to go out after spending the morning and part of the afternoon unwinding from the previous day, taking time to shower and reach out to their friends through the shared cell phone, no word from Lau yet.

Ayale threw on a clean black tank top and matching pants, the only cut of color coming from a silver chain belt around their waist. They brushed out their hair, each thin strand symmetrical over both shoulders.

Osiris didn't bother with the minor details of his outfit, sporting a random black tee from his bag, and the same finishing combination of black jeans as always. He carried his jacket in hand for when the sun eventually set, in case the night brought with it a cold breeze.

Eventually choosing a place to eat, the two of them decided to go back to the first café they visited the night they arrived. The overlook of the sea won them both over, as it did to everyone who visited Nalira, making the capital city a blooming tourist attraction. And yet, visiting the capital of the Cxai territory was anything but a vacation.

Ayale had reluctantly left their phone number with their older brother, anxiously awaiting to hear about their father's arrival back home. Their face shifted from expressive to stoic, going so much back and forth that Osiris could feel their nerves like secondhand smoke.

Their respective drinks quickly melted in the warmth of the sun, untouched by either of them. The table sat empty, neither with the stomach to eat while waiting for Ateno to reach out.

Osiris let the warm breeze bring some sort of relief to his worry, the salty air giving him a renewed sense of purpose as it flowed from behind him forward. But his line of sight still managed to drift back to the other. When Ayale looked up from the phone in their lap, they caught his stare. He shifted his gaze back to the ocean, the same timid look from when the two of them met.

Then the two heard the vibration of the phone against the metal table.

Ayale grabbed the phone and quickly placed it back down when they saw it wasn't Ateno, feeling the hesitant smile push itself forward in return to his, accompanied by the fluttering warmth in their unstill chest. "I think I've stared at the phone long enough." They leaned forward and outstretched their arms, placing their chin on the cold table. "We need food." They searched for someone before grabbing a menu from a passing server. It wasn't long before the two of them shared food along with miniscule conversations, from questions about family affairs to more humorous topics, anything to lighten the load of waiting for Ateno to respond.

Osiris felt a rush of curiosity from yesterday's events. He didn't bring up the elementals, nor any mention of affinities after finding out Ayale held two at once. Beyond not wanting to sound rude, he didn't want to push the topic.

But everything in him had so many questions. "What is it like with two kinds of elemental magic?"

Ayale swallowed their food and thought for a moment, putting their fork down onto their plate. They could only come up with one word. "Awful." They sat still, their hands flat on their lap. "Like something violent trying to crawl out of my body whenever I even think of my affinity, elemental, whatever. I thought that was normal for everyone, until I was an adult."

"What did your parents think?"

"One thought of me as weak, while the other said it out loud. Removal wasn't an option because they couldn't find anyone who would perform it on someone with two elementals. It's dangerous enough to remove one, but two could kill the people performing the rite." They sipped their tea as if their trauma were a common plot to a movie.

Osiris bit his cheek, recalling the moments when he thought his fate was sealed in Densriel. "That's awful."

Ayale shrugged. "Doesn't really matter to me since I don't really use my affinity. I'm an abomination."

"Ayale!" Osiris scolded louder than he wanted. He looked around, grateful for the thin crowd. "That's a terrible thing to say, you're not an abomination."

They blinked at him, their stare unchanging and unconvinced. "It's life. I'm not going to sit here and say I'm upset over a fact of life."

He shifted his chair to their side. His hand moved over theirs, taking it from their lap onto his.

"I am. I'm upset with everything here. Your family, your acceptance of their bullshit, and everything in between. I knew coming back would be hard but—"

"I'm used to this, you really don't need to get so upset."

Osiris stared back at them, recalling his earlier promise to be upset in their stead. He didn't think everything they said would still be prominent when they arrived in Cxai territory, but was quickly proven wrong, beginning at the border with Diori's sudden appearance. "Why should you be used to this treatment? You deserve better."

Ayale pulled their hand out of his and touched his cheek, feeling his dark complexion pulse with a warmth they knew so well. They wanted to do more than simply touch his cheek, but pulled back before they could act out of impulse. "I appreciate the thought. But you don't need to worry about me so much." They dropped their hand back to their lap.

Their time together was coming to an end, the fleeting seconds spent like this ready to become a set of distant memories when the Cxai leader arrived home. They had an inkling of what to expect from the meeting, if they knew their father well enough. While it was going to be difficult, he could ultimately be reasoned with if Ayale said the right words in the right order. Mention the invasion and request Osiris' asylum on the islands in response for his direct assistance of the Cxai clan, crediting him for the information.

And leave him be to start his life over in peace.

The rehearsal of their new plan in their head stole away Ayale's comfort, leaving another sharp pain in their stomach.

On the walk back to the inn, the sun's setting glow illuminated the skyline, leaving a dreamy mixture of orange, red, and deep pink tones reflecting along the darkening sea.

The silence between them had been filled with thoughts of what was to come for both of them. Ayale tried to accept their individual fates, bracing themself to go back to the lonely existence they lived before going on the run.

Osiris, though just as quiet, felt something far different. Instead of embracing the worst to come, he thought of ways he could speak from his heart, how to let his true feelings be known to Ayale. It was only a matter of how much longer he could stay silent. His hands impatiently tapped the sides of his legs, fidgeting with nerves far stronger than himself. He wondered for a second if he should simply say it and rip the words out from his heart.

In the split second he considered it, his mouth moving without his brain's consent. "Ayale, I don't want to be anywhere without you—"

The loud ringing of the phone in his pocket stopped everything.

Osiris saw the number when it slipped from his jacket pocket into Ayale's hands, instantly aware that this phone call was the beginning of the end.

"Hello?" Ayale frantically answered, the muffled voice of Ateno came off serious, words unending and equally indistinguishable. "Okay. Tonight." They agreed, nodding along before ending the call. Ayale looked up at Osiris, their stoic face returning.

To say the two of them were nervous was an understatement.

The soundless compound was devoid of guards. Something that left both Ayale and Osiris unsettled as they walked into the corridor leading to the other end of the house. With Osiris behind them, they thought they would be calmer.

They also thought they had more time before the call. Yet there they were, the echoes of their shoes on the dusty marble floors beneath them. A knot formed in their stomach, their breathing less than steady, air unable to sit in their lungs.

Osiris barely made it through the front door and was already flushed with anxiety, ready to take his jacket off. He swallowed hard, forcing himself to be strong, for Ayale's sake over his own.

When they turned the corner, the metal door at the end of the hall was guarded by two men in distinctly cream suits, the black shirts beneath them clad with small silver flowers on both sides of each collar. Both men did not significantly stand out, standing tall on either side of the door leading to the office of the Cxai clan leader. The guards watched as Ayale and Osiris stepped forward, stopping at the front of the door. Without so much as a moment of hesitation, the two men pushed open the double doors and followed them inside the office.

The room was considerably spacious, but the clutter was far beyond bad, worse than the rest of the house. Bookshelves along their left and right sides overflowed with books of all sizes, piles beginning and ending on the ground leading to the single large velvet chair in one corner of the room. Towards the middle was a desk where every Cxai order originated and ceased; where their father sat currently, staring at the two as they walked in. The mismatched chairs on the other side were askew, waiting for them to be seated.

"Enter." Mero declared, his brown eyes unblinking and straight faced at the two people before him. His white hair whipped to the right, peppered with grey and black strands. The wrinkles beneath eyes denoted that he hadn't slept in some time, his pale complexion reminiscent of Ayale and Ateno, yet somehow sicklier, as if he hadn't seen much daylight in recent days. His fixed stare was almost identical to Ayale's, leaving Osiris more nervous than ever.

As Ayale and Osiris sat in the chairs, they saw the clutter of the desk spill over into a pile of opened letters and various paperwork, their purpose for being on the floor unknown.

The doors behind them closed, the two guards now inside the room, along with Ateno along the back wall and the other set of Cxai guards behind Mero.

Ayale sat upright, their iconic stoic stare making itself known in the face of their most controversial adversary, their father.

"You look...different." The older man commented, his eyes falling from their hair back to their hazel stare.

"My looks aren't why I'm here. We need to talk about something much more important."

"Important enough that you have the audacity to force me back from my outing up north, is that right?"

Osiris glanced over at Ayale, immediately caught by Mero's eyes. "Who is this?" Mero asked with much more disdain than expected.

"Before we get into that, did Ateno tell you anything else?" Ayale asked, feeling their brother's eyes from the corner stick on them, hearing a faint, heavy exhale leaving him.

"No." Mero sat still, his daggering stare never straying from Osiris.

"Well." They put their hands together in their lap, carefully choosing their next words just like they planned. "The Matxha clan is planning an invasion of the Cxai territory, we suspect from the western Cxai border through the Oolonxg mountains. There's talk of them taking over our entire country and—"

"Get the fuck out. That cannot be why you are here." Mero waved off, shaking his head.

Osiris nodded softly to himself, both surprised and not. The whole family is unhinged, he found himself thinking.

"Don't treat this like a joke, we have intel. Osiris here bought us this time to prepare. I came this far to warn you, so we could prepare to fight back. The Matxha clan is not expecting us to be ready, so if we put together a small force at the western border, they shouldn't stand a chance." Ayale forced themself to sound as convincing of a leader as possible, not letting their frustration show through sheer willpower.

Mero held their gaze before he finally responded. "Nothing more stupid has ever come out of your mouth before." He said slowly, making sure every word trickled out with the same amount of emphasis.

"Coming back home to this is a close first for stupid." Ayale shot back, speaking loudly enough so he could hear. Ateno and Osiris's eyes widened, not daring to make a comment themselves.

Mero simply laughed. "Whatever war or invasion you think is coming isn't real. The Matxha clan would never come all this way for our land."

"They—everyone, actually—knows about the divorce. Everyone is fully aware you are struggling here by yourself." They gestured to the collapse of papers beside his desk.

"I wouldn't be struggling had you stayed here in the first place!" His voice raised, the guards behind him visibly nervous. "Is this the man who took you from here? Is he the one feeding you these lies? Why are you really here?" Mero shook his head, the repetitive words catching their attention.

"I already told you. I came back to tell you the Matxha are ready to invade, we only have maybe a week before they're at the border knocking on the front fucking door!" Ayale's tone became more and more frustrated as the conversation went on. They couldn't believe the once powerful Cxai leader couldn't hold it together long enough to understand the serious nature of the situation.

Almost instantly, Mero's eyes whipped to Osiris, who managed to mimic the straight face sitting beside him.

"What is your purpose for bringing back Ayale?" Mero's paranoia stung the air, leaving Ayale less and less sure of their plan.

"Are you delusional? He's with me, he didn't bring me back." Ayale's brow furrowed, taking another attempt to keep their father on track. "And we need to focus on the invasion."

"I asked for your purpose here." He pointed his words at Osiris again. His glare reminded him nothing of Ayale, but of a person who often relied on fear to lead. Simply by the look of his startling expression, Osiris could see Mero in Ayale's stories and felt a sense of understanding for their run to Densriel.

With everyone's eyes on Osiris, Ayale still answered instead. "We are here to ask for asylum in exchange for the information, once the invasion is thwarted. Osiris and I had come all this way to ask for protection from the Matxha clan, but ended up learning of the invasion along the way."

The office drew quiet, enough to hear the tick of the grandfather clock near the single large window behind Mero.

"Asylum from what?"

"The Matxha clan wants us both dead. I attacked their men."

Mero leaned back from his chair, his eyes widening. "You did what?"

Ateno made a signal with his hand and mouthed the words *shut the fuck up*. The guards beside him also changed expressions from their serious looks to one of intrigue, not expecting their meeting here to turn out like a family soap opera.

"I used my affinity to take out two of their men. They were going to kill Osiris so I got involved and we ran away. We found out about the invasion after speaking to one another." Ayale pushed their shoulders back.

Ateno could be heard sighing heavily in the back once more.

"What an idiotic thing to do, saving the man who kidnapped you." Mero face turned with disappointment.

Ayale blinked, unsure where his assumptions were coming from. "Osiris did not kidnap me, I left by my own volition. He's helped this far, not to mention he can help us know our enemy." They responded confidently, not allowing his skewed mental capacity to deter their point.

"I have no use for this street boy beside you, not after everything he's done against the Cxai clan."

Ayale shifted in their seat and clenched their fists in their lap, unsure what to do next, considering Mero's unfortunate state of being. The twist in their stomach began to knot, suddenly finding themself speaking out of turn. With full composure, Ayale wasn't ready to let the leader of the Cxai clan diminish Osiris for any reason.

"Please understand, Osiris isn't a kidnapper. If anything, he is the reason I am here and safe. He is far more useful beside us, especially from his time in the Matxha clan. After everything we saw coming back here, he gave me strength to face my fears, to sit in this decrepit room you call an office. He is smart, kind, funny, one of the sweetest, most patient people I have ever met..." Ayale trailed off before realizing what had come out of them. They stiffened before turning to find Osiris watching them carefully, their heart going faster with every passing second.

Osiris didn't know what to say, his gaze contemplative, unlike anything they had ever seen point at them. He looked ready to speak up himself.

Ayale had sung praises about Osiris before the entire Cxai family. His heart was ready to burst from his chest, ready to confess what it has held dear since his first night in the tea shoppe.

And so, Osiris didn't wait to speak out of turn.

"You give me strength I didn't know I had. No matter what territory we are in, whatever situation we get into, all I know is that I want to stay beside you. You bring me joy, you understand me like no one else can. There is no asylum without you there beside me. If there is, then I don't want it." Osiris leaned over the chair and took their balled-up fists into each of his hands, feeling them slowly unfurl. "I'm in love with you, Ayale Ceylonis."

The entire room; guards, Ateno, Ayale, and their father Mero, all stared at Osiris, whose dedicated stance did not falter. Even if he were to say anything else, no one would recall any of the words passed along the three of them quite like Osiris's confession.

One of the guards by the door wiped away a single stray tear from his eyes.

Ayale felt a smile curve on their lips, Osiris returning it tenfold.

"I think I understand plenty." Mero's brown eyes tore from Ayale, now disgusted. He briefly shared the look with Osiris. His voice rose as he looked to the guards behind them. "I want the boy gone. He has ruined my only heir. And take Ayale to the apartment, make sure they do not leave. Clearly, they have been on their own too long. No one with a clear head would bring a Matxha member home." Mero turned his back to the two of them, a wave of his hand being the last gesture of him either could see before he left the room.

Ateno followed him out, the serious expression breaking only for a short second to allow some sympathy to flow from himself to his sibling, who stared back with a stabbing look of betrayal.

A set of guards from the door walked over to grab Osiris, while the ones next to the desk reached carefully for Ayale's forearms. They shrunk back before standing from the chair, demands to stop being met with resistance. Osiris let go of Ayale's hands and took a swing at the guard behind them but missed, briefly noticing a massive red scar on his nose and a familiar glare in his piercing green eyes. The one behind Osiris took him in a full hold.

"Let him go, get off of him!" Ayale yelled, trying to rip themself out of the grip of the two remaining Cxai guards, who promptly dragged them toward the double doors. Osiris' head turned to their direction, desperately trying to break from their hold. One guard forced him up and against the desk, the fearful look in his eyes settled on Ayale's as they were taken out of the room.

The words echoed within everyone inside the room.

*I'm in love with you, Ayale Ceylonis.*

## XLI

Ayale's worst fears had come true.

They laid on the bed in their childhood room, inside a secluded apartment with no escape and newly added bars to the windows. Nothing but posters and memories of bands, movies, tv shows, random art from their younger years that once sparked joy surrounding them in the casket feeling of their room. The musty scent of age and dust had been adamant against their nose, until it settled into the background of their senses.

Every frightening thought, nightmare, the least likely of possibilities, all were happening before their very eyes.

To make matters worse, it felt as though the outcome had been entirely their fault. It wasn't long until they could barely register everything going on around them. All they once knew crumbled and gone, as though a distant memory.

In a moment of uncertainty and brief denial, they wondered if their captivity had been some kind of sick joke. For close to an hour, they sat up almost expectant that someone would come get them. Osiris, Diori, Katari, Visu. Somebody would come to get them.

As they sat around the small apartment, quiet and patient, they realized no one was coming.

A second wind of energy struck Ayale like nothing else, and they quickly tried to look around the apartment for some kind of escape. They scoured every corner, every room, crack and crevice. The first time they left, they were able to leave from the front door, but that was certainly no longer an option.

Soon, the sun had come to set, signaling the end of the first day of Ayale in captivity. A heavy guard presence had been placed on the other side of the apartment door, something they did not account for when they attempted a last-ditch effort to run out. They tried to subtly open the door and sneak out but was met with four men in Cxai uniform who forced them back in, even when they tried to solo fistfight the guard presence.

Ateno had been allowed to visit but Ayale quickly ejected him from the apartment, refusing to converse with the sibling who once again left them at the whim of their psychotic father.

At the peak of night, Ayale flopped into the bed, unsuccessful in trying to leave. They laid quietly in the dark, unable to sleep, to catch onto a train of thought that wasn't accompanied by a fleeting stream of memories.

Regret welled in their chest. They should have listened to Osiris, settled in what remained of the Rooiboux territory. Maybe in the capital of Odania, since the two of them were used to a city setting. It would have been difficult, but nothing the two of them couldn't have accomplished together.

They turned over to their side, pulling the old pillow closer to their face, working hard not to let the weight in their eyes spill over. They could hear Diori's voice, a simple plead to stay away, to go with her instead, aware her own child had no trust in her. It seemed everyone had the better idea, but they still came home to leave their father a warning, to do the right thing for their territory and the people who lived in it.

Every moment outside of their bedroom in the past few years felt made up. As if everything they had done no longer held any value.

As if they had never existed outside of these walls.

No more tea shoppe. No more riding across the continent in Lau's car. No more living the life they built from the bottom up.

Hours upon hours settled in a steady stream of time, but Ayale never slept.

After Ayale's first night alone passed, the weight of their insomnia began to quickly catch up. They tossed and turned in their bed, half expecting to awaken from a nightmare and continue on as if none of this was happening. Against their control, everything turned black, the rising red dawn sun no longer within their vision.

The next time their eyes opened, the sun seemed to be settling behind the tall trees outside their barred window.

For the first time since they slept, Ayale moved off the bed, feeling weight in their body as they tried to get up. Every step heavier than the last, they wandered towards the large window.

Their heavy-lidded eyes watched the overgrown gardens from a distance. Many of the apricot branches from their childhood hung over, bearing too much fruit to stand up straight. Vines left unattended grew against the side of the brick building below their window, while orange and red lilies grew wildly in one spot closer to the back of the house far across the courtyard. Their brilliant hues crossed into the bushed and hedges that bordered the high metal fencing. Its beauty unparalleled to anything else in the yard.

They rested their head on the sill of the open window.

Osiris didn't get a chance to see the garden in its full, overgrown glory.

The warm breeze sifting into their room was anything except comforting. The pain in their stomach returned, overly conscious and leaving Ayale wondering where Osiris could have possibly been taken. They gave up on being near the window, trudging back to the bed before flopping back onto it, sinking back into another depression sleep.

Day turned to night, before morning followed again. Ayale watched the ever-shifting time of day. Every thought more corrosive than the last, they slept through much of the day and night, before finally lying awake. They laid flat on their back in the ruffled bed, staring up at the ceiling without a single cohesive thought to linger more than a moment.

They had come all this way, only to fail and go back to the way things were before they left. Trapped, silent, scared of what was to come next.

There was no more painful thought than remembering everything they once held dear.

They lost their tea shoppe, their friends, their freedom, and the person who loved them as they were.

Ayale felt warm streaks of tears descend from both sides of their face, pooling onto the cotton bed sheets beneath them. Helpless and uncertain of every aspect of their current situation, Ayale cried until exhaustion forced them back to sleep.

*

Sitting at the other end of the Cxai compound past the overgrown garden was a set of stairs nearest the back door, leading into a basement area, designed similarly to that of the underground Rooiboux compound in Istanza. Though the floors and walls were anything but the fine marble that made the underground compound the two found an ally within. Much of the structure of the basement and its adjacent halls looked medieval, as if it had never been updated from the initial founding of the clan system after the downfall of the monarchy three hundred years prior.

The difference between the Rooiboux and the Cxai clans being that Osiris had been forcibly dragged down to the lowest floor rather than invited, nowhere near reminiscent of the first time he found himself in a clan compound. He was taken down three flights of stone stairs, cuffed and held by two Cxai guards. The two men uncuffed his wrists before they threw him in the nearest cell, pulling the solid door closed behind them.

Concrete on all walls, floor, and ceiling. The room had been devoid of any light except a single fog light above him. While he was glad his hands were no longer tied together, he sat in the corner of a not nearly a fancy enough cell that left him yearning for the Oolonxg prison cell more than ever before.

The compound may have been outdated but its cell system was certainly more modern than Osiris expected. The door crackled with electricity, a sound of whirring noises on the wall across. The bare bones window was small, high up towards the ceiling, making him feel like an actual prisoner for the first time since Odania.

At least he had Ayale to help get them out of their prison the first time.

Unsure of the time and fearful what would happen next, anxiety flooded into him. He couldn't stop the influx of unfortunate thoughts turned to quick breaths that pushed him over, feeling as if he failed not only himself but Ayale.

Osiris sank against the back wall, sliding down until he was seated on the concrete floor. He held his face in his hands, feeling the descent of tears even as he tried to force them back, his unheard sobbing leaving him in uncontrollable waves. The overall fear he would be left to rot held nothing to his feeling of failure and blame.

Hours passed, and his only coherent thoughts were that of memories. Exhaustion made its home in him, no longer able to do anything but sit in silence, watching the pulse of the light give out every so often.

He thought of the guard in Mero's office. Where he knew him from, he could barely place. But the image of his scarred nose and familiar face haunted him.

Osiris wanted nothing more than to breathe the air outside again, of salt and humidity and sweet scents that would linger more when the two of them discovered a new city or town. The adventures he shared with Ayale brought him to places he could only dream of.

Ayale brought him this far.

His friend, his trusted person, the one who won his heart.

Osiris pressed his back against the cold concrete walls behind him.

There had to be a way out of the prison cell, an answer to the puzzle. There always was in every situation he got himself in, and he was convinced there had to be one now.

He wiped away the remaining tears from his eyes with the back of his hand, his need to cry replaced with a moment of clarity. He did something beyond himself and began plotting an escape from the Cxai prison.

If Ayale could do it, then he could, too.

From there, he would find Ayale, and...well, the rest would eventually come to him, he thought. All he needed to start was to open the door in front of him.

Osiris shook off the fear he knew so well and embraced uncertainty.

He had someone waiting for him, someone he owed his life to.
Someone he needed to save.

*

The sound of scraping metal and machinery filled the room of the
small warehouse. The heavy scent of petroleum and gasoline lingered
in the air with that of cars and more vehicles. Eines took it upon
herself to walk around the brightly lit room, inspecting everything
inside, as well as everyone against the back wall.

She signaled with her hand for the soldiers behind them to form a
single line, each wearing a uniform etched with a special color and
symbol to specify their individual affinities, with special ones made
for elemental users. She would pick at random who would be
subjected to interrogation, just to keep things interesting for herself.
As she scanned the line, she spotted an older woman, back straight as
an arrow, a largely healed over scar on her face and the symbol of a
river, a sign of the water elemental patched over the heart of her
uniform.

Eines stared at her scar for a second before picking out the
woman beside her, walking past as if she never saw her at all.

# XLII

Diori shot up from her bed, eyes wide open, a silent nightmare shimmering against her glittery white eyes. Unaware herself that she was awake, her quickened heart rate and sweat filled clothes reminded her she was indeed alive and conscious. The gentle morning light slipped in between the closed blinds of the small hotel, giving her only a hint of the time at hand.

She thought about Ayale. As she did every morning since their escape from the Cxai compound three years ago.

The instinctive worry was a new part of her morning routine, prevalent since she saw them again for the first time in years at the Oolonxg – Cxai border.

The scent of fresh coffee swarmed the dark, unlit room, the only reason for leaving the bed at what she assumed was an ungodly early hour. When she peeked out from her room, Katari was fully dressed in a formal black jumpsuit with her curly hair up high, her signature gold necklace on, a set of matching red leather bracelets tight on both wrists, and flat black shoes to finish her look.

Beyond impressed, Diori snuck into the seat beside Katari before she handed over a full mug.

"They were captured. In the dream, I saw which rooms. I think I have an idea where they could be held inside the compound. Mero has decided to keep them separated from one another." Diori yawned, reaching out for the cup and promptly lifting it to her lips. "Someone told him to keep them away from one another."

"I heard. I believe the entire hotel heard. Was the sobbing truly what you saw?" Katari inquired, to which Diori nodded. "Awful. I could only imagine what Mero did with the two of them. We couldn't be more blessed to have your," Katari struggled with the right words in reference to Diori's extra talents, spanning beyond her affinity. "Expertise." She drank the last of her coffee and produced the handmade map from her bag beside her, laying it out flat on the kitchen table. She looked up and down the detailed ink map, making note of as many details as possible. "Do you think they will notice their map is missing?"

"Not our problem now." Diori shrugged. "I'm lucky I noticed the Matxha infiltration to begin with. For a new 'Cxai' member to have such a detailed blueprint of the house is bizarre."

"Agreed. But enough diversions, let's leave soon. We only have so much time to pick up our young stragglers." Katari stretched out her arms and back in the creaky wood kitchen chair.

Diori nodded and smiled through her nerves, beginning by pointing out where the two would sneak in from.

*

Osiris wasn't quite sure how much time had passed in his cell. With no sunlight to tell the time of day, he sat alone with his intrepid thoughts. Being someone who had a disorder in overthinking, his anxiety had settled for the moment.

His heart and mind were set on finding a way out.

The only question was how Osiris was going to get out of his prison cell.

He sat back against the cold concrete, feeling a chill run down his spine. A brief memory of their last time in a jail cell had him recalling how the two of them had gotten out the first time.

Ayale flexed their lineage, not an option for Osiris. To everyone in the compound, he was the kidnapper of their future Cxai clan leader. The idea of being some abductor was bizarre, even for everything he had done in the Matxha clan.

He wondered if he could put on an elaborate lie. Maybe he could tell them he was some higher up of the Matxha or Rooiboux clans.

He recalled the man with the scar on his nose, wondering why he struck him with such familiarity.

Otherwise, there wasn't much confidence in the plan, let alone in himself.

Osiris let out a frustrated sigh, leaning his back onto the concrete to force himself to sit upright. His eyes traveled to the ceiling, watching the fog light struggle to remain lit. With every shudder of light, a small buzz noise would follow. At one point, the light shut off entirely, only illuminating again seconds later. Its cover was a worn-out plastic, melted at one corner.

Osiris stood up, attempting to reach it by stretching out his arm as far as he could. He jumped up, able to touch it. He hopped up once more, whacking it with a slap. Part of it snagged at the melted corner, the plastic now within arm's reach. When he ripped it off, the heat of the bulb hit him like the sun to a flower.

An idea like none other suddenly presented itself.

Just like Ayale, Osiris needed to play to his strengths.

*

At the entrance of the Cxai family compound stood two still guards. Specifically, the two who had dragged away a less than compliant Ayale, who took swings at them while being taken from the office of the clan leader and transported to the apartment, a few bruises on their faces evidence that Ayale didn't always miss. The discolored parts of their faces rendered one of them worse than the other.

399

Neither knew what to expect when they were told Ayale had shown up again.

But for Mero to lock his own child in the apartment was odd. That would have been considered unusual had it been done prior to the day he kicked out Diori. Both guards agreed, anything was possible these days.

The rustle of leaves above them was loud enough to gather their collective attention. Leaves swung violently with the shifting branches, an unnaturally strong gust of wind taking its toll. The two guards looked around the area, blaming the strange winds on shifting weather.

To the right of the guards sat the overgrown gardens that were once the pride of Ateno and the Cxai compound. Around the same time as Mero's unfortunate mental change, Ateno could not find the strength to keep tending to the gardens.

Within the partially blooming hydrangeas, hid the odd pair of lifelong friends, carefully watching the guards. Diori and Katari shared a look, ready in waiting.

Diori's hand slowly rose up into an inch of the brush in front of her. Partly outstretched, and a subtle movement later, the wind picked up once more. She traced a pointed finger to the left, the resulting wind a sudden and harsh gust almost knocking over the two men. A loose branch above them fell over in front of door they guarded, its fruit whipping off into their suits. When the sudden gust subsided, the less than gentle breeze followed.

Diori's focus mirrored in her careful movements. With a short twitch of her hand, flitting from left to right, the waves of wind rustled the trees above the guards, who decided then that the outside was too much for them, the seemingly innocent sky clearly threatening an incoming storm. They both walked towards the main house, jaunting with a quick run, and leaving the back door officially unaccounted for.

The two women looked at one another. A sigh of relief left Katari, answered with a smile from Diori.

Both women made their way out of the brush and quietly stepped toward the unattended steel door. The two of them peered between the small opening, noting a pair of guards inside.

"When did Mero start to send people in pairs?" Katari whispered.

Diori shrugged, unsure herself. The guard presence was partly new but otherwise standard for Mero's leadership. Her only worry was getting through the door and down into the basement levels.

Diori looked to Katari for confirmation, whose brow furrowed.

"You aren't planning to go in alone, are you?"

She nodded, looking around the courtyard.

"Absolutely not." Katari retorted, her face not once changing. "I'll be fine."

"We go together or not at all." She said with thick finality.

Diori rolled her eyes before nodding reluctantly.

The two grabbed the door, preparing themselves for what was on the other side.

"If things shift out of our favor, take them both and get to the island. Do not come back for me, understood?"

Katari hesitated but nodded regardless. There was no chance she would leave her behind, even if things were to go south. Diori didn't leave her behind, so Katari would never seriously entertain the idea.

Her signal to move took her back to their mission, the creak of the metal door opening beside them. They rushed in the small opening, like wind through trees.

*

Osiris overthought for hours.

He could only come up with one plan; reach up as far as possible towards the light above him while utilizing his affinity, push out vines and try to feel for the locking mechanism attached to the door. Or for air. Whichever came first. One of them, he hoped.

The heat of the bulb emanated brightly. Since the door of the cell ran with the same unsteady electricity, it was worth a shot.

If he could get out, he was confident he would find Ayale, and it wouldn't take much to get the two of them out of there. He had some training in combat from the Matxha clan, hopefully enough to escape.

Osiris reached his arm up as far as he could and let his affinity guide him. His focus began on the strength of the vines, summoning with as much power as he could force. While it was slow, going inch by inch, he pushed on, until the overgrowth made its way into the ceiling. He closed his eyes, focusing on what he could feel with the vines. Lots of dust, a few bumps here and there against the rough metal ducts. Then, a short drop that he was confident led to the door.

The vines were held in place against the wall with small facets lining the inner workings of the cell door, a few with rust on them. He couldn't imagine how rust made its way inside a wall, shaking off the thought of moisture and possibly mold where his vines moved.

He tried to push through the metal cover, eventually hearing a faint click inside the wall as evidence of success. He focused more, pushing the wires forward and sneaking behind them. He braced himself, unsure what the results would be, and circling the vines around the set of wires. He held his breath before pulling them with all his remaining strength.

Everything in the room went black.

*

Diori made her way down the dim hallway, careful and quiet. The lights turned off, no longer having eyes on the guards. She backed up to the door leading to the courtyard, pulling Katari back with her. The two sat still, until the red emergency lights flickered on with a click.

"What happened?" Katari whispered as she looked around the long corridor.

"I don't know, but we need to get down to the third sublevel."

"Are you sure?"

Diori frantically nodded, pulling Katari alongside her as they began to sprint down the hallway, following behind a pair of guards down the first set of stairs.

*

Osiris heard the incessant buzz of the door, locking and unlocking as it struggled to maintain a consistent flow of electricity. He pulled open the door when it buzzed once more, watching a guard tapping frantically on a computer. He snuck behind, making a break for the stairs, when he felt a tight grip on his arm followed by a fierce yank, giving him whiplash when his back hit the floor. Another nearby guard threw his full weight down, aiming for his chest.

Osiris rolled to the side, grabbing the guard by the shoulders, and forcefully shoved him down onto the concrete floor. He pinned the man, face down with an elbow at the back of his neck, focusing his own weight on the pressure point to keep him still.

"Stay down or I incapacitate you, your choice." Osiris said in a low voice, warning him what he was capable of. The other guard watched from his computer, backing away and up the stairs, leaving the two of them alone. A shaky noise of agreement left the man beneath him before Osiris pulled the weapon off his belt and hurried up the stairs.



Diori and Katari ran down the dark hall as two guards ran past them in the opposite direction. The two of them were forced to rely on Diori's knowledge in the dark, occasionally stopping to look at the placement of rooms along the narrow hallways.

The moment she stopped in the middle of the hall and spotted the stairs, all she could see was a gun pointed in her direction coming out of the room beside her. Just as quickly, the gun whipped from the Cxai guard's hands and into the side of his head, leaving him unconscious on the ground. Two more ascended from the stairs, blocking the way down. Katari's iron grip of her affinity on the air around them could be felt throughout the hall, immediately taking the throats of the two guards under her unseen control.

Her power was an art form few could perfect like her. The flow of energy seamless, her stance behind Diori confident and unwavering. The illumination of her eyes matched the glow of the emergency lights, her hands curving and grabbing without so much as a moment of hesitation before she stepped out in front of Diori. She threw the two of the guards down beside another, making sure they stayed down.

The two of them ran past the fallen Cxai guards, running down the uneven stone stairs.

In the second sublevel, Diori and Katari watched as a familiar young man took on two of the men down the thin hallway, with two more bodies fallen behind him. Holding one soldier up as bait for the other, the second guard put down his gun and tried to reach around, but Osiris pushed them into one another against the wall. He used the chance to steal his dropped gun, pointing it at the two of them, his serious expression unchanged.

"Tell me where the apartments are on the compound, or I'll shoot you both without a second thought." Osiris' pointed gaze didn't waver, but neither Cxai guard were ready to take the risk. A glance at their chest pockets, Osiris spotted a singular flower, symbolizing they were entry-level grunts to the clan.

"Osiris?" Katari's voice echoed down the hall, grabbing his attention.

"Leave the compound and don't come back." He nodded to the exit, leaving the two guards scrambling past Diori and Katari. He put the stolen gun down and made his way over to the two of them, who were surprised, to put it simply.

"I almost forgot you were in the Matxha clan." Katari momentarily glanced at him, keeping her eyes on the end of the hall. "Is Ayale down there?"

Osiris shook his head, having recalled the words Mero said in his office. "I heard him say something about an apartment."

"Sounds like our next stop." Katari looked back and forth between the two of them.

"The apartments are going to be heavily guarded after this, I'm not even sure which one it is." Diori thought aloud.

"You don't even know what part of the house your own children live in?" Osiris asked, leaving Diori appalled before her face fell, unable to form a response.

Katari walked towards the upper stairs, ignoring the red lights. "We will figure it out. For now, let's get out of here."

As the three of them left the basement, the auburn sky and chilled air drastic against Osiris' face. Adrenaline gone, exhaustion falling over him in waves. He couldn't be more grateful to be outside. He waited for some grand plan to come from the conversation in front of him, leaning against the door to keep himself up. The sounds of their words were barely tangible, their discussion becoming an echo. His tired eyes struggled to take in the remaining daylight.

Looking around the overgrown gardens, Osiris found a fleeting sense of solace in the blooms and overgrowth everywhere. Beside him and the door sat wild red and orange lilies, blooming in their full beauty. When he looked to the windows across the courtyard, he saw the metal bars adorning each window, including one glass pane opened from the inside.

Without thinking, Osiris walked off across the garden, carefully approaching the open window. The vines stuck to the brick siding, thick with green roots and leaves all over.

Osiris' sleepy voice sounded out once, hopeful. "Aya?"

A few moments passed, with only the breeze shifting the leaves to make any sort of sound around him. Osiris wondered if luck could be on his side. There wasn't a time he felt unluckier, and yet, here he stood, four feet below the barred open window. He could have easily gotten the attention of guards from the act, but still he waited, and every minute that went by had him more scared than the next. His intuition remained.

"Ayale!" He yelled once more, cutting into Diori and Katari's conversation, and risking everyone's safety. Katari quickly came up from behind and placed a hand on his shoulder, pulling him away.

Until a half asleep Ayale approached the window, disheveled and exhausted as they looked down for the source of the voice.

Osiris slipped out of her hold. "Katari, tell me you can see them."

"Shouldn't that be my line?" Ayale yawned. Their groggy expression struggled to determine whether not any of this had been real, slow blinking as they watched Katari and Osiris struggle with the bars on the window.

"Ayale, darling, we are very much here." Katari already attempted to take control of the bars with her affinity, to no avail. "Diori, what do we do?"

"Is there a way to unscrew the bolts on the bars?" Diori frantically asked.

Osiris placed a hand on the wall, grazing the vines bundled and overlapping one another. He leaned against the wall, his flattened hand a strong grip on the base of the vines. In seconds, he forcefully bloomed every vine he could, twirling their threads towards the bars above him. When the bars slowly overcame with different shades of green, he turned to Katari with a desperate look in his eyes.

"I can't do this alone, I need your help." Osiris asked, unsure his affinity would be enough alone.

Katari cast aside her doubts on his plan, forcing the red glow back into her eyes, the air thickening with finite tension, the same power Osiris had been met with inside the Rooiboux compound. Her pull carried more weight on the bars, more pointed and focused than his own.

With their combined effort, the bars didn't shift.

Osiris placed the other hand on the wall, exuding more of his power, everything he could force out of himself in a last-ditch effort to get the metal to loosen. They didn't all need to come off, just a few and they could do the rest by hand.

His grip on the vines tightened, and Katari used that sense of resolve to push her own limits at the same time.

All Diori could do was stay on watch for guards while the two attempted to take down the bars keeping Ayale hostage.

The sound of a bolt clinking on the ground took her attention. Then another, and in quick succession, small screws, followed by a massive thud of the bars on the ground beside Osiris.

Collective relief came and went as Katari and Osiris stared at their newest dilemma.

An unblinking Ayale stood at the window, zoned out and unresponsive.

Osiris looked around for something to climb on, eventually settling on a discarded wheelbarrow. He propped himself up to the edge of the window with his hands. He pulled himself into the window and in the room, straining before he fell inside.

Ayale didn't believe he was there at all. Not until he forced them against his chest, embracing them tighter than anything they ever felt before. Osiris moved without thought, his heart racing alongside his unsteady breath. His lips met the top of their head, the side of their face, before kissing them gently on their lips. Ayale placed their hands on his face, wrapping them around the back of his neck and basking in the warmth Osiris brought them. Their chest rose with uneven breaths, realizing he was indeed in front of them, holding them close.

"I thought you were gone." Ayale drew in a long breath, pressing their face against his shoulder.

Osiris tightened his sore arms around them. "Not on my life. I told you I won't leave you behind."

"I didn't think I'd see you again." Ayale's voice crumbled, a small hiccup in their throat accompanied by their arms going up his back.

He didn't want to let go. Everything inside him screamed to never let go again. He stood still, feeling his shoulder moisten with tears, willing himself to stop from crying himself. "We need to go,

Diori and Katari are waiting." His arms moved down to their waist, trying to pull them towards the opening of the window.

Ayale jumped back when they heard a rustle outside. They peered out of the open window, his arm remaining protective around them. "Are we sure I'm not asleep?" They touched the bare brick of the outside window.

"Very. Let's get out of here before someone discovers us." Osiris took their bag from the floor onto his shoulders, throwing their jacket down for Katari to catch.

Diori helped steady Ayale as they lowered their legs first until they felt the metal beneath them. Osiris came out next, handling himself and their bag on his back as he hopped down.

Diori and Katari led the group quickly through the gardens, noting the sudden influx of guards, and barely made it out undetected into a side street beyond the gates.

Wherever they were going, Ayale nor Osiris knew, only relying on one another to keep moving forward.

# XLIII

Ayale and Osiris followed Diori and Katari down the long side street towards an unmarked car, to a massive ship, one meant to connect locals of the Cxai mainland to the plethora of islands, both near and far. While traveling by sea wasn't a common use by Ayale, ships never ceased to amaze (and terrify) them. The largest port in Nalira housed quite a few liners in the past, compared to the three sole ships that came and went from the old harbors presently. The orange hues of the sun sunk back into the ocean's distant horizon, leaving behind a waning red moon in its evening wake.

As the four of them boarded the old cruise liner, Diori brandished four one-way tickets in her hands. Ayale leaned forward to look, their eyes widening before shooting a confused look at their mother. "Craitani? Where is that?"

Diori peered over her shoulder, momentarily imagining Ayale in adolescence. "Capital island of the old Ceyxlon clan. Functioned almost entirely within the islands until…" She trailed off, pursing her lips together. "Your father."

"Oh." Ayale fell back in their spot, looking out at the darkening harbor. They felt a supportive nudge on their shoulder.

Osiris kept his eyes ahead at the small line in front of them, remaining silent since their initial run of the Cxai compound. He would say his piece once the two of them settled in for the ride.

This was going to be a long night.

*

The ship went full speed towards Craitani, leaving when the sun had fully set behind the Cxai mainland, night taking its place. Among both sides of the ship were public seating areas, both outside and in, with sections for private rooms, halls, and the occasional booth selling snacks.

The seats on the first and second floors of the ship had large windows, showing the outer balcony area and the scattered assortment of people on it.

While the group had two rooms for the night, Ayale took to the second floor's public balcony, sitting on an old white bench containing life jackets, stained with a thin layer of salt spray from the ocean. They took out a single cigarette, igniting it with a red lighter, given to them from their time in Istanza. They inhaled deeply, tasting the humid ocean air, its salt staining their arms as they rolled up their sleeves to their elbows.

Ayale looked around the barren area, the nearest person an old man who settled in an old white plastic chair at the opposite end of the open space, watching the flow of water ride against the ship.

For the time they were held in their room, Ayale had been so certain they wouldn't see the world outside ever again. But they were grateful for every second when it came. Hearing the noise of the ocean waves crash against the side of the ship, they closed their eyes and finished their cigarette in some semblance of tranquility.

Osiris approached and joined them on the bench, brandishing not one but two chocolate croissants and two peach juices, handing off one of each to Ayale.

"You look like you haven't eaten in a while." His subtle voice carried off by the breaking waves, his tired eyes flowing from the ocean back to Ayale.

"It's been a bit." They mumbled as they bit into the pastry.

"Same." He agreed, shifting closer to their side. Osiris took to his pastry shortly after, watching the red moon rise above the water, reflecting on its black waves. His side glances were his way of making sure they ate, suddenly unsure what to say.

Ayale dusted off their sweater from crumbs, fulfilled by some degree before puncturing their peach juice box next. The sound of the ocean would have pulled them away, had Osiris' hand not grazed theirs ever so slightly.

"I'm sorry for what I said in front of Mero."

"Osiris," Ayale said defensively. "I should be the one apologizing. I froze when I should have acted. Next thing I knew, I was being dragged away."

"You didn't do anything wrong."

"And neither did you." Ayale glanced from the side. "I failed you, in every aspect."

Osiris bit the inside of his cheek, forcing himself not to tear up.

"It was the longest three days of my life, but I learned a lot about myself in that prison cell." He choked back, wiping away at sparse tears. "I don't regret anything. Besides spilling my guts in front of the whole Cxai clan. And hurting a bunch of guards. And taking their weapons. And brandishing it against them."

Ayale looked up at him in mild horror, which then turned contemplative, and into an understanding nod. He was an exile from the Matxha clan, after all.

"I don't think I'm allowed back there." He whispered to himself.

"Me neither." Ayale half-laughed. "I wish circumstances were different."

After a moment of quiet and thoughts of the Cxai prison cell floated back to memory, Osiris nodded. "Me too. I wish they had at least kept us in the same room. Though I understand why Mero kept us separate."

Ayale sat still, a jumble of emotions and uncertainty slapped together in one sentient depressive episode. It wasn't as if they didn't feel the same way, either.

They felt his feelings towards them were simply undeserved. Even so, in their thoughtful silence, Ayale felt his arms wrap around them into a hug and leaned into him. His inviting warmth always knew how to slow their heart and settle them down. They inhaled, his arms tightening around their back as they let out a small breath.

In short moments like these, Ayale felt safe, even if temporarily. After everything they had gone through, they knew they could trust him with their life, proving so these last few days. Osiris managed to escape imprisonment from inside the Cxai prison, find Ayale, and get them both of them out of the compound.

Ayale's eyes closed, their exhausted body leaning too much into Osiris. Against the white noise of the ocean, the humid chill coming off the water, they found a fleeting solace in Osiris. "Don't leave me again." Ayale muttered, barely audible against the sounds of the crashing waves.

"They'll have to tear me away." Osiris pressed his lips against the side of their head. "And if they do, I'll always find my way back to you."

Ayale smiled, resting their head against his shoulder. Their arms found his back, feeling a light exhale escape him. Neither of the two dared to move.

"What comes next? There's no asylum, barred from Cxai territory, and an invasion to boot." They groaned, summing up the last few months in a mere sentence.

"We persist together." Osiris placed another light kiss on their cheek. "Nothing we can't handle. As long as I'm with you, nothing stands in our way."

Ayale snorted. "That's the cheesiest thing you've ever said."

"I have definitely said worse." Osiris felt his cheeks warm up, referring to his moments in front of Mero.

"Maybe." They pulled back and met his soft gaze, nothing less than loving towards them. "Come on, drink something. Been a long couple of days." They pushed the unopened peach juice in his direction.

"What is this anyways? I just picked whatever I saw first."

They nudged him again. "Not coffee, I promise."

Diori sat on the first-floor deck, eyes drifting with the crashing waves in the dark horizon. She felt her eyes close, her thoughts heavy on everything placed before her so suddenly. She worried about her children, her home island of Craitani, and now had a possible war to prepare for. In all her years of living, she had never dreamed of ending up in such a situation.

After all, she accepted an arranged marriage to unite the Ceyxlon and Cxai clans to avoid a war.

Everything felt surreal knowing what she knew now that no matter the path, all roads led to war regardless of her actions.

One child agreed to hesitantly accept her help, while the other barely spoke to her, only accepting her offer to act as a spy for their younger sibling.

As the cigarette slipped out from her pocket, Diori had no one else to blame but herself. Lack of involvement for so many years led to more problems than if she had just defended Ayale and Ateno when the two of them needed her most. She couldn't fix the past, only atonement as she moved forward.

How she would accomplish gaining Ayale's forgiveness, win a war, and gain independence for the Ceyxlon, she couldn't say.

At the end of it all, Diori was at the mercy of too many.

Katari sat inside the ship, watching from the nearest window the barely lit up islands that passed them by. She had wondered how simple life could be living on such a remote place, but her curiosity fell as she recalled the Ceyxlon territories being handed off to the Cxai clan not long ago. The day of Mero and Diori's wedding doubled as an acquisition. An unfortunate similarity of losing core identity shared among herself and Diori, if not an attestment to their trauma bonding experience.

She felt the right side of her forehead tense at the memory of her wedding and stood abruptly from her seat, refusing to give the thought room to grow. Katari wandered off from the seating area towards the rooms in the back of the ship.

The remainder of the night drifted alongside the ship, as the hours slowly progressed to midnight.

Ayale and Osiris bought out a mass of snacks from the shop inside, taking to the seats inside to stuff their faces and talk about everyone.

When Ayale inevitably turned on the phone in their bag, it took a full ten minutes to load up missed calls and frantic text messages from both Teryn and Visu, a few ominous texts from Lau, as well as a text from an unknown number they presumed was Ateno. They sighed and handed off the phone to Osiris, shaking their head. "Can you tell those two we aren't dead? I don't have the energy to even begin describing the last few days." They said, promptly stuffing their face with a fluffy sweet bread covered in sliced almonds up top.

"Any limits on how I phrase this?" He inquired, already beginning his typing.

"This is about to sound like a drama script, isn't it?"

"Only if you're okay with granting me creative freedom, then yes."

Katari turned the corner, spotting the two seated alone with their snacks everywhere, and sat herself beside Ayale, snatching a small bag of chips for herself. Eventually, Diori came over to join them, and the four idled amongst one another. She didn't earn so much as a word of acknowledgement from Ayale. The group slowly retired to their rooms, until it was just Ayale and Diori.

Ayale began cleaning up the mess they made, throwing out trash, actively avoiding the piercing gaze of their mother.

"We can't just leave things this way." Diori's voice was subtle but heard, watching Ayale pause as they grabbed their bag off the chair.

"We left them this way for twenty years, we can leave it for another day." Ayale shot a blank stare back at her and walked off towards their shared room with Osiris. "Have a good night, Diori." They made sure to use her name while they walked down the hall, regret welling up with every step.

Diori sank in her seat, realizing how large of a rift she created, and unsure where to begin to fix their relationship.

Ayale entered the small room, locking the door behind them. The sound of Osiris showering in the bathroom brought them a weird sense of relief, simply knowing he was present.

They switched out of their clothes, deciding to use the shower when he had finished. But before they could go in, Osiris placed a hand on their arm to stop them, already sure something was amiss by the blank stare on their face.

"I'll talk about it later." Ayale exhaled, knowing the question by the look on his face. They lowered his arm and walked into the bathroom.

When Ayale came back out, they sat beside him, earning an ever-patient smile from Osiris. "I had a feeling it was risky leaving you alone with Diori."

"I can't talk to her yet. I need some time to figure out how I really feel and put it into words. We both deserve that much." Ayale stared out at the glowing moon from the circular window. "I don't want to leave things this way, but I can't help feeling angry whenever I see her. I have way too much to think about, it's a problem."

"Is it a problem, or are you just not used to allowing yourself to feel anything?" Osiris reached out to touch their face, feeling them instinctively lean against his hand, their eyes practically refusing to meet his.

Just as he was ready to draw closer, Osiris remembered what he had confessed in front of everyone.

And that he never received an answer back.

Osiris felt his face flush, kissing their cheek before moving away from Ayale to find his sketchbook. It was no time to think of such things.

"Tomorrow is a new day." Ayale resigned, a yawn running through them before they stood back up and began to go through their bag, barely sure of what they should be doing while they fought against sleep.

# XLIV

The next morning came with a loudspeaker announcement that the ship was an hour away from land. Groggy and a bit lazy, Ayale hesitantly tore themself from Osiris, who groaned and pulled them back into his arms. The crack of dawn illuminated with a gentle orange glow into the room.

They almost fell back asleep, obliging to Osiris' pull for a few more minutes. Ayale pried themself away again, his arms finally giving them up. They rubbed their eyes, shifting to the other side of the small room, and began to clean up and pack their things into the backpack beside the bed.

Ayale leaned over Osiris, the warmth of their face so close to his rousing him from sleep. A gentle voice did the remainder. "We need to get up and meet with the others." They nudged him, receiving a light groan in return.

"Don't want to move yet."

"I'll get breakfast if you do, and if not, I'll make sure you only have coffee, like the one you had in Istanza."

Osiris forced himself up, letting the sheet fall away from his chest. His groggy face barely signaled that he awoke, if only for the threat looming over him.

The two of them slowly packed up and went back towards the seating area for breakfast, before Ayale pulled the two of them outside in a rush, citing how much the sight would be worth the wait. Ayale and Osiris settled on the small expanse of the white benches, sharing food that didn't only consist of snacks and drinks for the first time in days.

"Just wait." Ayale stared off at the sun's slow ascent over the island of Craitani. Crown of the once vibrant Ceyxlon clan, homeland of their mother Diori, and for now, their temporary home. Much of the island rose in distant mountainous waves, with colorful buildings of both businesses and residences clad in warm red tones, yellow and cream, and the occasional stark white in the mix. From where they sat, everything seemed so quaint, nothing like the cities the two of them had been used to seeing.

Beside them sat Diori and Katari, brandishing coffees in hand. Together, the four of them watched the red morning sky shift with the approach of the island. Craitani was close enough to see small details, particularly the uneven rising roads into the city, motorcyclists rising through the port, and a line of yellow taxis waiting to pick up people coming off the boat.

While they all waited to be told they could get off the ship, Diori glanced over at Ayale, who could feel her tired eyes on them.

The horn blared for the passengers to disembark, and a line formed of sluggish passengers ready to leave.

Osiris' hand slipped into Ayale's, walking off together behind Diori and Katari. The scent of diesel filled the air, a soreness filling Ayale's arms and legs.

Diori seemed to shift her face from the misery she wore on the ship to a soft smile as she hurried to her car parked in a distant lot, far from the ports entrance. "I'm finally home." She smiled brightly at her small lilac four-door car, looking out at the dry land around her. "Home and alive." Diori fumbled in her purse for her keys, Katari looking into the bag with her as if she might spot them before her.

"Right there, Diori." Katari eventually pointed out.

She snatched them up with a grateful smile. "Ah, thanks."

The four of them got into the car, Katari and Osiris in the back, forcing him to do a double take before meeting Katari's knowing gaze with one of understanding.

Ayale hesitantly sat in the passenger seat, placing their bag in their lap.

Diori placed a headband over her grey stricken black hair to pull it back. She turned on her car with a harsh crank, its loud start jarring everyone in the car.

"How old is this thing?" Ayale touched the hand crank lever for the window beside them, a subtle squeak coming from the window.

"Maybe older than Ateno." Diori answered, both looking down at the stick shift.

"It's a stick? Really?"

"Older than old, so yes!" She looked behind her seat to backup out of the dusty lot. The roads were less than steady, but heck, if this purple hell on wheels didn't go fast. The sounds of the car overtook whatever cassette was stuck in the sound system.

Diori took them down the main roads, everyone staring out the windows to look at the strange shape of the buildings. Many businesses functioned out of houses, the barebones city of Tiryi itself barely industrious enough to be considered a capital. Nalira of Cxai was four times the islands size with a much denser population.

"My real home, Ayale." Diori said. "When I first came back a few years ago, it felt as if I never left." She pulled down the windows and let the warm wind hit her face.

Ayale hesitantly did the same, pleasantly surprised by the warm sea air no longer diluted by the smell of gas.

Diori stopped and parked the car in front of a remote café, turning the car off in the process. "Before we go in, I have to ask something," Her voice dropped before turning around in her seat, a smile pointing at Osiris. "How long were you in the Matxha clan?"

Alarmed at the sudden question, Osiris shifted awkwardly in his seat. "Four years or so, why?"

"Curiosity." Diori turned back around and left the car, everyone following suit.

The four of them lined up inside the quiet coffee shop. The options weren't many for drinks, but their food menu was expansive. While everyone stared at the board, Osiris looked to Ayale, ready to ask them to order for him, but Diori stepped between them and chimed in instead.

"I want you to try something with me." She beamed, patting him on the shoulders.

While Diori spoke to the barista and ordered for the two of them, Ayale and Katari ordered their own drinks; iced coffees inspired by the culture of the Ceyxlon culture, made with a smooth tea-based foam, floating above a dark coffee, brewed with coffee beans grown on the island itself.

When they all sat down, Osiris stared longingly at Ayale's iced coffee, eyes begging for a single taste. He held his hot beverage with confusion before putting it down on the table in front of him. Diori encouraged him to drink up, sending a smile his way before taking a sip of her identical beverage.

Not willing to be rude to the only parent Ayale had left, he nodded and took a sip of the coffee, forcing himself not to make a face.

The coffee tasted identical to what Ayale gave him in Istanza. The drink burned going down his throat, yet he persisted, and soon his cup was empty, save for the thick layer swimming at the bottom of the white ceramic.

Katari sat idly with her iced coffee, impressed, while Diori's eyes remained fixed and unblinking in his direction. Diori took his cup out of his hands, looking at the bottom.

Ayale slid their iced coffee to Osiris, who happily took a few large sips to soothe his burning throat.

Diori took Osiris' cup from Katari, looking into it with a piercing stare, taking the saucer out from beneath the cup. She swished the remnants of the coffee grounds around the three times before placing the coffee upside down onto the saucer. She pushed it to the side and her smile returned.

"I think it is time we all have an open dialogue." Diori straightened her back. The opening line brought a certain level of tension to the table. "To clarify that we are all on the same page." She looked to Ayale. "I know about the invasion. Unlike Mero, I believe you. A war was inevitable once I discovered an interloper from the Matxha clan in the Cxai guard. Now that the marriage is dissolved, I would like to reform the Ceyxlon clan."

Ayale leaned on their elbows, seemingly unphased by the news. "Is that why Mero has so many more guards posted around the compound?"

Diori nodded, pulling Osiris' cup over to her. "There is a lot coming our way. We need to be ready for anything, and to be honest with each other." She looked at him with knowing eyes, flipping up his cup to investigate. Osiris' shoulders stiffened at the sight, recalling how Diori had been the one to discover and force his secret out in the open.

That was exactly what she had intended to do again.

"I imagine by now, all of us have our intentions painted in plain color. No reason for any of us to hide anything." Katari peered into his cup out of curiosity, though squinting her eyes. "Am I looking for symbols?" She muttered aloud.

Ayale made no effort to involve themself in whatever went on across from them, letting their estranged mother run her course. He looked at them with stark fear in his eyes, but they could only shrug and whisper just go with it. Osiris could experience Diori for himself. The tactic of buying someone coffee to investigate their deepest secrets, piecing together the person in front of you, was old school to the highest degree; A Ceyxlon clan talent.

Diori rotated the cup in her hand, the strange line over her middle brow beginning to twitch. Her eyes pierced with a subtle grey glow from their stasis brown. She stared deftly into the lining of the cup. "Nice heart at the bottom of this. And what looks like spattered blood stains next to it. Kat, see anything you want to point out?"

"Hm. What looks like a lightning strike to the side, keep moving to the left and there's a mountain."

"To the left?"

"What about this?" She pointed a red nail further along the wall of the cup. "Looks like a plant. Barely distinguishable but follows a very solid pattern around the rim of the cup. His affinity?"

"Correct. Anything else?"

Katari shook her head.

"Good." Diori put the cup down for all of them to see, keeping her eyes on Osiris. "For the journey you have made so far, all started on a bond made in blood. I saw cracked earth, so I am very sure that has something to do with my little one's affinity."

Ayale cringed, trying to shake off the embarrassment. "I'm in my twenties, you know."

"The human heart in the middle tells me the obvious, how much love you hold, and for whom. Happened early, didn't it, perhaps at first sight? Did you feel something before you left Densriel?" She looked directly at Osiris as if Ayale and Katari were not there. He nodded slowly, doing his best not to look embarrassed as well.

"The open road shows here. Fir trees to the side of the highway, distinct maples. Clouds coming towards the small sedan here." She pointed out to Osiris, who leaned over to see what she was looking at. "A lovely mountain range to the north after that, stars to the south above a set of plains." Her voice softened, and just as quickly, her demeanor sank into a thoughtful one, her eyes changing back to their original brown hue. "You two have quite the tale to tell."

The four of them drew quiet.

Ayale snuck their hand into Osiris' beneath the table, squeezing it to calm both of their nerves.

"I told you there was nothing left to find." Katari shifted her gaze to Diori, who let out a heavy sigh.

"Fine, you win." Diori conceded.

"My confidence in him does not wane. I know you fear for your child, but they have chosen good company."

"Alright, alright," She waved her off before Katari could begin lecturing Diori about trust again. "I suppose that is another thing I should work on." Diori looked up at Ayale, who stared off at the empty street.

"We're worried, too." Osiris confessed. "I think I speak for both of us when I say I genuinely didn't expect Mero to react so...poorly."

"We had no other choice. We talked about this once before in passing, but I never thought he would lock us up." Ayale took back their coffee from Osiris.

Diori looked at the bottom of her own cup and took in a sharp breath. "Let's head to the house."

Everyone followed behind Diori, packing into the small car once again.

Diori drove through the countryside, making their way through hills and small mountains. So much of the Ceyxlon island was similar to Cxai territory, with its own distinctive charms. Villages were built into mountain sides as they faced the ocean, farms and flatlands wedged in between hills that made up the island. For a moment, Ayale felt a flicker of familiarity strike them, fleeting as soon as they bore witness to the glittering ocean in the distance. The car followed the water closely, the sun's rays unobstructed by any clouds.

The group stopped at an odd house, the three-tier building looking so much like its own compound, Osiris felt his heart in his throat. Passing over a rocky driveway, Diori's car shook violently from the uneven road.

Osiris looked at the building in awe. He wondered how long it had been there to how it was still standing, especially after an acquisition. The foundation looked older than the building itself. The closer the car came to the compound, the road began to dip down further, into a sublevel parking lot.

"What exactly is this place?" Ayale asked, taking the words right out of Osiris' mouth.

"A piece of history." Katari answered from the back of the car while Diori parked the car closest to the entrance of the sublevel. A mass of empty, concrete space, walls lined with rough pieces of unexcavated marble stone. An unlit light up top buzzed with electricity.

"This is the Ceyxlon clan compound. Your grandfather rebuilt it just before his passing. The building stands on our land, passed down from the founding days of the clan system. It was a symbol of strength and resilience for the Ceyxlon clan," Diori stressed, leaving an odd tightness in Ayale's chest. "I grew up here, lived here my whole life until the allyship of the Ceyxlon and Cxai clans."

Katari placed a hand on her shoulder. "Even under allyship, nothing takes away your culture nor your name."

Diori nodded, the look on her face only partly comforted.

Among the strain of silence, Osiris chimed in. "Ohhhh, that's why your last name is Ceylonis."

Diori perked up, shooting a hopeful look at Ayale. "You changed your last name to mine?"

"Don't overthink it, my choices were limited and keeping his was like asking for someone to find me." Ayale turned back in their seat to Osiris, a deadly stare only meant for him. "Stop telling people my name, damn it. First Mero and now her, enough people know." They scolded.

"Sorry." Osiris mumbled an apology, not feeling quite as bad as he should.

Ayale forcefully opened the door to the passenger side of the car. "Everyone all set on exposition or is there anything else?"

"The Rooiboux guard is also on the island as well." Katari added quietly.

"Anything else?" Ayale asked once more but louder, their legs out of the open door.

Everyone sat quietly, Osiris himself trying to keep his smile to himself. Diori decided to keep her comments to herself, while Katari had nothing left to say.

"Good, we're all caught up." Ayale took their bag and left the car, the others following close behind.

While walking up the slanted concrete, the sudden warmth and sunlight almost blinded Ayale, forcing them to cover their eyes with their arm. They yearned for a time when life wasn't as complicated, before concluding that had never once been the case.

Diori showed the two around the Ceyxlon compound. The building was similar to that of a large house, each floor made almost entirely with a grey marble and granite color and rooms down both ends of each hall. The ground floor had been the only one with a kitchen, access to a gated back area that Ayale already had eyes for since the start of the tour. Night quickly followed, and Diori left the two to themselves.

Ayale and Osiris went back outside in the courtyard, where the ground had been covered in nothing but clay and overgrown, thick stone pines. An overgrown jasmine trellis sat partly broken behind an iron tea table, bordering the door to the inner house. The blooms seemed to be at their peak when Ayale looked at the flowers, causing them to wonder if Osiris' presence had anything to do with it.

The two shared the iron garden bench, watching night slowly fall on the dimming sky over them.

"How are you doing with everything going on?" Osiris extended his arm over the back of the bench.

"I should be asking you." Ayale peered from the side, their pin straight back barely relaxing. "But I'm okay. Struggling with how I feel about Diori."

He nodded, moving his arm onto their shoulders. "I don't want to overstep any more than I already have, but I do want to point out that she's trying." He shifted one leg over the other. "At the same time, and I wish I had said this earlier, but you don't owe her or anyone anything. Forgiveness included."

Ayale pulled their sleeves over their hands. "I don't hate her, I stand by that. But we have a long way to go. If I knew she felt bad for leaving us hanging in Odania, maybe…" They trailed off, unable to find the words.

"Wouldn't make you feel better, but a step in the right direction." Osiris finished, rubbing his hand on their shoulder.

They nodded. "The past is the past, but I want to move forward. I don't know where to start. Part of me feels like it's too late now." Ayale shifted closer to him, a small feeling of shame washing over them as they realized how selfish it was to feel calm at a time like this.

Osiris felt the same in that regard, reaching to touch their somber face with the back of his hand. How awful would it have been to say how much he loved them again, only for Ayale to be ripped away from him a second time.

Ayale enjoyed the warmth of his hand against their chilled face. A sigh of relief left their chest. "Osiris, I couldn't apologize enough for all of this, dragging you across the continent, bringing you all this way for a plan that didn't even work out in our favor."

"I don't regret a single moment." Osiris said a low tone, only loud enough for them to hear.

"No, I really mean it." Ayale made a frustrated noise. They pressed their forehead on his shoulder, trying their best to come up with the words. "I really meant everything I said in Mero's office. You really are the kindest, sweetest person I know. There is no one else I could imagine doing this with, and if I died tomorrow, I would want you to know how much you mean to me." Their hands balled up into fists, adamant to let everything out. But when Osiris heard the words, he tilted their face up, his eyes watching them carefully.

Ayale froze up, the sounds of the nightlife around them null to the look in his eyes when he gazed at them, waiting for them to continue. So many feelings came together all at once, the words could no longer come out of their mouth.

Osiris cupped their chin in his hand, turning their face to kiss their cheek, the side of their head, then their lips. Barely able to keep apart, he took one of their hands into his, feeling their fist unfurl.

A short noise caught their collective attention. The moment would have lasted longer if the two of them had not heard the shuffle of incoming steps behind them.

"Every time." Osiris laughed quietly, pulling away from them, but letting his arm remain around their shoulders.

Diori walked up the back of the bench the two of them shared, cautious as she eyed them separately. Fully aware she was intruding, she smiled as the two turned to look at her. "Mind if I interrupt?" She asked, hands clasped behind her back.

Osiris nodded, motioning to get up before Diori placed a hand on his shoulder. "I would rather speak to both of you, if I may."

The request took Ayale by surprise, reluctantly settling into the bench as Diori came around and pulled up one of the plastic chairs stacked away to the side of the courtyard. She seated herself across from them, cleared her throat, and smiled gracefully. It was clear she had no idea how to start.

"First, I want to express my gratitude to you," Diori looked at Osiris, a sense of guilt mixed in with her smile. "Thank you for taking care of my Ayale. I couldn't bear the thought of them driving alone through the territories."

"I owe them my life, it is the least I could do." Osiris said quietly, a subtle warmth crossing his face when Ayale placed their hand back over his.

"I think after what happened at the Cxai compound, we're even now." Ayale squeezed his hand.

"Regardless of circumstance, I am truly grateful to the both of you." She turned to Ayale, nervous to keep going. "I know you are trying hard and that is all I could ask of you. I know you might have questions for me, so know that I am here for you to ask anything." She fumbled with her hands, her bronze eyes setting on both Ayale and Osiris.

Surprising everyone, Ayale nodded. "I'm ready."

"I suppose I am, too." Diori nervously smiled, bracing herself for the worst.

The night was young, though for Ayale and Osiris, it felt as though they had only scratched the bare surface of the inner workings of the Cxai, the Ceyxlon, all among some family secrets.

# XLV

Ayale braced themself for what was to come, their only source of comfort coming from knowing Osiris was by their side, his arm remaining secure on their lower back.

Diori shifted uncomfortably, her sheer grey shawl covering her shoulders and her white long-sleeved shirt beneath. She found herself forcing out her next words. "This is difficult for me." She breathed out. "Because I don't want you to think it sits as an excuse for what I have done. And what I failed to do. I know I have disappointed you, done more bad than good, and I know this all too well. I think about how I have let you down so often, if not every day." Her eyes watered.

"I haven't been at peace with myself since I came back home. Every day in Cxai territory has been more painful than the next, since the day of my marriage to your father. This island is more than just my home, but of our family's domain." She told Ayale, wiping the tears from her eyes. "I am Diori of the Ceyxlon family. And I married Mero to ally both of our clans, for our people to be taken under the Cxai name. Subsequently, Mero made sure our culture had become fully erased from the face of the world, as if we never even existed.

"I don't harbor anything negative for you running away. I only wished I had done the same sooner. But I owed it to my people to stay, to protect the islands. Mero is out of his right mind now, but the psychopath used to be far quieter and vindictive. Anything against him, and the Ceyxlon people would be nothing more than on stakes. There is nothing more terrifying than being the one with a clan's survival on your back."

Ayale felt Osiris tense up, both remaining attentive. They squeezed his hand for reassurance.

"Our survival staked on this alliance, but at the end of the day, Mero wanted land and control, and that's exactly what he got. But it didn't stop there. His involvement in Ceyxlon politics ruined what little autonomy we had left. And when you ran, that's when I decided to take back control. I knew enough to sustain us, to grow the clan from the ground up. We existed again. From when you left until now, I have been pulling people from Mero, creating alliances everywhere I could. I am utterly and endlessly grateful for Katari and the Rooiboux clan, for everything they have done to help me, to help all of us. A few months ago, I was well on my way to reestablish the Ceyxlon clan and place us back on the map. Until the Matxha clan made a move so bold, none of us believed it to be true."

Diori leaned in close, a deathly serious look in her eyes. "I witnessed their leader's downfall in a vision that played like more of a nightmare than anything else. The young girl who leads now is the one who usurped well over a year ago, murdering the previous Matxha clan leader in cold blood. Their new leadership resides in the child as we speak. When I tried so graciously to warn Mero, who decided now would be the perfect time to doubt my visions, he did nothing but make life that much worse for those of us who remained at his side. My suspicions were that there was someone within the inner circle telling him otherwise, someone who knew what I had been able to see, and knew how to place that final wedge between us. The closest I came to figuring out who it was, I was kicked out not too long after. Whether by Mero's own choice or by the one whispering in his ear, I am uncertain."

"What about the invasion, why are the Matxha clan suddenly hell-bent on taking over the Cxai territory so suddenly?" Ayale asked, causing Diori to suck in a deep breath.

"I couldn't say. Even with everything happening around us, I barely understand it myself. Even with my visions." She gestured to the strange scar on her forehead. "All I could pick up was that it had something to do with Mero and the new leader, nothing else."

Ayale slowly nodded and rolled their eyes. Most of their problems seem to start the same way, they thought. "Did Mero do something to piss off the Matxha clan?"

Diori shook her head and shrugged. "He makes far too many enemies for me to keep count." Diori played with the ruffle at the edge of her sleeve, inching to continue. But the idea of delving into her next topic made her visibly scared, her hands tight on her knees. "I plan to take advantage of the invasion and reestablish the Ceyxlon clan once more."

Ayale and Osiris sat speechless, the sound of the cicadas filling the massive gap of silence.

"Does that mean you're going to let the Cxai clan fall to the Matxha clan?" Osiris asked out loud what the two of them were thinking.

Upon hearing that, what came after was a gentle, barely noticeable warm wind.

"No. That would spell the death of the Ceyxlon clan." She looked down to her hands, flat on both knees. "This means we fight the invasion off on our own."


After the conversation with Diori ended, both Ayale and Osiris wandered off to their rooms on the third floor of the unfamiliar compound. The stairs twirled upward with the building, bringing them up to an unlit floor, only the sounds of their steps echoing against the marble and walls. Ayale felt the walls for a light switch, revealing a barely developed common room with only two set up bedrooms, likely created for Ayale and Osiris. No one else slept on the highest floor, which left them both grateful for the space but offset just as much by the stark silence.

The odd curtains looked to cover a large expanse of the wall, leaving Ayale's curiosity piqued. A set of blackout curtains in faded reds cascaded down in an intricate pattern going down the sides. The two changed into sleep clothes within their respective rooms, while the other spaces across theirs remained abandoned and dark.

Osiris soon left his room and found his eyes wandering to the unusual curtains, questioning its placement, ultimately wondering what sat behind it.

Ayale peeked out of the worn door of their temporary bedroom, eyes narrowing on the red that spanned the entire back wall of the third-floor common room. They walked over, taking the thick fabric in hand, and pulling it to one side. Even in the dark, they could tell something was outside of the now exposed window. While pulling the other side of the curtains, Osiris came out from his room, helping to draw back the rest of the dense fabric.

Ayale walked over to the corner of the wall where they spotted a latch, pushing the lever in, a door suddenly popped open beside them.

Their eyes barely distinguished shapes in the darkness of the night, still making sure to be careful when going down the small set of stairs descending below. When they walked through the door, they felt the cold stone beneath them with each step forward. They reached the edge of the hidden balcony, the horizontal stone pillar adorning the whole area and the solid stonework all around them. It barely reached the height of Ayale's waist. To say they were in awe of the sights was an understatement.

Osiris made his way to their side, the two of them slowly adjusting to the night as he looked out at the expanse. He reached the edge of the balcony, leaning over the stone, trying to make out the horizon beyond them. He was soon met with the same sight as Ayale, a sea shimmering in faint moonlight, reflecting the clear night sky above them.

"The sea. I can't believe we can see it from here. I thought we were too far inland for that." Ayale said breathlessly. A soft smile crossed their face while they took in the rare view.

Osiris peered from the side of his glasses, his heart warming at the sight of their excitement. To his surprise, they turned and leaned back on the stone overhang to look up at the night sky above them. He followed their eyes, taking in another view unlike any other.

The lack of light pollution on the island allowed for a sight the two of them had never seen before. Small, glittering lights littered the sky, and the longer the two of them looked up, the more stars crossed their path.

Stargazing in its purest form, faint constellations coming to light, just as Ayale and Osiris saw during their first night on the road. But nothing could prepare either of them for the stars that streaked across the sky.

The sudden warmth of Osiris' hand took over Ayale's, comforting as it was unexpected. Ayale didn't so much as shift, making it seem as though it were a common occurrence. His star filled eyes fell onto them, drinking in every detail of their exploring eyes.

"I remember when you would flinch if I so much as looked at you too long." Osiris whispered to himself. To his surprise, Ayale snorted in response.

"I still might if you stare at me long enough." They felt a cold drift of air on their face, their smile not once wavering.

"Ayale Ceylonis, flirting with me? As I live and breathe." He drew closer, earning their immediate ire before his dreamlike smile softened their hard expression.

"Is there a problem with that?" They crossed their free arm over their chest.

"Never." Osiris said softly, his hand still on theirs. The other reached for their cheek as he did earlier, the warmth of his palm matching the flush of their face. His fingertips ran through their soft hair, feathering a few stray strands away from their eyes. "Reminds me of that night in Odania. The way you looked at the city, always with that thoughtful look in your eye," He openly observed. "You're always deep in thought."

"Sometimes if I stare off long enough, everything gets quiet. It is rare though."

Osiris lost himself within their soft gaze, drifting down from the night sky to him. Within their small space, he was close enough to feel the short, warm breaths taking up the gap between the two of them. While he tried to lean in, he felt Ayale's hand against his chest, their line of sight sinking to the stone beneath them.

"Are you okay? Have I gone too far?" Osiris asked, his hand immediately dropping to his side.

They hesitated to answer, a nervous look growing on their face. "I think we need to talk. About all of...this." Ayale exhaled, the small pain in their gut returning.

The phrase alone was enough to summon Osiris' anxiety, his stomach dropping instantly.

"I keep trying to get the words out, but it's difficult. Either we get interrupted, or we say them at the worst possible times. I want to say what I feel, but I don't want to mess this up." They took a deep breath in and held it for a moment before exhaling. "When I'm with you, I don't feel so alone. I'm understood as a person, like I don't need to hide who I am, or whatever complex emotions take hold of me," Ayale still struggled to look him in the eyes, especially when they felt his careful stare studying them. "You've seen my elemental atrocity and never said a word about it."

"In my defense, I was in the middle of getting my ass kicked both times you used your affinity." He spoke quietly, confused about the direction of this conversation. "I know I'm not in danger around you. You have more control than you give yourself credit for."

"You looked past my affinity defect, my relation to the Cxai clan, and I guess the Ceyxlon clan as well. You never made me feel bad about my own issues along the way. I dragged you across the goddamn continent, and you haven't so much as complained once."

Osiris short laughter filled the small gap between them. He leaned in, pressing a kiss to their cheek, then to the space below their ear.

"It's easy to accept these things when you're in love, Ayale." Osiris whispered in a low voice.

They slowly pushed him back, though harder than before and now creating a greater distance between them. The nervous look in their eyes distinct with wariness as they finally shifted back up to meet his uncertain gaze.

In that second, he felt his heart drop, the tension between them palpable.

"Osiris." Ayale said his name with emphasis, leaving him fearful for the next words to come out of their mouth. "You mean too much to me. Enough that it's almost a weakness. And yet, I would rather die than move from this spot right now!" They felt their voice grow, shifting their gaze directly to his wide eyes. Ayale felt their throat dry, swallowing hard to keep from coughing.

"I see the way the world looks at affinity users, regardless of what it is we hold. But the thing is, they don't get to see us the way I've seen you." Ayale slid their shaky hand from his chest to his heart, its feverish beat wild beneath their hand. "I've seen your silence, your worry, the height of your anxiety," Their hand moved to his jaw, tracing it with light strokes of their thumb. "I've seen your joy, the way you and your affinity work together to create art in your own medium. The way you look at mountaintops and coastlines, cityscapes and forests." They stepped forward, cupping his cheek with the same hand, his unsteady breath easily felt with his flushed gaze.

"And I see that all those things, they make you who you are. They come together to make you one of the kindest, smartest, most wonderful people I have ever met. I wonder how I got so lucky as to have you by my side this whole time." They met Osiris' teary-eyed gaze, pressing their forehead against his, their lips barely brushing against his own.

"I'm in love with you, Osiris Fyl. I only wish I told you sooner." Ayale confessed, their adamant eyes almost searching for an answer in Osiris' expression.

Osiris couldn't find the words to respond, yet relief washed over him all the same. Relief, tears, elation. Nothing would ever compare to this moment in his eyes. The tender touch of their hand gently swiping away the tears left him unable to hold any emotion back. He wrapped his arms around their lower back and pulled them close, pressing his lips against theirs in a feverish kiss that felt unlike any other they shared so far.

Ayale and Osiris spent so much of the night on the balcony, watching the night sky shift ever so slowly above them, sharing each other's company.

Beneath the stars, and for once, no interruptions.

## XLVI

The morning light came through the thin curtains of the guest room, though it barely stirred Ayale and Osiris, who struggled to awaken.

Ayale slept soundly against Osiris in one of the two guest rooms. His arms remained around them for the duration of the night, never daring to separate from its place on Ayale's back.

Most of the time, Osiris would have trouble finding sleep, waking at various points in the night. After the course of events last night, that problem seemed to disappear, even if only temporarily. He felt himself begin to awaken and tightened his arms around Ayale, taking a few more minutes to pretend the world hadn't been slowly crumbling around them.

Osiris listened to Ayale mumble in their sleep, their hand moving quickly on its own, barely missing his face as it slapped down on the pillow next to him. He turned over to face them, placing their hand back down to their side. Inches away from their face, he watched them for a moment before planting a kiss to their cheek, their jaw, and one to their lips, a homage to their admission to him last night, and now a habit.

They stirred once more, a subtle grumble leaving their lips. "Are you okay?" Ayale yawned midway, forcing their eyes open. When he didn't respond, Ayale felt their consciousness drift back towards sleep, mumbling something about the light bothering their eyes.

Osiris knew they could hear his heart race when they settled on his chest to sleep, but he didn't feel the need to hide it. "I couldn't be better, Aya." He said, kissing the top of their head.

And he meant it, no part of him could possibly be unhappy for as long as the morning light shined through the window.

The remainder of the morning was spent on the ground floor balcony with coffees and breakfast pastries, alongside Diori, Katari, and a handful of various Rooiboux, ex-Cxai, and current Ceyxlon soldiers that Diori had picked up after her exile.

While everyone donned formal suits, Ayale and Osiris showed up in casual wear. Ayale threw on the first black tank top from their bag and a matching bolero up top, coupled with black pants, while Osiris wore the same dynamic of black jeans and a tee shirt of some sort, both standing out in the sea of suits with little care.

Ayale didn't pay much mind to these clan ordeals before they left the Cxai clan, and they certainly weren't one to change their mind were it not for the circumstances at hand. Otherwise, meetings like these typically went in one ear and out the other.

Osiris shifted uncomfortably, not used to multiple major clan presences without a certain instinct of fear panging inside of him.

Katari noted his nerves during her short conversation with Mit, shifting her seat closer to Osiris, though neither felt particularly sociable.

"Diori saw something last night, so we are all here to make a plan, just in case it comes to fruition." She said, picking up her second cup of coffee.

"What did she see?" Ayale perked up from their inattentive state.

"A short young blonde girl, no older than a teen. She swears that her presence had been made up of different energy compared to the prior Matxha clan leader. Storm clouds swirled behind her, she said. Such a claim was alarming to say the least, especially knowing what we know already." Katari yawned, still beside herself over the meaning of the dream.

Ayale nodded, carefully thinking about the imagery of their mother's dream in their head. Nothing immediate came to mind except for what Diori had told her last night about the young girl usurping her own father from leadership.

Osiris shrugged, his alarm decreasing since Ayale didn't seem so worried. He felt his phone vibrate, taking it out of his pocket to check, and all he saw was a small popup text notification from an unknown number that said, look up at the door and nothing else. Extremely confused, he looked to the nearest door and was met with Visu's stoic face and iconic midnight blue suit. He tapped Ayale's arm, earning a stifled sound of annoyance, until they looked where he stared.

"Visu!" Ayale left their cup behind and scooted away from the full table, approaching the subtly smiling Oolonxg leader. "What the hell brings you out here?"

Visu pointed to Diori before waving back to Osiris. "I left the phone with Teryn and started using my own again. He was worried about me coming here." Visu looked past Osiris, nodding knowingly at Katari beside him. "Is that Katari of the Rooiboux clan? I thought the clan went extinct and disbanded after the Matxha clan invasion."

"You might want to give Katari more credit than that. The Rooiboux clan has been rebuilding since their invasion. Smaller territory now, but honestly, thriving in their own way. Their new area is beyond beautiful, too." Ayale stood tall beside him, eyeing the room as the two scanned everyone slowly trickling in. "Don't get any ideas." Ayale added, which Visu scoffed at, mildly offended.

"Do I look like a conqueror to you?"

"Just in case. I've seen her in action, she could take you in a second."

"I have heard the tales. Elemental user?"

"Nope." They motioned back to their seat and bringing Visu with them, pulling up a chair for him.

Around a large, rectangular cherry wood table, sat scattered soldiers from all different clans, staying close to their individual leaders. To the far left sat Katari and a few sparse Rooiboux soldiers, who managed to take up the full corner. In the other corner sat Osiris, Visu, with two familiar faces as far as Ayale noticed.

It took them a moment, but once they recognized the two cooks from the restaurant Teryn worked at, clad in identical Oolonxg uniforms, the message was clear how far the Oolonxg clan's reach extended. A small smile escaped them regardless, happy to know Visu had a few people on his side from the start.

Closest to Ayale stood Diori, making sure to leave a space beside her for Ayale, who chose to remain seated.

"I want to make certain that we are all on the same page. We are gathered to discuss the increasing concerns surrounding the actions of the Matxha clan. Currently speaking, what we know as far as their leadership standing, the child in charge is indeed the true descendent of the prior leader." She looked between Visu and Katari, before regarding the room once more. "The young daughter of the Matxha leader murdered him in cold blood and took over in less than a few days. A young girl named Eines."

Collective gasps and wide eyes filled the room.

"But that is as far as my intel has received. We know not a single motive nor a thought from the clan leader. She has yet to reach out to anyone directly, having only sent soldiers to the Oolonxg territory." Diori continued, and as if drawing strength from Katari, shared a look with the Rooiboux leader that spoke louder than her next words. "I have gathered you all here to work together for what is to come. The

Matxha clan is unstable under the leadership of this young lady, Eines. From here on, we need to put together our resources and support one another to get to the bottom of this. And if luck is on our side, to persuade the young girl to step down before someone else gets hurt."

Visu stood from his seat, partly reluctant to speak. "She has already gone ahead and requested for the assistance of the Oolonxg army, citing an old clause far beyond her or even her father's time. The Matxha did not disclose what for, only to prepare. Or else. The Matxha clansmen she sent over dared to threaten the Oolonxg clan in the same breath." Visu added, not allowing his nerves to show for even a moment. "We have done all we can to buy time, to learn their motives. Our soldiers have begun to be stationed all around the city and know to report anything these Matxha grunts do."

Diori nodded, forcing forward her next few words.

"My youngest has alerted me that Eines wishes to invade the Cxai territory in its entirety. I did all I could to warn Mero, as did Ayale, but to no avail. We are all that stands between the invading Matxha clan. If they take the Cxai clan, there is no telling what, or rather who, will be targeted next."

Ayale felt their stomach turn. Had they stayed in the Cxai compound, the likelihood that they would be representing the Cxai clan was a high one. The thought that they would have been the one to brunt the ambush of the Matxha clan sent shivers down their back.

They recalled being in the room with Mero, their walk down the hall leading to the compound's main office. The familiar faces they had seen all their life, except for one who had stood behind Mero just as they walked in with Osiris, making his way out of the room soon after the conversation began, only coming back in to help restrain and separate Ayale and Osiris, as if on cue.

Ayale stood abruptly, grabbing the undivided attention of Diori, the other leaders, and their soldiers in the room. They stared down at the table, their hands flat on the old wood.

"We were in the same room as the spy. There was only one man I didn't recognize from the old guard, but rather from when Osiris and I escaped Densriel. We stopped at a diner and were confronted by two men. And I... I think he was from the Matxha clan. With Mero in denial of everything coming our way, it only makes sense. But I think I speak for the Cxai clan when I say there is no chance we can handle an invasion by ourselves. We need everyone's hands on this task, we need to push the Matxha back before it's too late. I would rather not see their success in one invasion and decide to pursue another." Ayale found themself speaking on behalf of their clan, feeling a strange weight sit on their shoulders. Osiris placed a warm hand on their back, causing them to straighten up. Even in casual clothes, it couldn't take away the confident aura.

Visu stood from his seat, meeting Ayale's eyes. "I believe we can handle that."

"As do I. It is the least the Rooiboux can do for our friends in the east." Katari stood and nodded in agreement.

Diori smiled in her seat, letting the moment continue without her interruption. A prideful beam remained on her face, one that was unlike anything Ayale had seen before. And Ayale couldn't help but smile back.

A simple knock on the front door would bring change the course of the next seventy-two hours.

Diori's alarmed face was a sharp stab to the unity in the room. She nodded to herself, making brief eye contact with Katari before motioning to the door outside the hall. Ayale shared a look with Osiris before rushing off to her side, the two opening the front door together.

A young girl no older than thirteen wandered inside in a pale green dress, followed by Mero, who entered the building with no immediate regard to either Diori or Ayale. Five other soldiers clad in black, and a deep shade of green on each suit that followed behind the two.

Diori and Ayale froze, face to face with Mero and the girl respectively.

Mero stared daggers at Diori, ignoring Ayale entirely. "What are you doing on my property?" He said under his breath.

"It was never your property to begin with." Diori sneered, before lowering her voice to bicker more with Mero.

The young girl looked down the empty hall, shooting a glare back to Mero. "Find us a place to speak, Cxai leader." She said in a warning tone. Ayale watched the men behind her hold steady, the Matxha emblems symbolizing they were the highest-level guards, full bouquets of flowers over their chest pockets.

Ayale's heart began to beat fast in their chest as they realized who the identity of the young girl before them. When they turned back to her, Ayale quickly felt her bold green eyes searching them, staring at them up and down with no hesitation.

"Ayale." She said in a factual manner. "Child of Mero and Diori. Dissident and runaway of the Cxai clan." Her eyes never blinking once. The young girl abruptly put out a hand, waiting expectantly for Ayale to take it. They simply looked at her with a blank face, no words for the bizarre interaction.

"Eines. My name is Eines." She did not smile or frown but had a gentle upward curve of her lips.

"I would introduce myself, but you seem to know me already." Ayale hesitantly took her hand and shook it, noting the tight grasp of Eines' hand on theirs.

"You broke the nose of one of my best. Stole one of our soldiers away, hid in plain sight within the territory when my father was still alive, never once detected. I know far more than you might think. Now that someone was looking for you." Eines looked to Mero, whose aggressive expression had been pierced with one of fear. He regarded Ayale for the first time since arriving, keeping his mouth shut before letting a string of words slip out without a voice behind them. Ayale tried to read the words from his mouth until they were interrupted.

"Why are you standing there, find us a place to speak! I don't care for being interrupted by these extras, Mero." Eines shot a glare at Mero, who nodded briefly before leading the group down a set of stairs into the first level of the basement, towards an area of privacy.

"We need to get everyone out, now." Diori said, rushing back to the group in the common room.

Ayale grabbed her wrist to stop her. "What, and leave Mero with the fucking leader of the Matxha clan?"

"The invasion is here Ayale, we cannot spend another minute in this building. We need to regroup somewhere safer." Diori shook her arm out of Ayale's grasp before turning the corner into the room.

Ayale stood in the hallway, torn and worried all the same. Even if their father tossed them away into their room like some psych ward patient, the way he looked at them before walking away felt as though he was far more mentally present than he had been in years.

And Mero was scared. An expression of pure fear they had never seen before.

The words that left his mouth bothered them. Ayale could have sworn they read the word escape in their native language, a tongue neither of them had spoken to each other in years.

While contemplating the reason, Ayale heard the first gunshot fire, sounding out like an explosion throughout the house. Barely able to comprehend it, they turned to the source coming from the basement, unable to move.

The second and third registered, and Ayale ran towards the sound faster than they could comprehend, adrenaline fueling their every movement.

When the compound began to shake violently, Ayale could feel the source coming from the basement. They double backed and ran towards the meeting room, pulling together their earth elemental in a mindless heartbeat.

The last thing they could recollect before the ceiling started to cave in was blonde hair whipping past their peripheral vision.

# XLVII

Eines had always known she was different from a young age. Not in the sense of her deadly affinity discovered only a year ago, but far before affinities were seen as burdens in her eyes.

It wasn't long before she noticed the discrepancies between her mother and father. That is, while her mother had still been alive. She was always treated with love and kindness to no end, equal in that of her brother. There was never a moment she questioned the affection of her mother.

And when she died, so did a part of Eines.

Life had taken on a different tone, loss that shook their household, if not the entire structure of the Matxha clan. They not only lost a kind soul, but a blood relative to the direct founding family of the Matxha.

Eines' father had always been somewhat distant, his only role in the grand scheme to tend to his wife, never his children. After her passing, he immediately felt burdened by everything. He was left a clan to run and children to raise.

Memories came and went with Eines, as they always did. But in times of life and death, she was always reminded of her mother's sudden passing.

Eines found her eyes still burned, barely able to open without irritation since she had run out of crumbling Ceyxlon compound days prior. She was three days into an invasion: slowly making her way through the island of Craitani of the Cxai territory, all while struggling to recover from a building collapse caused by Mero of the Cxai clan.

What she recalled before the collapse was enough to cause her the same grief as losing her mother had done to her. Eines had planned to confront Mero, forcing a photo of her mother into his face. But it was the clear recognition of his expression that she would never forget.

But when he spoke, Mero pretended not to know the woman in the photo, asking who she was and what she had to do with him.

Eines, unable to not be taken seriously, fired not one, not two, but three shots after that.

The first for her mother, who bore his unfortunate child.

The second for the death of the child she once was.

The third for her dominance, as the new leader of the Matxha clan.

Three days later, Eines of the Matxha clan settled herself and her remaining army of only ten in the nearest city north of the island, biding their time and putting together her plans, as if she wasn't still coughing up dust from the rubble leftover, all after taking down the last parent she had left.

An invasion of the Cxai territory was supposed to fill the void remaining in her. The accomplishment that would put her on the map, as both the youngest leader in history and the most fearsome.

But Eines had never felt worse in her life.

*

Ayale Ceylonis had what many would call a curse; not one, but two elemental affinities that they abhorred since the day their powers came to them.

Somehow, the curse they had always loathed became the sole reason anyone made it out of the building collapse alive and unscathed from the Ceyxlon building. With their adrenaline rich elemental, they managed to close off the entryway to the underground compound, and keep a safe path open for everyone else on the first floor to escape.

After everyone scrambled outside of the compound, the group made way to a separate part of the southern island, far from the capital, a prior contingency planned on Diori's part. They only stayed there until the safe houses in a remote section of the island were ready.

For three days, Ayale did not speak, quietly grieving for Mero. They thought of their father's last words over and over, their complicated relationship stranger than ever, knowing that he was buried under the remnants of the Ceyxlon compound. Given the use of Diori's car, Osiris drove in place of Ayale, utilizing what little skills he had to give them some time to themself. On their way to the safe house, the rumble of the uneven road barely scathed either of them, remaining the only noise in the car.

Ayale didn't move their face from where they looked out the window. In the same breath, they saw a glimpse of their reflection, one that showed them the stoic expression of their father on their face.

"There is still a chance—" Osiris started but Ayale put their hand up to stop him.

"It was him who forced the collapse. I know it was." Ayale said quietly. "He knew what was going to happen and planned to kill himself and everyone with him."

Osiris struggled to brake without throwing the two of them forward, still not entirely sure how the stick shift of the car functioned, running on vague directions given to him by Diori.

"Did you catch a glimpse of Eines?" Ayale grabbed the handle above them.

Osiris shook his head, keeping his eyes on the road. "I didn't."

"That girl...she knew so much about me."

"And what do we know about her?"

"Her name is Eines, and she is the Leader of the Matxha clan. She killed not only her own father but now mine. Feels like a vendetta of some sort if I had any sense."

Osiris pressed the brakes a lot rougher than he intended. "She did what to her own father? We thought he just up and disappeared!"

"Doesn't explain anything about why she took out my father now, too."

"Sounds like we have two dead and no motive." He began his drive once more, keeping a good distance behind Diori and Katari.

Back to the burden of silence, Ayale glazed over the long highway and the steep mountains beside them. The free roaming sheep collected to the sides of the road without so much as a care for the caravan of cars around them drew out envy. Part of them had been convinced that coming back home had caused this, as if they brought all the strife home with them. Another thought plagued them terribly, wondering if they had stayed away, whether Mero would still be alive or not.

Osiris placed a hand on their lower back and rubbed slowly, trying to bring some form of comfort to them. There wasn't much he could say to them. Nothing like "Mero lit up the room" or anything of the sort could describe the Cxai clan leader. His first interaction with Ayale's father took a total of ten minutes, left Mero thinking he was a kidnapper, and ended with him imprisoned in the Cxai compound, adding to his third time being arrested in the last year.

Knowing everything he had done to Ayale and their family, Osiris felt he was the worst one to give any words of comfort. All he did was sit in misery with them and drive on to the next place.

An hour of silence passed with the two almost at their newest destination. The two saw a steep decline in the road ahead, the rugged terrain becoming lusher as they came closer to the ocean. A long stretch of concrete beach homes sat beyond large boulders, likely pieces from the mountain beside them. The further they drove on, the flatter the dry roads became, earning an outward sigh of relief from Osiris, whose first full drive was an hour through and between the mountain ranges.

It wasn't until the road led from gnarled olive trees and occasional farmland to a string of single-story summer homes, one right after the other, where the beach was a mere ten-foot walk.

Diori came out of the passenger side of the car in front and signaled for the two to park on a tiny driveway up ahead. Ayale met Osiris' nervous face with reassurance. "You'll be fine, just don't ding my mom's car." They said, watching his face crumple with anxiety. "I'm kidding." They started to direct him, to make sure he parked with enough room for the two of them to maneuver.

Ayale and Osiris left the car, making their way to the end of the brick driveway, in search of Diori among the scattered people of different clans. They had a million questions welling up in their head, sudden flutters of distant memories coming and going, and an odd feeling of familiarity sprouting with them as they went to approach her.

"Where are we and why does this seem familiar?" Ayale asked Diori, who took off her sunglasses and placed them on her head.

Diori smiled unexpectedly, before her expression disappeared the next second. "Your great aunt's home. He brought you here as a small child, both you and Ateno. Mero would drive you both through the mountains to visit her in the late summertime."

Ayale nodded, the mention of Mero so casually bringing them nothing but numbness. They let Diori go about directing people with her tactical retreat, who goes where and the like, listening to her voice linger like the ocean waves crashing across from them.

Nothing stayed in the numb flow of their thoughts. Only sounds and the sweat from their forehead was all their senses could take on.

After meeting and checking in on the other leaders, it was already late afternoon when Ayale and Osiris were left alone to look around the small beach house. The two set up and cleaned the room they were to sleep in for later, tested the lights, and even planned to walk down the road to eat at one of the small restaurants out of someone's home that they had driven by earlier.

The two started to slow down for the day, but Ayale almost refused to sit still. They looked around the small, one-story home aimlessly in an attempt to find something to do, no matter how tedious.

Osiris had already put his bag down, unpacked his clothes and art supplies, noticing Ayale's mindless wandering around the house, staring at portraits and strewn trinkets along a dusty fireplace. He thought to himself, wanting to come up with something for the two of them to do.

The sound of the ocean across the street was more than enough to inspire a plan.

"Let's go to the beach. Right now." Osiris grabbed one of the antiquated towels from the closet nearest him, took Ayale's hand, and walked the two of them over to the empty beach across from the small villa style home. He laid down the towel, sitting on one side and urged Ayale to sit down beside him.

They cautiously sat down on the towel, unsure what to do with themself.

When Ayale glanced at Osiris from the side, they could see the green glimmering in his hazel eyes, far more distinct than usual. His eyes reflected parts of the red sunset across the beach, its radiant hues laid bare among the green.

Ayale turned fully to look at him, watching as he looked to the incoming waves across from them.

Osiris was unlike anyone else in their life, and every moment with him proved that more and more each day.

"Are you doing okay? I know a lot's happened in the last few days." Ayale asked softly, breaking from their mournful silence to brush one of his braids back from his face. The act clearly took him aback, startled out of his deepest thoughts.

"I feel like I should be asking you that," Osiris partly smiled, his face soon turning solemn, as if readying to say something else. "Did I tell you that when those shots went off, I thought it was you who was shot?"

"What?" Ayale stared back in disbelief.

"I thought the Matxha or maybe even one of the Cxai had come to kill you. I was terrified, couldn't move, and then I saw you. But in those moments after, I didn't know what to think." His voice broke but refused to turn back to them. "Wasn't enough to lose you once, so life tried a second time. Makes sense, right?" He tried to laugh, choking back the few tears threatening to spill.

"I'm alright, and alive to boot. I didn't expect to have to hold open a path in a crumbling building though. Didn't think I could use my elemental in such a way," Ayale shifted towards him, wiping a stream of tears coming down his cheek with their thumb. He took their hand into his, struggling to face them. "I've never felt such a thing in my life. My affinity flowed through my veins, as if a dam had broken."

Osiris smiled, genuine with almost relief lining his tear-stricken eyes. "Sounds like an affinity to me."

Ayale nodded, one hand digging into the sand beneath them before an incoming breeze tousled the sand away from their hand.

"I want to stop running, Ayale. From everything." Osiris squeezed their hand tight in his. "When all of this is done, I want to go back to Densriel. I think we have a few things to settle there."

"We?" Ayale asked, amused by the plural.

Osiris nodded, swallowing hard before he continued. "I guess what I'm asking is that you come back with me. I-If you want to, of course. Might try to reconcile the remnants of my life before the Matxha clan took me in. Find my parents." He stumbled on his words.

Ayale found themself lost in thought. Besides questioning the desire to go back, they weren't sure if the Matxha clan would be a consistent problem, waiting to ambush them.

To add fuel to the fire, with Mero gone, any chance of secondary asylum had vanished with him.

For either Ayale or Osiris.

That was a hard thought alone. The idea that neither would see peace. But the words that left their mouth next would have to suffice, until the day came.

"We will go wherever we need to, and wherever we end up is secondary." Ayale whispered to him, barely audible over the crashing ocean waves.

"Anywhere we may roam." Osiris emphasized, glancing at their lesser solemn expression.

Their hand tightened over his, a promise to stay together, through and through, no matter what might come for them next.

Later in the night, as the two set up for bed in the barely lit bedroom, one that scented with musty fabrics and old wood. A singular bed had its place in the corner, a giant window barely cracked open above where the two sat. Ayale found their intrigue strike up when they noticed an old wooden vanity with three mirrors extended outward. They were half tempted to go through the drawers and see if anything remained, wondering like some child what they could find.

Instead, they opted for the bed, sitting along the edge of the bed while they took in the sounds of the cicadas nesting in the trees outside the open window. A small box made visible beneath the gap of the stone bed frame and the linoleum floor. Osiris noticed the strange wooden box and slid it out from underneath the bed.

Ayale had readied to scold him, until he opened the clasp and the two looked inside.

Photos of Ayale and Ateno as children spilled over on its unsteady stack, backdrops of the beach behind them that they had just returned from. Same as the photo the two saw hanging in the halls of the Cxai compound. Rocks and seashells scattered around the box, the jumble of childhood memories taking them back to a time they hadn't thought of in years.

An unstable intake of breath shuddered through Ayale, and the rest was history. They choked back a sob, heavy and unsteady breaths leaving their lungs as if they had been punched out of them. They barely felt Osiris' arm reach around their shoulders, pulling them into his embrace.

Ayale brushed their hand against the small rocks inside, the jagged edges a brief flashback of pride when they first touched them. They felt that same odd pulse in that moment that they felt that same day, before quickly recalling the crumble of stone and cement left burying their father at the Ceyxlon compound.

To think Mero would be buried by his own affinity was crueler than any karma they could imagine.

Ayale remained inconsolable for a better part of the night. They promised to try and sleep, with no way to shut down their rampant thoughts.

Even as Osiris tried to stay awake for their sake, he could not manage more than an hour after midnight. Considering the last week the two shared, it was no surprise he was exhausted.

Beyond sorrow crept regrets, what-ifs, uncertainty for the future; all of which came from the same place, the Matxha clan. Hour after hour, they did not find peace.

Ayale pulled their knees up to their chest, the moonlight's glow illuminating the room. The burning sensation in their eyes became a permanent fixture on their warm cheeks. How they traded one problematic clan for the next was beyond all reasoning. They ran to get away from all these things, but as cruel as life could be, they were instead thrown into the eye of the storm.

Everybody they ever met was now in danger, and worst of all, they didn't have a clear answer as to why.

Ayale's stomach churned nervously, lifting their head up from their knees. An odd wave of realization washed over them, an unstable breath leaving them once more.

If all their issues stemmed from the Matxha clan leader, what if they took out the person behind it all?

Ayale had never once considered taking a life. But if it meant securing the future, what other options were left?

And thus, Ayale began to plot a murder.

# XLVIII

Before the morning dawn could awaken Osiris, Ayale had woken up and slid out of the bed undetected, silently preparing for the journey to come. They put together their bag, took the keys, and stole a black plaid leather jacket from their great aunt's wardrobe.

They stalled at the entryway of the house. A weight settled on them as they watched Osiris sleep, the subtle rise and fall of his chest among all the chaos in their lives right now.

To leave him behind with no explanation was almost damnable.

Ayale walked back in, ripping a piece of paper out from their small notebook. They started scribbling together a note, making sure to cover all they wanted to say. In one part of the page, they asked Diori and Katari to keep an eye on Osiris, to give him a life to live without worry.

*Diori, I see you trying to change, to make up for everything that has come and passed. Thank you for doing your best.*

*Katari, take care of Osiris for me, so he can thrive and be himself.*

*Visu, be the great leader I know you can be.*

*Lau & Rae; thank you for taking me in and giving me the family I never had.*

*Ateno, I'm sorry for leaving you behind again.*

They began to write on a separate piece of paper.

*Osiris, I haven't always been the most open type of person. A lot of me simply doesn't know how to be that way. But you accepted me regardless, for being related to the Cxai clan (and now the Ceyxlon, I suppose), for all the baggage I carried throughout this trip, for being two pieces of an elemental neither of us could understand.*

*It is that which makes me wonder how you look past it all, to see me for more than the trauma I let take hold of me.*

*I'm going to go solve the source of our problems. Whether I make it back or not, know that you made me happier than anything else. My final wish is that you start over, be the artist I know you're capable of being.*

At the bottom of the page, they drew a small arrow, so Osiris would know to flip the page.

*I love you, Osiris. Find happiness wherever you may roam.*

*Signed,*

*Ayale Ceyxlonis,*
*of no clan.*

A half smile curved on their lips, the placement of the 'x' deliberate, a symbol of their lost clan. They placed the note on the mirror, leaving the house and hurrying over to the lilac car.

Ayale shifted the gear of the car into forced neutral, carefully pushing the small car out of its parking spot. They shifted it into park once it was on the street, only starting it once they had considered everything on their person.

In a matter of minutes, they hit the road, driving off into the guise of early dawn, making their way back to the old Ceyxlon compound. If they were correct in remembering what they had seen while the compound was collapsing around them, Eines escaped.

They wondered how far from the collapse she had gone. Some part of them hoped Eines and those who made it out remained close to the scene so they wouldn't have to look far.

If not, Ayale would go look for clues and find a way to track her down.

If not, they would do whatever it took to find her.

The feeling of the car accelerating beneath them, the morning light leaving partial trails of shadows on the passenger seat brought the reality of their coming actions to light. Ayale felt oddly calm, the notion of death bringing nothing more than a passing thought.

When it came down to whether they would be able to go through with the act, a hesitant jump in their throat rendered them inconclusive. They gripped the steering wheel tight, a groan rumbling in their chest turning into a yawn. They only slept a handful of hours, easily countable on one hand. Though the lack of sleep wasn't nearly as invasive as they expected.

Ayale shook their head of any doubts. This was the only way to freedom, to peace.

Take out Eines, stop the Matxha clan invasion, and pick up all the pieces left over.

If they survived the ordeal, of course.

The potholes shook the small car and Ayale in the driver's seat, wincing in the process. Day had barely broken by the time they saw the ruins of the partially collapsed Ceyxlon compound begin to rise in the distance.

*

Osiris reached over Ayale's side, finding no warmth, no one beside him. He slid his hand along the bed, feeling the entirety of the mattress and its empty space. He shot up from the bed, looking down at their vacant spot. He frantically looked around the bedroom, hoping they would simply walk in, but once his eyes set on the note taped on the mirror on the other end of the room, his heart dropped. He got out of the bed and ripped the note down, reading the note on the back first. An affectionate line that never ceased to leave him a flustered mess now stared back at him, agonizing and knowing what the remainder of the note stood for.

He still flipped open the note, quickly reading what he already knew, to reaffirm his worst fear. His breath shook, forcing himself to shove back all the tears forming in his eyes.

Osiris frantically threw on yesterday's clothes, and sprinted out the door, running to get Diori and an already awake Katari.

*

Ayale parked the car as far away as they could while keeping the crumbled compound in view. Out of the three buildings that made up the Ceyxlon compound, only the abandoned entry house remained. They pulled the keys from the ignition, dropping the set into the side compartment of the door. The morning light was far more distinct, its warmth at Ayale's back, their heart beating harder than the day they left the Cxai territory.

Upon taking their first step out of the car, the gravel crunched loud beneath their boots. The air felt cool against their flared cheeks, prompting them to take off their coat and toss it into the back seat. They turned their eyes towards the scattered rubble that remained of the Ceyxlon compound, surprised to see no cars or otherwise proof that anyone had remained at the scene. Their apprehension rose, scanning the area for any sign of life. One foot in front of the other, they looked all around them, keeping a careful ear out for any Matxha guards or henchmen lurking about.

Ayale moved forward every step a reminder of what they came here to do. The people at risk, the lives lost along the way, and every civilian in between.

No longer did Ayale Ceylonis want to run away from conflict, so for the first time in their life, they walked towards what scared them the most.

And in another first, the conflict appeared from the entry house and started walking towards them.

Eines came out from the short building alone, the only one left somewhat intact. Gravel and clay made up the ground around them, its crunch sounding out from her short steps. Her green eyes kept to Ayale as she made her way over.

"I had a feeling one of you would come back, but I didn't expect the runaway to act so...persistent." Eines thought aloud, her stare embedding itself not only in Ayale's face, but their stance, their clothes, and everything around them. It left a raw, vulnerable feeling crawl over their skin, knowing there was no place to hide. "I'm only here to make sure Mero is truly dead." She shrugged nonchalantly.

"Why?" Ayale stared back, swallowing back the lump forming in their throat. "Why did you shoot Mero? What could he have possibly done to warrant an execution style death to begin with?" They asked, willing themself to remain civil for a little longer to gain some kind of answer to Mero's death.

Eines remained fixed on Ayale, taking a few more steps forward. Her shoulders shrugged back, but her face told a far more elaborate tale than her words. The closer she advanced towards them, the more Ayale noticed the dismal details in her eyes. Her green eyes sat along the bloodshot whites of her eyes, the pale skin beneath them irritated and puffy, a few healed over scars disappearing into the side of her head, covered by strands of thin blonde hair.

In the exhaustion of their eyes, Ayale saw a bit of themself in the young girl, reminiscent of abuse they once endured. They recalled the fate of their father and shook off the prior thought, refusing to humanize the terror standing before them.

"What do you believe he did to deserve his fate?" She asked Ayale, her face forming a subtle but knowing smile.

Ayale did not answer, scowling at her audacity.

Eines' expression did not shift. "Then let me ask you this; how well did you know Mero? His stance on you and Ateno?"

"Old man had a habit of making it clear he never wanted kids for any reason except as an heir to the Cxai clan. One of the reasons I left, which you seem to know." Ayale's shoulders tightened.

"And yet, he spawned three of them." Eines watched Ayale carefully, the look of confusion on their face morphing into one of realization.

They inhaled a sharp breath, holding it in their chest before forcing out a long exhale. "Mero, why?" They seemingly asked themself.

"Because he felt like it. And his one act would haunt me, from the day of my mother's death until his own downfall. He deserved every shot I put into his body." Her voice grew increasingly agitated. "I have waited my whole life to see change, but all I experienced was agony, at the hands of my own father until I took fate into my own hands. Ayale Ceylonis, when I tell you there is nothing like watching the light fade from their eyes, I mean every part of it. Have you ever taken control of your life by taking someone else's?"

"Eines." Ayale's heart raced, unable to keep from staring at the young girl in horror.

"I swore when my father died, I would make a new name for myself, unlike anyone in the Matxha clan's history. To surpass not only my father, but my biological Cxai father. If not by force, then by elimination, of blood rights, as our world was once built upon."

They shook their head, unable to listen to any more of what Eines had to say. "That's enough. You won't be taking another inch of Cxai or Ceyxlon land." Ayale said with finality. "You have taken enough lives, taken the title of leader, what more could you want?"

Eines met their wary eyes with a stare unlike any other Ayale had seen before. "Everything." She said before the air between the two fueled with tension. The young girl abruptly stepped forward, a distinct glow in her eyes following her sudden movement.

Ayale moved back, barely given a moment's notice to use their earthly affinity throw up a short wall in between them, pulled up from the clay and gravel beneath them.

The time for talking had come and passed, leaving Ayale and Eines at their final standoff.

## XLIX

Ayale swallowed hard, the sudden hot air around them bringing a flush to their face. They pushed all excess thoughts out of their head, bracing themself for whatever came next. Their wall crumbled back down, revealing a flash of fear in Ayale's eyes before reverting to their stoic expression.

Neither of them moved for some time, watching one another closely. Ayale shook their head, a stare of warning meant for the young girl across from them.

Eines threw her arms out, her small, pale fists tightening. Each hand crackled with electricity. Her eyes lent an eerie glow, staring daggers at Ayale, as if facing a threat.

Just her eyes alone left Ayale bracing, throwing out a hand, and raising a thin wall from the clay below, meeting the brunt of Eines' attack before the wall crumbled back into the dirt. They held onto their breath, wide eyed at the remains on the ground.

"Eines, we don't have to do this." Ayale shifted their weight to the right side, placing their shoulder forward, and painfully aware their words would not be received by the seething teenager across from them.

"*Fuck you*. Fuck Mero and fuck the rest of your clan!" Eines exclaimed, launching herself forward, blocked off by a lone risen wall, two, then three.

Ayale struggled with the idea of attacking Eines. If not for the fact that she was a child, then for the fact that she was their half-sister. They continued to remain defensive instead, hoping her frantic attacks would eventually tire her out. The hesitation that made its home in their mind during the drive quickly turned into the hardest '*no*' there could have been. There was absolutely no way they could kill one of their own blood relatives.

Not even in their worst days did they ever entertain the idea.

Eines pressed forward, letting her dominant hand linger in the air, eyes glowing at the never shifting elemental user before her. A small cloud formed in the middle of the circle, the almost distant, muffled sounds of thunder in her hands being the barest form of a cue for Ayale to throw out another barrier of clay between themself and the girl. They hardly dodged in time for a strike of artificial lightning directed at their face.

"Please don't do this." Ayale huffed, losing steam from every use of their earth affinity.

"Shut up! Shut the fuck up!" Eines screamed, taking a step back before launching forward once more. A sharp wind whipped her blonde hair back, stealing her momentum, and nearly pushing her over.

Ayale's left hand shifted, reminiscent of what they had once seen their mother do, and waved ever so subtly by their side, keeping their line of sight focused on Eines. With their right hand, they raised another wall, far more thick and jagged compared to the last one, pulled from deeper within the earth. They created it knowing she would use it as a punching bag, doing what they could to buy more time. Ayale took the distraction to catch their ragged breath, kneeling behind the large wall to come up with something, anything that could turn the battle around and end it all peacefully.

Ayale's own elementals were barely stable enough as they were. With so little practice under their belt in controlling either wind or earth, they were forced to fight with the skillset of a child, and the fear of one, too.

A fight that truly meant life or death.

Their mind raced, trying to figure out some way to disarm Eines, to stop her from hurting them or herself in the process.

Turn around. Mero's words sounded into their head, as if he stood right behind them.

Ayale quickly turned around to find Eines behind them, her electrified fist mid-swing toward their neck. They grabbed her fist with their bare hand, their boots digging into the dirt below them, letting go of the faux wall now behind them. They shoved her back, pushing through the pain of the electrical current, trying to follow through on their hands until they successfully pushed her down to the ground.

Eines took seconds to bounce back, instantly rushing to get her hands on Ayale.

They ducked back and fell to one side, avoiding every attempted hit, save for one in which they threw out their arm against one of her strikes to protect their face.

The blood in their arm felt as if it were on fire, fighting through the searing pain seizing in their veins as they continued to dodge the barrage of electric currents coming from Eines' small fists. Ayale forced and pushed through the singeing of their skin, doing all they could to avoid any more of her strikes from landing. They couldn't imagine the consequences if she was able to land a direct hit on their body.

Eines' eyes glowed, a symptom of an affinity user with substantial power, a fearsome warning for what was to come. An achievement Ayale had never accomplished with either of their affinities. Nothing they yearned for either, except in moments when their life was on the line.

A stray punch aimed for their other arm, leaving Ayale barely able to escape. Another barrier came up between them, a last-ditch effort for defense. Ayale knew they could only avoid Eines for so long. How could they push their elementals to become the force of nature they needed them to be?

Ayale pulled together another collection of short walls to hide behind. Punch after punch, followed by the sound of crackles hit the thick clay walls, their only source of protection from the rampaging Matxha leader on the other side.

Thinking back to Osiris, his own glow only came after an anxiety attack or spike of adrenaline. He had passion for his power though, for nature as an affinity.

Ayale's only passion had been for survival. There were no binds or ties with either elemental that they could tap into. The only correlation between Ayale and their affinities was their shame for them. A shame built from their parents, the ones who passed down both of their strange magic to Ayale, bad genetics beyond bad luck.

Between Mero's disdain for their wind elemental and Diori's blatant disgust for their earth elemental, mixed with their mutual hatred of one another, neither affinity had a chance to grow with Ayale.

And Ayale had never given either a chance, even after they ran away.

"Come out and fight me!" Eines screamed, throwing an assault of punches at a barely hidden Ayale, clay slowly crumbling.

Ayale had thought of themself a freak of nature. The repression and shame of merely existing, of having two sides was no more their fault than anyone else's.

But their time for contemplation grew shorter by the second.

To push their elementals to the same level as Osiris, they had to move forward with their affinities.

Both were a part of their core being.

Osiris had accepted them as they were, so why couldn't they?

In a single, shaken breath, they closed their eyes, feeling the wall behind them thin with every passing second, and asked themself for forgiveness.

Ayale turned towards their shield, breaking through the crumbling wall of clay, and throwing their whole body towards Eines, tackling her back to the ground. They towered over her, pressing her wrists into the ground. She struggled against them, her violent green eyes expanding with fear, a sight Ayale didn't expect.

They felt a strange warmth settle behind one of their own eyes and an equally cold weight in the other.

Her eyes tremored with terror, all but the last thing Ayale needed to see.

And then, for the briefest moment, silence.

"What kind of disgusting hybrid are you?" Eines whispered aloud.

"Wouldn't you like to know?" Ayale gritted through their teeth, tightening their grip on her wrists.

"Grey and gold, one eye each," She stared, her intensity falling in both her face and her struggle. "I don't understand." Her voice broke, arms settling on the ground beneath her.

Ayale felt tears instinctively fall down their cheek and onto her. "Eines, please stop this."

"Why couldn't it have been me? To have an elemental affinity?" She broke down, tears flooding from her eyes. "To have a family?"

Ayale pulled back and unknowingly retracted their hands back to their side. "Your affinity is more than enough. You don't want any of this. Believe me, Eines."

Ayale was thrown backward onto the ground, shards of rocks pressing into their back. They felt the wind knock out of their lungs.

A ball of fog manifested between the two of them, crackling and rumbling its subtle threats.

"You're right, I don't want any of this. Not anymore," Eines smiled, wiping her tears away with her sleeve. "But it wouldn't hurt to get a few problems out of the way. If I can expand the Matxha clan to the coast, I can surpass the old assholes' legacy. The Cxai are all that stand in my way."

Ayale's glowing eyes widened before their vision had been overcome by white, the ball between them erupting into electrical currents that shook through their body. Their hand instinctively reached out and grabbed onto Eines' throat, holding with more strength than they had left. They held onto her neck like their life depended on it, braving through the pain and the electrified atmosphere that Eines created with her affinity.

The currents exploded, ripples of electricity taking over every one of their senses, burning its way through their stomach, chest, into their arms. The scream that ripped itself from Ayale's throat was unlike anything they ever felt. Their body felt as if a power line had run through them.

Eines pushed them over, freeing their hands from her throat. She stumbled before standing over them and coughed profusely, taking sharp inhales of air into her lungs, while Ayale convulsed on the ground before her.

They struggled to gain control of their hands, grasping at the rocks on the ground beside them, unable to so much as keep a hand still. The air couldn't get into their chest fast enough, their vision barely holding on to the scene in front of them.

Eines almost tripped over herself as she began to walk away, stumbling on her own two feet. Beside her, Ayale hyperventilated, blood-stained tears leaving their glowing eyes. Even when they could finally see again, they laid still, having lost too much control of their body. The taste of iron settled on their tongue, no longer convulsing to the degree they began at.

Their glazed eyes watched the clouds float above an all too bright blue sky. A sight they had seen many times; not once did it look so vivid.

The mountains in the background they would never explore again, the odd formations that made up Ceyxlon land.

The incoming breeze cooled their burned face. The same wind that shifted the clouds in the sky.

The same wind that, since birth, had made its home in their veins, never to be used, for the shame of simply coexisting with the earth within them.

Ayale felt the clay gravel shift in their hands, in little control again. Their fingers didn't respond, their palm unable to steady their hand muscles. The muddy brown clay responded to their numb touch, bringing with it a cold hardness, completely unlike the wind on their face.

For the first time in their life, Ayale Ceylonis felt and heard their elemental affinities. The sweet sound of the howling wind, the pulse of the earth beneath them, both singing different parts of the same song, one that had survived centuries. Before the rise of the Alqueris empire, before the rise of the clan system, before their birth and existence.

Before everything.

At the creation of the world came the birth of affinities, of all kinds, of elementals, made of the magic that created everything.

All of it.

Everything that had been and will be, all of it was more than a simple squabble, than a little girl who wanted vengeance and to take land out of spite and anger.

Ayale felt the small rocks, pieces of dust and clay and rubble, grasping at the ground around them, the warm wail of wind shifting their disheveled and bloodied hair. They twitched uncontrollably, but they managed to move, sitting upward through all the pain searing their body, inside and out.

The sounds of both elementals played their song in their head, more clearly than if someone had begun speaking to them. They dug their boots into the ground, rocks shifting and shaking beneath them. The light breeze evolved into a wild gale, helping them lift their unsteady hand, doing whatever it took to stand back up.

With Eines' back turned and barely in their sight, Ayale stood up, exhausted beyond all means. They put their right foot forward, tucked their left hand behind their back, open and tilted upward, while the other flexed, slowly and shakily moving up toward their chest.

Unable to hear nor comprehend anything outside the song in their head, Ayale's vision turned black.

*

Diori drove faster than manageable, cutting turns and signs with no regard, with Osiris in the front seat and Katari seated behind them. The loud rev of the engine was the only noise around, the car going well past everything in their vicinity. The three of them looked out for anything or anyone for that matter, looking for Ayale along the way.

Osiris felt his anxiety in his throat. His nerves were far worse than they had been since the beginning of their journey when the Matxha were hunting him down. He could only think of every terrible possibility, running through so many at once. His hand tapped an equally restless leg, eyes unblinking.

What if Ayale was injured? Or even dead? The one who killed Mero and the Matxha leader could easily still be at the site of the compound.

As if thinking the same thought, Diori found herself holding back her emotions, stoic and focused on the road before her.

"Are you sure they would go back to the compound?" Katari watched the scenery pass by the car, as if hoping to spot Ayale on the side of the road.

"Yes." Osiris clutched the paper tight in his hand, his eyes focused on the surrounding area outside his window.

It was half a mile down the road that the trio saw the remnants of the Ceyxlon compound and two figures in the distance. When Diori began to slow down, she recognized Eines standing, and suddenly slammed on the brakes, unwilling to get any closer.

"Why are you stopping now?" Osiris frantically tried the latch on the passenger side, violently pulling on it to open the locked door. But Diori's fearful stare remained on the young girl in the distance, placing a hand on Osiris' shoulder.

"That is Eines of the Matxha clan, you are not going anywhere. She would kill you in an instant." Diori's voice shook, swallowing hard. "I will handle her."

Osiris dislodged his shoulder from her hand and kicked open the car door, leaving everyone, save for Katari following close behind him.

"Osiris, please stay back and do not approach her, the girl will kill you!" She tried to take his arm, but he shook her off and made off towards the ruins of the Ceyxlon compound, until Katari pulled her affinity onto him, taking control of his body in seconds and forcing him to stop.

The three of them heard an explosion, followed by a widespread rumble in the air around them, though no storm followed. No one was visible in the dust cloud that came next, surrounding the entire area around the car and the buildings.

When the dust settled, all of them saw Ayale, unmoving on the ground behind Eines, who slowly but surely had spotted the trio and began to make her way over to the group.

"Aya?" Osiris whimpered, knowing he could not be heard.

Katari's abjuration shut down, leaving Osiris to stare at the sight of Ayale collapsed behind Eines. He froze, his eyes waiting to see some sort of movement from Ayale, but as each second passed him, they didn't move.

"Ayale. Ayale, please." Osiris barely whispered. He fell to his knees, numb and unresponsive to the chaos around him as he waited for them to move. "You promised me we would go back home. Don't leave me like this."

Everything moved without him, because Osiris was no longer present to the danger coming towards him.

Katari looked between him and Eines, whose glowing eyes focused on Osiris. She went into action, shoving him back behind her and standing tall in front of him, the gentle red in her eyes ready for combat.

Diori moved to her side, eyes glowing a gentle grey, one that distinguished the rain from the storm. With no hesitation left in her body, she threw forward her hands and let out a deep, foreboding scream from her chest, one of someone regretful, mourning, and ultimately, full of wrath. Diori continuously pushed out gales of wind from her shaken hands, her aim for the girl struggling to walk toward their group.

But Diori soon froze, unmoving as her eyes moved to the sight behind Eines.

"Ayale!" Diori cried out, loud enough to pull everyone's attention to Ayale barely standing behind Eines.

The earth beneath them began to rumble violently. The unnatural tremor followed a heavy gale of wind, whipping out from behind her towards Eines. The ground beneath her spasmed violently, bending and shifting, throwing her into the air, while the next gust of wind pulled up a rising wall of deep earth and clay, encasing her in a tomb of rocks.

A loud thud and red dust were all that remained of Eines of the Matxha clan.

Osiris didn't hesitate to stand back up and sprint forward to Ayale, who promptly fell back to the ground, the tremors and gusts ceasing with them.

# L

For the first time in forever, Ayale had a peaceful dream. Barely considered a dream, with the high probability that they were dead, they thought in the darkness that made up their consciousness.

But the song in their mind kept going. Their eyes slowly opened, the sight of a reddish orange landscape where the Ceyxlon compound had once stood, but not even the ruins of the remains were in its place. No remnants, no...anything. Just rock, more so the reddish clay that surrounded them earlier, and a light breeze on their cheeks.

They carefully sat up from their place on the ground, eyeing the mountains in the distance that were capped with the same reddish hue as the clay beneath them.

Ayale stretched their arms forward, their sleeves lifting slightly, revealing light-colored markings on their left arm and darker ones on their right. Confused, they frantically pulled up both sleeves, the intricate details on each arm taking them by surprise to say the least. They stared at their left arm, taking in the light grey to white ink moving up their forearm surrounded what looked like a bird, at least a creature with wings. On their right arm sat a dark brown to black set of lines, seemingly drawn over their veins on their wrist surrounding a mountain shape, drawn up their forearm.

Ayale watched as a flock of birds shaped all too similarly to the one on their left arm flew by them, mentally noting each detail.

Looking around them, they came to one of two conclusions.

This wasn't their time, nor the place they just fought for their life.

Ayale touched their face, tapping it a few times, wondering if they were truly dead.

"Not dead, my dear." A voice whispered from behind them.

Ayale turned their head and met with a set of warm eyes, from a sitting figure in a far too formal black to white halter dress, unsleeved but flowing at the bottom where the light fabric met the earth. The dress had been made up with the same detail work from their arms spanning the entire garb, top to bottom.

Ayale's eyes darted back up to their eyes, seeing the gold and silver color in each, a warm smile grabbing their attention. "How I have waited." Their soft voice rang through them with an unhindered sense of familiarity. They motioned to sit beside Ayale, taking in the marks over both arms. "I wish these were better circumstances." They spoke with a softness that almost settled Ayale's uncertainty.

"But better late than never. To see another one of us after so long makes me..." They trailed off, placing a hand through their silver stung black hair. "I am not so sure such a word exists! I feel hopeful, surprised, so many things all at once." The odd person took Ayale's hand into theirs, a detailed sleeve of tattoos on them almost matching their own.

Ayale gawked, taking in each detail when the other person's laughter brought them back to the one-sided conversation.

"A display of our affinities. When the world was young, we had pride over our magic. Far before the days where your society made it commonplace to remove their affinities." Their excitement died down, keeping their eyes on Ayale. "Most now believe having one elemental is a pain but imagine two. Most believe such a thing could ever coexist. One and done," The other squeezed their hand. "But not us. We have two. Two of the oldest forms of affinities, ones that shaped the world you see now. Primals were the name coined for people like us, far before the concept of elementals."

Ayale went to speak but found their mouth had opened, but no words came out.

"There is far more to what you know than simple affinities and elementals. Their functions are beyond simple understanding. There are other people like us, who control the primal forms with the snap of a finger. Incredible how different the world becomes as time passes by." They sighed, a weight in their chest forming as their eyes watched the sunset in the expanse of the distance ahead.

"Where are we?" Ayale finally felt their ragged voice ask. "Who are you, for that matter? I feel like I know you but I certainly can't. That's just not possible."

The figure beside them held tight to their hand, pushing away their hair to the side with their free hand. A short smile grew back on the stranger's face. "A place between time, between realms. Dreamers, the deceased, and everyone in between make their way here," they said before stealing another glance. "I think you know how you arrived here, darling descendant."

"Oh." Was the only word to come out, leaving them pulling their legs up to their chest. Certainly answered the question as to why they didn't feel any of the pain overwhelming them as they did before they fell. Ayale rested their head on their knees, letting the warmth of the resting sun linger on their skin. They peered down at their arms, the strange markings taking over their curiosity.

A warm hand touched Ayale's shoulder, pulling them out of their thoughts. "You need to go back home."

"I have a feeling we'll speak again." Ayale looked over to the other, a short smile bubbling to the surface.

With no hesitation, they were pulled into the stranger's arms. Their embrace felt as warm as a parent's, careful and caring, as though they knew each other forever. They were squeezed tight, letting their own arms carefully situate around their back.

"You need not have to choose, contrary to what you were taught. Know that I love you as you are, Ayale Ceylonis." They said, their soft voice swimming in their consciousness.

~

Ayale gasped and forced out a breath, a violent cough coming forth instead as their eyes shot open. The first thing they saw had been Osiris' arms, warm against the full body ache that followed with consciousness. They met his fearful eyes with a confused stare back, cold and stoic as always, before softening.

They reached out a shaken hand and touched his cheek, wiping away the unspoken tears that dripped down at his chin. But the simple act made him cry even harder, though he tried so very hard to make sure it wasn't audible, lest he draw unneeded attention.

Ayale painfully drew their body up from the ground, pushed up from the red clay beneath them, and leaned in close to Osiris, softly kissing his cheek. A flurry of comforting words spilled out of them a moment after, trying hard to wrap their sore arm around his torso, willing themself to keep their own tears at bay. "I'm here Osiris, I'm not going anywhere." Ayale felt his arms tighten around them, unwilling to let the pain stop them from embracing him. They leaned their head into his shoulder, resting for a breath. Their eyes began to burn, the reality of the situation barely unfolding while they started to sob into his shoulder. "I'm sorry, I just wanted to fix all of this. You've dealt with so much, you and everyone around us. I thought I could reason with her, but she kept going on and on about...about..." Ayale lost their train of thought, hurled back into the very moment Eines tried to kill them. The recollection left them curling further into Osiris for comfort.

Osiris didn't say anything, focusing on Ayale rather than the adrenaline in his veins. He could barely feel relief at their awakening, only an anger that he refused to justify. He looked across the field of ruins, spotting Eines' unresponsive body being investigated by Diori and Katari, who took careful measures of looking at the young Matxha clan leader.

The thought that Ayale could do such a thing was too unrealistic for him, until he considered the life and death situation they had been in not too long ago. Osiris had been ready to do anything that night he escaped the Cxai compound. He could only imagine the circumstance of being under attack by such an unstable affinity user.

He carefully picked Ayale up, bringing them to Diori's car. The thought of Eines alone was enough for him to utterly forget his anger on their way to the car. "Why didn't you take me with you?" He asked without thinking.

"Not for your life to be put on the line again. I think you've dealt with enough of the Matxha clan." Ayale held onto Osiris, keeping an arm around his neck as he took them back to the car. Osiris didn't respond to their answer, not when they got to the car, nor even when they made it back to the temporary placement of their collective friends and whoever else.

Ayale passed out soon after arriving, in the same house they slept in the night before. People had come in and out of the house, tending to them and helping in any way they could. The worst of the damage came from their arms and legs, discolored tendrils in place of the where electricity had once run through them at the hands of Eines. Their arms had been wrapped up tight, compressing some strong menthol scented ointment all over both sides of their body, chest, and most of their legs.

Osiris remained by their bedside while they slept, watching various people from different clan's drift in and out of the room. Katari eventually made her way in to check on him hours later, seeing if she could do anything for him. But soon enough, she too left, leaving Ayale and Osiris alone once more. He found a small sense of peace in drawing but couldn't focus for more than a mere doodle here nor there in his sketchbook.

It was only twenty-four hours ago that the two of them had been side by side on the beach out front, discussing what the two of them wanted when all of this was over. Osiris pulled his knees up to his chest, letting his head fall on his lap, curled up in the old piece of furniture. He could not fathom what sacrificial mentality went through their head when they made a note and left. Unsure what else to do, he reached out and carefully took their hand into his. He inspected the visible singes along their wrist, a part of him cringing at what they might have felt like on his skin.

The small act caused them to stir, their hand instantly squeezing his back.

Ayale turned to the side he sat, eyes fluttering open. "You alright?" They yawned partway into their question, a tired strain in their voice.

He shook his head, his eyes barely lifting from the floor.

"I know today's been a lot on us both."

"*Stop*. Just stop." Osiris interrupted, his hand remaining still in theirs. "You ran. While I was asleep, and you left me behind nothing more than a note. A note that had your last will in it. That said you *loved* me." His voice shook with the last words, pulling himself upright in his chair. He took his hand back, holding his hands together on his lap.

"I don't—" He took a sharp breath. "I hate feeling like this. Angry doesn't even scratch the surface right now, but damn if it isn't close. I'm pissed, Ayale."

Ayale nodded, having sort of expected the reaction, and sat up slowly in the bed to a sitting position.

"What the hell were you thinking? Why the fuck did you leave me behind like that and think a note was enough?" Osiris kept his voice low, but every word remained sharp.

Ayale looked down at their lap, letting him vent as much as he needed. Truth be told, a very small part of them had been certain they wouldn't make it back. "I didn't know what else to do." They responded softly.

Osiris nodded, biting the inside of his cheek. "Well, great choice you made." He looked up at them, his harsh feelings subsiding at the sight of their very outward guilt. "Ayale, that note was... a lot to handle."

"I'm sorry, Osiris."

He wasn't sure what else to say. He was still upset, even more so that he just went off on them after they just woke up.

"Leaving you behind was the worst feeling in the world. More than when I left Nalira. But it felt like something I had to do. You deserve to feel safe, and all I've done is put us in peril every other day." Ayale pushed their hair back, refusing to look back at Osiris just yet. "I meant what I said in that note. All I want is for you to be happy. I'm sorry I couldn't do that for you."

Osiris groaned, a heavy, long breath leaving his chest. "Ayale." He said, emphasizing their name. "All this self-sacrifice bullshit, it needs to stop. I can't keep doing this."

When they turned to look at him, a short smile graced their worn-out face. "Were you worried about me?"

"Of course I was, am, will be! You think you can put on some stupid, stoic mask on, as if it fools me like it does everyone else. But I refuse to fall for it!" He exclaimed, trying to keep his voice quiet in the late hour.

Ayale kept their eyes on him, their smile not once wavering as they slowly tried to pull the thin cover off their body. They tried to swing their legs off the side of the bed, stepping on the old linoleum and making every effort to keep steady. The second they moved off the bed, Osiris caught their shoulders, his scowl clear as ever, even in the nighttime. "Stay in bed." He begged, but Ayale leaned up and pushed forward, barely steady on their feet. They put out their arms, wrapping their shaky arms around his lower back. "What the hell are you doing?" Osiris made sure to hold them steady, practically holding them up altogether.

Their hands stayed flat on his back, one barely making Its way to the back of his head. They leaned on him, pressing their forehead against his, ignoring the shooting pain erupting around various parts of their body. Entrusting him to keep them steady, Ayale wouldn't have dared to ask for help at the beginning of all of this.

Osiris knew how bold a move that had to be, doing everything in his power to keep them up. This level of trust was enough to dissolve his anger into a threat of tears instead.

"Be as mad as you need to be." Ayale spoke softly. "Thank you for being with me regardless of everything that comes our way. I know you're upset at me because you care."

"Nothing you do could ever change the way I feel about you, Ayale." Osiris' arms tightened around their lower back, drawing closer, his voice soft. "But I thought you died today. Again. I wasn't ready to see your body on the ground, with Eines standing over you. It was too much for me." His voice shook, tears spilling over.

"I wasn't going to let her kill me so easily. Not today, not here. I knew I had to make it back to everyone. To you." They touched his face, his flushed cheek warming their cold hand.

Osiris felt his racing heart settle down. He closed his eyes, inhaling the air around the two of them. Just knowing Ayale was alive was enough for him to pull through what made him upset. Not once did he think a small tea shoppe crush could bring him this far, to bring him to tears. His frustration melted away with them in his arms.

As shaken as the two of them were, Ayale and Osiris found solace in one another.

Ayale had been ready to fall asleep in his arms, not letting the weight of what was to come their way shake them. For the first time, they felt understood, having revealed their full self to someone who accepted them as they were.

For now, for the night, it was the two of them, and no one else.

Nothing except the tales they created together along the way.

# Acknowledgments

If you had told me this short story from a random summer years ago would become something so expansive, a project that would begin at my job one winter morning and take me years to organize and fulfill, I would not have believed you. If you know me, you may know this wasn't my first major project. You might even know I threw out one of my very first manuscripts.

Bounds of the Forest would become my first redemption project. Until Next Time would become my first short story collection. Of Indomitable Desire would become my first novella.

But Tales of the Tea Shoppe was meant to be something greater. Something different. It gave me the opportunity to be creative in a way I hadn't experienced since my first manuscript.

My thanks and appreciation stretch so far, further than you might expect. To the teller line all the way to Greece, to my coworkers, my family members, my friends who kept me caffeinated and hopeful, especially in times of doubt. My significant other who worked hard and honestly on helping me achieve my dream. My sister who made sure I knew my work was worth the time and effort. My cat, Cleopatra, for being my support since the start of my writing career.

And so, to make this short, thank you for picking up my latest work! I'm honored beyond words to say one more thing; this tale isn't the end for Ayale and Osiris.

This is only the beginning.